THE
HOARDER

JESS KIDD

CANONGATE

This paperback edition published in 2018 by Canongate Books

First published in Great Britain in 2018 by Canongate Books Ltd,
14 High Street, Edinburgh, EH1 1TE

canongate.co.uk

1

British Library Cataloguing-in-Publication Data
A catalogue record for this book is available on
request from the British Library

ISBN 978 1 78211 852 7

Typeset in Bembo by Palimpsest Book Production Ltd,
Falkirk, Stirlingshire

Printed and bound in Great Britain by Clays Ltd, Elcograf S.p.A.

For Eva

Chapter 1

He has a curious way of moving through his rubbish. He leans into it, skimming down the corridors like a fearless biker on a hairpin bend. He gallops and vaults through the valleys and hills, canters and bobs through the outcrops and gorges of his improbable hoardings. Now and then he stops to climb over an obstacle, folding his long legs like picnic chairs. And all the while his chin juts up and out and his body hangs beneath it, as if his grizzled jaw is wired to an invisible puppeteer. And all the while the backs of his big gnarly hands brush over the surfaces. For a tall man and an old man he can shift himself when he wants to.

I don't move like that. I wade, tripping over boxes and piles of mildewing curtains, getting caught in cables, hooked on hat stands and assaulted by rutting ironing boards. I flounder over records, books, stained blankets, greasy collections of plastic bags, garden forks, antique mangles, a woman's patent leather shoe and an unopened blender that also grates and peels. And cats, cats, cats.

Cats of all kinds: ginger, black, brindled, tabby and piebald. Cats sleeping, eyeing, scratching and licking their arses on sour cushions, humping under upturned boxes and crapping on great drifts of newspaper.

I try not to look at the details but some little thing always catches my eye. A dead mouse curled in a teacup, a headless ceramic dray horse, a mannequin's pink severed limb: that sort of thing. I have a morbid bent.

This morning I am excavating the northwest corner of the kitchen. Taking as modern topsoil a pile of local papers dated September 2015, I have traced back through layers and layers of history. On reaching a sprinkling of betting slips stuck to the linoleum (dated March 1990) I was able to estimate that this filth hole has not been cleaned for at least twenty-five years. Having opened several speculative trenches and located an oven, I am now enthusiastically cleaning its hob.

I count (sing with me):

Seven withered woodlice
Six shrivelled spiders
Five black bags
Four kitchen rolls
Three dishcloths
Two scouring pads
And industrial grade thick bleach.

I am wearing a disposable apron, extra-safe rubber gloves and a facemask for the smell and for the spores.

He's staring at me from the kitchen door, Mr Cathal Flood, three feet taller than usual because he is standing on a mound of discarded carpet tiles. This makes him a giant because he is already a fair height: a long, thin, raw-boned, polluted old giant. The set of eyes he has trained on me are deep-socketed and unnervingly pale: the pale, pale, boreal blue of an Arctic hound.

'You had no business throwing out the cartons and so forth.' He talks slowly and over-loudly, as if he's testing his voice. 'All my things gone and I had a need for them.'

I turn to him, breathing like Darth Vader through my mask, and shrug. I hope my shrug communicates a profound respect for his discarded possessions (twenty refuse sacks of empty sardine tins) combined with the regretful need for practical living.

He narrows his gimlet eyes. 'You're a little shit, aren't you?'

I pull off my mask. 'I wanted to find your cooker, Mr Flood. I thought we might branch out, give the microwave a bit of a break.'

He watches me, his mouth tight with venom. 'I could curse you,' he says, a hint of a sob in his frayed brogue. 'I could curse you to hell.'

Be my fecking guest, I say to my Brillo pad.

I draw hearts on the rotten hob with bleach and then start scrubbing again. Mr Flood mutters in broken Irish on the other side of the kitchen.

'That's lovely,' I murmur. 'You have a poet's voice, Mr Flood. Loaded with foreboding and misery.'

I flick the dishcloth blithely into the corners of the grill as Mr Flood switches to English. He wishes me a barren womb (no changes there, then), eating without ever shitting, sodomy by all of hell's demons (simultaneously and one after another), fierce constrictions of the throat, a relentless smouldering of the groin and an eternity in hell with my eyes on fire.

Then he stops and I look up. He is pushing his hand through the spun floss of his hair (white halo, cobweb magnet, subject to static) patting it down, as if making himself presentable.

Then he raises the still-dark caterpillars of his eyebrows a fraction of an inch and dips his head to one side. The effect is oddly charming; it has something of an ancient misanthropic squirrel about it. His mouth starts to work, in a series of stifled contortions, like a ventriloquist with hiccups.

'Are you OK, Mr Flood?'

He takes a deep breath and bares his tarnished dentures at me. I realise that he's smiling.

I venture a tentative smile of my own.

'Don't you ever lose your temper?' he asks.

I study his face for signs of attack. 'No, Mr Flood, I have a sunny disposition.'

'Isn't that a grand thing for the both of us, Drennan?' he says, and with a quick pat of the wall he climbs down from the carpet tiles and swims back through the hallway.

I stare at the damp patch on the seat of his trousers.

I have worked at Mr Flood's house for just over a week and he's finally said my name.

I consider this a relative success.

Sam Hebden, a geriatric whisperer brought in at great expense from a better agency than ours, lasted three days before Mr Flood ran him off the property with a hurling stick. I haven't had the pleasure, but I gather Sam was in tatters.

Perhaps Biba Morel, Case Manager, was right after all in pairing us: Cathal Flood meet Maud Drennan. Biba's cake-saturated voice was full of glee when she phoned me that day. I could picture her, squeezed behind the desk, sucking on a cream éclair. Her jowls wobbling with delight as she rifled through her agency files, performing that alchemic magic she was renowned for: matching geriatric hell-raisers with minimum-waged staff. Biba the social-care cupid, dressed in a stretch-waisted suit and floral scarf. Her voice honeyed with the joy of facilitating yet another spectacular client–care worker relationship.

I hardly listened, but if I had, I would have heard the words: *attracts a higher pay rate, challenging, assault, hoarding* and *common ground*. I would certainly have agreed that Mr Flood and myself, both being Irish, share a love of fiddle music, warm firesides and a staunch belief in the malevolence of fairies. Not to mention the innate racial capacity to drink any man alive under the table whilst we dwell, in soft melancholy, on the lost wild beauty of our homeland.

But now, as I survey the scene before me, my optimism falters.

Even the cloakroom in Mr Flood's straight-up, falling-down, Gothic crap heap is on a grand scale. Part-ballroom, part-cave, with a great black marble horse trough of a sink and wall sconces three feet high topped with whipped glass flames. An antiquated tin cistern roosts high above a monumental throne – a masterpiece in crenulated ceramic. The colour palette of this room is unremittingly unwholesome. the paintwork is lurid sphagnum and the tiles are veined the blue-black-green of an overripe cheese. The linoleum, where I've swept the floor, is patterned with brown lozenges like ancient orderly blood stains.

In one corner a limbless Barbie doll floats on an ocean of takeaway menus. Her smile is a picture of buoyant fortitude. I wonder if she is part of some sort of art installation, like the abstract expressionist shit that splatters the wall and the mug tree lodged in the toilet bowl.

Perhaps this is a job for another day. Perhaps this is a job for never.

A low-grade grumbling tells me that Mr Flood is haunting the corridor outside. He has been watching me all afternoon, lurking behind stacked boxes and disembowelled televisions as I crinkle through his house in my disposable plastic apron.

I'm certain he's working up to something.

Out of the corner of my eye I see him dragging a filing cabinet to the mouth of the door. He arranges himself on top of it, ruffling his many layers of clothing and folding his rangy limbs like an ancient disdainful crane.

Then: 'I've been thinking, Drennan.'

'Good for you, Mr Flood.'

Then: nothing.

I glance across at him, waiting. He is staring down at the hands resting on his knees, so I consider them too. Palms big enough to span a melon, fingers slim and dextrous-looking: a pianist's or a surgeon's fingers. A smear of paint on the knuckle of his wrist, and long, curved nails, as strong as horn. He wears several checked shirts, each with over-stuffed patch pockets, which give him the appearance of having multiple lopsided breasts. A woollen scarf is wound haphazardly about his head. On his feet he wears a pair of winkle-pickers laced with string. The toes alone are a metre long. They curl at the end with all the coiled threat of a scorpion's tail.

I put on my safety goggles and turn back to the toilet, hastily extracting the mug tree from the bowl. I triple bag it without breathing, tie the handles and get ready to start my bleach offensive.

'Maud Drennan.' He says my name slowly, as if tasting it, savouring it. 'There you are with your head down the toilet. Will you come out and let me talk to you?'

Now here's a departure: it wants to talk.

I pull the chain on the old-fashioned cistern. The thing flushes with a rush of rust-coloured water.

'What do you want to talk about, Mr Flood?'

'The house: how are you finding it?'

I glance up at him. He has an expression of twisted playfulness, as if he's pulled half the legs off a spider and is now going to watch it reel round in circles.

'The house is grand.'

He narrows his eyes. 'You're rattled by it and by me. I can tell by your pinched little face.'

'My face is in no way rattled or pinched, Mr Flood.'

'I make you nervous.' His voice softens. 'Don't lie to me now, Drennan. I can see it in your eyes.'

'Don't flatter yourself,' I growl into the toilet bowl.

He sits in silence for a while, then, softer still: 'You have a beautiful set of eyes. The brown of a newly split conker.'

I squeeze bleach under the rim.

'Or a polished walnut table.'

I start to scrub.

'An amber glow to them in the light, like fine Cognac.'

I scrub harder.

'Had a little sister with eyes just like yours,' he says. 'Could bore through the chest of a fella at ten paces and grab him by the heart at five. Eyes a man could drown in. Like hot treacle.'

I straighten up and throw him a withering look. He looks back at me gravely, sucking solemnly on his dentures, without even a hint of a smirk.

'Of course, it was miraculous that she had a pair of eyes at all,' he says. 'Considering . . .'

'Considering what?'

He takes cigarette papers and a pouch of tobacco out of his breast pocket and puts them on his knees. He regards me slyly. 'Do you want to know why my sister's eyes were miraculous?'

I give a half-shrug, which means not especially, and turn

back to the cistern, giving the chain a pull for something to do. But it's too early: the mechanism clanks and there's nothing. I'll have to wait.

Mr Flood waits too. With calm, practised movements he starts to roll a cigarette against his long thigh. His big hands are gentle, adept. I try not to watch him. He deftly licks the gummed strip on the paper, pinches the loose tobacco from the ends and puts the cigarette between his lips.

'It all started with the wasps.' He lights his cigarette and takes a drag.

'The wasps?'

He exhales. 'It's quite a story; do you want to hear it?'

'Is it a long story?'

'Not at all.' He gives me a crafty smile, his blue eyes lit. 'In my boyhood I was a great one for a dare.'

'Were you now?'

'There was nothing I wouldn't do if you bet me to do it. I'd bite into the belly of a dead frog, shit on the priest's doorstep, or sleep the night on the grave of the terrifying Mrs Gillespie.'

'You did all those things?' I give up on the cistern, shut the lid of the toilet and sit down on it.

'I did. I was a holy terror.'

I laugh, despite myself.

He laughs too, delightedly. 'Now one day the town's children bet me I wouldn't climb up the tree in Mrs Clancy's yard and belt the hell out of her wasp's nest. It was the biggest nest anyone had ever seen. For years it had grown unchecked, a great whorled bunion of a thing.'

Mr Flood pauses for effect, taking another drag on his cigarette. 'Mr Clancy had been forever promising Mrs Clancy that he'd deal with it. But it was well known that he was terrified of wasps, having been stung on the end of his gooter whilst pissing in a hedgerow.' Mr Flood opens his legs and points emphatically at the drooping crotch of his trousers.

'I know what a gooter is, Mr Flood.'

As if laughing, the cistern gives a sick gurgle.

He grins. 'So you do. One day, word began to go around that Cathal Flood was going head to head with Clancy's wasps. There was nothing for it but to take a length of rope and a sturdy belting stick and set out for Clancy's.'

For a long moment he sits smiling at his knees. 'Every child in the neighbourhood came to watch me climb that tree. Up I went, and soon enough I got a proper look at the nest.' He frowns. 'There they were, these great long feckers. Flying in and out, crawling over each other with their arses fat with venom.'

Above me, a nervous dribble of water runs down through the pipes.

'But I held firm and gave the nest a bit of a poke with my stick. All the children below roared and hopped as the wasps woke up and began to spill out of the nest.'

He eyes me belligerently. 'My next move was fearless. I stood up on the bough of the tree and gave the nest a good clout. It peeled from the trunk like a rotten blister and fell down to the ground amongst the children, who scattered to the four corners of the yard. We all stared at the nest in surprise.' Mr Flood hesitates, looking at me expectantly, waiting for the question.

'Why? What did you see?' I ask.

Mr Flood leans forward, his eyes wide. '*Nothing.*'

'Nothing?'

'That's just it,' he says. 'Nothing happened. The nest lay there motionless. Dented but intact. And quiet. Not a peep from it. So the children drew nearer. And nothing happened. So the children drew nearer. And still nothing happened.'

'The wasps were dead?'

A smile plays on his lips. 'I jumped down out of the tree and everyone gathered around me and we began to debate whether I ought to stamp on the nest or set it on fire. And that's when Ruth heard it.'

'Heard what?'

He looks like he's enjoying this. He has the voice for it: blarney-coated. 'As we debated, my baby sister had toddled up to the nest and crouched on the ground. She dipped her head to it and listened. Do you know what she heard?'

I nod slowly.

'A low angry drone. The sound of a thousand wasps protesting,' he says. 'Ruth, in her innocence, picked up the nest. She cradled it in her arms and began to sing it a lullaby.'

He relights his roll-up, tapping ash into a nearby broken soup tureen. 'Of course, I'd noticed none of this for by now a fight had broken out. I was refusing to have anything further to do with the nest but the children had come to see a daring spectacle. I was just about to agree to eat a dead wasp, minus the sting, for I was not a total fecking eejit, when one of the children pulled on my sleeve and pointed across the yard in horror.'

I'm on the edge of the toilet seat; the cistern too is riveted: it is holding its drips. 'What was it?'

Mr Flood frowns. 'Ruth. Sitting on the ground, no bigger than a milk pail. Her face a mask of furious insects.'

I shake my head.

He leans forward, his voice clotted with disgust. 'They were swarming all over her. No sound came from her mouth, which was opened as if in a scream, only wasps crawling in and out of it.'

'Bloody hell,' I whisper.

'The wasps began to spread, coating her a hundred deep,

writing, teeming. Soon all that was left uncovered was one tiny outstretched finger.' He mimics Ruth's pose with his horn-nailed old digit.

And it strikes me how utterly convincing he is, his pale eyes filled with emotion and a distressed look about his jowls.

'Then, God help me, I acted, Drennan. I took up my stick and began to beat the feckers off her. The others watched, horrified, behind walls and ditches. But I stood my ground, holding my arm over my face, belting the wasps until Ruth fell over and Mrs Clancy came screaming out into the yard.'

He passes his hand over his forehead, frowning deeply. 'Mr Clancy tried to pull me away and Mrs Clancy tried to cover Ruth with a blanket, but I swung my stick again and again.'

I realise that I'm gripping the toilet brush. I put it down.

He regards me with a grave expression. 'And then, and I swear this to God, all at once the creatures lifted up in one great maddened cloud and droned off across the field. I threw down my stick, slung Ruth over my shoulder and, without thinking, carried her up to the holy well.'

'The holy well?'

'A horse trough on the road out of town, but it was said to have powers.' He glances at me. 'God bless Ireland in the olden days; if water collected in a teacup it was said to have curative powers. Ours was a great well for curing scrofula.'

'Scrofula?'

'Five miles down the coast, there was a pond that relieved pharyngitis. I ran up the road, threw the baby into the water and held her under.' He frowns. 'If she still had eyes in her head I couldn't see them. Her face was pulp, a mess of poison. Her little arm floated up and out of the water as if she was waving to me, although I was sure she had gone.'

He looks at the cigarette end forgotten in his fingers. He finds his lighter. 'But the saints were listening that day and the water in that trough was truly holy. For as I raised her up out of the water Ruth took a deep breath and began to wail. And I saw there wasn't a mark on the child. Not a sting. Not a bruise. I pulled her outfit off and turned her around and around. There she was, shivering and turning before my eyes, a perfect little unmarked girl.'

'St Gobnait,' I mutter.

St Gobnait with her pale hair and calm face, lovely in her golden robe and diadem. Smiling down at the friendly bee that has alighted on her finger. I glance around, half expecting to see her leaning against the sink, but she isn't of course. No reasonable saint would come into this house.

Mr Flood frowns. 'What?'

'The listening saint would have been St Gobnait. Although, she's bees really, but she'd have been a great one to help with the stings.'

He looks puzzled. I've dropped a pebble in his story; it has made ripples and clouded the picture.

'So Ruth survived?' I ask.

He nods. 'But things were never the same with her. She had changed. She began to talk to herself.' He gives me a twisted half-smile. 'She said she was speaking to the dead.'

'The dead?'

The cistern gives a resonant burble.

Mr Flood looks up at it distractedly. 'Mammy took her before the priest and Daddy offered to knock the corners off her but still Ruth twittered on. Until I sat her down and told her that if she wanted to survive her childhood she must keep her abilities to herself.'

'And did she?'

'She did. From that day, whenever the urge was upon her, Ruth crept outside and whispered to the fence post. So it all ended well in a way.'

'In a way,' I say flatly.

'But the biggest change was in her eyes and Ruth couldn't hide that.' He smiles at me. 'They were lit with a kind of sorrowful gleam, a kind of tragic lustre, like *pearls*, you know.'

Something moves deep in the heart of me, as lithe and unwholesome as an old snake turning over in the sand. My breath snags; my nerves catch.

I keep my voice light. 'Not conkers?'

A faraway look settles on Mr Flood's face. 'Do you know how pearls are made? A tiny bit of grit works its way inside the shell, into the softest place.' He twists his fingertips into his cupped hand. 'The oyster coats this irritant to make it smooth, to make it bearable.'

I can't answer.

'A pearl is an everlasting tear,' he whispers. 'A swaddled hurt.'

I stare at him.

'Likewise, the loveliest eyes are found in the heads of women who have suffered.' He smiles. 'Damage lies at their shining core. As I said, Drennan, you have beautiful eyes.'

The cistern gives a tense gurgle and I remind myself that this old man has no idea what damage lies at my shining core. Away with his reveries, prodding at his palm, murmuring nonsense; he hasn't a clue what he's saying.

'Stick to the story, Mr Flood,' I say.

He narrows his eyes. 'But you've a better one . . . ?'

'If I had I wouldn't tell you.'

'Fair play.' He smiles. 'So because of me, Ruth went to the brink of death, was saved, learnt to keep her cracked ways to herself and became better-looking.'

'And because of you the nest came down and the wasps nearly killed her in the first place.'

'Shit happens. Mind, Ruth did predict that I'd marry Mary.'

The cistern comes alive with the happy gushing of water. I glance up at it.

'Your wife?'

He nods. 'Although my sister didn't need second sight to work that out.'

'Why not?'

Mr Flood hesitates. 'Mary had this fiery hair like the sun setting on autumn. Born to a farmer but built for the drawing room. You'd never imagine she wasn't a lady, a queen, Helen of Troy, any day.'

'You must have loved her very much.'

His body stiffens. 'Must I?'

'You must miss her.'

Brows lower over a blue glare. 'Must I?'

'You've been on your own for a while now, haven't you?'

'Have you even read the fucking care plan?' He affects a sing-song snarl. 'Mr Cathal Flood, retired artist, mechanical engineer and dealer in curiosities, lives *alone* in his substantial Victorian Grade II listed villa.'

'But you have a son. He must be some comfort to you?'

'What do you know about my son?'

'What I read in the care plan.'

He pauses, his face a picture of disgust. 'Spill.'

'Dr Gabriel Flood is a Drama and Theatre Arts lecturer and an active member of West Ealing Choral Society.'

'Dr Gabriel Flood is a gobshite.'

I frown. 'Who wishes very strongly for his father to continue to reside at Bridlemere, with the best possible care, pending Mr Flood's admission to a suitable residential home.'

Mr Flood smiles sourly. 'Which will prove a challenging placement because the old bastard has threatened trouble on a *biblical* scale – dirty protest, arson and ruin – if he is moved to a residential home.'

'It doesn't say that in the care plan. So you're not planning on moving to a residential home, Mr Flood?'

'Not while there's a hole in my arse,' he says.

He throws me a look of loathing as he unfurls his limbs in a series of spasms. Hauling himself to his feet, restacking bone and joint. Setting his great head wobbling at the top, all hinged jaw and glowering brows.

He's halfway down the corridor when I say it.

'I'm sure your son only wants the best for you, Mr Flood.'

With remarkable speed, in one blurred bound he's back in through the door and across the floor.

Bolt upright his height is stunning.

He is a gigantic longbow: body held taut, every sinew trembling with tension. He points down at me, the arrow of his index finger aimed between my eyes.

'*Fucker*,' he hisses.

He backs out of the room, still pointing, drops his arm and casts off down the hallway. Piles of rubbish slump and tumble in his wake.

I wonder if I should make a run for it. I sit down on the toilet while I think about this, my legs not being quite trustworthy yet. Above me water races through the pipes, a sudden deluge into the cistern, as if it has been waiting with its breath held.

Then this happens, in this order: the cloakroom door slams shut, a low moan sounds deep in the cistern, a toilet roll unspools itself across the floor.

I glance over at limbless Barbie. She looks alarmed, despite the winning smile.

I cross the room at a half-run, try the door handle and find it locked.

The wall lights flare with a sudden tungsten glow. Burning bright, then dipping low.

I wait, still holding the handle with my heart flapping, counting down and then up again in little panicky scales of numbers.

On high, the top of the old tin cistern begins to hop like the lid of a pan on the boil, dribbles of water bubbling over. This is followed by a concentrated hiss like the pressurised song of a coal-fired train. Streams of water spurt from the joints of the pipework in a series of gushes. I press myself against the door. Airborne arcs of water whip and fall from the cistern. Dashing and collapsing, twisting and falling, like dropped skipping ropes.

The water in the toilet bowl starts to rock.

The handbasin taps join in, opening with a metallic grind, vomiting water. In moments the sink is full, overspill pouring onto the floor.

I watch as a milk bottle, of all things, bobs up from the depths of the handbasin. The milk bottle treads water in a slow revolve, as if, fully aware of its inexplicable entry into the scene, it is waiting for the audience to catch up. Then it launches, decisively, over the side of the basin in a cascade of water to skim across the wet linoleum and knock gently against the side of my trainer.

The torrent halts as suddenly as it started. The last jet from the cistern arrested in mid-air falls, scattering droplets on the linoleum. The handbasin drains.

The room is silent but for the odd coy drip and contrite burble and sheepish plash. As if the plumbing is embarrassed about its outburst.

Behind me the cloakroom door opens.

The milk bottle is old-fashioned, shoddily stoppered with a taped-on foil top. It is empty but for a photograph. I dry my hands and the bottle and poke the picture out.

Two children stand, hand in hand, beside an ornate fountain. The stone nymph at the centre of the fountain watches them with languorous curiosity whilst pretending to listen to her conch shell. The water in her pond looks solid, dark. Icicles hang from the tiered rims. The branches on the bushes in the background are frostbitten and bare.

The boy scowls up at the camera. No more than four, his face translucently pale and his hair vivid auburn.

The girl is taller, no less than seven, and has no face. Instead there is a burn that goes right through the photograph. Edges melted, a raised welt, as if from a cigarette.

An army of spiders march across my scalp. I feel cursed even to be holding this. Drop it, I say to myself.

But I don't. I look at the frizz of hair that surrounds the space where her face should be: russet hair, unnaturally bright, backlit by the setting winter sun. I look at the girl's patent shoes and her legs in red patterned tights and her navy coat. The toes of her feet meet. Pigeon-toed.

I turn the photograph over. The first word is scored out, a series of deeply etched kisses. The caption reads:

Xxxxxxxxxx and Gabriel, Bridlemere, 1977.

An artefact has washed up, knocking, on my shore.

Why my shore?

My shore is strange, inhospitable terrain. It is rock-ringed and uninviting and ruled by odd, unfathomable tides.

Another person, in another time, put their faith in the unknown – in the unseen me. They rolled and stoppered and hoped their message would get through. Someone transmitted: I received.

Would it be churlish to throw it back amongst the flotsam and jetsam and let someone else find it?

Would I dare? In all the mad swill of objects, the house gave me this.

The photograph lies on my palm, turning up at the ends like a fortune-telling fish. It's telling a bad kind of fortune, of that I've no doubt.

I glance around me. At the sodden rubbish, the soaked walls; at limbless Barbie watching me from the corner with one eyebrow raised. Her fuchsia-pink lips mouth one word. *Run.*

Chapter 2

I don't run at all. I go into the kitchen, close the door, prop a chair against it and select a cast-iron skillet. Testing the heft of it in my hand and placing it within easy reach on the Formica-topped table.

I am professionally obliged to leave Mr Flood a nutritious dinner. Then I can run.

Today it is steak and kidney pie and potatoes; for afters there is jelly and mandarin oranges. My landlady, Renata Sparks, says I ought to pocket Mr Flood's money and serve him dog food and crackers. I tell her I derive a sense of occupational pride from finding a clean plate every morning. Besides, the old man is looking a lot less peaky, still cadaverous, but filling out a little around the eye sockets. Renata laughs through her nose at me.

I also have to feed his clutter of cats before I run.

I've named them for all the top writers. Hemingway has half an ear and a rousing meow, Dame Cartland is a sociable Persian with a matted rear-end, and Burroughs, dour and sneaky, hisses suspiciously in corners. They are starting to come when I call; they twist themselves around my legs, giving me bubonic constellations of fleabites.

Once or twice I stop, hearing something at the door: a faint cry, a scratching, perhaps not of cats. Once or twice my hand reaches for the skillet. But after all it is nothing. Away from the confinement of the downstairs cloakroom I remind myself of the following:

1. There are more things in heaven and earth, but rarely are they this direct or comprehensible in their methods.
2. I hardly read Biba Morel's legal disclaimer, but if I had paid more attention I would have noted the words: *council raid, booby traps, ingenious mechanisms, police caution*.
3. Quick reflexes and heavy cookware will turn the tide in all but the most desperate situations.

Keeping a calm, steady pace, I wash up, put my jacket on and lock the back door behind me. Fighting the urge to break into a run, I make my way sedately down the garden path. Congratulating myself for reaching the gate in a serene and orderly fashion, I step out onto the street.

And take a deep breath.

Here the pavement is certain beneath my feet and nothing heaves or scurries. Here smells are simple, uncomplicated: the scent of bus fumes, the dwindling waft of a cigarette. Rather than the thick, fierce, mind-shattering, stomach-lifting stench of decades of hoarded refuse, one unwashed old man, one hundred cats, the shit from one hundred cats and the fecund wreckage of a decaying garden.

It's funny how humans and care workers adapt. On my first day I thought the reek of Mr Flood's house would take the top of my head off. By the end of my shift I could eat a fig roll if I breathed through my mouth.

But I haven't got used to the uneasiness that haunts me

as I catch the bus to work, or the foreboding that grows as I walk from the bus stop, or the dread that drowns me as I step over Mr Flood's threshold.

I look back at Bridlemere from the gate. From the street it's a wall of dark green, a forest of leylandii grown up around Sleeping Beauty's castle.

The only way in now is through the back gate, past satellites of sheds and decaying outhouses. Along a path lined with dismembered bicycles, eviscerated mattresses and abandoned car batteries. Step off the path and you will allegedly find a walled garden, an ice house, a well and a gate lodge with mullioned windows. Keep to the path and you'll reach the rear of the house with the conservatory to your right. A miniature glass cathedral, all pointed spires and arches, its panes fogged with whorls of whitewash and greened with moss. The lower windows of the house have been blinded: shuttered or newspapered to a height. A flight of iron steps leads to the back door, the kitchen, the scullery and the pantry.

The house has four storeys and at the top there is a belvedere, a long glazed gallery, which, if I ever got to it, would give me a view of the whole of London. From there I would see the wing tips of the planes landing at Heathrow or the masts of the boats in Greenwich. From there I would see the changing of the guards at Buckingham Palace or a pigeon shit on Nelson's Column.

To the left of the house is a narrow path that continues to the front of the house, where you can still discern, amongst the riotous undergrowth and suppurating bin bags, the ghost of a driveway. It circles a pond with a fountain where a nymph wilts with moss in her crevices.

The place where two children stood in 1977, one with a face and one without. (I check my bag. The photograph is there, rolled and furled and back in its bottle for now.)

The nymph still holds a conch to her ear, pretending to listen. At her feet, stone fish with gibbous eyes cavort and unspeakable pond creatures turn in water clotted with algae, a soup of ooze. She gazes languidly towards the porch, as if waiting for the occupants of the house to come outside, which they don't, for the front door is painted closed. Walk up the wide, flat steps and look through the letterbox – you can't: it's nailed shut.

There's an underwater quality to the light at Bridlemere, a greenish cast from the forest of foliage that surrounds the house. Sound changes too, noise fades, so that you hardly hear the traffic outside. At Bridlemere there is only the slow settling of rubbish and the patter of cats, and, when he is not roaring a lungful, the subtle sounds of Mr Flood moving, or the silence of him standing still. Sometimes there is a kind of hushed rustling, a sort of whispering. Like a sheaf of leaves blown, or a prayer breathed, rushed and desperate, just out of earshot.

Time wavers and retreats at Bridlemere, coughing and shambling. Here is history mutely putrefying and elegance politely withering.

But for all this, the quiet house is not at peace, for there is a watched and watchful feeling, a shifting shiftless feeling. As if more than cats track your moves, as if nameless eyes follow you about your business.

At Bridlemere objects disappear and reappear somewhere else at will. Put your wristwatch on the windowsill, you'll find it hanging from a hook on the dresser. Turn your back and the teapot you left on the table is now on a shelf in the pantry.

At Bridlemere cats startle and hiss at nothing, bouncing down the hallway with their hackles lifted and their ears flat. Or else they rub themselves, purring, against patches of air.

At Bridlemere spiders spin webs like Baroque masterpieces. They hang all through the house like coded warnings.

But it doesn't do to dwell on it.

Sam Hebden, Senior Care Worker, no doubt dwelt on it and that is how Bridlemere broke his nerve. Mr Flood's attempted assault with a hurley would have been the final straw; the house would have got to Sam first.

Sam Hebden was armed with an NVQ in Social Care and a diploma in Geriatric Conflict Resolution. He didn't need an induction; he merely glanced at the risk assessment. He worked alone. Some said that Sam was a tall man with a topknot like a Samurai. Some said he rode a Ducati and had a tattoo of a cobra on his neck. The truth is, only Biba had seen him and she spoke his name low and with a barely contained excitement. Sam was the human embodiment of a care plan successfully coming together; he was untouchable.

Then he came to Bridlemere.

Then he was gone.

Maybe he climbed on a homeward-bound motorbike. Or maybe he was detained at a local mental-health establishment, frothing at the mouth and ranting about sentient rubbish.

Who knows?

It wouldn't do to take the fate of Sam Hebden lightly. Here are working conditions the likes of which have not been seen since Charles Booth's day. Whole days trapped in a maze of clutter with a bockety old maniac liable to rear up at any moment, all clacking dentures and spittle-flecked gizzards. Despite his age, with his speed and long legs he would run me to ground in an instant, if today was anything to go by. My only defence is a constant vigilance and a willingness to kick an octogenarian right up his hole.

As I close the gate, I catch sight of a sudden movement

in the garden. Mr Flood is emerging chin-first from behind the bushes. He throws a furtive glance towards the back door and limps across the path holding a length of rope and a sink plunger. I thank the saints in heaven I've made it out alive.

I don't thank St Dymphna (family harmony, madness and runaways) specifically, although she is waiting outside the gate for me, as she does most days, shimmering dimly. She is chewing the plait that hangs down inside her veil. She does this when she's bored; it gives her a ruminative look and leaves the ends of her invisible hair spiky. St Dymphna catches sight of me, widens her eyes in mock surprise and blesses herself in an ironic kind of way. Framed against the verdant backdrop of Bridlemere's hedge, she glows and is beautiful. They always paint her with fair hair, but it's brown. She resembles a very young Kate O'Mara, only transparent and world-weary (which is remarkable considering Dymphna was consecrated to Christ at fourteen and dead by fifteen).

I ignore her, hoping she might just dissipate, but she hitches up her robe and trails behind me. I can hear the faint slap and saunter of her sandals. From this sound I can tell she's affecting her jaded gait.

St Dymphna won't set foot in Bridlemere. She refuses to come any further than the gate. The only other time she balked this badly was during a trip to the National Wax Museum in Dublin. She said the place was too bloody heathen for her; there was no way she'd go inside, even though she was mad to view the likenesses of Wolfe Tone and de Valera. She flew up onto the roof and waited it out with the pigeons, sending invisible spits down onto the heads of visitors. Faced with Bridlemere St Dymphna narrows her eyes and sucks air in through her teeth like a plumber condemning a boiler.

I glance over my shoulder at her as I walk to the bus stop. She wanders through pushchairs and litterbins. She makes a beeline for every pedestrian to drift through them. I see them shudder and look around, like someone has walked over their grave. It is not a pleasant feeling. I've felt it.

At the bus stop St Dymphna draws level and flicks back her veil. 'What's that about?' she points at my bag. 'In there?'

'A message in a bottle washed up in the downstairs cloakroom. Under strange circumstances.'

St Dymphna frowns. 'Don't.'

'Almost like a kind of haunting.'

'Just. Bloody. Don't.'

St Dymphna is all talk: all dark flashing eyes and righteous swords and sulking and bluster and challenge. But underneath this she is terrified by anything out of the ordinary, or overly mundane, or pitiful, or unpleasant. Death scares her, as do people who are terminally sick, crying loudly, or depressed. She is frightened of the dark and of enclosed spaces and will barely even hazard an alcove. St Dymphna likes very little other than bagpipe music, stories about herself and dirty limericks.

'I feel like this job could kill me,' I say, more to myself than to her.

'Jobs are very dangerous.' She closes her eyes. 'Disappointment, lung disorders, boredom, stress, futility, suicide, heart disease, disillusionment, diabetes, strokes.'

'And you know this, how?'

She shrugs, keeping her eyes closed.

'So I am in danger at Bridlemere?'

She opens her eyes. 'How the hell would I know?'

We wait in silence for the bus.

Her voice, when it comes, is weary. 'Occupationally or spiritually?'

'Both. Either.'

'In that house?' St Dymphna pouts. 'What do you bloody think?'

'Then I should leave?'

'Do what you want. I wouldn't bloody stay there.'

'Why?'

She hesitates.

'What's in there? Ghosts? Demons?'

She rolls her eyes. 'There's no such thing.'

'Just hoary old Mr Flood and his cats up at the house?'

She says nothing.

'Go on, give me a hint,' I say. I tap my bag. 'This photo—'

'Don't even bloody ask.'

We stand in silence for a while.

'They have the look of siblings.' She gestures towards my bag with a flap of her arm.

'And you'd know that how? One of them doesn't have a face.'

St Dymphna steps out into the path of a man in a cheap suit with a carrier bag in his hand. He falters as he moves through her, as if he's tripped on a crack in the pavement. He looks around himself, glancing at me briefly with hunted eyes. Then he's off down the road clutching his bag a little tighter.

St Dymphna wears a pleased expression. 'It's in the way they are standing, you know, for their picture to be taken.'

'How do siblings stand?'

'Oh, I don't bloody know.' She inspects the end of her tattered plait. 'Like they are part of the same suite of furniture. Sort of unaware of each other, like a table and a lamp.'

'There's only one child in the care plan, the boy, Gabriel. The Floods only had the one son.'

'And they put every bloody thing in the care plan? What about all the stuff a family leaves out?'

Cars go past but no buses.

'All the skeletons, you mean?'

'I warned you.' She straightens her crown pettishly. It sparks and glows a little brighter in the places touched by her fingertips. She has no visible halo, although in dim light, when her veil slips back, you can sometimes see a glow radiate from her centre parting.

'So I shouldn't go back then?'

St Dymphna rolls her eyes. 'Jesus, I told you: do what you like.'

I tap the bottle in my handbag. 'What if this is a cry for help?'

'So what if it is?' she mumbles.

'It's strange though, a little girl with her face burnt out of a photograph.'

She pulls her veil around her ears. 'I don't want to *hear* it, all right?'

'What if I found this photograph for a reason?'

'What bloody reason? Drop it,' she says. 'Walk away.'

'But someone might need my help?'

'You'll only cause bloody trouble. Like you did before.'

I stare at her.

With a sour glance over her shoulder, St Dymphna steps out through the bus stop and into the path of the oncoming bus.

Chapter 3

There is a photograph that lies inside the flyleaf of a book, under old coats and school reports, at the bottom of a suitcase, on top of my wardrobe. Two girls, in summer dresses, at the beach; both have faces and names. Turn the picture over, there is nothing written on the back, but these facts I know:

Names (left to right): Deirdre Drennan, Maud Drennan
Place: Pearl Strand, County Donegal
Date: July or August 1989

This photograph wasn't found furled in a milk bottle in a handbasin in the Gothic lair of a geriatric hoarder in West London. Its finding was far less extraordinary but just as inexplicable. The guards came across this photograph on the road to Ballyshannon in Jimmy O'Donnell's car, under the passenger seat.

It is as ordinary and complicated as any family snapshot.

A girl, no more than fifteen, stands on a boarded walkway flanked by sand dunes. She leans against the railing with her hip jutting out, her mouth unsmiling. Beside her stands a smaller girl, no less than seven. Her hair is tucked behind her ears and she is wearing an uncertain smile. Their hair is brown and they wear the same white sandals. Otherwise they hardly look related. It is a day of warm skies and settled winds. I can tell this because the marram grass that fringes the mounds around them is upright and they do not have that brittle look of people frozen to the bone.

I have no recollection of this photograph being taken. In fact, it couldn't have been taken because we never saw another soul on that beach through the whole of that summer.

It was a wild empty place, that beach. A place where the ocean met the sky and the seabirds screamed and reeled in wide, wide, borderless blue. The dunes were three storeys high or no bigger than an anthill, great ancient breakers or new little hillocks. It was a place of shifting sand, singing sand, sinking sand, hard-packed made-for-running-on sand. Sand with a sheen to it, a certain lustre in the right light (moonlight, starlight, dawnlight). A long crescent swoon of a beach, even its name was magical: Pearl Strand.

My sister said that when the tide was out you could walk all the way to America; the waves pulled back that far. So far that the starfish forgot there ever was an ocean and stiffened with dismay. So far that the seaweed wept itself dry on the rocks with nostalgia.

Pearl Strand was a place of great beauty and great treachery.

You needed to know where to put your foot, which direction home was in, and where to take shelter when the wind blew horizontally. The tides were fickle and the weather could change at any moment. Sometimes the wind dropped down and hid behind the dunes, sometimes it sent playful handfuls of sand skipping. Sometimes it raised colossal storms to scour your arse all along the strand. A gyre of needles abrading your cheeks and legs and arms. Closing your eyes and ears and mouth, plugging them shut.

You could escape into the caves.

These were not kindly, welcoming caves. They were purse-lipped, sinister fissures. Squeeze and duck, plash through freezing rock pools, over surfaces perilously slippery or rough enough to cut the feet off you. Follow inlets of wave-ridged sand into dank, secret places with fierce briny smells – the armpits of the sea!

Sometimes you found the empty throne room of a mermaid with bum-tail hollowed-out rocks and starry limpets studding the ceiling. Sometimes you found the mermaid's salty larder, littered with dismembered crabs and frayed rope, and once a floundered eyeless fish.

Ten paces on, the cave might open up to a cathedral. An echoing masterpiece carved by the sea's savage love, with ledges and striations and a year-round mineral winter.

Only that summer the caves were out of bounds, Deirdre said.

Chapter 4

I rarely make it up the stairs to my first-floor, purpose-built, rented maisonette in the arse-end of Whitton without my landlady emerging like a New Age butterfly from her ground-floor cocoon. Although she doesn't quite emerge; she rather sniffs the air with her heavily powdered proboscis from just inside the doorway.

I've long given up trying to sneak by her. The front gate, kept rusty, heralds my return with its grating alarm. What happens next is a well-rehearsed dance. I walk down the path. She raps on her kitchen window with a knuckle full of dress rings. I nod in a polite and faraway manner or put my head down and run. The result is the same: the kitchen window is thrown open and Renata's voice issues forth with a velvety authority.

'Maud, darling, come inside.'

Each word glides out, enrobed in plush. Delivered with the precisely modulated, perfectly intonated accent usually found in the BBC archives. The speech equivalent of 'Rule Britannia' at Last Night of the Proms: a cut-glass, cannon-firing, wave-ruling, plummy stridency. A stridency Renata employs in arguments with the meter man. I've seen him edging away, bowing and grimacing with involuntary class deference.

One would never believe she came from Rotherhithe.

As I round the house I see Renata at the bathroom window, bobbing up and down behind the frosted glass. By the time I reach her door she's standing there, wearing a rueful scowl and a kaftan.

'Maud, darling, come inside.'

I don't mind visiting. Renata's home provides the antidote to Mr Flood's apocalyptic squalor that my own flat doesn't offer. At Renata's, tea towels are ironed and the carpet is mown in straight lines. Renata once told me that housework was the only way her sister, Lillian, can express her love. Lillian comes twice a week to demonstrate her affection and they argue until Lillian slams the door in disgust, taking the washing with her.

I follow Renata into the hallway. The outdoor shoes she will never wear again are lined up on a rack. The twin icons of her life, Jesus Christ and Johnny Cash, look down from the wall, bestowing their mixed blessings.

Jesus Christ reveals his Sacred Heart: a rinsed orb of holy light. His eyes are gentle with mercy and his bright curls fall softly onto his robed shoulders.

Johnny Cash reveals nothing; his face is dyspeptic. He purses his lips against life's fairground ride of moral vicissitude, damnation and the dwindling hope of redemption.

Our money is on Cash.

'The kettle is on; will you step in?' Renata widens her eyes, which are already theatrically wide with a feline stroke of eyeliner along her top lashes.

Renata favours the more is more approach when it comes to make-up, but it is artfully applied. It's the make-up she wore all her working life, only modified to create a kind of off-duty screen-goddess look. It isn't natural but, as she says, it gets off one stop short of destination drag queen. Renata's greatest fear, amongst all her other great fears, is to die without make-up on. In the event of an accident or congestive heart failure I am to administer make-up before I even call the ambulance, although Renata fears the effect will be more Pablo Picasso than Vivien Leigh.

She pulls up her sleeve and points to the place her watch would be if she lived a practical existence, ruled by anything other than the moon and her whims. 'Do you have time?'

I always have time. 'Go on and sit down. I'll finish making the tea.' I slip off my trainers with a respectful salute to Johnny Cash.

She frowns. 'What about the ginger twins? You know, if you finish making the tea another individual has started? The risk of red-haired babies?'

I have taught her all the Irish superstitions I can think of. She likes them very much. She has added them to her own cockeyed beliefs and now the universe has become even more fickle and absurd.

I nod sagely. 'There's always a risk. Did you measure the tea leaves into the pot already?'

She shakes her head.

'It should be fine then; anyway, I haven't had a ride for years.'

'And I've never owned a uterus,' she says with a lurid wink and sashays off down the hall, leaving a trail of frangipani behind her.

'Good for you.'

Renata has the tray ready in the kitchen. I love the way she does it properly, with the little milk jug and tongs, although neither of us takes sugar. When I carry the tray in she smiles up at me from the sofa.

Even when she's smiling Renata has a formidable look about her, despite her gentle Aquarian soul. Her cheekbones are brutal, and her dark eyes, an unexpected gift to her mother from a Portuguese sailor, have a simmering tarry depth. In Renata's eyes there is the creak and pitch of a thousand ships and the moon on the water and the song of a sad drunken deckhand.

Amongst friends, a wry half-smile is common to Renata and a candid grin is not rare. With strangers Renata has the countenance of an occupational hangman or locum doctor: knowing, dour and vaguely resentful. I have seen many a tentative smile flounder and break against her foreboding expression, for Renata only smiles when she wants to and never to make friends.

Renata draws her eyebrows on by hand, giving them the devastating curve of a committed femme fatale. She wears a headscarf tight to her forehead, with the tail ends twisted at the back to form a kind of dancer's bun. Sometimes she trades her headscarf for a felt turban. Occasionally she adds a beret or a fedora. In the spare room three wigs perch on disembodied polystyrene heads. They are called Liza, Rita and Lauren and are black, red and blonde respectively. These are worn rarely and only when she has guests. For everyday wear she chooses a kaftan or kimono, enjoying their carefree bohemian glamour. She inclines towards fabulous prints and startling colours.

Although her passport puts her at sixty, Renata will admit to no more than forty-five. Born Lemuel Sewell, she was working on a building site and wearing frocks in her spare time when she met Bernie Sparks in a pub in Catford in 1972. She spent the remaining years of Bernie's life as his wife, sexpot and magician's assistant, as the occasion demanded. For Bernie she shaved three times a day and forsook friends, family and her own name. Bernie's magic act guaranteed a lucrative summer season at holiday camps and seaside theatres. In winter Bernie took to the betting shop. He drank perennially.

For a fine-boned boy from Rotherhithe there was the compensatory lure of ostrich feathers, gold stilettos and being sawn in half twice nightly. But Renata had wanted a different life, as a geologist or a holistic private detective. Or even a life that combined both, allowing her to solve gemstone-related misdemeanours mindfully.

This is the path Renata would follow today, she says, if she were able to go outside. For a free spirit Renata is grievously confined.

Her fears are, in ascending order:

The pubic hair of strangers.
Bridges.
Tuberculosis on doorknobs.
Rabid dogs.
Helium balloons.

The certain likelihood of one, or all, of these factors being present beyond the front doorstep of her maisonette makes going outside inadvisable. This is because Renata's universe, like most people's, is constructed on a Sod's Law principle.

I put the tray on the occasional table next to her and sit down on the plastic sheeting she spreads on the sofa for visitors.

Renata lifts the lid of the teapot and pokes warily at the tea leaves. 'So, how was Flood today?'

'He said my name.'

'*See You Next Tuesday?*'

'No,' I say. 'He used my actual name and then he sort of smiled at me. I was cleaning cat shit off his hob.'

'You bear these crosses.'

'Not as many as you, with your mortifying corns.'

'I'm a martyr to fashion footwear.' She waves a feathered mule.

'We never learn. How was your day?'

Renata closes her eyes and tilts her head up to the light. Her eyelids are a vivid shade of blue. 'Blended sockets.'

'Arresting. So a full and productive afternoon then?'

'I could do your roots for you and sort out your eyebrows, a little makeover. Put yourself in my hands.'

'If I were mad I would.'

She sighs and shakes her head. 'You could do so much with yourself; you are really not as plain as you look.'

This is true. Physically I am small with a negligible chest and commonplace backside, although I'm a great catch for a leg man for I have a pair of those. My face is pale with an overly strong jawline and a habitual look of confusion. Eyes are standard issue with a tendency to squint. My hair is long, thick and wayward; a romance novel would describe it as my chief beauty. Sometimes I plait it like Mona Darkfeather. And my ears are small, inordinately sweet, and neat to the sides of my head. With training and effort I could be a siren.

'Would it kill you, darling, to put on a little lipstick?'

'No make-up. I can't risk inflaming my clients,' I say.

Renata wrinkles her nose. 'Balls.'

'Have you forgotten old Mr Polya's stroke event? That was the day I went to work wearing a push-up bra.'

'Pervert.'

'Undoubtedly.'

'Touching himself?'

'Usually.'

Renata shakes her head. 'And still refusing to wear pyjamas?'

'Always. Although that's largely due to his sweat-induced eczema: his daughter refuses to buy him cotton.'

Renata looks thoughtful. 'He's a marked man. Why would his daughter waste her inheritance on new pyjamas?'

'It would be a waste, with him being not long for the world.'

'You see why it's better not to have children?' she says. 'For one day you will be worth more to them dead than alive.'

'It's likely.'

'It's inevitable. Pretend to be dead in the chair and they are happy. Pretend to wake up . . . disappointment.' Renata pulls a disappointed face.

'They're delighted when you trip on loose stair carpet.'

'Gleeful when you break your hip on greased linoleum,' adds Renata.

'Before your rigor mortis sets in they'll be arguing over your premium bonds.'

Renata looks smug. 'I am glad I have no vultures waiting to strip me.'

'What about Lillian? She'll be in here with her elbows out.'

'Before they've even swathed me in my shroud. Just look at all I have.'

I glance around the room. There is a wide-screen television, a sideboard with a built-in cocktail cabinet containing at least six half-empty bottles of Advocaat. There is a bookcase full of crime novels and a Moroccan leather pouffe. Above the fireplace there is an ugly picture of two fighting cockerels made from string. On the opposite wall there is a mirror in a gilt frame and, next to it, a glass cabinet full of rock samples.

'Your moon rock alone is worth a fortune,' I say.

'My rocks are yours. All of them.' She wiggles her fingers and her fake diamonds reflect the light.

'Thanks. Change your will then; I don't want your sister coming after me.'

She smiles. 'Mr Flood will get you first.'

'Don't even joke about that.'

She studies me with a mournful regard. 'I don't know why you do it, Maud; you're such a clever girl.'

'I'm hardly a girl. I'm slaloming towards forty.'

'Nonsense. You've barely cleared thirty. Besides, you're very young-looking.'

'Thank you, back at you.'

Renata's smile is munificent; either an even greater compliment is coming or a shining ingot of wisdom. 'You look after all these people because you think you're a bad person.'

At the words *bad person* St Dymphna emerges from the chimney breast. She moves out across the carpet, treading slowly, carefully, as if she's testing every step with her pale, sandaled feet. She holds her face like a martyr, with her mouth pursed and her eyelids heavy.

'Your job is a kind of penance,' says Renata, who is happily oblivious to the saint trailing through her coffee table.

At the word *penance* St Dymphna glances over at me meaningfully.

I frown. 'Let's change the subject.'

'I'm right though, aren't I?' Renata frowns. 'You always say you are a bad person. You, bad, really?'

St Dymphna drifts over to the corner, where she stands with her hands tucked up the dim sleeves of her robe and her head drooping piously.

'I can't believe you have anything to atone for, Maud.'

St Dymphna shoots me a scathing look from under her veil.

I choose my words carefully. 'There's always something to atone for.'

Renata leans across and pats my arm. 'Go easy with the old man. You can't save them all; you'll break your heart trying.'

'You get me wrong. I don't set out to help anyone; I'm in it for the money.'

'That is not true. Look how kind you are to all people, even spiders,' she says in a soft kind of voice. 'You've helped me so much in my life.'

Detecting a note of impassioned daytime television confession, I dive for the remote control and the blessed distraction of *Inspector Morse*.

Halfway through *Inspector Morse*, when I could have sworn she was asleep, Renata pipes up.

'Something else happened today, Maud. Something you didn't tell me about.'

'Whatever do you mean?'

'You're acting shifty, darling.'

'I am not.'

'You are. You're biting your nails. And when you're not biting your nails you're looking in your handbag.' Renata is scrutinising me; she has even put on her varifocals. 'Well?'

I glance over at the standard lamp. St Dymphna seems to have melted back into the wall.

'Out with it,' says Renata.

Where's the harm?

★   ★   ★

'It's so deliberate, malicious.' Renata looks up from the photograph. 'And you found this just by chance, in the downstairs cloakroom?'

I keep scrupulous eye contact. 'When I was cleaning.'

Renata seems satisfied. 'And the old boy's wife has passed over?'

'She died, yes.'

'He was disgruntled, when you talked about her?'

'He was.'

Renata bites her lip. 'Then he hopped and pointed? When you spoke about his son?'

'He hops quite a lot.'

'But does he point, Maud?'

'Not usually so vehemently.'

'How did the wife die?'

I hesitate. 'Does it matter?'

'Of course it matters.'

For a moment I wish for a straightforward coronary, an innocuous bout of pneumonia, a nice, seemly stroke.

'A fall, up at the house,' I say.

Renata throws me a look. 'A fall killed her, is that so?'

'That's what it says in the care plan. Mr Flood suffered from depression after Mrs Flood's tragic and untimely death. It was held to be pertinent.'

Renata is riveted. 'When did this happen?'

'Twenty-odd years ago.'

'And I suppose it was properly followed up, Mrs Flood's fall?' I notice that Renata is using her investigatory tone of voice, somewhere between hectoring and badgering.

'Now, Renata.'

She reaches for a bottle behind the footstall.

I groan, but I know better than to protest, so I get up and go to the sideboard for two of the smallest glasses I can find.

I was hoping to avoid the krupnik tonight. Especially this krupnik, a unique variety aged in oil drums in the shed of the painter and decorator named Józef who lives at number seven. The resulting concoction is strained against rust through Józef's wife's pop socks and decanted into plastic juice bottles. The result is considered by Renata to be a powerful tonic promoting health and vitality; it's certain that Józef also uses it to clean his brushes.

I pour us both a shot.

Renata motions to me to sit next to her on the sofa, and when I am seated, with the devil's own cocktail in my hand, she begins.

'And do we know who the mystery girl is in the photograph?'

'We don't.'

'But we know the identity of the little boy?'

'Mr Flood's son, Gabriel. He's referred to in the care plan.'

'The son the old man didn't like you mentioning?'

'The same.'

'I smell a rat, Maud.'

'I smell nothing of the sort.'

'You just haven't a nose for crime,' she mutters. 'A hated son, a defaced photograph and the tragedy of Mrs Flood's fatal fall.'

I look at her and she looks back at me with an expression of wily playfulness. I feel suddenly weary. 'I know what you're thinking.'

She smiles.

I study the glass of krupnik in my hand: it is an unwholesome yellow, like something distilled in a renal ward. I wonder how I should approach it.

'What am I thinking?' Her smile widens.

'It was an accident, Renata. It says so in the care plan.'

'Heaven forefend that the care plan be wrong. I'd want to look into that if I were you.'

'Not a chance.'

She raises her eyebrows at me.

I raise mine back, haughtily.

I nod at the bookcase where popular crime novels with mauled pages and cracked spines slump in dog-eared rows.

'Do you not think you read too much in the way of crime?' I say. 'Real life isn't like that. You really think people are out there murdering the hell out of each other like they do in your novels?'

'Don't be flippant; drink the krupnik.'

I look at the glass in front of me. 'It will kill me.'

Renata points at it. 'It's good for the intellect. It burns the fat from the brain. Detectives have lean minds, honed, you see.' She pulls in her cheeks for emphasis. 'From herding clues all day long.'

St Dymphna laughs from somewhere just above the fireplace. It's not a nice laugh. St Dymphna doesn't approve of Renata for reasons unknown to me.

If I finish my drink I can leave. If my legs no longer work I can go on my elbows; I can slither up the stairs to my flat by increments. I will have peace and the cessation of this lunacy. I steel myself and manage half the glass with no more discomfort than a melted oesophagus.

Renata savours her drink a while, then she turns to me, her eyes lit. 'A case is unfolding, I'm sure of it.'

My lips, mouth, teeth, tongue: all benumbed. I manage a groan.

'Let me have my dream,' she says, gazing coquettishly through dark eyelashes. 'A house, a labyrinth of rubbish, a crazy old man and a message in a bottle: all the ingredients of a twisted crime story.'

'In future I'll be telling you nothing about my day.'

'That's cruel. You're my eyes and ears, Maud, my window onto the world. You tell me everything; you always have.'

I never have.

There's a note of wistfulness in her voice. Perhaps she's aware of this holding back, of the unreported elements of my workaday life. I study her face. She's wearing a knowing expression, but that's habitual.

I knock back the rest of the krupnik, wait until I can speak, then say, 'Wind your beak in, Renata. I'm there to do a job only.'

Renata pours us both another glass and makes a joyful toast. 'Here's to you doing your job only, up at Bluebeard's castle.'

In my mind I stray, as the television flickers and murmurs with the sound on low and Renata dozes in her wing-backed chair, a slumbering silver-screen siren. Her lovely face illuminated by the glowing embers of the coal-effect gas fire. A milk bottle stands motionless on the coffee table with its genie furled inside. And a long-gone, invisible saint sits cross-legged on the hearthrug, picking the soles of her sandals.

In my mind, I stray to Bridlemere.

Not to the known spaces: the kitchen, the hall and the downstairs cloakroom.

Tonight I step through the Bridlemere of my imagination.

I'm holding an oil lantern, which is in no way practical (sudden draughts, inconstant light, malfunctioning wicks). I'm barefoot and wearing, of all things, a voluminous white Victorian nightie which is just asking for trouble.

I start at the bottom of the house, below stairs, for this is where secrets usually lie, approaching the cellar door down a flight of overgrown steps. The ivy peels back from the doorframe, sucker by sucker. The padlock swings open; the chain snaps and falls. I hardly even have to touch the handle.

It's just a step over the threshold (feeling the cobwebs brush against my face and arms) and I'm in, padding through subterranean hallways. The lantern in my hand flares and burns brighter, sending shadows dancing into corners. Above me hang the dusty curls of unrung servant bells.

I take in the cellar, where undrinkable wines lie entombed in catacombs. Forgotten bottles, shrouded with dust, their sediments settling and corks rotting. I see the marble shelves in the pantry, which are for the mice to skate on, and a Belfast sink in the scullery where colossal powdery moths go to die.

I track up through hidden stairways and corridors, emerging through secret doors (clad in tapestries and wall-paper – you can hardly see the join!). This backstage trickery is the cause of every vanishing maid and materialising butler.

Luckily every door I try is unlocked, as I carry no key. I've checked, of course; the pockets of my imaginary night-dress are empty.

There is a library full of black leather-bound esoteric books, with an easy chair by the fire and a skull on the hearth. There is a dining room set for dinner where the only guests are the rats that gnaw the napkin rings and the spiders that swing from the candelabra.

The staircase that coils up through the house is dark wood and the wallpaper that peels down from the landing is crimson flock, as bright as a blood surge above the lacquered black wainscoting. There are portraits too: of ladies in silk dresses, of children with big heads and men in tights with jaunty hand gestures. I lift my lantern to see them. They pretend to stand still but their eyes follow me. There are endless bedrooms where four-posters sag and chamber pots squat and windows are swagged with mouldering velvet. There is a nursery with china-faced dolls and a still-creaking cradle. I watch it rock with blithe interest.

I tiptoe over to the window seat and press my face against the bars at the nursery window. I see the fountain below in the moonlit garden. The nymph clutches her shell and hunches her shoulders against the night. In the pond, at her feet, something turns in the water.

I climb the last set of steps.

At the very top of the house there is an attic. With trunks full of pin-tucked dresses, furs with glass eyes, and the yellowed gowns of long-ago brides. Where bats nap among the rafters, wrapped in the scent of dusty voile and the perpetual incense of mothballs.

Across the room is the very last door. But it is locked.

A sudden heaviness in my pocket: what could it be? I look down and see a key in my hand – a fairy-tale key!

A key made of bright-black iron, heavy and long-shanked. The head of it adorned with an emblem: a flower maybe, or a mouth, or a mollusc. The key glows a sudden red and whispers to me in the hot rushing tongue of the forge:

Here is a door that we mustn't open.

The key blazes. Searing pain. I drop it.

My palm is branded. A pattern – not a flower or a mouth or a mollusc, but intertwined letters: a monogram.

M F

Chapter 5

I have added Mr Flood's downstairs cloakroom to my domain, the precarious realm claimed back from the wilderness by the civilising effects of bleach and bin bags. My domain measures approximately one-sixth of the ground floor of Bridlemere, an area that spreads from the kitchen, pantry and scullery and out along the hallway. Up to, but not including, the Great Wall of *National Geographics*.

The Great Wall of *National Geographics* is the gateway to the rest of the ground floor, the staircase and beyond. This remarkable structure is not only a barrier to my progress but also a fitting monument to compulsive collecting. It is over twelve feet high and formed by close-packed strata (yellow spines aligned uniformly outwards) of the widely informative magazine. Each copy has been placed carefully, with aptitude and instinct, so that the whole has the arcane strength of a dry stone wall.

At the dead centre there is a mended breach, a gap in the defences backfilled by VHS cassettes.

Over this repair a sign has been pasted up:

The wall is patrolled. Run your fingers across it, give the magazines the smallest tap and you'll see what I mean. The door to Mr Flood's workshop, lying just across the hallway, will fly open. And from this door he will emerge with the uncanny speed of a trapdoor spider.

During the raid on Mr Flood's hoard it is alleged that council workers broke through this wall. No doubt with the same trepidation as Howard Carter and the Earl of Carnarvon knocking on Tutankhamen's tomb. One party of stalwart volunteers lured Mr Flood away from his lair with malt whiskey and endeavoured to keep him distracted. The other party jimmied away at Mr Flood's defences. Eventually the wall yielded and they were through with a rush of stale air, and, as the dust settled, a nervous troop of men in high-visibility jackets briefly glimpsed the wonders beyond.

Before the wrath of Mr Flood descended on them.

In the days that followed many of the men took sick, some handed in their resignation, all of them chain-smoked cigarettes with shaking hands and stared into space. The wall was hurriedly resealed and the rest of the house went uncharted.

I stand in the hallway looking up at the Great Wall of *National Geographic*s most days, like David turning up at Goliath's with rubber gloves and a risk assessment and wondering where the hell to aim.

On my very first day at Bridlemere I vowed to open it again, to pass through it and find a bathroom. And on finding one, make the filthy old bastard take a bath.

Experimentally, I run my hands along the barricade. I

glance at the door to the workshop and steel myself, waiting for Mr Flood to come springing out, gnashing his dentures and rolling his eyes, like a grizzled jack-in-the-box.

Not a peep.

I try pushing at the stacked piles and rumpling the sign a bit, then I walk up and down, stepping heavily and coughing.

Still nothing. The door to the workshop remains firmly shut.

Then I see him, and only because he moves his eyes.

He is standing behind a pile of packing crates. Disguised as a bundle of clothes and a hat stand. I only just stop myself from blessing the heart that has turned crossways in my chest.

It's hard to tell but I think he could be smiling; at least his lips are pulled back and his dentures are bared. Perhaps he has forgotten our altercation yesterday. Or perhaps he is about to start a new one.

Perhaps he's going to have another hop and a point.

'Can I help you, Drennan?'

I point to the barricade. 'Bath through there, upstairs?'

He leans forward very slightly into the light so that the scarves that are wound about his head slip a little. 'There's no bath.'

'No bath, in the whole of this house?'

He fixes me with a stern blue eye but the corners of his mouth betray amusement. 'There's no bath.'

I don't believe a word of it. 'So what's beyond then?'

Mr Flood frowns slightly, as if I have asked him a complicated question. He thinks for a while. 'The past, Maud, and we don't go there.'

'Not even for a wash?' I ask, but he has melted back into the shadows.

There is no sign of Mr Flood in the kitchen. I have checked the pantry and under the table, although a tall old fella would have to go some to curl up under there. Even so, I have a strong feeling I am being watched as I set about making his dinner: sausages and mashed potato with onion gravy. But perhaps the cats are my only observers. They lie stretched out on the doormat or sit on chairs around the kitchen table, as if waiting to be served. We have reached an agreement: the hob and the work surfaces are out of bounds and anywhere else is fair game.

As I stand at the sink by the window peeling potatoes I see a flash of colour outside. There's a fox on the path, its coat lit to copper in the afternoon sun. It is prick-eared, sharp snouted and looking straight at me.

I walk to the door. It glances into the bushes, then back at me, *meaningfully*.

I'm halfway down the stairs with a potato in my hand before the fox moves. Even then it just sidles, weaving its bright flank through an abandoned bed frame, glancing over its shoulder, dog-like, as if willing me to follow. Like Lassie but with more stealth and less barking.

I follow, past rusting bikes and decaying sheds, through bushes and forests of saplings, into a small clearing. In the clearing is a caravan. The fox bounces up onto the roof and disappears.

The caravan is old, circa 1950s, the bottom half baby blue and the top half dirty cream, with a lick of chrome in the middle. It was once a thing of utilitarian beauty; now it is painted with mildew and moss. There is an oval window at the side and a rectangular window at the nose. Both have been boarded up from the inside, although the glazing is still intact. There are two new padlocks on the door.

I hear a scratching sound and listen, a faint scrabbling coming from inside; maybe the fox has got in and made its lair there. I look down at the half-peeled potato in my hand

and throw it into the weeds, under the van. The noise stops but no fox comes out.

As I walk back to the house I see it straight away, stuck to the kitchen window. I go inside, cross the room, climb up on a chair and balancing on the edge of the sink I make a grab for it. It flutters unstuck; I catch it before it lands amongst the dishes.

A photograph: a field in sunlight, a woman holding a little boy by the hand.

The woman's face is gone. A hole, a burn, circled by a raised welt.

Otherwise she is untouched, from her white patent shoes and long pale legs to her yellow dress. The cloud of red hair that surrounds the space where her face should be is unnaturally bright, backlit.

Beside her a boy looks up at the camera with a familiar scowl.

Gabriel is a little older here. His face and the knees below his shorts are translucently pale. His hair is the same unlikely red as the woman's. Behind them is the caravan. The same windows, the same shape, the same colours, but glowing with the warm cast of a long-forgotten Kodak summer. The sun belts down on field and trees, on the roof of the caravan, and the bright ellipse of water in a paddling pool. I turn the photo over. There is no tape or glue. I glance up at the kitchen window.

Static. Magic.

On the back, written in small neat letters, are the words:

Mary and Gabriel, Langton Cheney, 1980.

At the end of the garden path, by the garden gate, the leylandii is smoking.

This is not the work of a saint. A saint will not cross into Bridlemere, if Dymphna is anything to go by. Moreover, saints, to my knowledge, do not smoke (although Padre Pio was partial to snuff and likely still partakes in the afterlife, peppering his soutane with invisible flecks).

Then I notice boots, not sandals. This confirms my previous observations: I have never seen closed-toe footwear on a saint.

The boots shuffle and smoke drifts into the air.

'You there,' I say. 'I can see you.'

The trees shake and a stranger steps out onto the path.

I rapidly consider my arsenal of personal weaponry: a dangerously sharp crossword pencil, a swift right knee and a Wing Chun taster session.

The stranger holds up his hands in a gesture of supplication and possibly pacification.

'Maud, are you Maud?' he asks.

I nod.

He smiles at me.

Consider the smile of this perfect stranger: at the epicentre is an eyetooth. A singular snaggle-arsed tooth set in an otherwise straight white row of teeth.

This one rebellious, rank-breaking tooth, which, combined with a jaunty scar above the right eyebrow, imparts a powerful variety of roguish charm. I smile back, immediately and without reserve.

Then I wonder how this mugger knows my name and if he'll still mug me knowing it and if I'll let him. I think about asking him as I gaze into the lustrous depths of his grey eyes.

Or should I know him after all?
Then it strikes me. I know exactly who he is.
'You're Sam Hebden,' I say.
His smile widens.
My kneecaps melt.

He lets me do the talking all the way to the bus stop. He won't admit to a topknot, although his dark blond hair is past his ears; his tattoo isn't of a cobra (and it's not on his neck) and he doesn't ride a motorbike. Otherwise we had him pegged, he admits.

All of this with a twist of a half-smile and laughing glances.

Sam Hebden is in his early forties and, fair play to him, he has a shirt tight enough to display a wholesome set of shoulders. In every movement of his body there is that animal alertness that comes from running fast and lifting things. Of time spent, sweat-bathed and naked to the waist, delivering uppercuts to punchbags in dirty cellars or bench-pressing small cars.

Or playing rugby. Almost certainly playing rugby.

Running down the pitch in a snug pair of shorts, the roped muscles in his thighs glistening, the ball nuzzled in the crook of his iron bicep, his eyes blazing icily as he scores a try.

He's nearly a foot taller than me. If we slow-danced right now he could rest his chin on top of my head comfortably. He would have to stoop in order to put his hands on my backside, if he felt so inclined. I would need to be wearing heels with this man, not the second-hand gardening trainers of an agoraphobic transvestite.

'I'm sorry if I startled you, hiding in the hedge there.' He throws a sly look at me with the corners of his lips curled.

'Were you waiting to see me or casing the joint?' I ask.

'Both.' He laughs.

'You're off the case with Mr Flood?' I lower my voice. 'After what happened with the hurley and all that.'

'Yep, and all that.'

'So what brings you back?'

Sam shrugs and looks away. I fill in the gaps.

He has returned to exact revenge on the old man. For blotting his immaculate work record and for sending him mad.

Although Sam Hebden doesn't appear mad, but then if he has escaped from an asylum he'd need to be disguising the old lunacy. I eye him carefully, thoroughly. He still has his shoes and a belt on his trousers, which, in my experience, is a good sign.

He points down the road. 'Is that your bus?'

'I can miss the bus.'

'I've somewhere to be,' he says kindly, apologetically.

'Of course you have, that's grand.' I nod.

Sam glances at me. 'Look, can I meet you again? Not here, somewhere we can talk?'

Where to meet? A cafe? A pub? As a care worker Sam Hebden will have full disclosure from the Criminal Records Bureau. He will have references and a traceable history. He will have passed through multiple checks and safeguards. He will have been cleared to work with the vulnerable and the needy, unsupervised, in their own homes. I am neither vulner able nor needy.

I write down my address on his cigarette packet with my fatal crossword pencil.

As the bus pulls away I watch him turn and walk down the road with the easy stride of an honest cowboy. He could be at a rodeo, the sun beating down on his leather chaps, his shirt open at the neck, his hair golden in the late-afternoon light.

He licks his lips, narrows his eyes and mounts his horse in one easy, effortless move. He swings his horse round, his hands on the reins, masterful, yet relaxed, and surveys the horizon with his grey-eyed gaze—

'Watch yourself,' says Renata. She's sitting in a kimono at her kitchen table supervising the unwrapping of the chips. 'He's on to you; he knows that you suspect him of killing his wife and that you're on the hunt for evidence.'

St Rita of Cascia (marital strife, spousal abuse, lost and impossible causes) is standing sentinel in the corner by the fridge freezer. She is of grave appearance: dressed in mono-chrome robes. Far fainter than St Dymphna, less fully realised, with the slippery transparency of onion skin. St Rita never talks, although she often exudes sympathy.

'I don't suspect Mr Flood of anything of the kind,' I say. 'And I'll hunt for nothing in that house.'

St Rita shuffles slightly. Her face is a little pained inside her veil. She has the medieval style about her: all heavy eyelids and negligible eyebrows. Her stigmata, an ulcerated thorn wound on her forehead the size of a two pence piece, turns from dull mulberry to raw crimson. She glances around her and draws her cape over her shoulders.

We eat in the kitchen most evenings. Its distinguishing feature is its liberal use of wood cladding. Anything that isn't clad in wood is tiled with a representation of a Victorian street scene. Like the rest of Renata's flat, the kitchen is unreason-ably clean. Renata doesn't believe in labour-saving devices because she never cooks, barring the fondue she serves at her monthly Transgender Friends evenings, otherwise it's a mixture of takeaways and what Lillian leaves foiled in the fridge.

'Don't deny it, Maud.' Renata accepts a jumbo saveloy and half the chips, inspecting them carefully in her phobic little way. 'I've told you, there's a case unfolding up at Bridlemere.'

The two photographs and the milk bottle lie on the kitchen table in plastic freezer bags; they are labelled with the date of their discovery, like police exhibits.

'Mrs Flood wasn't murdered, Renata. She fell.'

'So you say. But what about this?' Renata gestures at the freezer bags. 'Nasty, no?'

I glance down at Mary Flood: her yellow dress, her pale legs, her cloud of russet hair and her burnt-out face. Then I look at the little girl: her navy coat, her red patterned tights, her cloud of russet hair and her burnt-out face.

'The boy, though, he is perfectly unscathed,' observes Renata.

I look at Gabriel, scowling at the camera in both instances.

We sit in silence for a while. St Rita is motionless but for her lips, which betray a speechless prayer. Now and again her halo, an understated burst of rays, glows with a pleasant light.

Renata regards me slyly. 'Mr Flood told the police that his wife had climbed up on a chair on the first-floor landing to dust a light fitting.'

St Rita's halo flares and gutters. She stops mid-prayer and blesses herself.

'According to Mr Flood,' says Renata, 'Mary lost her balance and went straight down the stairs. She died in hospital as a result of her injuries.'

I frown. 'And you know this, how?'

'Lillian looked it up. Mary Flood's tragic death was in the local paper.'

'You told Lillian? Now why would you tell Lillian?'

'Why not? She's very discreet and she likes solving murder mysteries.'

'Renata, what are you even talking about?'

Renata pauses. 'He pushed her, Maud.'

'Ah no—'

'He did. He killed her and made it look like an accident.'

'I'm losing the will—'

'You ought to keep an open mind.' Renata sifts through her chips. 'Murder is possible even in nice parts of West London, you know.'

'Look,' I say, 'Mr Flood is a malignant old fecker but that doesn't make him a murderer.'

'But still, there's something not right up at that house. The old man builds a labyrinth of junk and then defends it.' Renata blows on a chip, then eats it with an air of distaste. 'Beating up care workers, threatening council staff. Now I would say that those are the actions of a man with something to hide.'

'He's a hoarder; they were coming for his rubbish!'

'Well, I fail to—'

'They had a skip, Renata.'

Renata finishes her chips and starts to scrutinise her saveloy. 'You don't see?' she asks finally.

'See what?'

'Flood has been sizing you up. He suspects you are psychic and that his murdered wife may well try to communicate with you.'

'Get a grip.'

'Why else did he tell you about his sister's second sight?'

'Honestly? I've no idea. He was making polite conversation?'

Renata stabs at her saveloy with a fork. 'A man like Cathal Flood doesn't make polite conversation—'

'You don't even know Cathal Flood.'

'Darling, you must watch your back in case the old man is considering finishing you off too. He won't want to run the risk of you gathering supernatural evidence against him.'

I nearly choke. 'You're as mad as a spoon.'

'Haven't I always said that you are gifted? It's obvious from your aura.'

'What's wrong with my aura?' I ask.

'Things happen to you, Maud. Messages in milk bottles.'

'Mr Flood probably set the whole thing up.'

Renata thinks for a while. Then: 'This has nothing to do with Mr Flood. This is the work of Mrs Flood. These are clues from the afterlife.'

I laugh, but not comfortably.

'Mary Flood wants us to solve her murder.' Renata's face is grave. 'She is a woman silenced, a woman faceless. To say nothing of this little girl; who is she even?'

St Rita adjusts her veil. My eyes are drawn to the movement. She drops her hands before her and suddenly they are very clear to me, her hands, very sharply in focus. Gentle, capable hands with strong fingers and neat, square nails – hands so real I could reach out and touch them.

I look up at her in surprise and she looks back at me, her prominent hazel eyes bright with a suffering kind of lustre. She smiles sadly and is gone.

'You're cracked,' I murmur.

Renata bites her lip. 'We are dealing with a poltergeist of course.'

I roll my eyes. 'Of course.'

'Have you been bitten, Maud?'

'By fleas I have.'

'Poltergeists are attention seekers; this type of spirit is accompanied by moving or levitating objects.' She muses. 'You have difficulty finding things in the house, when you put them down?'

'There's a lot of shit in there.'

Renata nods sagely. 'A tip-top poltergeist can turn a

room upside down in minutes. Are there cold corners?'

'Yes.'

'Inexplicable noises?'

'Sometimes.'

Renata narrows her eyes. 'Strange behaviour from the animals in the house, barking or hissing?'

'Hissing, definitely.'

'A brooding malignity?'

I glance at her, wondering where she gets these words. 'Only when Mr Flood is about.'

'What you have to realise is that a poltergeist has almost always had a traumatic end. Being pushed down a flight of stairs would do it.' Renata lowers her voice, undoubtedly for dramatic effect, and puts her hand on my arm. 'Don't be frightened. Poor Mrs Flood is only making herself known, avenging her death and all that.'

'Let's not have any more avenging spirits tonight, Renata,' I suggest.

I am mindful that one type of spirit might lead to another and I may not survive another evening of Józef's home brew. But Renata pays no mind. She carefully takes the photographs out of their plastic bags and lays them on the table. Then she squints at them: first one, then the other. Then she gets up and wanders into the sitting room and returns holding the magnifying glass she keeps in the magazine rack for spot the differences.

After a while she says, 'Look here, there's a child in the doorway.'

I take the magnifying glass from her.

She's right. Just inside the caravan, behind the multicoloured fly-strips, stands a child in a blue dress. Her face is obscured by a pinned-back swag of plastic ribbons. She holds her fist outstretched as if to catch the loose strips that blow in the wind.

Renata looks triumphant. 'You said the Floods only have the one son?'

'That I know of: Gabriel.'

Renata taps the photographs. 'So these little girls—'

'It's the same girl,' I say, inexplicably sure. Then I think of St Dymphna's comment. 'They look like siblings, the two children.'

'The colour of their hair?'

I nod. 'Just like Mary's.'

Renata sighs. 'None of this is normal. Who finds photographs in milk bottles and stuck to windows? And why are these faces burnt away?' She purses her lips. 'And what kind of person stays in a caravan?'

I laugh. 'I don't think you can consider caravanning pathological behaviour.'

'No?' Her face wears an expression of profound disgust. 'A wealthy family who live in a great big mansion, going to – where is this place even?'

'Dorset, it's in Dorset. I looked it up in your road map of Great Britain.'

She grunts. 'A caravan, Maud, is that a holiday? If you loved your family would you make them stay in a caravan?'

I glance at my chips, getting cold in their wrapper 'You've never even been inside a caravan, have you?'

'That's hardly the point.' Renata throws me a caustic look and picks up the latest photograph. She dangles it between her thumb and her forefinger. 'So what do we do with this evidence?'

'Nothing.'

'Maud—'

'If it's a trick I'll have played into his hands.'

'And if it's not a trick?' asks Renata.

'I can't think of any other way this photograph could have got there. It wasn't there before I went into the garden. If Mr Flood didn't put it there who did?'

'So whoever planted this photograph was already in the house?'

'I suppose there would have been time for someone to slip inside, but I was only outside for moments.' I remember Sam. 'I did meet Sam Hebden when I was leaving, but that was hours later.'

Renata frowns. 'Sam Hebden?'

'Mr Flood's last care worker.'

Renata looks delighted. 'The care worker the old man threatened? He was at the house?'

'He was outside, waiting at the gate.'

'Living proof of Mr Flood's murderous rage.'

'Not entirely murderous if Sam's still living.'

'He had a breakdown or went to Hull. Isn't that what the agency said?'

'Whatever happened he's back again,' I say breezily. 'And he wants to talk to me.'

Renata sits up in her chair. 'Does he indeed?'

I try to appear nonchalant. 'I gave him my address, told him to come round.'

There's an expression of high intrigue on her lovely painted face. 'He found something out, up at the house.'

'Now he didn't say that.'

I finish my chips and Renata's saveloy while she studies the disfigured photographs with her magnifying glass.

'It's so deliberate, malicious,' she remarks. 'The old man is very sick.'

'We don't know he burnt them.'

'Oh, he burnt them all right,' Renata says coolly. 'And much worse.'

'Let's not get carried away. After all, what's to suggest that there isn't some kind of innocent explanation?'

Renata fixes me with a steady gaze. 'Instinct.'

I clear the plates and make coffee whilst Renata lays a length of black velvet on the kitchen table and gets out her tarot cards.

'They would have burnt you as a witch for that, Renata.'

'Lillian still would. She's never liked them.'

'Is that the root of her antagonism?'

'The cards?' Renata raises a pencilled eyebrow. 'No. Jealousy. I stole all her boyfriends. I was twice as pretty and five times more fun. Anyway, siblings usually hate each other, don't they?'

'I wouldn't know,' I say.

'You're blessed to be an only child.' Renata holds her cards to her chest and closes her eyes. 'Sisters are the worst, like a bag of close-knit snakes, all venom and envy.'

Squaring the cards, she puts them down. 'Do you want a reading?'

'Do I have to?'

'It can't hurt.'

I secretly love to watch Renata read her cards. A kind of languorous grace comes over her, a happy abstraction. Her movements are serene and easy, the fears that rule her waking moments, keeping her trapped and grounded, forgotten for a while.

'Don't you ever want to go outside?' I once asked, watching a shadow pass across her immaculately made-up face.

'I do go outside.' She smiled wryly. 'Have you ever heard of astral projection? It is when your spiritual body leaves your material body to wander freely on the astral plane. In my case it started with my feet.'

'Astral feet?'

She nodded with complete sincerity.

'Sounds like the name of a prog rock band,' I said, and we laughed together.

I once asked Lillian what had happened to Renata to cause her to stay inside. Lillian, red-faced and tearful from an afternoon of arguments and oven cleaner, stopped scrubbing the grill. She straightened up and pulled her mouth down at each corner, carp-like, as if she were mulling something complicated and bitter.

I waited for some kind of insight.

She narrowed her eyes and delivered her verdict with the same spiteful delight as a cat getting sick on the carpet.

'The real world,' Lillian said. 'He's too good for it.'

There was a world of venom in that pronoun.

Renata asks me to cut the cards into three piles and pick one. She lays out the cards in a cross on the table and frowns at them.

Enigmatic characters go about their business in a palette of glowing colours. The cards are thick, black and edged in gold. They are worn and scuffed and a little dog-eared. I look out for the Devil and Death. These are my favourites: the Devil for his leather gimp mask, sexy abdominals and the flames of hell leaping round his hairy goat flanks; Death for his skeletal smirk and luminous blue scythe.

Neither are there, but I recognise a mounted figure Renata calls Mr Darcy, the Knight of Swords. This is a man with a fast horse and a keen intellect who is prone to dogmatism and aloofness. I also spot the Tower, a large stone phallus on a rocky outcrop being struck by lightning. Two jesters in tights fall grinning through the air.

Renata glances up at me. 'A tall dark handsome stranger will come into your life and turn it upside down.'

I think, briefly, of the quarried slate of Sam Hebden's eyes. 'I think we've heard that one before, Renata.'

'And the satellite TV repairman came, didn't he?'

'He was short and bald and you sent him upstairs.'

'Details, darling,' says Renata stiffly.

'So, no murdered wives and faceless children, no communications from beyond the grave?'

Renata wrinkles her nose. 'No, but there's something else: this.' She taps the card second from the top. A man in a cape is waving a wand. 'And this.' A naked woman dances with a curtain pole in each hand.

'There's a lot of wand-waving going on there.'

'Of course, there's a magician in our midst and a riddle to be solved; whether the two are linked or the outcome is favourable I cannot tell.' She peers up at me with mischief in her eyes.

'Before you start, I'm not giving Mrs Flood another thought.'

'Just answer one question, Maud. When did Mr Flood's hoarding habit start?'

'Around twenty-five years ago I think.'

'After Mrs Flood took a tumble? I'd put money on it.' Renata is triumphant: I can tell from the uplift of her eyebrows. 'It's grief, you see, Maud.'

'What is?'

'That causes people never to throw anything else away, ever again. Not even a crisp packet. They can't take another loss. Believe me. I'm no stranger to bereavement.'

'Not with the late Bernie Sparks in an urn in your spare room.'

We sit in silence for a while, looking at the cards.

She straightens the edges of the black velvet cloth, smoothing invisible wrinkles. 'It could have been very simple,' she says, 'a crime of passion. Mary was planning to leave him and in the heat of the moment Cathal killed her and made it look like an accident.'

'Just like that?'

Renata nods. 'He didn't want to part with her.'

'Like a crisp packet?'

'With his history of violent mood swings, I think murder is the most likely outcome for Mrs Flood.'

'You would.'

'And as for the girl . . .' Renata bites her lip.

I narrow my eyes at her. 'Don't even think it.'

'Maud,' she says, her voice a steely purr. 'You and I both know that something isn't right up at that house. Just have a little poke around, eh? See what else floats to the surface.'

I look at the magician on the card. He's about to let rip with some powerful conjuring; he has his wand gripped tight and one eye narrowed. This is someone who means business.

Chapter 6

Dr Gabriel Flood has joined us for afternoon tea. He says he normally visits at night, which is why I thought he was selling conservatories or Jesus; else I would have been more polite when he materialised on the back doorstep. He could easily be a confidence trickster or God-botherer, but right now he's masquerading as a college lecturer with a leather manbag. He tells me to call him Gabriel and gives me a handshake of unnecessary firmness.

It is not unusual for relatives to turn up unexpected; they do this in order to catch care workers pocketing heirlooms and beating their loved ones senseless. Today, Gabriel was disappointed, because on his arrival I was making sandwiches and Mr Flood was doing a sudoku in a cleared corner of the garden.

I have finally lured the old fecker outside where I can see him, in the same way that you would encourage any wild creature into the garden: by providing a suitable habitat. I set out a sunlounger and on a table next to it I left a half-ounce of tobacco, a puzzle book and a flask of tea. Sure enough, after a while, Mr Flood landed there and began to roost, enjoying a bit of fresh air as he squinted at the book and picked his dentures. I was confident that if I made no sudden movements he might stay.

Gabriel sits down at the kitchen table and sets his manbag on the chair next to him. He doesn't look a bit like his father; there's no trace of bedraggled Irish giant in him. Neither are there echoes of the pale little boy scowling in the photographs. Grown Gabriel is a small man and a discordant amalgamation of the doughy and the angular. A sharp nose and pointed chin protrude from an otherwise round, flabby head, which, together with his close-set eyes, give the impression that Gabriel's features are being irresistibly drawn to the middle of his face. Gabriel's body runs with the doughy theme, although he seems light on his feet for all that. As if he's a nimble weasel of a man dressed up in a plump man's skin. His hair is black, not the searing red of his childhood, and badly thinning, although it has been artfully heaped into a peaked cone to make the most of it. Gabriel colours his hair then. I can just imagine him dripping dye under plastic.

He offers to help, so I set him slicing tomatoes at the kitchen table and study him out of the corner of my eye as I mash the eggs. He approaches the tomatoes fussily, getting up, moving the chair further round the table, inspecting the chopping board, making a big show of taking off his jacket and rolling up his cuffs. He is unused to manual labour and it's all a great novelty for him, chopping.

He picks up a tomato. 'Maud,' he says, 'you are working wonders, really you are. I can't believe the old man has let you clear all of this.'

He waves the tomato at the kitchen.

Gabriel has a generic doctor-lawyer-teacher-airline pilot voice. A voice calibrated to suggest trustworthiness and serene authority when some sort of shit is going down. I don't buy it, not least because his voice is at odds with his eyes, which dart from one door to the other.

Then I realise: he's not supposed to be here. The old man will scour him if he catches him in the house.

Gabriel's smile is strained. 'Really, it's incredible what you've done. Others have fought him for a week to throw out a milk bottle top.' He lowers his voice conspiratorially. 'I can't tell you what a relief it is to have you here.'

'Thanks.'

Gabriel picks up another tomato and studies it. 'May I speak plainly, Maud?'

'If you want.'

He starts to slice the tomato with a peevish kind of face on him. 'How can I say this?' He glances up at me. 'The agency will have told you that my father sometimes gets *enamoured* with female staff.'

I frown.

He gives the tomato his undivided attention. 'And of course you know there have been *incidents*.'

I know nothing of the sort.

Gabriel continues, pushing the tomato into a bowl. 'In the past my father has made *strenuous advances* on female care workers, district nurses, meals-on-wheels volunteers, that sort of thing. Which is why the agency usually send a male carer.' He smiles lugubriously. 'I was surprised to find out that you aren't male.'

I think of Biba Morel wedged behind her desk, cackling over her list of expendable care workers, with my name at the top of it.

Gabriel bayonets the last tomato, carves it deftly and then puts down the knife. 'I hope I'm not speaking out of turn here. The agency no doubt thinks you can handle the old man, or else they wouldn't have sent you.'

'Of course.' I smile grimly. In my mind I am getting ready to give Biba a kick right up her extensive arse.

He wipes his hands gingerly on the edge of my clean tablecloth. 'I'm sure your manager wouldn't put your personal safety at risk.'

'I'm sure she wouldn't.' Biba is squealing as I take a run up.

'I just wanted to warn you to be careful.' He adopts an expression of concern. 'My father is not normally as tractable as this, you see.'

I withhold a snort.

'I just hope, Maud, he isn't getting – *notions*.'

I withhold a laugh.

Gabriel's brow furrows. 'Perhaps the threat of the residential home is making him behave? Perhaps he finally understands that he needs to comply with support to remain living independently.'

'So a residential home is on the cards?'

'Not if I can help it,' he says quietly. 'The old man mustn't leave Bridlemere.'

'Why not?'

The knife on the chopping board at Gabriel's elbow twitches.

'It would kill him, Maud.'

The knife begins to wobble imperceptibly.

'But it's very hard for me to help him,' says Gabriel. 'He has quite a dislike of me.'

The knife turns, infinitesimally slowly, on the pivot of its handle.

'He often denies I'm his son.'

The knife stops with its blade pointing in the region of Gabriel's important organs.

'He's told people I'm dead before, or that I've come to value the house.'

'That's bleak,' I venture.

'Sometimes I wonder if his mind is going. He's so often on his own.' Gabriel smiles at me brightly. 'But not now that you're here with him, practically every day, going through his worldly goods.'

His smile is a long way off reaching his eyes.

We look at each other for a long moment.

While we do, I think about the spurious shade of Gabriel's dye job, the defaced photograph of two children standing next to a fountain and whether or not I should try to pick up the sentient knife.

'Do you happen to have a sister, Gabriel?'

This happens, in this order: a cat jumps through the kitchen window and slides the length of the work surface, the knife flies off the table and Gabriel leaps up from his chair.

'Christ Almighty,' cries Gabriel, pointing at the cat. 'How do you put up with this shit?'

I head Burroughs off before he reaches the hob and shoo him to the back door. He slinks out on bony haunches, snaking his whip-thin tail.

With the knife stuck fast in the lino I try again. 'Do you have a sister, Gabriel?'

'No.' He eyes the kitchen door. 'I hate cats.'

'I found a photograph of Bridlemere dated 1977. In it you and a little girl hold hands next to the fountain. Only her name is crossed out on the back.' I choose my words carefully. 'And it's damaged where her face should be.'

He frowns. 'You have it here, this photograph?'

I hesitate. 'Not to hand. Can you tell me who she is?'

'No idea.'

'Do you remember? Yourself and this little girl, next to the fountain?'

He regards me, sourly. 'I don't remember.'

'Could she be a relative? A friend of the family?'

'I told you. I don't remember.' Gabriel rolls down his sleeves, his face closed.

I motion to the sandwiches on the tray. 'Will we? Or the flies will be hopping.'

Gabriel picks up his manbag.

Mr Flood looks up. 'And you can fuck off.'

Gabriel walks down the garden path behind me, carrying a plate of bite-sized Scotch eggs.

He nods at the old man with a resentful kind of deference. 'I'm here for a little visit with you, Flood Senior. A chat and a bit of news about what your son has been up to.'

'My son can go to hell.' He fixes Gabriel with a baleful eye. 'Get off my property, toad.'

Gabriel smiles as if charmed by his father's wit. 'A moment of your time, sir, and then I'll go. No quibbles. No dramatics.'

'I want her to stay.' It is no more than a growl, low in Mr Flood's throat.

Gabriel's smile stiffens. 'Of course you do. I'll grab another chair.'

He picks his way back down the garden path through broken flowerpots and abandoned standard lamps.

Mr Flood glares at me. 'Who are you to be letting this Antichrist in?'

'Was I to turn him away from the door?'

The old man snarls. We watch Gabriel rummaging cautiously behind a tarpaulin.

'I'll go back inside,' I say.

'You fucking won't.'

'Don't you want some time alone with your son, Mr Flood?'

He looks at me aghast. 'That unctuous gobshite is not my son. If he told you he's my son then he's a lying bastard.'

'I know you're estranged—'

'Estranged, my arse. I tell you that fucker is no son of mine.'

I decide not to press it, for the old man seems truly riled. Instead I busy myself arranging the sandwiches and bits on the table.

'Stay here. Talk to him.'

'But, Mr Flood, I've work to do—'

Mr Flood shifts in his deckchair and groans. 'Please. Just distract him for a while.'

I notice that his big hands are shaking.

He clamps them between his knees and tries to smile. His smile is agitated, imploring. 'Please.'

Gabriel comes back with a sawn-off barstool. 'It's all I could find,' he says.

He puts it down and tries to sit on it but the legs are uneven. The effort of balancing gives him an uneasy, fretful air.

Mr Flood gives me a tenuous nod. I start talking.

For the best part of an hour I hold forth on subjects as diverse as spray tans, euthanasia, Copenhagen and potted shrimp. Gabriel looks startled. Mr Flood looks glazed. At some point Gabriel asks for coffee.

I am pretending to make coffee while keeping an old pair of binoculars trained on Father and Son Flood from the kitchen window. They are arguing fiercely. Gabriel rubs his forehead from time to time and flicks through the papers he's pulled out of his manbag. Mr Flood looks to be spitting: I can see foam. I can't lip-read but I'm sure there are expletives on both sides. Gabriel jumps up and paces between the toolshed and the bank of black bags awaiting council collection. He looks back towards the house. I have the presence of mind to duck. It was always a flash of light on the lenses that gave the Famous Five away.

They stop talking when I return with a tray and Gabriel checks the cuff of his shirt.

'Maud, I must be off.'

'No coffee?'

'Next time,' he says. He nods at his father and is off down the path, sidestepping cat shit in his loafers.

Mr Flood is very pale. 'And I wish you knob rot. A biblical dose of it.'

I fancy that I see Gabriel's hand tighten around the strap of his manbag.

'That's hardly nice, is it, Mr Flood?'

'They would have me dead, Drennan. They would kill me and make it look like an accident.'

Mary Flood, red-haired and faceless, scales a wobbly stepladder on the first-floor landing with a feather duster in her hand . . .

'Is that so?' I push the last of the sandwiches onto his plate. 'Who are *they*, Mr Flood?'

He ignores me. 'But I have something Gabriel wants, the shitehawk, and he can't risk anything happening to the old man before he gets his hands on it.'

A splenetic expression haunts his face, a bitter kind of gloating. 'We'll call it my life insurance policy.'

'What is it?' I affect an innocent, disinterested kind of appearance.

Mr Flood glances at me. 'And I would tell you?'

There's a sudden movement from shrubbery to table, a streak of colour and the sharp russet face of a young fox is nosing the sandwich from Mr Flood's hand.

'Drennan, meet Larkin.' He grins. 'I raised him from a cub.'

The fox takes the sandwich away a few steps and drops it on the ground. This close it is obvious that he is far more beautiful than any fox I've ever seen. His coat is rich orange, pale-flecked in places, with a white tip to his tail. His eyes are molten honey. I catch the smell from him: a fierce musky reek.

Mr Flood studies him with pride. 'He's a fine fella. Too young for vixens, not a vice on him.'

'He lives under the caravan, doesn't he?'

For a moment I don't think Mr Flood has heard, then he turns in his seat to face me. 'Do you ever think to wind your fecking beak in?' he says. He makes a shape with his hand; with his fingers and thumb pursed together, pointed, he stabs at the air. 'Before you go sticking it, here, here and here?'

'I followed the fox, only.'

'Slinkeens the pair of you.' He mutters and picks up another sandwich. He throws it into the bushes, sending Larkin leaping after it.

I pick up the puzzle book and feign nonchalance. 'It could do with a wash, that caravan. Been anywhere nice in it?'

I can hear a faint clacking noise as Mr Flood sucks his dentures. 'It was already here when we came, marooned in the bushes.'

'And you've never taken it away, on holiday perhaps?

'It's never moved from that spot.'

'Not even to the countryside, the southwest coast maybe? Dorset is first-rate for a break, not too far from London.' I glance at him.

He stares at me. 'Now what are you saying?'

'Only that—'

'Only that you're going to give your fecking beak a rest.'

'Just making conversation.' I turn back to my crossword but I can feel his eyes on me. His long legs are jiggling. I wait until his knees stop hopping.

'So you've never taken the caravan anywhere?'

His roar sends cats scattering from sunny corners. 'Why in the name of God—'

'Just making conversation, Mr Flood.'

'Don't. Sit me back a bit in this contraption.'

I help him put back the sunlounger and adjust the blanket over his legs.

'Now feck away with yourself.'

I sit back down and pretend to finish a crossword. Oddly jubilant that he's ruffled. Like I've won a turn of a game I don't know the rules of.

But then, if he's set the game up in the first place he'd *want* me to ask these questions.

I steal a look at Bluebeard on his sunlounger: his eyes are closed and his still-dark brows have unknitted and his big hands have unfolded on his lap. He lies lulled by the hum of the bluebottles round the rubbish bags, the breeze and the warm early-autumn sun.

It's a golden afternoon.

Even the cats have settled down and stopped fighting over wheelbarrows and upended mattresses. They lie stretched out here and there, a patchwork of purring furs.

Larkin noses back out through the bushes. Mr Flood opens one eye. 'There you are now. Give me those sandwiches over for this man.'

He holds the plate on his lap and throws one high into the air. It lands in dense bushes and Larkin shoots after it.

'Did your mammy not tell you never to follow a fox in life?'

'That particular piece of advice never came up.'

'Don't smartarse me, Drennan. Have you not heard the tale of the fox and the owl, the Irish version?'

'Is this another story?'

'It is. Is that a problem for you?'

'So you want a bit of conversation now, Mr Flood?'

'Away to hell.'

I stifle a smile. 'A story would be grand.'

He stretches out his legs and squints up at the sun. 'There was once a village on the west coast of Ireland. A wild, lonely place it was, battered by the sea on one side and surrounded by bog on all others. This village was held in thrall by an owl.'

'Not much in the way of entertainment then?'

'Sure, you'd know the kind of place,' he says, offhand. 'Wouldn't it be the kind of backward hole you'd find in Mayo? Isn't it Mayo you're from?'

'It is.'

He throws another sandwich into the bushes and seems gratified to hear the fox rustle through the undergrowth. 'Once a year, on the first night of spring, a great owl would settle at the top of the tallest tree in the village and wait there until nightfall. Her eyes were the size of hubcaps and her wingspan the height of a man. She wore her plumage like a cloak, her feathered shoulders as broad as any general's.'

'That's some class of owl.'

He narrows his eyes at me. 'None of your shit.'

'I was only saying.'

'Well, don't.' He fishes in his breast pocket and pulls out a half-smoked cigarette end. 'Now I've lost me place.'

'The big owl sat in the tree.' I'm straight-faced.

He lights the stump of his cigarette. 'When dusk fell and

night settled on the village the owl would fly down from the tree with her great wings spread and her white face staring. "Death is coming," she would hoot, "death is coming."'

He studies his spent dog-end with a frown. 'I'll need to make a fresh one of these lads.'

'You could give them up.'

He shoots me a look and pats down his pockets for his tobacco. 'The villagers were terrified of the owl. Some hid indoors with their windows closed and doors bolted.'

He extracts a cigarette paper and smoothes it flat on his knee, then he takes a pinch of tobacco and lays it along the strip. 'Others, a little braver, stood outside and watched as the owl flew around the village, as she banked and rose, her face a second moon in the sky.'

He rolls the paper and licks the seam. 'The bird's flight was a thing of beauty and of terror. For when it ended so too would the life of one of the villagers.'

He twists a few flakes from each end of his cigarette then tucks it behind his ear. Ignoring my smile, he continues. 'Every year the villagers held their breath and waited, until, with claws outstretched, the owl landed on the roof of a house. It was then that the villagers sent up a cry of grief or relief, for the owl had chosen her yearly tribute. She would send a soft hoot down the chimney and in a week's time, to that moment, the owl would return to carry away the purest soul in the household.'

Larkin stalks back through the bushes, ready to give chase to another sandwich.

Mr Flood smiles benevolently at him. 'Have you found it then? Good man yourself.' The fox licks his snout in answer then drops to his hindquarters and stretches out on the ground. Mr Flood turns to me. 'Over the years the families of the accursed tried everything. They'd pack their innocents off to Canada, or hide them down the well, or up at the church. Nothing saved them. Within a week the owl would return, then babies, mothers, grandfathers, all, would sigh once and die.'

Larkin flops onto his side, his plumed brush tapping the ground like an angry cat's.

'So it was that time of year again,' resumes Mr Flood. 'As usual, the villagers were praying for the owl to pass them by and land on their neighbour's roof. This time the owl circled round and headed out over the trees.

'On the edge of town there lived a woman and her son. The husband was a great gallivanter who rarely came home. When she saw the owl scrabbling on her chimney she nearly died. The owl had come for her son, but she loved her son and was not ready to lose him. Now this woman was no ordinary woman; she was a gifted enchantress, so she set about making a quick spell. She ran into the house on feet and she jumped out again on paws, in the form of a sleek vixen.

'The owl took fright and the fox followed, her trim red body weaving through field and bog after the swoop and rise of the great white bird. From time to time the owl drew near the ground to feed, but the fox jumped up and snapped at the owl, so the owl flew on.

'The fox was tireless: she ran day and night. Until she ran so fast that her feet no longer touched the ground. The owl heard no footsteps and believed she had lost her pursuer, and so, flying over a forest, she landed in a tree to rest awhile.

'The fox hardly stopped to draw breath; she drove up the trunk of the tree.' Mr Flood stops. 'I've a throat on me, Drennan.'

'There's tea in your flask there,' I say.

'Grand so, and where would that be?'

'There, in front of your eyes. Get on with the story and I'll pour it.'

He grins at me as I unscrew the lid. 'The fox climbed the tree and saw the owl perched on a bough. The fox crept nearer. But before the fox could get her maw around it, the owl spun her head round and started to talk. And the owl told the fox she hadn't come for the boy's soul at all, for she only harvested pure souls and his was evil to the root.'

He pauses for the longest time. I glance at him. He looks to be gazing at Larkin, who is turning over again and again on the path, dust dulling his coat. But then I see Mr Flood is not looking at anything, not really.

'Are you all right, Mr Flood?'

He nods and drains his cup of tea, spilling it on the grey fuzz of his chin. 'When the fox learnt that her son was wicked, her heart broke and, unable to stand it, she jumped.'

Larkin stretches, watching Mr Flood intently, as if he's listening too.

'The owl peered down through the boughs of the tree to the dead woman on the ground below and screeched in disappointment. For one who had died by her own actions was no good to the owl. Later that night the owl would fly back to the village and claim the boy. For the owl needed her tribute.'

'But he wasn't pure, the son.'

'Well, he would have to do anyway.'

Larkin springs to his feet and runs off through the bushes.

'What about the husband?'

He looks up at me. 'What about him?'

'The enchantress had a gallivanting husband, couldn't the owl have taken him instead of the son?'

'She couldn't.'

'Why not?'

The old man smiles sadly. 'He was even worse.'

I glance at him. 'And was there a daughter?'

He hesitates. Then he puts down his cup, his movements slow and deliberate. 'No,' he says. 'Only a son.'

We sit in silence. I wonder if I believe him.

'What's the moral?' I ask.

'What?'

'Doesn't that kind of story always have a moral?'

'Of course.' Mr Flood picks up his sudoku pad. 'Now I'd have thought a bright young inquisitive gobshite like yourself would have that easily worked out.'

'Maybe you overestimate me?'

Mr Flood squints at me. 'For being a gobshite, never.'

Chapter 7

There were two ways to reach Pearl Strand and both of them involved jeopardy. One way was the long way, out along the lane that ran by the side of Boland's place, then down through his field. An area patrolled by Mister Boland's Lady, a collie fully likely to rip the face off you. Sometimes Lady was chained up, sometimes she wasn't. There was a gap in the fence halfway down that she could come out if she wanted. She never did, but she could if she wanted. We knew it and she knew it too.

The best thing to do was take bacon rinds or, if not, a few crusts that had been in the fat. Bread and jam would also work. Oranges wouldn't cut it. You threw the scrap at her bastarding paws just before you got to the gap in the fence. She would put her muzzle down to eat and you could get past with your legs intact. She'd look up and realise you were getting away and rush down alongside the fence barking. Sometimes we heard Mister Boland's voice telling Lady to shut the fuck up, sometimes we didn't. Sometimes we saw Mister Boland himself, sometimes we didn't. If we saw him he would nod fiercely at us. The top of his head was narrower than the bottom, his neck went unshaven and his eyebrows went in a straight line. He had a gap in his front teeth and a big burgundy bulb of a nose.

Mister Boland had shot his wife and four children and cemented them into the floor of his pigpen. He was looking for a new wife and children now; this was common knowledge.

He would watch us pass, all the way down the lane, his eyes on Deirdre, taking in her swagger and her summer dress, her white sandals and her red heart-shaped leather bag. Lady watched too, slunk low at his side, all hackles and stare. Deirdre would keep her head up, her nose in the air. At the bottom of the lane she would flick her hair and look back at Mister Boland over her shoulder.

The other way to Pearl Strand was through the car park and past Noel Noone's kiosk. Old Noel had a wall eye. So, he could keep one eye on Deirdre and one eye on me as we went down to the beach, even if we walked five feet apart.

There were two main dangers with Old Noel. The first danger was getting his spittle on you, for the man had only three teeth in his head and when excited, as he always was when he saw us, his chat was peppered with spit. The second danger was being caught inside the kiosk with him. Go too near and he would hem you in and before you knew it you'd be stuck between the buckets and spades and the bamboo beach mats. Then he would put his old, dry, spatulate fingers on your arm, or your face, or your hair. And he would tug and pinch and stroke. All the time talking nonsense in his strange, high, giddy voice, flecking your face with saliva.

'Now think about it really, really carefully, Maud,' said the guard. 'Don't rush now.'

· 81 ·

I waited, not rushing.

'So apart from Mr Boland you're saying you never saw anyone else when you went to the beach?'

'We saw the old fella in the kiosk.'

'Noel Noone? So apart from Mr Boland and Mr Noone you never saw anyone else?'

'Never.'

'And you're certain your sister never met anyone down on the beach?'

'There was only ever the two of us.'

'Yourself and Deirdre?'

I nodded.

'Every single time you went?'

I nodded.

'You're sure of that, Maud?'

I nodded.

The guard nodded too, but with less certainty, as if she wasn't convinced by my answer but it would have to do for now. 'You're off to your new school now?'

'I am.'

We were staying with Granny until Deirdre came back. Granny had enrolled me at the local school because just waiting for Deirdre all day every day wasn't healthy for anyone.

The guard gestured at the brush and the bobble in my hand. 'Will I do your hair?'

I nodded.

She had me stand in front of her chair as she plaited. Then she turned me to face her and put the plait forward on my shoulder and brushed out the tail end, curling it around her finger. I watched her hands move: gentle, capable hands with strong fingers and neat, square nails.

'There.'

'Thank you.' I felt my plait. This would be the nicest my hair had been since Mammy had stopped doing it.

The guard smiled so that it lit up her eyes. Her eyes were hazel and bulgy and kind. I liked her.

'Do you get to drive the car fast with the sirens on?' I asked.

Mammy walked into the kitchen. She had shadow-ringed, inward-looking eyes and a mouth she held pressed in a thin hard line, as if she was trying to stop flies getting into it. She'd ruined her good cream dressing gown with a coffee stain down the front. She exhaled cigarette smoke and threw the guard a look.

The guard smiled at me. 'We take turns driving the car.'

'You an' him?' I pointed at the other guard who was outside the back door talking into his radio.

The guard nodded.

'Could you get me to school on time for my first lesson?'

Mammy let out a hiss of air and looked up at the heavens. She screwed her cigarette out vehemently in a saucer and leant up against the sink.

'Mrs Drennan?'

Mammy turned on the tap and put her hands under it, palms upward, as if she was trying to catch water.

'Mrs Drennan?'

'Just get her out of my sight,' she said.

Chapter 8

'And you say Gabriel Flood wore loafers?'

'Yes, but how is that relevant, Renata?'

Renata is especially glamorous today, clad in an appliquéd romper suit and feathered mules. Instead of her usual head-scarf she has plumped for her Rita wig, the deep auburn chiming perfectly with the emerald rhinestones on her epaulettes. She looks out of place against the homely backdrop of her kitchen; she really ought to be propping up a slot machine in Las Vegas with a pocketful of dimes.

'Loafers are a murderer's choice of footwear. Don't you know that, Maud? Quiet footsteps and hardly a trace of a print, especially when you tie plastic bags around your feet.'

Her make-up is more extravagant than usual too. To her workaday face she has added shimmering cheekbones and fake eyelashes, which give her the appearance of having harnessed a pair of fitful spiders. I vaguely wonder what the occasion is.

'A nice smart flat-soled loafer is easy to hose down. None of those grips you get on a trainer that just hog the DNA,' Renata continues, sure in her convictions.

'Now Gabriel is a murderer too?'

Renata fixes me with a glare, as if I'm wilfully annoying her. 'I didn't say that. But murdering usually runs in the family; it's an inherited condition, like a squint.'

'Is that really the case, Renata?'

She takes a handkerchief from her sleeve and dabs her forehead. Wigs often make her overheated and bad-tempered.

'It's a scientific fact,' she says. 'So the old man is right: his son probably does want to kill him.'

'Then he can get in line,' I murmur.

'You have to ask *why* his son wants to kill him?'

'Because his son is a psychopath, like his daddy?'

'He still needs a motive, Maud.'

I take a biscuit from the tin on the kitchen table. 'Since when do psychopaths need a motive?'

'Since always; even if it's because it's a Thursday or the voices just said so. Gabriel's motive is easy.' Renata is solemn-eyed. 'He wants to kill Daddy in retribution for murdering his mummy and the little faceless girl.'

'The girl Gabriel has no recollection of?'

'He's lying. You said yourself, Maud, that the children look like siblings.'

'Conjecture only.'

Renata frowns. 'Well, both Mary and the little girl have had their faces erased on the photographs. Mary met with a fishy accident. It stands to reason that the girl was wiped out too.'

'And you'd put your money on the savage old misanthrope up at the house there?'

Renata looks superior. 'Bluebeard? Why not?'

'Two defaced snapshots and Mr Flood is a serial killer. Really, Renata?'

Renata smiles benignly. 'Don't believe me. It is only a

matter of time before more clues surface. The identity, perhaps, of the little girl.'

'Don't bank on it.'

'Or her whereabouts.' She waits for me to take the bait. When I don't, she continues. 'Bluebeard is guarding far more than just rubbish.'

'I don't want to discuss this, Renata.'

'Corpses are like stones, Maud. They want to be found. Ask any farmer and they'll tell you: stones always rise. Look at the victims of Arctic Bob.'

'Renata—'

'Arctic Bob: the Colorado truck driver who kept his victims in chest freezers. When he went on holiday to Florida one year the electricity supply to his carport broke down. His neighbours found the remains.' She glances at me. 'It was the smell.'

'That's enough,' I say.

'Some of his victims broke their fingers trying to get out. Even grown police officers cried when they found those poor people defrosting, all twelve of them. It was the terror in their eyes, you see, staring out through the bags of discounted chicken wings. And the air thick with flies and the ground awash with the worst kind of melt water.'

'I'm leaving—'

'Has Mr Flood got a chest freezer? Maybe the little girl is in there? You should check the outbuildings, Maud.'

'I'll do no such thing. There are no dead children in chest freezers.'

Renata roots around in the biscuit tin. 'Would it kill you to search around the place a bit? You know, be proactive and not wait for Mary Flood to drop hints in your lap?'

She avoids my eyes, picking out a garibaldi and dipping it in her coffee. She is a picture of indifference.

'Why would I want to do that?'

'To prove you are right and I am wrong and that the little faceless girl is alive and well and Mary really did take an accidental tumble. To lay this case to rest, darling, so to speak.'

'And then you'll stop harassing me with your fictional crime case and telling me your horrible tales of murder?'

Her grin is lavish. 'Absolutely.'

'You swear on the immortal soul of Johnny Cash?'

Renata looks gravely up to Heaven. 'May God Preserve and Keep Him.' She crosses the glittery breast of her jumpsuit, just like a good Catholic would.

True to her word Renata refrains from discussing murder and we enjoy a peaceful evening. Now and again she peers over at me and bites her lip as she sits on the living room sofa knitting gloves for retired fishermen. It is appropriate that Renata cares for old seafarers; sometimes I wonder about her rolling landlocked gait and her black brigand's eyes. All she needs is a parrot and an eyepatch.

I close my eyes. The room is silent but for the television on low and the pernickety click of Renata's needles.

Mostly Renata knits to keep her hands busy when she misses her pipe. To her credit she stays off the Borkum Riff these days, although now and again I catch a bitter smoky waft and I feel sure that Renata has kept her pipe, carefully stowed away where her sister can't find it. Pipe-smoking was a habit Renata developed hanging around shipyards during her Rotherhithe boyhood, along with her ability to eat eels with relish. Renata's past is complicated and surprising; I have never asked where she learnt to knit.

I watch her fingers move with an implausible deftness. It

is as if her hands are operating independently from her, cursed to fuss and jab at the wool for all eternity.

But her mind isn't on the wool: it's on Mary Flood and the faceless child. Her happy scowl tells me my friend is thinking of dark deeds.

'So, no word from Mary Flood today?'

'I thought we were talking about something other than death and murder and bones for a change? You swore.'

Renata puts down her knitting. 'We'll talk about the living then.' She regards me coyly. 'A man called today for you; he was very *alive*.' She puts a lewd spin on the word.

'The satellite TV repairman?'

The satellite TV repairman lives with his mother and participates in historical re-enactments (Roundhead). When he last visited, two pairs of knickers went missing from my bathroom radiator. Renata has encouraged this match due to some folkloric notion of warding off the certain evils visited on our community by my prolonged spinsterhood.

Renata shakes her head. 'No, this one was a hunky blondie.' She returns to her knitting.

'Did he leave his name?' I ask, although I already know it.

'He did. Then we drank vermouth and he fixed the bathroom blind. Lovely man. Well-muscled.' Renata looks at me. 'It was Sam, you know, the threatened care worker who went mad or back to Hull.'

Hence the wig and the glad rags. I can just imagine her scuttling off to change then returning to drape herself nonchalantly over furniture. A woman transformed, exuding sudden star quality.

'And you're only telling me this now?'

She shrugs, not in the least repentant.

'Did Sam say what he wanted to talk to me about?'

'At first it wasn't clear why he was here, either to Sam or to me. Until we did his cards.' She frowns. 'Major Arcana and Swords such as you wouldn't believe. Justice, Judgement and the Wheel of Fortune, all upside down.' She purses her lips. 'But he took it well.'

'Did he say anything about the house? About Mr Flood?'

'No, but I told him that we're on to Mr Flood for killing his wife, along with a young unidentified female relative.' She keeps her head down, rummaging in her knitting bag.

'Why did you tell him that? What if he's still in a delicate state of mind, after the assault? He could believe it.'

Renata pulls out a ball of lurid pink wool; she squeezes it, then, satisfied, picks up her needles. 'Sam isn't delicate at all. If by *delicate* you mean *mental*.'

I stare at her in despair.

She begins to cast off. 'He came here today to tell you to stop working at Bridlemere. He likes you.' She smirks. 'He's worried for your safety.'

'Sam said that?' I ask.

She pettishly knits a few more stitches, then glances up at me. 'He thinks you are in grave danger from Mr Flood.'

I can't help but smile. 'And aren't you worried for my safety, Renata? Sending me off digging around Bluebeard's lair.'

'I know you; why would I be worried?'

'Thanks.'

'You are like me, Maud. Drop us, we bounce. Kick us, we bounce.' She puts her knitting down. 'Besides. There's a puzzle to be solved here, an intrigue. Do we run away?'

I don't answer.

Renata nods, gratified. 'As you know, the best things in life are usually a little dangerous.' She extracts a full bottle of krupnik from the side of her chair with a smile.

Chapter 9

'Meeting her boyfriend, is she? In a rush to get down there, is she? End of your visit to Granny's, is it? Making the most of it, is she?'

Noel Noone always asked four questions to one, for he never had anyone to talk to. Nobody ever visited his kiosk. Even so, he was there all day, every day.

Old Noel sold cigarettes, sweets, deckchairs (try putting one of those up; the wind would laugh its bollocks off), fishing nets with cane handles and buckets and spades (blue or pink, square or round turrets). He had a kettle out the back and he'd make you a tea but the milk was chancy and you had to stay and drink it in front of him so he could have the cup back. The cups had drippings on the outside; we were uncertain as to whether he ever washed them.

Old Noel called Deirdre Sugarcheeks and Deirdre called him a dirty old fecker.

He had cornered me near the second-hand books, pinching the top of my arm, squeezing my earlobe and circling my wrist with his grabbling fingers. And all the while talking in his strange, high, giddy voice with the spits coming out of his bluish lips.

Old Noel regarded me intently with one eye. His other eye was trained on Deirdre as she stood outside the door to the kiosk. Deirdre had her back to us. An angel framed against the sunlit tarmac of the car park, her brown hair burnished, pinned up, wispy curls falling on her narrow neck nape.

I saw him see this with his wall eye.

He saw her slim shoulder blades under her dress and the rouge on her cheeks. She'd picked a spot on her chin; he saw this too. For after all Deirdre wasn't perfect, although she looked it in some lights.

Deirdre kicked the doorframe with her sandal, surveyed the sky with an expression of profound boredom and then opened her handbag. It was beautiful: heart-shaped and made from red leather. Deirdre let me touch it once and showed me the inside. It was lined with pink silk and had a gold popper to keep it closed. The strap was a fine slim ribbon of a thing. Jimmy O'Donnell had given it to her, for no other reason than he felt like it.

Jimmy O'Donnell was Mammy's special friend. They had gone to the pictures together when they were kids. Then they grew up and Mammy moved away, married Daddy and had us. One day, when we were back visiting Granny, Jimmy asked Mammy to go to the pictures with him again. After that, Jimmy was around all the time.

Deirdre said she would rip the head off me if I breathed a word to anyone about Jimmy giving her the bag.

I loved Jimmy O'Donnell less from that moment.

Jimmy with his long hair and dark laughing eyes and the fast car that he'd drive from town to coast and back again just to spend an hour with us.

It was a curse, Deirdre's handbag, for with its arrival came the departure of Jimmy.

Now Jimmy no longer gave us piggybacks out along the field, or sat with us in the kitchen pulling faces behind Mammy's back, or gave us money to buy sweets. Now Jimmy visited less and less, and when he did, he and Mammy argued and he left with his tyres tearing up the gravel.

Deirdre took bubblegum out of her handbag and snapped it shut. She chewed, moving from heel to toe on the tarmac, wanting to be gone. She blew a few experimental bubbles; they grew and collapsed, sticky pink. She gathered the ruptured gum with thumb and forefinger and pushed it back into her mouth.

Old Noel wet his lip and gave my wrist a quick press. He was waiting for a reply, impatient for a reply. One of his eyes watched Deirdre and the other watched me.

I spoke the words Deirdre told me to speak slowly and carefully. 'We have never seen another living soul on the beach. There is only ever us.'

Deirdre turned and looked at me over her shoulder. Perhaps she narrowed her eyes. Perhaps she gave me a half-smile or a scowl. I can't remember.

I can hardly even remember her face now, just the bag. A heart of red leather and pink silk, a gold popper and a thin, thin, strawberry-shoelace strap.

Old Noel bent closer and spat in my ear. '*I don't believe you, Twinkle.*'

Then he straightened up and winked at Deirdre, as well he might, for in less than a week she would be gone.

Chapter 10

I will kill Larkin, for he is driving me insane. Like his master he torments me from morning to afternoon. Both of them, skulking and nosing in shopping bags, leaving their foxy reek in corridors and corners, tripping me up and watching me. I threaten them both outside. Mr Flood, in a coat and a pair of ratty slippers, roosts on the sunlounger. Larkin stretches out at his feet. Sometimes one or other of the cats joins them, prancing just near enough to cause offence or jumping in the branches of the overhanging trees. Sometimes Larkin gives chase, causing caterwauls.

They both seem to be immune to the smell emanating from the wall of rubbish bags I have been stealthily lining up along the pathway in readiness for the skip that is coming tomorrow.

'Will you come out, Drennan, and sit with me?' Mr Flood shouts.

When I take him out his lime cordial he winks at me.

Since Gabriel's visit we have developed an uneasy sort of camaraderie. I laugh at his jokes and he tolerates my whole-sale disposal of his possessions.

Only sometimes I catch a certain look in his eye as he watches me clearing and sorting, bagging and dragging. Then I realise: I'm like a bird, a busy bird, hopping between a lion's paws, inches away from tooth and claw. One wrong move and I'll get it.

So I don't drop my guard: if he comes at me with a hurley I'll be ready.

I pull up Gabriel's wonky barstool and sit down.

Mr Flood salutes me with his glass and gives me the alligator smile of a TV advert denture-wearer: jauntily fraudulent. Larkin peers down from the roof of the toolshed where he's been giving chase.

'Get him a pork pie. Go on.' Mr Flood points at the fox.

'I won't; they're for your tea with a bit of potato salad.'

He shakes his head. 'I'm fine and fat. I can spare it.' He pats his chest, which is savagely thin. His arms are worse.

Earlier, when he peeled off his clothes for laundering, the man went from gaunt to skeletal in a moment. I had two pairs of trousers, four shirts and three jumpers off him. He had stood in his vest and underpants in the scullery, with a curve to his back like a bent bow. The shocking thinness of his limbs made his joints, feet, hands and head look disproportionately large. A giant buckled by famine. His skin hung on his long frame like a flag on a pole on a windless day.

'You had a fair few clothes on, Mr Flood,' I'd said to him.

'I had.'

'Do you feel better for wearing them all at the same time?'

He shrugged. 'I get attached to my bits and pieces.'

'And will you be doing that again, wearing all your things at once, when I've laundered and pressed them?'

'I will, Drennan.'

'There's your coat over the door there; you can put that on for a bit of decency while I deal with these.'

And as tractable as a good child he'd wandered off with his white head wobbling and his gangling arms held stiffly askew from his body and his elbows jutting at a sharp angle. Like the picked and bleached carcass of an ancient buzzard struggling to take flight.

Pity caught in my throat for him and, in that moment, I doubted every one of Renata's theories. This was no murderer, just some abandoned old man. But then I studied him closely: the breadth of his shoulders, the size of his hands and his pitiless pale, pale eyes. In his prime this man would have been terrifying.

I sit quietly on the barstool next to him, turning my face up to the sun, relaxed now that I know where he is. After a while I glance at him. He's kept hold of the coat, I notice; the pockets are full already.

'How's the clean shirt? It's a pity Gabriel didn't see his old fella looking so fine.'

'I've told you. That fat arsewipe is not my son. *Capiche?*' There's a wild gleam in his eyes, so I just nod.

'He's a solicitor, you know, that pestilent fucker.'

'Is he? I thought he was a university lecturer?'

Mr Flood looks at me witheringly. 'Jesus, do you people ever listen? Or do you just prefer the sound of your own fecking mouths flapping?'

Another fight is breaking out on the roof of the toolshed. A ginger tom scales down the side, his tale snaking.

'He told you to leave?' he asks.

'He didn't.'

'But he said that I was a pervert?' There is a dangerous hint of a smile on his face.

I say nothing.

'He told you I'd tried it on with one of the carers? Molested her? Tried to finger her?' He bares his dentures in a bitter sneer.

'Any more of that and I'll be out of here. Straight up.'

'You will in your arse,' he says, but he stops sneering. 'So what did he say?'

'Look, I don't want to get involved in any dispute here.'

'Of course you don't – and you earwigging with binoculars when I was talking to that bollix in the garden.'

I look at him. 'Now why would I do that? On your private business?'

'Because you have a beak you like to stick into other people's private business. Fecking snipe.'

'I don't at all. I keep my head down and get on with my work. Which is what I should be doing now, so if you've finished your drink?'

He nods. 'Good girl yourself, off you go. I wouldn't dream of distracting you from your important work. Thieving away my few things and selling them, right under the old caubogue's nose. Spending my bit of shopping money on yourself and feeding me the cat's leftovers.'

'You really are a nasty old bastard.' I've said it before I realise it.

As I walk down the path I hear him chuckling with delight.

I take his glass into the kitchen to wash it. When I look out again he has put down the back of the sunlounger and is lying dead to the world, his twiggy old arms stretched out above him. Larkin has crawled underneath the chair and is curled up like a dog.

It's a nice day for it. The sun shines down on a garden that looks like Armageddon has come to a municipal dump. But the sun doesn't mind. She burnishes rusty paint tins full of rainwater and warms abandoned mattresses for sleeping cats. Her rays are indiscriminate: they fall on wooden pallets and stacked roof tiles as well as the late daisies and crocosmia that bring pockets of colour to this blighted land. I stand at the sink watching Mr Flood's old checked shirts flutter on the line I've strung between the house and the toolshed. It's good drying weather for autumn; if I knew where Mr Flood's bed was I could tackle his sheets. God only knows the condition of them.

Somewhere in the house above me a door slams, hard. Then it does it again, and again.

Then there is silence.

I grab a pair of salad tongs and run into the hall.

Nothing is moving; even the clutter is waiting, holding its breath.

On a box of tangled electrical leads a black handbag purses its leathery mouth and a knitted spider frowns. In a laundry basket a troupe of china ladies grip their parasols and hats.

Dame Cartland peers out from behind a tea chest, big-eyed. We listen hard, the shabby-arsed cat and myself. We listen to the silence.

There is definitely silence. But what class of silence is it?

The rubbish is still and the mice are dead in the teacups. Mr Flood is asleep on the lounger and Larkin is curled up in his shade.

Holding the salad tongs, I edge along the hallway and stare in astonishment at the Great Wall of *National Geographics*.

Backlit with afternoon sun, there is a crack of radiant light right down the middle.

Dame Cartland sits back on her haunches and shakes out a paw. She starts cleaning it nonchalantly, biting between the pink pads.

'Will I go through? I could just about fit.'

She throws me a look of majestic indifference, then turns to lick her flank.

I grip the salad tongs and take a deep breath.

Everything is different on the other side. On the other side there are no cobwebs, cat hairs or drifts of newspapers. There are no piles of pizza menus or heaps of sardine cans. Instead there are objects that glisten as if they are newly minted, like pristine treasures on a beach when the tide goes out. But these objects are not new or remotely lovely; I have stepped through the Great Wall into a museum of terrible wonders.

Glass cases of differing sizes are stacked all along the hallway. In one, a pale Botticelli Venus reclines, spooling out her gastric organs with a smile. In the case above her is a severed foot with bubbling skin and wizened toes. I peer at the label: *gangrenous necrosis*. Next door is a female pudendum with an advanced case of syphilis. I hum a little song and remind myself that I am not squeamish: I have entry-level training in bedsores.

Dame Cartland comes slinking through the gap in the Great Wall with her rear low to the floor. She glances around and, hearing a rustle, gives chase, her tattered rump shaking as she runs. I watch her disappear out of sight at the end of the corridor.

Further along, under a magnificent domed bell jar, is a tray of glass eyes. As I draw nearer I hear a click. The click is followed by a whirr.

I watch in horror as the tray begins to move and tip, causing each eyeball to turn in its own small hole. As I pass by, the eyes follow me. A hundred lidless glares, each one pale, pale, boreal blue.

On a nearby stand sits a shrunken head, a sinister coconut

in a hellish shy. It cries trails of thread from its sewn-up eyes, on its wrinkled lips a stitched pout. A plume of hair spills down and around its stand.

There is a card tacked to the plinth, it reads:

Cathal T. Flood
Purveyor of Antiques and Curiosities
Flora and Fauna, Medical, Scientific
Specialist in Taxidermy and Victorian Automata.

Out of the corner of my eye I see movement. Along the corridor a pack of stoats are playing poker. The dealer wears a visor and a cigar in its twisted smile and deals a rackety hand. Across the hallway there is a raven in a Yeoman Warder's hat. It shifts on its perch, ruffling its wings with a noise like the grinding down of gears, the black beads of its eyes glittering.

Certain words return to me from Biba Morel's legal disclaimer (hardly read). *Council raid, booby traps, ingenious mechanisms—*

I freeze and wait for the feathered darts with fatal poisons to hit, the net to drop, the whetted axe to fall.

The floor beneath my feet is covered with Turkish rugs. There are trapdoors lying under them. A headlong route onto bloodstained stone flags in a dank cellar, cranium smashed, splattering skull shards and jelly. I move slowly, treading carefully, keeping my eyes open for tripwires. I pass doors obscured by drawers and cabinets. I creep gingerly between them to try locked handles.

The corridor gives way to a grand entrance hall with a sweeping dark-wood staircase. A stained-glass window, graced with knights with pointed feet and ladies with great ropes of hair, throws a kaleidoscope of jewelled colours on the stairs below.

And there, perched on the newel post, is a nightmare.

I would consider running if I could move my legs. For here is a horror that not even Jason and a whole rake of Argonauts would take on.

A four-headed beast keeps watch in every direction.

The exact species that contributed their heads is uncertain, but I hazard a guess at dog, horse, pig and deer. Each creature appears to have met its death through a collision. The heads are set on the body of a carved wooden figurehead, full-breasted, arms by its side. Swan's wings, moulting badly and yellow with age, curve from the shoulders of this terrible, raddled guardian angel.

As I inch nearer to the bottom of the staircase the wings flutter stiffly and the heads begin a slow revolve. Each set of eyes, in their respective mashed orbits, addressing me in turn. I stand firm and expect the worst. The mechanism comes to a tottering halt with the head of a pig facing me.

I wait. The pig has a flinty twinkle in its eyes and a haughty wrinkle to its nose.

Nice pig. Good pig.

I force myself to look away – at a staircase awash with curiosities.

There are oddly shaped parcels and baskets of furled rolls of paper. A prosthetic arm sticks out from one of them as if hailing a cab. There are specimen jars containing slivers of gristle and boxes of contraptions with rubber nozzles, like distant relations of the sink plunger. On the bottom step a plaster model of a human heart lies broken.

There is a rustle and a clank above me. A shadow flits along the first-floor landing. Every last hair on my neck nape stands up.

I watch, riveted, as an object begins to roll down the stairs. It pitches unhurriedly from step to step. Sometimes falling with a dull thud, sometimes with the chink of glass on china or metal. Occasionally it loses momentum and wobbles on the spot for a while. Then it musters strength and continues. Eventually it lands at the bottom of the stairs where it knocks against my feet.

Something wrapped in newspaper.

I pick it up. Unwrap it. It's a paperweight. Cut glass, a carved starburst on the base. I stare at it in my hand for the longest time and wonder what the message is.

Then I realise.

I put the paperweight down and look at the newspaper cutting in my other hand. I read the headline:

Missing Dorset Schoolgirl

A girl with fair hair looks at the camera with a wide, rakish grin. She has her arm around a goat and seems to be intent on feeding it a crisp packet. Underneath is a name: *Maggie Dunne*.

Chapter 11

At Pearl Strand the tide would arrive in a sly fashion. Insinuating itself in snaky rivulets carved in the sand, at first lazy, then rushing in with a pace that terrified me. If I wanted to survive I should stay exactly where Deirdre said. To the left of me was sinking sand, to the right, a nest of horseflies. Behind me Old Noel was taking his afternoon stroll with his fingers just twitching for a feel. And before me the Atlantic was always sneaking nearer.

Deirdre shaved her legs with Mammy's razor. When she cycled she tucked her dress into her drawers. She stole lipstick and money and cigarettes. Deirdre was wild. This was common knowledge. That summer Mammy made her take me everywhere with her, for wouldn't that take the wind out of Deirdre's sails?

Once upon a time we had chased each other up and down the beach, Deirdre and me. She had chased me one way and I had chased her the other. That was the summer that Deirdre lived only for horses. We had a stable full of them, with golden manes and diamond hooves and we rode them fast along the hem of the sea.

The next summer, castles were the thing. We banked sand and built forts with the treasure the sea left behind. Crab Death Castle with its portcullis of pincers and broken legs waving from the battlements. A place with a cursed aspect. Bladderwrack crawled down its walls and its moat was infested with deadly rope octopuses. Princess Castle had stained-glass windows made from smooth-edged fragments of bottles, clear, green and brown. Its drawbridge was paved with a million shells. Its wildflower garden had been picked from the dunes—

Dunes creep. Deirdre told me as much. They could move inches when you weren't looking. If you annoyed them by running over them, or snooping round them, or digging into them they would simply glide over you and you would never be seen again. The sand would fill your mouth, plug your nose and squash your eyes. You'd suffocate with the whole massive weight of the dune above you. You'd die in the dark, listening to the sound of your ribs breaking and the sand rushing into your ears.

The best thing to do was not to annoy the dunes but rather to sit still and read your book and keep your fecking mouth shut.

I couldn't read and watch the dunes at the same time. So I brought a book I knew so well I wouldn't have to look at it. That way I could keep my eyes on the dunes. The book was called *The Illustrated Book of Saints*; it had been Granny's and then it was mine. I knew it by heart, words and pictures both.

I liked the pictures best.

St Joseph of Cupertino flying over the wall of the monastery with an unflattering tonsure and a look of amazement on his face (as well he might – a plump monk clearing eight feet). St Dymphna, with her laughing eyes and gold crown, walking over a field with her feet white against the green. St George, a secret favourite of mine just for his glinting armour and smirking yellow-eyed dragon. I knew every habit and robe, halo and attribute of the major saints and many of the minor ones.

The saints were brilliant. There they all were having revelations, or building churches, or being fed to lions. I loved their veils and coronets, coifs and birettas, their holy expressions and long pale hands. If I closed my eyes (quickly, because of the dunes) I could hear their voices – soft supplications and whispered prayers – in the wind coming in off the bay and the waves washing the shore. Sometimes I could even smell the saints. A subtle smell that came and went. Starched wimples and elderly velvet, spicy incense and the odour of sanctity – like the sweet, sad scent of overblown roses.

On cold days, or on wet days, or when the dunes moved and my heart stopped with the fear of being smothered, I imagined it was all part of my nun training, such as the wearing of itchy knickers or the eating of soup. I would suffer these privations willingly: it would be worth it to join a convent. Granny said a nun's life was dull, but I knew better. At a convent you had your own room and coach outings every weekend. Depending on the order, you could grow flowers, play with chickens or go out helping people. And best of all, if you had enough misfortune and didn't whine or moan about it, you had a cast-iron shot at becoming a saint.

St Maud. Imagine the picture in *The Illustrated Book of Saints*. I am no less than seven. My eyes, blurred with tears of anguish, are raised to the heavens. My hands are clasped, my face paler than pale.

Forgive me, Father for I have sinned. I made my sister disappear.

Chapter 12

'It's from Mary Flood,' says Renata, gazing at the newspaper cutting through her varifocals. 'Voiceless as only the dead are voiceless, she communicates with us by sending material clues from beyond the grave.'

I don't even try to contradict her, for Renata is particularly strident tonight. She is favouring Liza, her most flattering wig: the black fringe sets off her burning pirate eyes. She has teamed it with a wiggle skirt and a pair of kitten heels. The effect is that of a retired 1950s vixen, all in honour of our guest, no doubt.

Sam Hebden looks baffled.

This afternoon Sam and Renata discovered that they are kindred spirits, for they both have chakras, share the same animal totem (the goat) and worship Johnny Cash. They also learnt that Sam has little recollection of Mr Flood's assault with a hurley. Renata interprets this as evidence of post-traumatic stress and Sam seems happy to go along with it. In hushed tones in the hallway Renata informed me that I am not to plague Sam with questions. He will tell us what happened in his own good time, when his fractured psyche repairs itself, memory loss being common to victims of trauma.

To be fair, Sam doesn't appear to have suffered any great trauma. An absent air sometimes comes over him but this could be due to Renata's experimental cocktails. Otherwise Sam gives the impression that he's very well in himself, lolling on the easy chair with his stubble and his grey eyes and his devilish smile.

'Maud.' Renata clicks her fingers under my nose. 'You must keep an open mind. The trouble with Western thinking is that it sets science at odds with the supernatural. These are simply different, but equally valid, ways of telling a story.'

I grimace. Renata has memorised entire articles on true spectral crimes and the science behind them. She has shared every one of them with me. I have contemplated for hours pictures of middle-aged bearded virgins called Dave with machines made out of tinfoil and kitchen probes.

'To solve a crime,' Renata continues, 'the canny detective will use everything at her disposal, both modern and archaic. She may cast an electronic web or consult her age-old tools of divination – either can offer her guidance.' She bites her lip. 'I prefer the archaic. More reliable.'

Sam glances at me.

'Renata is unable to use a computer,' I mutter. 'Except in dire emergencies.'

'The electromagnetic fields play havoc with my third eye,' Renata says defensively.

'The tarot is her main investigative tool, heavy on the Suit of Swords at the moment, I believe.'

Renata throws me a black look. 'Signifying responsibility and intellect, violence and struggle.' She smiles radiantly at Sam. 'So, you see, Maud can't ditch her job, certainly not with this new development.'

I glance at her. 'Excuse me: "Maud can't ditch her job"?'

Renata seems to choose her words carefully. 'Sam came here to persuade you to stop working at Bridlemere.'

I turn to Sam. 'Is that why you're here?'

Sam shrugs and leans back in the chair.

St Valentine (love, the plague) wanders into the room uninvited. He's an old, sly class of saint with a roving wall eye. He fixes Sam with one eye and trains the other on me. His robes have a second-hand look about them. The braiding is frayed around the hem and the cuffs. His halo, the size and shape of a tea tray, is worn to the back of the head like a casual sombrero. It burns with a smoky orange flame. St Valentine settles on the pouffe with a smirk, showing that he has three teeth in his head and a tendency towards spittle.

'Sam is here to tell you,' Renata glances across at Sam, 'that the house and the old man are best left well alone.'

'You think I should leave?'

Sam looks a little sheepish. 'I do. But then that's your decision, Maud.'

Renata angles the newspaper cutting towards the light and starts to read aloud. '"Police are continuing their search for Maggie Dunne, aged fifteen, who has been missing from the village of Langton Cheney since last Tuesday."'

St Valentine lets out a whistle.

'"Maggie is five feet, six inches tall,"' Renata reads. '"Slim build, blue eyes, blonde hair."' She puts the newspaper cutting down. 'Dated Monday, 26 August 1985.'

'With all due respect' – Sam leans forward with his palms open in a conciliatory gesture – 'what has this got to do with Maud working up at the house?'

Renata taps the newspaper. 'We know the Floods visited this place five years before.'

'A coincidence,' suggests Sam.

'I think not. There's a connection here, between that old man and this case.' Renata frowns. 'We ought to show this to the police.'

Sam sits up. 'I wouldn't do that.'

St Valentine looks at Sam with interest.

'Given Cathal Flood's track record as a troublemaker I doubt if the police would take this seriously,' says Sam evenly. 'Let's face it, he may even have set this whole thing up.'

Renata looks doubtful. 'I don't know, Sam—'

'Really, Renata, I've been in that house. There are no ghosts, or ghouls, or missing schoolgirls. Just an old man and his hoard of rubbish.'

'Then why these clues, one after the other?'

Sam hesitates. 'Who says they are clues? I think you are letting your imagination run riot.'

Renata fixes Sam with a steely stare.

'There'll be wigs on the green,' murmurs St Valentine, almost audibly.

'We already know the old man has a violent temper—'

'But this is probably no more than a prank, Renata,' says Sam. 'You know that he booby-trapped the house for the council workers?'

'Well, if it's a prank then we catch him at his own game,' Renata concedes. 'Either way, we must find out who is behind these communications.'

'Cathal Flood may be old, but he's unpredictable. What about Maud in all of this?' Sam studies me. 'What are you, five foot three? A slight woman pitched against a six-foot-nine man with a history of assault.'

Renata's eyes widen. 'Is he that tall?'

I nod. 'He's an Irish giant.'

'Like the skeleton in the museum? The one John Hunter boiled?' Renata seems impressed.

'Identical,' I mutter. 'Only this one's animated: it roars and it swears.'

Renata turns to Sam. 'What's Maud's height got to do with it?' she says coolly. 'And what's her being a woman got to do with it?'

Sam appears to be at a loss, as well he should be. 'I'm just saying Mr Flood is no ordinary pensioner; don't underestimate him.'

Renata narrows her eyes. 'To that I would say: Maud is no ordinary slight woman. Don't underestimate her. If anyone can get to the bottom of this, Maud can. Unshakable tenacity in the face of stacked odds is one of her key traits.'

I glance at her. 'Thanks, Renata.'

She nods. 'She's a beaver, you know, totem-wise. I meditated and her spirit animal came forward. It's a wonder, really, how Maud's complex and resolute nature can be summed up by one small hairy emblem.'

Sam looks at us in dismay. Then he runs his hands through his dark golden hair. I wonder if his memories are coming back to him: the labyrinthine clutter, the marauding cats and the rabid pensioner coming towards him with a fighting grip on a hurley . . .

But maybe Sam isn't traumatised; maybe he's ashamed, as I would be if I let an ancient scarecrow of a man run me out of town.

Sam turns to me, his face kind, serious. 'You're really going to risk stirring up that old man, and the consequences that might bring, by playing detective in a fictional crime case?'

Put this way it doesn't sound like such a good idea.

Renata glowers. 'This isn't fictional and we're not playing.'

Sam looks suitably impressed.

St Valentine sniggers.

'We are going to get to the bottom of this, Sam Hebden,' she says. 'All we need is a plan.'

We focus on the flip chart Renata has set up in the living room. In the middle of a blank page she has written MARY FLOOD in red capital letters and drawn a black cloud around it.

She has also drawn two zigzag arrows coming out of the cloud like lightning bolts, only in green. One lightning bolt points to the word ACCIDENT and the other to the word MURDER.

Beneath all of this Renata has written the words MISSING SCHOOLGIRL MAGGIE DUNNE in luminous pink with no cloud but with a wavy line under it.

Renata scratches under her wig with a marker pen. 'My firm belief is that Mary Flood knew something about this case.' She taps MAGGIE DUNNE with her knuckle. 'This girl was never found, dead or alive.'

'How can you know that?' I ask.

'Lillian looked it up. She used the computer in Petersham library.'

'Of course, you told Lillian.' I glance over at Sam. 'Renata's sister loves a murder mystery.'

Sam frowns. Renata looks shifty.

'Just come out with it, Renata,' I say.

'We think that Mary found out about her husband's part in Maggie's disappearance and down the stairs she went.'

St Valentine leans forward. 'This just gets better.'

Renata's pirate eyes are lit.

'What else, Renata?'

'It's a mansion, Maud, set in extensive grounds. A labyrinth – you've said so yourself. There would be plenty of places to hide a missing girl,' she pauses, 'living or dead. Just think about it: cellar, basement, attic, rooms galore and a whole range of outhouses. Take your pick.'

'There is no schoolgirl hidden up in that house,' says Sam with surprising firmness.

Renata turns to him. 'And you've been through every inch of that house, Sam?'

Sam swirls his drink dubiously; from its acetone bouquet I can tell it's Józef's finest. 'Of course not, but this is some conclusion to jump to.'

'I haven't jumped to a conclusion.' Renata looks aggrieved. 'Mary Flood is giving us clear evidence. A girl went missing; the Floods had previously visited her village. There's a connection between these two events.'

St Valentine throws up his hands. 'This one will have the whole thing solved!'

Renata bites her lip. 'Of course, we might be too late.'

St Valentine nods enthusiastically. 'You will be of course.'

'The best we can hope for is that Flood hasn't killed her; he may have just kept her imprisoned all these years.' Renata adjusts her wig, pulling down the edges against an imaginary spell of blustery weather. Something contentious is coming. 'As a sex slave, you know, that kind of thing.'

St Valentine grins.

Sam lets out a groan of despair.

'It happens all the time,' says Renata defensively.

'Even in nice parts of West London?'

'Maud, this is serious.' Renata's face is grave, her voice low and urgent. 'If there's even a slight chance Maggie Dunne is still alive we have to find her.'

St Valentine starts to clap. 'Bravo! That's the spirit. Good man yourself!'

I glare at him.

He shrugs.

Renata looks at me with sudden horror. 'What if anything happened to the old man? Maggie could starve, or die of thirst.'

Sam gets up and pours himself another krupnik. He waves the bottle at me. I shake my head; alcohol poisoning won't make this any easier.

Renata turns over a page to a fresh sheet of paper and writes WHO IS CATHAL FLOOD???

Then she paces up and down the floor like a real detective.

'We now have three tasks.' She pauses in front of the flip chart. 'One: we find the missing girl. Two: we discover if Mrs Flood's death really was an accident. Three: we hand Mr Flood over to the police.'

'Or four: we leave well alone.' Sam downs his drink in one and wipes the tears from his eyes.

St Valentine looks at Sam admiringly. He sidles nearer and pokes an old, dry, spatulate finger through the glass in Sam's hand. Then St Valentine retracts his finger and licks it. He pulls a face.

I daren't ask. But I do. 'So what next?'

'We search the house,' says Renata firmly.

Sam glances over at me. There's real concern in his lovely eyes. 'You mean Maud searches the house.'

'Of course.' Renata replies. 'And we find a medium. You know, a really good one. Get a direct line to Mary Flood, find out what she's trying to tell us.'

Sam bites his lip.

Renata writes: TALK TO MARY.

'There are no such things as ghosts,' I point out.

St Valentine raises his eyebrows.

Renata snaps the lid on her marker pen. 'Of course there are; mediums see them all the time.'

'When you pay them.'

'That's not true, Maud. They grow up seeing them. They see them everywhere. Even at the supermarket.'

Why wouldn't the dead be found roaming in supermarkets? Death, like life, is probably quite routine. Not unpleasant, just a bit dreary, the best any of us can hope for.

I see Sam to the door. Keeping my voice low, I ask him the two questions I've waited all evening to hear him answer, memory loss or no memory loss.

Question 1: 'Did anything odd happen to you up at the house?'

He pushes his feet into his trainers and straightens himself up. 'Not at all.'

I think about this. No bobbing bottles and flickering lights, strange noises and sentient rubbish? Then I remember that denial is the cornerstone to mental health.

Question 2: 'Why did Mr Flood go for you with a hurley?'

'He just turned; I've no idea what set him off.'

'You didn't provoke him in some way?'

Sam laughs. 'Of course not.' He studies me closely, his face suddenly serious. 'Look, I love Renata, I think she's fantastic, but she's a great one to spin a tale, create a drama.'

I feel suddenly defensive. 'She's got a point though: that place is odd and he's odd—'

'Humour your friend, if you want; let her solve an imaginary case, but don't take this any further, Maud.'

I look at him.

'Leave the old man alone. Don't go prying into his business.' He kisses me on the cheek. With his breath in my hair and his mouth against my ear he murmurs, '*You don't know what you're dealing with.*'

I feel his low notes heating the base of my spine. I smell soap, citrus and expensive, tinged only slightly with cigarette smoke.

He pulls back and squeezes my arm.

I watch him walk down the path. He shuts the gate, raises his hand and then he's gone into the night, turning up his collar, lighting a cigarette.

As I go to close the door I see St Valentine sitting on Renata's dustbin, illuminated by the light from the hallway and his own unearthly glow.

He looks at me with one eye; he has the other trained on the garden gate. 'Your man's very vigorous,' he says, his voice high and giddy with delight. 'Is he a hopper and a leaper? Is he an honest cowboy? Would he be any use in the sack? Would you say he's a definite ride?'

St Valentine will ask four questions to one when he's over-excited. If he were close enough and not incorporeal he would fleck my face with saliva. Small mercies. St Valentine waits, wet-lipped, grinning.

I frown at him in disgust. 'Now that's crossing the line.'

He holds his hands up and chuckles. 'All I'm saying is I'd watch meself if I were you; compatibility-wise this is a difficult match.'

'Who said anything about a match?'

St Valentine snorts. 'He's a stallion, a hot-wired, fierce-blooded, honest-to-goodness stallion. You should know, you've had the full of your eye on him.'

'Whereas I'm?'

'A fervent donkey at best.'

I narrow my eyes. 'And I asked for your opinion?'

'You didn't, but where love is involved—'

'Then with all due respect, we've no further business.'

St Valentine roars laughing. 'Oh, there'll be further business all right, Twinkle, just you wait.'

I quickly close the door.

Chapter 13

A storm is coming in over the Atlantic. Above me the sky is sheet metal. With the thunder the rain falls in quick needling bursts, hardly enough to wet the dunes and hardly enough to make me put my hood up. But still, I zipper my anorak and shove my book up the front to keep it dry. This gives me a big square tummy.

And that's when I see them breathe, the dunes.

I watch in horror as their sandy skirts begin to buzz and waft. They start to move, floating towards me like hovercraft, churning up the beach in their path, ripping out the marram grass.

I never took my eyes from them, I never nosed around them, I never ran over them – they have no right to attack!

To my left: sinking sand; to my right: horseflies; before me; the sea, behind me—

Morning has happened. Weak light shines through my curtains. St Dymphna is sitting on the end of my bed. She cradles a lamp in her lap. It is slipper-shaped, pinched and smoothed from clay, a thing of loveliness that perfectly fits her little white hand. She blows on it and it sparks with a sudden flame. Her face is illuminated, her eyes glittering, a half-smile on her lips.

She glances up at me. 'It's all fiction you know, what you think you remember about that day.'

'I know what I remember.'

'You know better than to trust your memory, Maud. What have I told you?'

I don't answer.

She sets the lamp on the bedside table. The flame lengthens and flickers. 'What were you? Six, ten?'

'Seven.'

She leans forward, her voice a whisper. 'She left with him, in the car that day. They caught the ferry and moved to Rhyl. She was having a baby for him. That was the plan.'

'What about the guards? Why couldn't they find her?'

'There were no guards. She never went missing.'

I frown. 'There were the ones that sat in the kitchen, the ones that talked with Mammy.'

St Dymphna smiles bitterly. 'Mammy never had guards in the kitchen. Didn't she help Deirdre pack and give them a tin of sandwiches for the journey?' She tucks her brown plait back under her veil. 'Didn't Mammy give them her blessing?'

'That's not what happened.'

St Dymphna stretches her legs out on the bed, smoothing her robe around her lovely dim ankles. 'Do you remember Tommy McLaughlin?'

'No.'

'Early fifties, bald, butcher's assistant?'

'No.'

'A dirty feely old fella?' She rolls her eyes. 'Jesus, there was enough of them.'

'No.'

'He came out from the back of the shop and showed you

his little flabby flute, wiggled it, when Granny was up at the counter buying liver?'

I think back, to the smell of fresh sawdust and old blood, the green plastic parsley between smeared trays of red, the joints hanging in the window: bone, sinew, tissue, flesh. And Tommy McLaughlin with his white coat open just a little. His trousers undone just a little, pale slug, greying mound. He stared down at me, lips parted, breathing through his nose.

'I remember.'

'Well, that didn't happen either,' St Dymphna says, with a cold kind of delight in her eyes. 'Memories are fickle creatures, you ought to know that, skittish and in no ways trustworthy.'

'I know what I remember.'

St Dymphna holds up her hands. 'You do of course! After all, weren't you there with your big round child's eyes?' She mimes a vacant expression. 'Looking around yourself, spying at things that didn't concern you, *taking it all in*.'

'I was scared, there in the dunes. I was only small.'

'You'd do well to tighten the screws,' she murmurs, right in my ear. 'Or the nightmares will start again.'

When I look up she's gone.

* * *

Mr Flood has been tucked away in his workshop all morning. I've not heard step nor roar from him. The *National Geographics* present a solid wall today. I could have dreamt the land beyond, where stuffed stoats play cards, four-headed taxidermy angels keep watch and paperweights move of their own volition.

The house has a locked-down, shuttered, tight-lipped vigilance today.

The cats feel it: they are acting skittishly, flattening their ears and thrashing their tails, skulking low and jumping at nothing. I stand at the kitchen door, listening, watching. Not knowing what I'm listening or watching for.

The house is ominously quiet: it's holding its breath.
I turn to put the kettle on and then I hear it.
My blood stops flowing.

A girl is singing in the hallway, her voice high and lovely, with the hint of a caught sob. Half a phrase, four words at the most, and I understand none of them.

Then: nothing. Only ringing silence.

The crack in the Great Wall of *National Geographic*s has reopened, wider than before, and I am stepping right through it. Just watch me. I am a beaver. I am tenacious in the face of stacked odds and singing ghosts.

Botticelli's Venus winks at me as she unravels her duodenum. The glass eyes spin and the stoats smirk into their playing cards. The raven is nowhere to be seen and the shrunken head smiles as if it's nursing a nasty joke. The four-headed angel appears to be looking in any direction but mine. I stand at the bottom of the stairs, biting my lip, hesitating.

'What now, Mary?' I whisper and survey the staircase.

The staircase Mary Flood fell down.

Did she hit the floor headfirst and black out? Or did she lie at the foot of the stairs drifting in and out of consciousness? A wheezing bag of broken bones and haemorrhages. Perhaps she landed right here, where I'm standing?

Does her ghost fall still, over and over again in the after-life? Reliving, in perpetuity, those terrible moments? The accusations, the look in his eye, the step backwards, the brief tussle—

Where do schoolgirls go when they disappear? Into a cave, into the sea, into a basement with the windows boarded, into a bedsit in Rhyl?

It's a vanishing trick.

I imagine Mary standing next to me at the foot of the stairs, an urgent, silent presence. She turns the melted hole where her face once was to me. I can see right through it. She points up the staircase.

I am a fecking beaver, and so, with my breath held and my heart beating backwards, I climb the stairs.

The flood of objects flows to the top step, then stops and laps there, rising no higher. Before me is an empty landing. I count six doors obstructed by nothing and a table that holds nothing more than a silk-shaded lamp.

I survey the hall below and I'm staggered.

I am Ariadne: I have made it through the maze, without even a ball of string. Through an ocean of glazed cases and taxidermy, polished wood and medical curiosities. I have eluded the raddled old Minotaur.

The air is different up here at the top of the stairs. Neutral, unused, as if no one has ever breathed it. I have the strongest feeling that if I go any further I will be trespassing somewhere secret, somewhere private.

The light changes; the sun shines through the stained-glass window. Dappled colours, sudden and dazzling, fall on the wall opposite.

A woman in black is watching me.

The portrait is life-sized and painted in astoundingly beautiful hues. Skin the colour of chalk and copper hair so vivid it looks lit from the inside. Her chin is tilted up, defiantly, so that she stares down the bridge of her nose. Her eyes are large, green, alarmed. Dots of bright paint capture their liquid brilliance.

Despite her stern grandeur she is an untamed hare: long

in limb, her gaze crazed with panic. She is frozen, captured in mid-flight – one naked heel lifting. Nerve alone holds her; she wants to turn and run.

In one hand she grasps a posy of red and white roses, the other plucks at them. The petals are scattered behind her, a trail of blood and snowflakes.

I suddenly realise: I am now in the domain of Mary Flood.

I sit on the top step stroking Samuel Beckett. I have never seen him before but naming him is the work of a moment. He is a Siamese beauty with a forthright expression in his powder-blue eyes. I wonder if he's a neighbour's cat, attracted by the herds of mice that run along the skirting boards.

Beckett looks up at me and yawns.

'You're an intelligent feline, should I go any further?'

He blinks at me disdainfully and, as if sensing my cowardice, flounces across the hallway. Mary Flood's portrait shows no reaction. The sun has gone in and the colours are muted now. She is still scattering rose petals but no longer looks alarmed, just vaguely bored.

Beckett flicks a succession of question marks with his tail, then walks over to a door on the right. If he were a dog he would paw at it and whimper, but being a cat he nonchalantly runs his flank along it.

I take this as a sign and get up and walk over to the door. I touch it carefully, pressing my palm against it, like a firefighter feeling for heat, trying to guess what's behind it – perhaps the ghost of a blazing-haired woman, perhaps a long-lost girl?

I try the handle. The door isn't locked but there's resistance. The stickiness of a door unopened for years, then the sigh of something pent-up undone as a whisper of air rushes past me.

A genie let out of the bottle.

Beckett pushes in front of me and weaves inside.

The room is large and dark; the air is cold. Heavy curtains are drawn over the windows, shadowy shapes of furniture huddle. The light switch doesn't work, so I cross the carpet, thick underfoot, to open the curtains.

Daylight and dust motes set in dizzying motion.

The room is lovely, with a faded opulence that still dazzles.

On the wallpapered walls snowy doves coo in cages against an oyster background. In the spaces between, repeated at intervals, twist love knots and delicate nooses. The carpet is deep and soft and aged to off-white.

In the centre of the room is a bed fit for a princess. Stacked with feather mattresses, cushions and bolsters. Dressed in velvet and brocade, in shades of vanilla and magnolia, seashell and bone. Beckett jumps up on the bed and spirals around, blissfully kneading the counterpane with his paws. Above the bed is a silver-framed picture. I draw nearer and see that it is exquisite and horrible in equal measure: a dozen pale moths, splayed and pinned. At the centre, a beast the size of a teacup with black-spotted wings as plush as an ermine cape. She is flanked, either side, by smaller beauties with wings of creamy gauze or crenulated lace.

Opposite the bed, in front of the window, is a dressing table with a stool. Along the wall, on a striped grey and white chaise longue, legions of china dolls look on in watchful stiffness. Some are the size of toddlers, bonneted in blanched straw with dusty curls falling onto pale sprigged cotton.

Others are smaller and dressed in white coats with pearly buttons and fur-trimmed hats. Without exception they are sinister: their expressions ranging from blank spite to thin-lipped malice.

One of the line-up catches my attention. She is hatless and bootless with a high-necked lace dress and pale hair. Her face has a look of thwarted evil. Her lips reveal sharp porcelain teeth. Frayed bandages hang from her tiny wrists, like an escapee from an asylum. I have no doubt she's the ringleader.

I ignore her and her friends and sit down in front of the dressing table and its ancient liver-spotted mirror, a triptych thick with dust. I see three hazy Mauds, loitering and blinking, peering and nosing, in their polyester tabards with their dark hair scraped back. Their expressions are uneasy but there's a resolute set to their jaws, fair play to them.

I open the drawer and see a long velvet box. I lift it out carefully; inside, there is a delicate pearl necklace nestled in satin. The clasp, a crescent moon set with opals. I close the box and put it back. Next to it there is a mother-of-pearl backed brush and comb set and some silver-topped bottles, their contents solidified.

I get up and walk over to the door to the right of the room and try the handle. It is not an en suite as I expected but a dressing room, painted white with fitted wardrobes along one side. There's a mirror and a silver bentwood chair.

I glance back into the bedroom. Beckett is cleaning his backside with one leg sticking vertically in the air.

I open the wardrobe door.

For Mary Flood I envisaged tweed skirts and raincoats, low-heeled shoes and headscarves. Here are dresses of vermillion and emerald, indigo and magenta, in satin, silk and lace. And here is the scent – not of mothballs or stale old clothes – but of summer air.

These clothes are as inviolable as the bodies of saints.

I hesitate. I daren't touch.

But then I do touch – a dress of blue slub silk.

I lift it out and hold it up and see that Mary Flood was as slim as she looked in the painting, but less tall.

Here are several lifetimes of dresses, on padded hangers, shrouded in plastic. There is a silver 1930s flapper dress with a scalloped hem, heavy with beadwork. A knee-length, sugar-pink 1950s ballerina with a stiff tulle skirt and a bodice dotted with roses. There are drawers full of gloves and stockings and rows of bags: jewel-studded opera purses and tiny golden clutches.

It is like a girl's dressing-up-box dream.

The final door conceals a wall of shoeboxes. I open box after box of shoes, finding black kitten heels and gold sandals, nude pumps and ruby-red slippers.

My heart leaps. I lift the ruby slippers out with awe; they shimmer just like Dorothy's. The same magical glitz, the same irrepressible sparkle.

I turn them round; they catch the light from the window. They have little bows on the toes and look like they could fit me.

Knowing how treacherous red shoes can be, I think for a moment before I slip them on. They could dance me to death or take me all the way home. Which would be worse?

I will be careful to not think of home and not click my heels.

I have one trainer off when I notice, at the bottom of the wardrobe, a shoebox different from the rest. It's battered and bound round with string. I take it out. Neatly packed inside are rows and rows of cards.

I sit down on the chair with the shoebox on my lap. I take out a card and look at the picture on the front: the Virgin and Child.

A Mass Offering

I open it; neat ink fills the gaps between printed copper-plate:

> *At the request of* MARY *The Holy Sacrifice of the Mass will be offered for the intentions of* GABRIEL.

I flick through the cards, finding Mass after Mass offered for Gabriel, until:

> *At the request of* MARY *The Holy Sacrifice of the Mass will be offered for* MARGUERITE.

Marguerite? I touch the name. Who is Marguerite?

I hear a noise, a faint scratching in the other room. I grab handfuls of cards and slip them into the pocket of my tabard. Glancing out of the door I see Beckett crouching on the bed; his ears point forwards and his tail sweeps across the counterpane. His fur stands rigid along his back.

When I follow his gaze my heart stops. Traced in the dust on the dressing table mirror are two letters:

M F

I collide with Cathal in the hallway just outside the kitchen door. He has a broken television aerial in one hand and a bicycle inner tube in the other. He looks down at them as if he's trying to work out the relationship between these two objects, as if each holds the clue to the other's potential.

'You went through,' he says, gesturing over my shoulder at the Great Wall of *National Geographic*s.

It's a statement, not a question.

I nod.

Close up I realise the size of him. When he's creeping or watching he has little presence. He is insubstantial, invisible. But right now he is immovably solid, as undeniable as a slagheap or a piano. He bares his massive tarnished dentures, making a snapping sound with his lips like a disgruntled horse.

'No one goes through,' he says. 'Do you hear me?'

'I went through to find the bathroom,' I say, in my defence.

'Don't lie to me.'

'It's like a museum, all that stuff—'

'And you didn't think to ask first?'

I look down at my trainers. 'I thought you'd have said no.'

'I would have,' he says sourly.

'Then I'm sorry.' I venture a smile of reconciliation.

'You're not sorry at all.' Mr Flood's face is expressionless, his voice flat. 'You broke in.'

'I did not. There was already a gap there; I just went through.'

'You're lying again.'

'I'm not, I swear to God . . . '

He looks at me coldly. 'You have the kitchen, the scullery

and the pantry. No more. If I catch you going through there again you'll be gone.'

*　*　*

I'll be gone. I ponder this with an opened tin of corned beef in one hand and a knife in the other.

What'll he do?

I think about it. He didn't appear malicious, just practical and even a little jaded. What he was saying is that he wouldn't *want* to kill me and chop me up, *but he'd have to*. I slice the corned beef, arrange it on the lettuce and pick up a radish. I cut its whiskery tail hair off and quarter it.

If I catch you, you'll be gone.

There it is then. If he catches me he'll have to kill me and if he doesn't he won't. So in a way he's given me his blessing: as long as he doesn't see what I'm up to I can come and go as I please without being murdered.

Like Mary Flood.

Like Maggie Dunne.

Turning back to the sink, I see him out of the corner of my eye, leaning against the dresser, watching me. And then I smell it. The sudden stink of fish. He has an open can and is hooking out sardines with his fingernails. Oil flecks his grizzled chin. I stare at him with revulsion.

A decrepit, fish-guzzling giant with feet as big as dustbin lids and I didn't even know he was there. Melting into the plates and the saucers and the milk jugs, half-invisible.

How?

'Can I help you, Mr Flood?' I sound abnormally bright.

He must have seen me jump. I quickly wash the knife, dry it and put it in the drawer, in case he's tempted to start right away with the murdering.

'I'll paint you, Drennan.'

My heart is in my mouth. 'I don't know—'

'Wear your hair up,' he says. 'We'll start tomorrow.'

I'm halfway down the garden path with a bin bag in each hand when I see Gabriel Flood up ahead. He's in jeans with a white shirt tucked in over the bulge of his stomach. He is still wearing loafers.

'Let me take that for you.' He smiles and holds out his hand. 'How's the old bugger today?'

'He's grand. I'll leave you to go in and see him now.'

Gabriel walks ahead, gallant with the rubbish. 'Actually, it's you I came to see, Maud. I wondered if we could have a word.'

'I need to be somewhere.'

He puts the rubbish into one of the wheelie bins and follows me out of the gate. 'I could give you a lift.'

'No, thanks,' I say.

'My car's just there.'

Renata's voice in my ear cautions me against accepting a lift from a man in loafers. 'The bus is fine.'

'But a lift would make a nice change? We could go for a quick coffee on the way.' He motions at a brand-new black BMW across the road.

I'm surprised. I had my money on something more prudent for a lecturer. A Škoda, perhaps, with tweed uphol-stery, hot-wired to Radio Four.

'I'm sorry, Gabriel, but—'

'Please, Maud.' He fixes me with a desperate, harassed kind of look. 'I need to talk to you about something. Something that concerns Dad.'

I assess the likelihood of Gabriel Flood driving me to the yard of a disused warehouse, bargaining for illicit sex and then beating me to death with a car jack.

Then I narrow my eyes and speak like a woman armed with a dangerously sharp crossword pencil, a swift right knee and a Wing Chun taster session.

'All right.'

At the coffee shop Gabriel takes a seat in a corner away from the window and waves the waiter over. He orders coffee and an all-day breakfast sandwich without looking at the menu. He's making an effort to seem calm and controlled, but the red face on him and the wet top lip betray the real state of affairs.

He scans the room surreptitiously, then leans towards me. 'I need a favour, Maud. It's a bit sensitive.'

I watch his fat fingers as he plays with the top of the ketchup bottle.

The waiter brings the coffee over. Gabriel looks pained by the interruption. He runs a hand over his thinning hair, as if checking it's still there, a quick frisk. Then he fiddles with the sugar bowl until the waiter walks away again.

He lowers his voice. 'I need to find something, in the house.'

'Oh yes?' I sound disinterested.

His top lip is becoming wetter; he dabs at it with a paper napkin. 'Nothing of any *material* worth, only sentimental value.'

'Can you not just ask your father for it?'

He frowns. 'You saw what the old man was like with me the other day. He hardly lets me step foot in the door.'

He looks crestfallen for a moment, then he licks the back of the spoon with his fleshy tongue.

'I'm not quite sure how I can help, Gabriel.'

Gabriel takes a sip of his coffee and pretends he's just had a thought. 'Is it too devious to ask if you would take Dad out of the house for the day? Then I could swing by and search for it myself?'

I smile at Gabriel, wondering if he realises that I have the advanced bullshit warning system which comes from working with the mad, bad and cantankerous day in, day out. This is how I can tell that someone is lying about eating the last custard cream, wilfully shitting their knickers, or hiding my handbag.

'I wasn't aware that your father ever went out.'

'You could convince him, surely; you are so good with him.'

He laughs; the small points of his teeth remind me of some kind of sinister fish. He has a pale clamminess to him, as if he's spent his life skulking around in the bottom of a tank avoiding daylight.

'What about a day trip?' he ventures. 'To the coast perhaps?'

I appear to consider it. 'It would do him the power of good. You'd want me to take him?'

Gabriel grins. 'Of course, all expenses paid.'

'Wonderful! Mr Flood will be so excited. I'm sure he'll be grateful to you for wanting to treat him.'

Gabriel's grin falters. 'Let's not tell him it was my idea. You know, he might think there's something cloak-and-dagger going on. Which there's not, of course.'

I smile benignly. 'Of course not, but there will be procedures. I'll have to write a risk assessment and run it past the agency for permission.' Just to see him hop, I add, 'It should only take a couple of weeks to set up.'

And hop he does. 'Would you really need to go to all that trouble, Maud?' he asks, the pitch of his voice rising with a pleasing note of hysteria.

The waiter arrives with his all-day breakfast sandwich.

Gabriel studies it with dismay until the waiter is back behind the counter. Suddenly a thought appears to hit him. He feels around in his breast pocket and pulls out his wallet.

'What if I gave you an advance, you know, to help you get

started planning the trip. Would that speed things up a bit?'

As I watch him count out a pile of notes I wonder what he wants from Bridlemere. It must be something really valuable: a big rock of an uncut diamond, the Holy Grail in a presentation box? If the *Antiques Roadshow* ever featured weird shit there would be ten episodes on the bottom step of the staircase alone.

Gabriel puts his wallet back in his pocket and picks up his sandwich. He eats with a kind of passive guzzle while he watches me. He gestures to the pile of money on the table. 'Take it. For your expenses.'

'What is it you're looking for, may I ask? Maybe I've come across it when I've been clearing the house?'

He smiles patronisingly. 'I doubt it.'

'I've had a good root around.' I pause for dramatic effect. 'I've even gone upstairs.'

'Really?' An expression of panic crosses his face.

'Really.'

He squints at me as if he is making a quick calculation. Then takes another bite of his sandwich. 'As I said,' he says, chewing, 'I doubt it. It's just something trifling.'

'Your father . . .' I hesitate.

'Yes, Maud?'

I look into his eyes, wondering if I can trust him. 'Would you say he is largely harmless?'

A smile stretches thinly across his suddenly reptilian face. Perhaps there's really a little green lizard inside his fat man's suit.

'Of course. Utterly harmless,' he says. 'A pussycat.'

I frown.

'So, Maud,' he says. 'All I need is one day and a key. You have the back-door key? If you lend it to me I can have one cut ready.'

'You don't have a key to your father's house?'

'No. He's a little paranoid about that. He doesn't want people spying about the place.'

'Why is that?'

'Why? No reason. He likes to keep himself to himself.' He smiles sourly. 'Or else maybe he thinks I want to lie in wait, bump him off.'

Gabriel lays into his sandwich.

I imagine him, loafers oiled, his footstep quieter than a light-stepping mouse. It's the dead of night and the new-cut key turns silently in the lock. Then Gabriel is inside, slinking through the house with his nasty father-murdering ways. Clad in a black polo neck and a balaclava, plump and deadly, like a homicidal blood pudding. A length of fuse wire and a filleting knife in his manbag.

Does Cathal Flood deserve that?

I look at Gabriel and he looks back at me, as rancid as the fried egg that decorates his chin.

He finishes his sandwich and wipes his fingers on a napkin. 'Of course, who wouldn't want to bump him off at times? He's a difficult man.' He taps the money on the table. 'So, Maud. Do we have a deal or not?'

I see the look in his eyes – cold, dead eyes. I may be about to swim in a dirty ocean with a badly coiffured shark.

'For work like this you need a relic.' The knight puts down the sack in his hand and lowers himself into Gabriel's vacated seat with a great clanking and scraping of invisible armour. 'Just think of the level of protection you could achieve with the hem of St Bernadette's shroud or St Joseph's phalanges.'

I glance up at the waiter; he's playing with his mobile

phone and looking bored. I'm the only customer and I've been nursing my coffee for nearly an hour.

St George (cavalry, chivalry, herpes) levers off his helmet and pushes his gauntleted fingers through his mid-length bob. It's a style that doesn't suit him and that he wears resentfully; it strikes an incongruous note against his unshaven jowls and the great burgundy bulb of his drinker's nose.

He studies me; his gaze is pitiless. 'You think you're tough, kiddo, but you're not.'

'I do all right.'

'Do you know what you're taking on, Maud?'

He looks over his shoulder then heaves up the sack, unties the mouth of it and rolls the contents out onto the table. The teaspoons and the saucers are undisturbed by the bloody head of a mammoth reptile that comes to rest with one glazed yellow eye staring up at me. Its mouth is open in a razor-toothed smirk; its forked tongue flops through the sugar bowl.

'Killed that.' St George produces a rag from the skirts of his chain mail and wipes his hands. 'Slippery little shit. Quick on its claws.'

'Fair play to you.'

'Could you do the same? Don't lie to me now, Maud, look at its teeth.'

'With the right equipment, a lance and so forth.'

St George gives a cynical laugh. 'You have grit.' Then he stops and leans forward, his face deadly serious. 'Which is just as well: I've seen your dragons.'

He stands up with the grating sound of wrenching iron, bangs his breastplate and lurches off through the window of the cafe. The reptile head fades too, its grin last of all. It hangs a while in the air, ancient and malevolent amongst the dirty coffee cups.

Chapter 14

I help Renata fill the vol-au-vents. From time to time we study Sam through the serving hatch. He is on his knees fixing Renata's video recorder; he has the television unit pulled out and is swearing softly. St Valentine is standing behind him making encouraging remarks he can't hear.

Today Renata told Sam a story about a boy from Rotherhithe. A boy who loved to feel, from a very early age, the swish of nylons, the delightful pinch of a bra strap and the silky bliss of a slip. A boy who found solace in make-up and the thrill of accessorising freely. Who enjoyed moving his hands, swinging his hips and talking in a widely modulating pitch. It was a story about a boy, who, through many trials and tribulations, grew up to become an originative, yet tastefully understated, woman.

I glance at Renata's sparkle-dazzled cheekbones as she adjusts her headscarf. Tonight she's relaxing in a pair of cork wedges and a kaleidoscopic viscose kaftan. Sam is an old friend now, so she has dispensed with the wigs.

'And Sam's response to your story?' I ask, shovelling an unidentifiable filling into its pastry home.

'He told me that he was aged five when he first set eyes on his big sister's swimsuit. Red polka dot, with a frilled skirt and a halter neck.' Renata smiles. 'He said it was a garment of incomparable cuteness and if he could have got hold of it he would have put it on there and then and never taken it off again.'

'Good answer.'

'He was very close to his sister growing up.'

'He said that?'

'It's obvious. It's why he's so in touch with his yin.'

We watch Sam crawl round the television set. St Valentine points at Sam's backside then gives me the thumbs up.

I raise my eyebrows and snip the spring onions.

I tell them about Mary Flood's portrait in the hallway, the white bedroom and the gowns in the dressing room. I don't tell them about the sound of the song sung in the hallway, half a phrase: high and pure, sad and wistful. Or about the letters written in the dust. Or about how I ran from the room like a gobdaw.

Over by the sideboard Renata is mixing a Staten Island Ferry and frowning.

St Valentine, however, looks to be enjoying himself immensely. He is stretched out on the hearthrug, his halo flaring from time to time with smoky orange light.

Renata tastes her drink with a flinty eye on me. 'And that's all that happened?'

I stop biting my nails and shrug.

'No sign of Maggie Dunne?'

I shake my head.

St Valentine scratches his chin thoughtfully. 'She'll have been dispatched long ago.' His eyes wander to the bookcase where Renata's crime novels roost in their shabby jackets.

'You'll never find that wee girl. He'll have her hidden away in some dark corner.'

Renata spears a pineapple garnish. 'So, can we draw any conclusions from Mary Flood's clothes?'

St Valentine starts up. 'She's likely scattered through the house, poor kid. Feet in the basement, arse in the bedroom, scalp in the attic.'

I throw him a look of unmitigated disgust. He winks back.

'They weren't the kind of things I expected Mary Flood to own. I mean, they weren't everyday.'

'She liked to dress up, all power to her elbow.' Renata adds more rum and sits down with her glass. I wonder if she's a little drunk. 'Well, eyes peeled.'

'A delicacy.' St Valentine grins.

'More clues will appear.' Renata purses her lips. 'Mary won't let us down.'

'Enough with the pleasantries,' mutters St Valentine. 'Tell 'em about the bribe.'

'I'm not surprised,' says Sam. 'Gabriel Flood is a piece of work.'

'You've met him?' Renata asks.

'I threw him off the property. Flood Senior told me he was an imposter.' Sam's face is grim. 'Gabriel Flood caused a lot of trouble for me at the agency.'

'Then I think you ought to go along with Gabriel's plan, Maud.' Renata wavers. 'Or at least make him think you are likely to.'

'I agree,' says Sam. 'Don't make an enemy of him.'

I decide not to answer.

St Valentine, sitting cross-legged picking his remaining teeth, pipes up. 'You should have taken his money, Twinkle. Didn't I tell you to pocket it?' He points at me with his toothpick. 'What's he even looking for?'

'You have to wonder what he's after, from the house,' I volunteer.

Renata looks thoughtful. 'Mr Flood's insurance policy, that's what he wants. The old man said the son couldn't touch him, that he had something on him.'

'I don't trust Gabriel. I haven't heard a true word from him yet.'

Renata turns to Sam. 'Maud can always spot a liar, even a very good one. That's why we had to stop playing poker.'

'Is that so?' Sam smiles.

'Even with this.' Renata waves her hand in front of her face. 'Inscrutable.'

Sam laughs. 'So you won't let Gabriel into the house, Maud, fair enough. But if you took the old man out for the day maybe we could look around.'

'We?'

'Well, me. For the sake of the investigation,' he adds.

St Valentine stops picking his teeth. 'It's a plan.'

'It wouldn't be right,' I say, before I change my mind. 'I can't let anyone in without Mr Flood's permission.'

St Valentine rolls his eyes.

'I understand how you feel, Maud.' Sam's face is easy, reasonable. 'But wouldn't a quick search of the house set everyone's mind at rest?'

'As much as I disagree with her, Maud's right.'

'Thank you, Renata.'

'And she won't be persuaded otherwise, Sam; she has great integrity when she isn't playing poker.' Renata adjusts her headscarf. 'So now we have three questions: what does the old man have on his son, what does Gabriel want so badly from the house and what have the Floods to do with the disappearance of Maggie Dunne?'

I take a small square bundle from my handbag and untie

it, spreading the Mass cards out on the coffee table.

'Maybe these will help to enlighten us. Let's see if you can read another set of cards, Renata.'

Sam studies the notepad in his hand. 'So now we have it. The Mass cards were issued by four different churches in London and two in the southwest of England, specifically Dorset. The earliest card was issued in March 1977 and the last card was issued in January 1990, just weeks before Mary Flood's death.' He glances up at me. 'We are all agreed that, for the most part, the majority of the Masses were offered by two churches.'

Renata nods. 'St Joseph's, East Twickenham, and Our Lady of Lourdes, Wareham.'

Sam continues. 'Most of the Masses were requested on Gabriel's behalf between August 1985 and January 1990. Many were offered on consecutive days or even on the same day at different churches.' He glances up at us. 'In addition, there were a number of Masses offered for Marguerite between 1977 and 1990.'

'At Our Lady of Lourdes,' adds Renata.

'With difficulty we have made out the signatures of the priests who issued these cards: Father Quigley and Father Creedo.'

'Good,' says Renata. 'So we start with these two priests and see what they can tell us.'

Sam puts down the pad. 'I'll take Father Quigley.'

'No,' I say, 'I'll do a detour on my way home.'

Sam smiles. 'Maud, let me. We're a team, aren't we?'

St Valentine turns over and leans on his elbow. 'Go on, Maud,' he leers. 'You're a team, aren't you?'

'It's okay, Sam,' I murmur grimly. 'I have a priest-wrangling background.'

Chapter 15

The age spots are moving on Cathal Flood's face. See them slipping down his nose and sliding under his chin. They travel across his temples to meet between his brows, flickering moth-wing patterns and praying-mantis shapes. He grins, a geriatric Rorschach, and touches his finger to his lips. Then he turns his back to me and waves his arms and soon much more than his face is in motion.

All around him objects start to flutter and shake; anatomical wax models and broken lampshades take to the air, to be joined by yowling cats and revolving spiders. Glass jars bob by, filled with scrolled notes, or jittering eyeballs, or butcher's gristle. Milk bottle tops and sardine tins twinkle and turn in starry constellations. Startling taxidermy creations hop, drag and flutter by with odd mechanical actions. Unholy medleys, from farmyard and zoo, assemble and reassemble mid-air. Photographs of red-haired children spontaneously combust and drop, smouldering, into a pond where a coy nymph holds to her ear not a conch but a skull. She winks knowingly and drinks from it. Newspaper cuttings join in the furore, waltzing round the fountain, screwing themselves up into little balls and unfurling again, on each a smiling blonde schoolgirl.

In the middle of it all stands Cathal Flood, conducting, with wet seeping through the arse of his trousers.

A woman in a yellow dress flies over, her face on fire. She turns her head with rapid jabbing motions. No eyes, no nose, no mouth, only a mask of flames that billow and spark with every movement. She is looking for something. She spots the old man, halts in mid-air, then plunges, feet first, her toes curved like claws.

I sit up in the bed. In a few hours it will be time to get up. I won't sleep again, I know that. There is no sign of St Dymphna. Small mercies.

★   ★   ★

As I get off the bus I think about Mr Flood's stark warning, of the consequences of going where I'm not supposed to go, even if it is to rescue a Siamese cat.

I will be gone.

And what if Maggie Dunne is living still? Holed up in some dusty corner of the house, in the attic, or in the basement?

Maud Drennan, the last hope of Maggie Dunne.

If I don't find her no one will.

I will have blood on my hands either way.

Maggie's or Beckett's. Take your pick.

I'll be saving neither: the back door is barricaded.

It opens less than three inches on the safety catch, just enough for me to shout through. So I holler for a while then straighten up to find Mr Flood standing behind me. He has picked up my handbag and is rifling through it. He is wearing a raincoat over paint-stained pyjamas. His white hair sticks upright on his head.

'What's all this, Mr Flood?'

He glances up at me and flicks my bus pass into the buddleia.

'Put the bag down, Mr Flood.'

He bares his dentures in a defiant grimace and continues digging, taking out a lipstick and throwing it over the toolshed.

Somewhere deep inside me there is sure to be anger but in this job normal responses callus over. So I sit down on the doorstep and take a half-packet of cough sweets out of the pocket of my fleece. I hold them out to him.

'Menthol eucalyptus?'

He stops rifling and looks at me.

I prise a sweet from the weathered roll. 'They've been through the wash a few times but they're grand.'

He droops a little. 'I don't want you here. You can feck right away. Go on. Go.'

'What about my portrait? You said you'd paint me today. Look. Hair up, brushed even.'

I peel the wrapper from the sweet; it has an ancient bloom to it. I pop it in my mouth; it is strangely tarry.

He drops my handbag with a sudden look of noble shame, like a wild bear caught stealing junk food from a skip.

I pat the step next to me. 'Take the weight off.'

He studies me suspiciously, his great fists clenched, his boreal eyes gleaming under low brows.

Then, to my surprise, and with great difficulty, he lowers himself down onto the steps and sits with his long, long legs stretched out before him. His pyjama jacket is buttoned up wrongly to reveal his stomach, as soft and pale as the underbelly of a fish. There's a powerful unwashed odour from him, strong enough to fight the medicinal ferocity of a vintage cough sweet. I breathe through my mouth. He takes the packet from my hand and puts it in his coat pocket.

'I saw you with him,' he says. 'You're in league with him, you sneaky bitch. You're in league with all of them.'

I glance at him: his hands are shaking and there's spittle on his lips and chin.

'In league with who?'

'That unctuous fat fucker.'

'What makes you think that?'

'He's charmed your knickers off. You've probably had him in your snatch.' I feel his breath on my cheek, the threat in his low growl.

'Then I'm easily charmed. He helped me take the rubbish out, just.' I spit out the sweet and fold it in the wrapper.

'He came to ask you to spy on me and you said yes.' He puts on a sing-song voice. '*Oh yes, I'll spy on the old eejit for you*, like the weasel you are. And he'll be reporting back all the time to the other one.'

'What other one? Biba?'

Mr Flood lets out a howl. 'Don't fucking pretend. You're here to spy on me.'

I hold up my hand. 'Stop it now, calm yourself and talk to me. It's too early in the morning to be giving out. Jesus, all I've had for breakfast is a cough sweet.'

He shakes his head and my heart goes out to him because the old man is crying. And whichever way you cut it, it's hard to see an old man cry. He looks away, wiping his eyes with his coat sleeve.

There's a rustle by the bin bags and Larkin comes nosing to the back steps, tripping lightly, flicking his ears.

Mr Flood makes small soft noises through his sobs.

The fox moves forwards, almost touching Mr Flood's outstretched hand with his sharp snout, ready to run but wanting to be near. I can see that in the lovely russet face he turns up to the old man.

'I'm no spy,' I say gently, 'I'm just here to clear some of your stuff so you don't get buried alive and to nag you to change your underpants.'

May God and all the saints forgive me for lying through my teeth.

Mr Flood exhales, and shuffles and struggles as if to get up. I offer him an arm. He stands, stringing his ramshackle bones together again. His feet turned out, legs thin like stilts, shoulders slumped as if with the weight of his great gnarled hands. The concave chest and the head set wobbling at the top with the big hinged jaw and glowering brow. When he's steady he pats me on the shoulder and limps away towards the conservatory. Larkin bolts out from behind an upturned wheelbarrow to run ahead on dancing paws, his bright face curving back to Mr Flood.

The old man stops and turns. 'And it's Cathal to you.' He frowns. 'Are you coming then, you little gobshite?'

Beckett will have to wait a while longer for his freedom.

Cathal leads me into the conservatory through a heavy iron door, which he immediately locks behind us, slipping the key into the pocket of his coat. He crosses the room to a door on the far side of the conservatory and disappears through it, leaving me to explore the glass room alone.

Locked inside, like a spider in a jar.

The morning sunlight illuminates the room. There's a marine cast thrown down from the panes above, which are glazed with algae. The lower windows cast a milkier light, having been painted with whitewash. The whole effect is like looking up from the bottom of the sea. Inside the conservatory there is a damp, mineral smell, tinged with linseed oil and turpentine.

The conservatory has a honed beauty, its grace intact despite years of decay. An octagon drawn in fine iron. I can still imagine it in its Victorian heyday, with palms and wicker chairs and trailing orchids. From the cupola an ornate lamp hangs with most of its glass globes intact, like little creamy moons.

I am surrounded by canvases, stacked twenty deep around the edges of the tiled floor, covered in cobwebs and blossoming with mildew. All of them are executed in bright colours, as if they record light strong enough to burn the shadows away. But the shadows haven't gone; they are there, inside the subjects.

They give me a strange feeling, these paintings.

They are like sunlit happy scenes moments before a disaster. A fairground ride with a bolt loose, a day at the beach before the wave hit, a lazy row along the Thames before the splash, struggle and sweep of the undertow.

A fox roams through many of them with its honeyed eyes glinting. Its fur meticulously picked out in shades of brown madder and Indian red, coarse on top with a soft snowy front bib. Maybe it's Larkin, or one of Larkin's predecessors.

A canvas hung on the wall above the door catches my eye: a painting of a red-haired woman in a yellow dress. She walks holding a little boy's hand, turning away from him to look down at the flower in her other hand, a sunny-eyed daisy with white petals. The boy's face is suggested by a few rapid brushstrokes, a tangle of hair, a scowl. But the woman's face is drawn in perfect luminous detail. Her face holds no tension; it is full of the peace and gladness of a long summer's day, lulled and captivated by the weather and by nature all around her. Here is the same delicacy of touch as the portrait on the landing, but this is a very different woman. She is as light as that woman is dark.

And she is beautiful, with a calm, unwatched kind of beauty. There is the slightest blush of colour on the lips and cheeks, the nostrils and earlobes and on the pale long slants of her eyebrows. Her hair is swept up and back to tumble around her shoulders; a strand blows across her face. And it burns, her hair, backlit by the dying fire of the sun that sets in a molten strip in the field behind her. In the background there is a blue and cream caravan.

Only the child in the doorway is missing.

We pull an armchair from the corner of the conservatory and drape it with an old curtain, and Cathal positions an easel and a trestle table opposite.

He lays the table with a surgeon's precision. Unpacking a box of glass bottles, labelled with pencilled writing on strips of masking tape. Soon there is a palette with tiny worms of colour squeezed out on it, a clean palette knife and brushes all in a line. Cathal disappears into the other room again and brings out a canvas, closing the door quickly behind him.

He motions for me to sit in the armchair.

'Mary is very beautiful in that painting,' I say. 'That is Mary, isn't it?'

He follows my eyes. 'She wanted the boy in it. He fidgeted too much.'

'That was painted from a photograph. Mary and Gabriel in Langton Cheney.'

He ignores me, fiddling with the nuts and bolts on the easel legs.

I realise I'm shaking. Full of adrenaline and ready to run, keen on the flight aspect more than anything. But the door is locked. I could smash through the glass, with my arm over my head like a stunt girl. Or I could take a run up and trapeze out of the open skylight. But no doubt I would need spandex and the natural bounce of an acrobat for that.

'I found the photograph in the kitchen.'

Cathal glances up at me with an expression of bored confusion, as if I keep asking him questions in a language he can't comprehend. 'There are no photographs of Mary.'

'There's one.'

'Where is it?'

On Renata Sparks's coffee table in a plastic bag labelled *Exhibit 2*. 'It was badly damaged.'

'Oh yes,' he says without interest.

'Her face was burnt out of the picture.'

'Was it?' His tone is flat, unsurprised. 'Well, Mary would do that.' He picks up a stick of charcoal. 'She didn't like the way the camera captured her.'

'Mary would burn her own face out of photographs?'

'Lean back and put your head on your arm. Look up with your eyes – not your face, your eyes.' He gestures at me from behind the easel. 'Keep your mouth closed, and stop clenching your fecking jaw. Jesus, you've a jaw on you.'

I move in the chair, turning myself this way and that for him. I have two thoughts racing neck and neck: do I believe him? Do I not believe him?

I look at him, holding up his charcoal stick, squinting. Shuffling about in his slippers and raincoat with his hair on end, like some wild old Druid conducting some forgotten rite. Or a humbug wizard making up the magic as he goes along.

Without another thought I say it: 'I found a photograph of two children too: Gabriel and a little girl standing next to the fountain. Her face was burnt away just like Mary's.'

No answer.

'Who is she?'

He frowns at the canvas. 'No idea.'

'So Mary defaced that picture too? Then crossed the little girl's name out on the back?'

'Keep still now.' He holds up his charcoal. 'As I said, she would do that, when the mood took her. Mary suffered with her nerves.'

'In what way?'

'She imagined things.'

'What sort of things?'

'Would you close your fecking mouth until I draw you,' he growls.

I sit in silence, listening to the slap of Cathal's slippers as he wanders backwards and forwards in a one-sided dance with the easel.

Outside this strange marine-lit world, life is happening. Buses and cars are driving up and down, people are going to the shops. A thousand million miles away. The Devil's Triangle has been transplanted from just south of Bermuda; it's here in West London. At Bridlemere navigational instruments are dashed and logic fails. Watches stop and phones don't work and inanimate objects are possessed. Even a saint won't step over the threshold.

And here I sit, locked in a glass room with a cantankerous old giant who might be a murderer, or worse even, but then again he might not be. If he is a killer he might beat me to death with the easel or cut my throat with the palette knife.

Now why did I wait until I was locked in a fish bowl to ask him questions?

Perhaps because it shows that I trust him not to slaughter me?

He glances up, a quick sharp look under his shaggy brows.

I could believe Renata: that this man finished off his wife and, most likely, a Dorset schoolgirl. I could believe Sam: that I'm the victim of some kind of prank and I should steer clear. I could believe Gabriel: that he doesn't remember posing for a wintertime photo with a little girl with the same fierce red hair as him.

I could believe Cathal: that Mary suffered with her nerves and defaced photographs.

I could try.

If not for letters traced in dust in an empty bedroom and

the slamming doors and the sound of singing. If not for the feeling that skewers my stomach whenever I think about Mary Flood and Maggie Dunne.

'Did Mary get treatment for her nerves?'

Cathal makes a swipe at the canvas and stands back. 'She did, thank you. Now will you hold yourself still?'

He can't object to me moving my eyes, so I examine the painting above the door. I think of the child missing from the painted scene. The caravan door is shut tight. And then I see it, the meaning in the picture.

'What kind of flower is that, the one that Mary is holding?'

He glances at the painting. 'No idea.'

'Isn't it a marguerite?'

'If you say so.'

Would it be anything else? 'Does it have a special meaning? It's a girl's name, isn't it?'

He looks at me, his face empty. 'It has no meaning. It's just a flower.'

It is a strange sensation, being painted by Cathal Flood. Of being measured with an unconscious kind of scrutiny. He peers often through one narrowed eye, frequently grimaces and sometimes looks amused, his eyebrows shooting up his forehead. But this play of emotions is pre-thought, I'm sure of it. Devoid of consciousness, like the expressions on the face of a sleeping baby.

I wonder how he sees me. 'What do I look like, in your drawing?'

'A dark-eyed terrier; keep your mouth shut.'

'That doesn't sound very complimentary.'

He smiles. 'You've a look of something that would dig up fence posts if you had a mind to.'

We continue in silence. The shadow of a cloud passes by, dimming the light overhead.

'What about a story?' I ask. 'You could tell me a story while you draw me. To pass the time.'

'I could.'

'You could tell me a story about Mary.'

I steel myself for the fallout, for the roaring and pointing. His expression is one of chronic indigestion, but to my surprise it passes quickly.

'The demands from it. No hounding; I tell what I tell.'

'No hounding.'

I wait, listening to the sound of his brush moving with a faint rasp, catching the raised texture of the canvas. He seems to be focusing on the line from my shoulder to my wrist.

'The first time I noticed Mary was at her husband's wake,' he says.

'Really?'

He nods. 'She was a wealthy widow of seventeen who was just after burying a man five times her age. Rumour had it that the old fool had killed himself on top of her.' Cathal smiles grimly. 'On account of his exertions.'

'That's awful.'

'They'd been married less than a year and the whole of his estate went to her. She'd been his housemaid. Of course his children were disgusted; they said she'd put a spell on the old fool.' He looks across at me. 'It was her tits that bewitched him.'

'None of that.'

'So the old fool's family were all there at the wake with these long faces on them having lost their inheritance to the little widoween who was planning on having them packed and out of the house by the end of the day. For hadn't she seen the way the old man's children had fleeced him for money?' He pulls a mock-sad face. 'Oh, and hadn't that hurt her? For she had loved the old devil in her own

· 149 ·

way. Wasn't that clear to everyone at the wake? With her eyes raw from crying?'

'So what happened?'

'I danced with the little widow, she copped a feel of a brave young man and we were married. Me without a pot to my name, for all my wealth had been lost by my father.' He reminisces. 'The big house was sold and we moved to London where we cut quite a dash.' He bows. 'I was a catch then, can you believe?'

I smile.

'We were the handsome Floods. She was a queen, with her grave penitent beauty. The upstart daughter of a drunken blacksmith.'

'And you were her king?'

'No. I was a gallery of a man.' He smiles back at me bitterly. 'She had this face you'd never forget. These green eyes; there was great piety in those eyes looking up.'

He puts down his brush, shuffles to the corner of the room and searches through canvases. He pulls one out, brings it back and props it near my chair.

In the painting Mary is very young; she wears a high-necked, short-sleeved blue dress with her searing red hair coiled over one shoulder. Her eyes are averted, gazing up to the heavens, like those of a saint. A fox cub sleeps curled in the crook of her arm, a froth of fur and snout. Behind them, perched by an open window, is an owl with a heart-shaped face and dappled feathers.

'The fox and the owl,' I murmur. 'Have you ever heard of a girl called Maggie Dunne?'

He goes back to the easel and picks up his brush. 'I haven't.'

'She went missing from a village called Langton Cheney in August 1985. She was fifteen. You took your caravan there a few years previously.'

'Never heard of her.'

'Are you sure, Cathal?' I ask softly.

He leans over the canvas. 'We're done,' he says. 'Get out, go home.'

His eyes are terrible, lupine, a sudden searing blue. For a moment I fear he'll vault his easel and have my throat out. Instead he looks away, fumbles the key from his coat pocket and stalks over to the door of the conservatory.

'You want me to leave?'

'That's what I said.'

'But your meal—'

'Get out, I said.' His face is white, as closed and hard as a fist.

I don't argue. I'm relieved to step out into the garden and hear the lock turn behind me.

I walk round to the kitchen door; it's latched still.

There's nothing left to do but go home. I look up at the house. There's a balcony outside what could be the white bedroom, if I could just find a ladder—

A shadow passes across one of the newspapered windows and an eye draws nearer to a peephole.

Or that could just be my imagination.

St Monica (disappointing children, victims of adultery) is waiting for me outside the gate. She nods curtly and falls in beside me as I walk to the bus stop. We exchange no words for she appears to be deep in thought. She's a pensive, abstracted kind of saint, given to drifting and staring into the distance. She has shadow-ringed eyes that look inwards and a thin, pained line of a mouth, lips pressed together as if to stop flies getting in. St Monica would be a little dreary if it weren't for her robes: they are cream, with a nice pale glow to them.

I form sentences in my head about missing schoolgirls and wives that have fallen to suspicious deaths but find I can't speak any of them. St Monica seems to understand, because now and again she glances up at me with a sour smile.

At the bus stop she arranges her robes around her feet with peevish delicacy and surveys the traffic.

'I don't know what to do.'

St Monica rolls her eyes.

'Is Maggie Dunne dead?'

St Monica frowns.

'If you could just let me know one way or the other? You don't have to say it out loud if it's against the rules. You could just cough once for yes, twice for no.'

St Monica folds her arms and looks disenchanted.

We wait in silence and I listen, just in case she decides to cough anyway.

After a while I say, 'Have you any practical advice for me? On finding Maggie and saving the cat?'

St Monica is staring out past the bus shelter. A muscle twitches in her jaw and the ghost of a grimace crosses her face as if some deep memory has suddenly snagged.

'I could do with backup in there,' I say. 'It's not likely though, is it?'

St Monica shrugs; there's a whole world of disinterest in her gesture.

'So that's it then. It's just part of my life's rich tapestry?'

St Monica, with her eyes on some dim distance, smiles. It's not a nice smile.

Chapter 16

I didn't know who Deirdre was meeting, who was at the beach, who wasn't at the beach, who drove a car out of the car park or what the number plate on that car was.

I couldn't remember what my sister was wearing. All I was certain of was what she was carrying: a red leather heart-shaped bag.

Mammy moved from the sink to the table and pointed her cigarette at me and asked if I had eyes in my fucking head.

We looked at each other in surprise, Mammy and me. I had never heard her swear before. Then she took up the ashtray and threw it.

I could hear Mammy crying next door. Granny was in with her. I went over my spellings.

The lady guard opened the car door for me. I sat in the back and we waited for the man guard to come out. They were taking me back to Pearl Strand to see if my memory could be jogged.

'Will you put the sirens on?' I asked.

The lady guard smiled into the back, her hazel eyes tired and kind. 'It's not an emergency, Maud.'

As we drove along they asked me questions about school. Had I settled in all right now?

My old school was over three hours away, where our own house was. Jimmy O'Donnell could drive it in less than two, I said to the guards. The guards glanced at each other in the front seats. Then I remembered I didn't love Jimmy any more. So I stopped talking and looked out of the window, watching the wet fields go by.

Chapter 17

There is no customary welcome dance from Renata today, which can only mean one thing. As I pass by her kitchen window I hear two voices: a high-pitched jabbing and an exhausted monotone. I ring the doorbell.

There's a temporary lull, then the skittering of feet along the plastic mat in the hall. Lillian answers the door, head down, showing two inches of grey roots. She doesn't want me to see her cry.

I bend down to take off my shoes while she composes herself.

'I am not coming back,' she announces, red-faced and defiant, her eyes blurred with tears of frustration and industrial oven cleaner. 'This is the last time.' She points down the hallway with a shaking finger. 'That thing in there, it's inhuman. It wears me out.'

She stands wiping her hands absent-mindedly on a pillowcase with her blouse on inside out. Then she puts the pillowcase in one of the laundry bags she has lined up in the hallway and puts on her jacket.

'One day, God forgive me, I will kill it in its sleep. I will poison it like a rat in a dress.'

She picks up the bags and leaves without a backward glance.

Renata is sitting at the kitchen table. Her lipstick has worn off and one of her eyebrows is smudged. She has a coat on over her kimono. I wonder if she attempted to storm off again, or just locked herself in the bathroom like she usually does. In an argument an agoraphobic is always at a disadvantage.

'I will change the locks and keep her out.' She pulls at the edges of her headscarf. 'I will never let her in again.'

'You always say that.'

'She wanted to throw away my magic costumes.'

'Why would she want to do that?'

'She says there's damp in the dressing room and she can't bring her builder round with my hooker's outfits on display.' She shakes her head. 'All it needs is a little paint maybe.'

I follow Renata into a room that's half-bordello and half-boudoir, with a rococo dressing table, beaded lamps and three bow-fronted deco wardrobes. Renata pushes a heap of clothes off a plush sofa and we sit down and survey the havoc.

Fishnets and leotards, furs and corsets, bras and feather boas are strewn across the floor or bundled into rubbish bags. Renata's working wardrobe, the costumes she wore when she toured with Bernie Sparks, the fast-burning, early-dimming light of her life.

'God, your waist,' I say, picking up a costume in mermaid green. Fronds of net bustle from the backside.

Renata laughs. 'And that bust, look at it.'

The costume is engineered to provide a lethal chest. I turn it around on its hanger. Ghost bosoms fill it still, straining voluptuously at the seams.

There is a faint smell of show business: sweat and panstick, singed hair and stage dust, and stale, stale dreams. I hold up a ringmaster's outfit: black satin tails and a bustier. A sequinned bow tie dangles from a buttonhole.

'I wore that the night Bernie died onstage in Weston-super-Mare,' says Renata.

I look up at her, aghast. 'Bernie died onstage? You never told me that.'

'We were going up for an Asrah levitation.'

'Christ, is that what killed him?'

Renata laughs and shakes her head. 'No, it's an old trick. The magician hypnotises his assistant and she lies down, all in a dream. Then he covers her with a cloth and she floats up, up, up. When he pulls off the cloth – she's vanished!'

'It sounds complicated.'

'Chicken wire and a sideboard on wheels.'

'You did well to earn a living from that.'

'Only just.' She frowns. 'We were halfway through the act that night when Bernie collapsed.'

'Jesus, that's terrible.'

She nods sagely. 'The audience didn't see a thing. He fell down and as quick as a flash I bundled him up and stuffed him into the sideboard.' She points. 'Top drawer of the dressing table, darling.'

I find the framed photograph she's after and I sit back down next to her. We study it. Renata, barely twenty, a wisp of a waist, stands in a corset with her hands on her hips. She is wearing an ironic smile and a top hat at a raffish angle. Stage right is a small man with the slippery air of a pickpocket about him. He has one eye narrowed and is reaching inside his jacket.

She touches the photograph. 'If you look closely you can see his Cuban heels.' She smiles. 'People were shorter then because of the rationing.' She glances towards the mantelpiece. 'You should feel the weight of Bernie's urn. It's pitiful.'

I have no intention of manhandling the earthly remains of Bernie Sparks. 'What happened next?' I ask.

'I finished the act, got a round of applause and pushed my darling off the stage.'

'Heavens.'

We sit in silence for a while.

'You still miss him, don't you?'

She nods. 'He was difficult, as all creative artists are. But he always stood by me, whether I was a boy or a girl.'

'And you never came unstuck, living as a woman I mean? Those were less forgiving times, surely?'

'You'd be surprised.' She thinks for a while. 'I was very good at it, but everyone fears being read. Being found out. Everyone has their secrets.'

I say nothing.

She taps me on the arm. 'Do you know what I've learnt from life?'

'Is it profound?'

'Not at all; it's very simple. Just be sincere and everything else will follow.'

I think about this. 'Do you think Sam is sincere?' I hazard.

'Yes.' She looks at me closely. 'I do. Why do you ask?'

'He seems too good to be true, you know, with his yin and everything.'

She smiles. 'Sam is a diamond.'

'You're the expert.'

'In men – not at all, but I am an expert detective's assistant.'

'Do you have to wear fishnets for that?'

She laughs. 'Father Quigley from St Joseph's has just returned from Fuengirola. He's been on retreat, apparently.'

'Really? In Fuengirola?'

'That's what the housekeeper said.'

'Then I'd better pay him a visit.'

Chapter 18

I look at the priest and then I look at the plate of biscuits. I wonder how many I should take, or if I should take any at all. The housekeeper wears spectacles smeared with finger-prints. She has a hint of frog about her, sticky wide-ended fingers and big soft-boiled eyes blinking behind cloudy lenses. She has a habit of licking her bottom lip with a quick dab of her tongue, just like a frog. The priest's house has a thick air of damp that I blame on the housekeeper; she would no doubt thrive in such an environment. I wonder if she mists the curtains and waters the carpets. I imagine the biscuits to be soft. I take a malted milk and I'm proved right.

Father Tom Quigley looks at me with concern. 'Let me get this straight, Maud. You are here to ask me questions about a deceased parishioner?'

I nod and chew. 'That's right, Father.'

'And you would prefer to talk to me about this matter, rather than the family of the deceased? Now why is that?'

I think about whether I should drink the tea, for the cup, stained with old dribbles, is none too clean. I wonder if the housekeeper even washes them. She probably just licks them with her nervous tongue. I glance across at her; she's pretending to pick the fluff off the antimacassars.

The priest follows my gaze. 'Thank you, Mrs O'Leary; I think we have everything we need. I'm sure the housekeeping can wait until after our visitor has gone.'

Mrs O'Leary straightens herself up, sends a sneer in my direction and ambles out of the room on a rackety set of legs.

Father Quigley leans back in his chair. He is a jovial, well-put-together old man and no doubt a credit to the priesthood. He has a tanned, happy face, a frequent laugh and a generous shape to him, all of which attest to a willingness to enjoy life, despite his pastoral responsibilities. Mrs O'Leary said I was lucky to see him without an appointment as he had only just returned from a pilgrimage: to lie on a beach by the looks of it.

He smiles at me. 'And do you have a name for this individual?'

'I do, Father,' I say. 'Mary Flood.'

He sits up in the chair. 'Mary Flood?'

'You said a fair few Masses for her.' I take Mary's Mass cards out of my bag and hand them to him. 'Do you remember?'

He flicks through the cards. 'I do of course. Fire away.'

'Did you know Mary well?'

'Quite well.'

'And the rest of the family?'

He shakes his head. 'Not at all. When Mary passed away it was impossible to keep in contact with the family. Cathal wrote and warned me not to contact them again. A curious note.'

The priest eases himself out of the chair and goes over to a filing cabinet by the window. 'It'll be in here somewhere. Under *F*, no doubt, after *Flanagan* and before *Foley*.'

The priest bends over, straining the arse of his black trousers.

'That's a big Irish contingent you have there, Father.'

'Here it is.' He smiles and straightens up. 'I'm a great man for the organisation of things.'

He hands me a one-sided letter on the back of a betting slip that reads:

Dear Priest,

I'll thank you not to call at the house or make further ingratiations or gestures of sympathy. Similarly, please inform your congregation that well-wishers, professional commiserators and prying old biddies bearing casseroles and unidentifiable crap in Tupperware boxes are not welcome at Bridlemere. Neither myself nor the boy are interested in the ministries of you or your church. In fact, if any of your number darkens my door again you'll receive the toe of my shoe right up your hole.

Yours, etc.,
Cathal T. Flood

I feel the priest watching me. I look up to catch him re-adjusting his expression from excited mirth to diligent calm.

'Mary had a fall, Father Quigley?'

'She did indeed.'

'A tragic fall, up at the house?'

The priest nods. 'Yes. It was entirely tragic.'

'An accident, was it?'

A flicker of understanding crosses the priest's face. He holds his hands up. 'Now as much as I love answering your questions, Maud,' he leans forward and lowers his voice, 'in what capacity are you making your enquiries?'

'In a professional capacity.'

I smile at him and he smiles back.

We sit looking at each other, smiling, for a long moment.

'Let me properly introduce myself,' I say, with all the conviction I can muster, 'I'm *Inspector* Maud Drennan.'

'Inspector, is it?'

I nod and smile again, with utter sincerity.

'Well now. Fair play to you,' says the priest.

I continue, breezily, 'I'm investigating links between the Flood family and a missing-persons case.' Remembering my uniform I reveal the name badge under my cardigan. 'I'm undercover, posing as a care worker.'

The priest looks pleasantly aghast. 'Missing persons?'

The door to the room moves slightly, as if blown by a sticky-fingered wind; Mrs O'Smeary is no doubt getting an earful.

'Did Mary ever mention the name Maggie Dunne?'

The priest shakes his head.

'Or a village called Langton Cheney in Dorset?'

The priest shakes his head.

'Do you know who Marguerite might be?'

The priest frowns. 'Now that I do know.' He takes a deep breath. 'The Flood family experienced a terrible blow long before the tragic death of Mary.'

'What sort of blow?'

'The death of the daughter, Marguerite,' says Father Quigley.

My heart pitches.

'Of course, Mary refused to talk about it. After Marguerite's death Mary hardly spoke a word to anyone.'

'What happened?'

'The Floods left one summer with the two children and returned with only the boy, Gabriel.' He looks downcast.

'Marguerite was a lovely girl. She had just turned seven years old. Very sturdy and exuberant, with this mass of red curls.'

Marguerite: the faceless girl in the photograph. The girl no one talks about.

'That's terrible.' I pause. 'How did Marguerite die?'

'The Floods went home for a visit and while they were there the child drowned in the sea. She's buried in Wexford, so they say.'

'Mary told you this?'

'No, as I said, Mary never mentioned her daughter again.' He opens his hands apologetically. 'And we didn't ask. We heard it on the grapevine, you understand. People talk.'

We sit for a while in silence.

'Would you say that Mary was of sound mind?'

The priest smiles sadly. 'I'd say she was a little delicate. Especially afterwards.'

I watch the priest. He sits with his hands folded and his eyes lowered, relaxed and full of post-pilgrimage contentment, despite all of the mothers and daughters dying of tragic accidents in the world.

Then I come out with it. 'Did Mary ever feel threatened, do you think, living in that house?'

Father Quigley falters. 'I can't answer that, Maud.'

'Did she ever ask you, or a member of your congregation, for help?'

He frowns. 'Not that I'm aware of.'

I study him. He looks out of the window, his jaw tight. My newfound police instinct tells me he's holding something back.

I go to hand him the note.

'Keep it,' he says. 'If it can help with your investigation.'

I fold it and put it in my handbag. 'Thank you for your time, Father. If you think of anything else.'

The priest looks relieved. 'I'll phone the station.'

I rummage in my bag and pull out a pen and a scrap of paper and dash off Renata's number. 'This is my direct line, at the station. Please don't hesitate to call.'

The priest calls out. 'Mrs O'Leary, will you please show Inspector Drennan out?'

Mrs O'Leary shuffles instantly through the door.

In the hallway Mrs O'Leary whispers, low and vicious, 'You're never a police.'

I glare down the full length of my nose at her. 'And you're never a housekeeper. Those cups were filthy dirty rotten; you ought to be ashamed of yourself.'

She pulls down the corners of her wide toad mouth, blinking at me behind her smeared glasses. 'And you ought to be ashamed of yourself for bothering the Father and raking up old coals.'

'Did you know Mary Flood?'

She nods resentfully. 'The Father was ever so upset about her accident. He'd been ever so worried about her leading up to it.'

As soon as she says it she knows she has made a mistake. I can see it.

'He was worried about her?'

'I wouldn't know about that.'

'But that's what you just said.'

She ferrets up her sleeve for a handkerchief and looks away, making a big point of blowing her nose.

'Mary was unravelled. Father Quigley told the husband to get her some help.'

'What gave Father Quigley that idea?'

The housekeeper frowns. She seems to be fighting against her natural bent to gossip.

'That's not for me to say.'

'Look, if you tell me I'll leave.'

'And you won't return to bother the Father?'

'No.'

Mrs O'Leary narrows her eyes. 'They say the daughter was destined for a home for the bewildered. Lord knows she was unhinged. If Mary brought her to Mass the girl would snap at people's ankles and crawl under the pews. That's if Mary could even drag her through the door.'

'So Marguerite was unruly?'

'Marguerite was an Antichrist. They say that when the Floods took her to the beach the child ran into the sea and drowned herself. Foaming at the mouth she was and seeing monsters.' Mrs O'Leary snorts. 'Monsters, she saw, in County Wexford. Mary, who'd been having a nap for herself on the sand, nearly died with the grief.'

'They say a lot of things about the Floods.'

The housekeeper opens the door and points up the path. 'Now aim yourself in that direction and don't come back. Pretending to be a police without even making an appointment.'

When I'm halfway down the path I glance back at the house. Mrs Frog has closed the door and hopped off to squat in the kitchen and encourage the flies, but I feel certain that Father Quigley is watching me from behind the net-curtained window of his study.

As I wait for the bus I think about Father Quigley and his housekeeper, each holding a portrait of Mary in their minds. Mary the good woman, the grieving mother, the woman astray in the head, who slept on the beach while her child drowned.

I add their memories to my own portrait of Mary. The regal beauty who married a rich old widower and cried when he died. Who burnt faces from photographs and wore Dorothy-red shoes and carried gold clutch bags. Who fell down, down a staircase, from top to bottom and never woke up again.

But then I think about what St Dymphna says about the memory. And I wonder: in all these long years of remembering Mary has she changed at all for the people who knew her? Have they welded new bits onto their memory of her, or revised it completely? Or have the details stayed sharp and clear and true?

Should I tell them, if they don't already know? Memory is like a wayward dog. Sometimes it drops the ball and sometimes it brings it, and sometimes it doesn't bring a ball at all; it brings a shoe.

Chapter 19

The wind grabbed a handful of sand and scattered it like bright confetti along the hard-packed, sea-scoured, deserted beach. The sky had a newly rinsed look, the clouds spun and wrung out on high.

I remember now what she was wearing: a halter-neck dress in pale-blue lace.

We slipped off our sandals when we reached the planked walkway through the dune field. The wood was warm and weatherworn. She told me to wait and then she walked off across the sand.

A scowling angel, shoulder blades like wing buds. Blown brown halo of hair.

Three things were different on the day Deirdre disappeared: it was properly hot (for the first and only time that summer), the sky was empty of seabirds (when usually they screamed and tumbled above us with clamorous joy), and Old Noel's kiosk was closed.

Chapter 20

I'd have a job to hear Cathal creeping up behind me with the sound of my own heart thumping in my ears. I climb quickly, picking my way through the landslide of curiosities on the staircase. I only hope Beckett has survived his incarceration and I'm not risking my life for a dead cat.

Mary Flood still haunts the portrait on the landing with her burning hair and fugitive beauty. Frozen by conflicting impulses: should she stay or should she run?

This must have been how Cathal first saw her: a stricken young widow dressed in black. I edge along the landing and open the door to the white room.

There is no sign of Beckett, other than a dip in the counterpane and a few pale hairs. Otherwise the room is exactly as I left it, with the door to the dressing room open and Mary's gowns slung over the chair.

And her initials still on the mirror, etched in dust.

M F

I don't know why, but I expected the letters to be gone. I walk over and study them closely. As I'd rummaged through the frocks next door, had a ghost drifted into the room, glided up to this mirror and traced these letters in the dust?

I touch nothing; although I feel bad leaving Mary's things strewn around, tidying up could incriminate me. I leave the room, closing the door quietly.

I'm at the top of the stairs when I hear a scratching noise. I stop and listen. Next I hear a faint plaintive meowing. Swearing softly to myself, I track back along the landing. A few doors on from the white room there's the muffled scrabbling of claws against wood.

'Beckett?' I whisper.

I try the handle. The cat bounds past me and down the stairs without a backward glance, knocking over artefacts and instruments.

The sound reverberates through the house.

In the musty depths of Cathal's lair, one eye flicks open.

Noise has pulled on the strings of his web, setting his long limbs twitching. He'll be slinking out of his trapdoor and threading through the rubbish. Crawling up the staircase with a knife clamped between his dentures and a lasso of fuse wire in his hand, ready to garrotte me and hack me to pieces.

I listen. Nothing moves below.

I step inside the room and close the door behind me. The curtains are closed and the light switch doesn't work. I cross the carpet and pull the drapes open.

My retinas are awash.

It is a mirror image of the white room. On the left is the door I know will lead to a dressing room. There is a bed fit for a princess and a dressing table before the window.

Only the colour is different. This room is red, as red as the devil's own dancing shoes. All shades are represented here, from carmine to garnet, ruby to cardinal, maroon to vermillion. On the walls a pattern as big as a tea tray is repeated, gouts of claret arc from three-tiered fountains silhouetted in black. The bed is dressed with red brocades, satins and velvets. On the wall above in a lacquered frame, a line of splayed and pinned moths, every insect a dark clot of a warning. At the centre is a furred beast of monumental proportions, the fat stalk of its body covered in plush. One white spot on each outstretched wing of black funeral crepe: two blind eyes. On either side smaller insects are ranged, their wings showing deco patterns, filigrees of red on black, like blood vessels.

On the chaise, upholstered in black velvet, a chorus of Pierrot dolls regard me balefully. A heavy black teardrop rests on every white cheek and each wears a wilting ruff. Every red mouth is painted with a downturned smile. And there it is: the Pierrot with a torn ruff and a malevolent stare, with its cap gone and a fuzz of fair hair. Bandages trail from its wrists.

I sit down at the dressing table and open the drawer. Inside a velvet box I find a remarkable piece of jewellery. A spider, its abdomen a bulging garnet, feeds on a fly held in the cradle of its mandible. I touch it and the fly falls out of the spider's grip to hang on a fine chain, swinging beneath, free again. There is a tiny pin on each so that the wearer can grant the spider a meal or allow the fly to hover under its predator's nose. I put the brooch back, alongside a brush and comb set inlaid with polished jet and smoky glass bottles with mouldering contents.

I get up and open the door to the dressing room. There's a mirror and an ebony bentwood chair.

The wardrobe is disappointing. Inside there are no bright gowns, only a few coats smelling of mothballs. Big buttoned and fur-trimmed and uniformly bedraggled.

But this room is a mirror image.

Something must be hidden in this wardrobe. Some counterpart to the Mass cards: another clue. I take out the coats and lay them on the chair, methodically checking the pockets, feeling around the lining.

Then I hear a bang.

I am intact.

Not dead.

I come out of the dressing room.

On the bed, broken apart, is the moth-filled frame. I open the door a fraction and peer out into the hallway. There is no sign of Cathal roaring up the stairs yet. I close the door and turn back to the bed.

The glass has shattered extravagantly, as if the frame has been blown open by an incendiary device. It has landed moth side up with some of the insects thrown clear of the wreckage. The mother of all moths lies in the middle of the bed; she has lost part of her wing and her legs on one side. With the glass gone she looks even more horribly alive. As if, at any moment, she might start limping over the counterpane, trying out her tattered wings.

Something catches my eye. Just under the broken frame, a wisp of ribbon. I pull it and beneath the blasted moths something comes slithering. The string is attached to an envelope: medium-sized, manila.

I work swiftly, pulling up my shirt and tucking the envelope into the waistband of my jeans. I pick up the counterpane, knot the ends together and, moving the broken glass as quietly as I can, bundle it up and put it in the bottom of the wardrobe. I straighten the bed and hang the remaining coats back up unchecked.

As I step out of the room I look towards the dressing table mirror.

It's undisturbed. It appears I've got the message now.

Chapter 21

I look at Renata and she looks back at me. We both look at the manila envelope on the coffee table.

An unlit pipe is between her lips. She's promised not to light it, only that she needs something to clamp her jaw around to calm her nerves.

'Open the envelope, Maud,' she murmurs.

I don't think I want to.

I stand up and walk over to the kitchen window. She is still there, St Dymphna, flitting after the neighbourhood cat.

She has abandoned her crown and veil and her sandals. They lie shining on the rockery. Her brown hair flies behind her; now and again she stops, catches up her unravelling plait and chews the end of it absorbedly, watching for the cat's next move. Then the nimbus of light that surrounds her lovely head sparks and flares and her face glows with delight and she makes a grab. There's a flash of bare feet and a peal of wicked laughter.

The flap is taped down. I walk the knife carefully along it. Inside there are newspaper cuttings. I unfold them, smoothing them down and laying them out on the table.

Picture after picture of Maggie Dunne.

There are other pictures too. Of the police searching a furrowed field, of a wooded copse with tree roots gnarling the banks, and of an old sanatorium set in lawned gardens.

I pick up a cutting towards the top of the pile and read it out loud, 'Thursday, 29 August 1985, "Chief Constable Frank Gaunt has confirmed that Dorset police are widening the search for Maggie Dunne amid increasing concerns for her welfare. Maggie, a resident of Cedar House children's home, was last seen around midday on Tuesday, 20 August."' As I flick through the rest of the cuttings I notice the articles getting smaller, dwindling to no more than a line in the *Dorset Echo* six months later reporting an unconfirmed sighting of Maggie in Dover. There the trail ends.

'So Maggie was in care?' says Renata.

'Looks like it.'

I glance out of the window. St Dymphna is nowhere to be seen. An uneasy feeling is growing in my stomach: a queasy sense of excitement, with a dash of inevitability about it.

'Don't you think it's strange that Mary kept these cuttings?' asks Renata.

'Perhaps no stranger than your collection of true-life crime magazines. What's stranger is that she went to such lengths to hide them.'

St Dymphna peers in at the window; she presses her face through the glass and frowns. Then she stalks into the room and flops down in front of the television.

Renata turns to me, her expression solemn. 'Mary was onto something. She was trying to solve the mystery of Maggie's disappearance. She couldn't save her own child, Marguerite, so she was driven by a need to save someone else's, to try to set things right on some level, in some way.'

I inadvertently glance towards St Dymphna. She sits on the hearthrug, small and still and suddenly far older than her fifteen years, with her dark eyes burning and her face unearthly pale.

'We need to find Maggie,' says Renata. 'There's something we could try.'

'What is it?'

'We could try asking Mary.'

St Dymphna watches me closely, coldly.

'I'll do whatever it takes,' I whisper.

St Dymphna scrabbles to her feet and is gone.

Chapter 22

The best place to start is right here in the kitchen at Bridlemere. Supernatural occurrences have taken place in this room. The best time to start is right now, when there is no sign of the old man.

I push a chair in front of the kitchen door. If Cathal tries to come in I'll have time to cover everything up and pretend I'm washing the floor. Otherwise the back door is locked and there are no cats in the scullery.

These are the perfect conditions for working a spirit board.

I have a shot glass from Renata's sideboard and two cereal boxes opened up and stuck together. I have drawn letters from the alphabet and numbers and written *YES* and *NO* in the two top corners. I sit down on the kitchen floor and wait, with my fingertips on the top of the glass.

This happens, in this order: my nose itches, the crack of my arse itches, the tap drips. Then: nothing.

I take out the photo of Mary and Gabriel and look into the space where Mary's face should be.

I close my eyes.

'Are you there, Mary?'

The tap drips, the clock ticks, a cat scratches at the back door. After a while my fingertips cramp on the edge of the glass and one of my legs falls asleep.

'Mary, if you have a minute?'

I stretch out my leg and rub it. Then I look around the kitchen, edified by the immaculate floor. If only I could get my own home into this kind of order. I put my fingers back on the glass, close my eyes and concentrate. I throw out a question.

'Do you know what happened to Maggie Dunne?'

This happens, in this order: the kettle switches itself on and starts to boil, the door to the pantry opens and the glass begins to move, slowly, jerkily towards—

YES.

The glass stops and waits, shuddering under my fingertips; the kettle switches itself off.

I close my eyes.

'Was she murdered?'

Nothing. Then a powerful smell of earth and leaf mould as a sudden mist of moisture hits my face. I open my eyes. The room darkens abruptly, although it is still sunny outside the kitchen window.

The glass begins to tremble, drawing my attention back to the spirit board. My finger does nothing; it merely goes along for the ride as the glass moves in slow circles around the word . . .

YES.

The top pops off a lemonade bottle and the clock falls off the wall. The kitchen lights turn themselves on and off and crockery starts to shake on the dresser. A milk jug skips from its hook and crashes to the floor and the knife drawer slowly opens.

I would run if I could take my finger off the glass, but it is held rooted to the spot by a strange quivering magnetism.

YES. YES. YES.

I take a deep breath. The glass bucks under my finger, as if it knows what I'm about to ask.

'Were you murdered, Mary?'

The glass hops and the door to the pantry slams shut and flies open. The packets of rice and sugar and semolina, the tins of ham and peach slices, begin to fling themselves off the shelves. Bags hit the ground, bursting and rupturing; jars explode into shards.

'Who did it, Mary?'

The table judders and the kettle switches itself on again, with the noise of water rushing to the boil.

The glass cleaves to the board and refuses to move.

I wait.

'Was it Cathal?'

Nothing.

I try another question. 'Is Maggie here?'

The glass spins, wrenches itself out from under my finger and shatters itself against the wall.

I fold the spirit board, put the packets and tins back on the shelves and take up the broom.

And then I see them. Heading towards the back door, two sets of footprints in the mess that dusts the floor. They pull apart, each on their own trajectory halfway across the kitchen. As they draw closer to the back door they change. The last prints, just near the threshold, are the dabbed pattern of toes and no heel: the prints of two people running.

Chapter 23

At the cafe Sam takes a seat, not in the corner but over near the window. I head to the lavatory, past the waiter who narrows his eyes at me in greeting. I ignore him. I am buoyed up by a great and happy coincidence: this morning I put on a dress.

A rare choice born not from some unearthly premonition but because the dress was the only clean garment available besides a pair of ungainly culottes of unknown provenance. I thank any and all listening saints for this premium stroke of good fortune as I slip off my tabard and rummage in my bag for a lipstick.

Then I look at myself in the mirror.

Then I immediately revoke my thanks in case any of the saints are listening and think twice about the lipstick. Then I tighten my ponytail and remember Renata's disparaging comments about this exact same ensemble when I presented myself, some months ago, with great reluctance and even greater misgivings, for a conscripted date with the satellite TV repairman. Renata said that in this dress (grey shift, stylishly demure) with my hair pulled back I looked like an uptight novitiate knocking at Mother Superior's gates. I took that as a compliment.

I sit down opposite Sam with the late-afternoon sun behind me, feeling like a backlit Deborah Kerr, but without the wimple.

The cafe is empty apart from me and Sam, and the saints squabbling into nearby seats, elbowing each other and hissing in a bid to appear unobtrusive.

St Valentine settles in the seat next to me. 'Steady, Twinkle,' he says. 'I've got your back.'

St Rita and St George take seats at the table opposite. St Monica, liverish in cream, arranges her robes sourly in a corner. St Dymphna is nowhere to be seen. Small mercies.

I smile at Sam and Sam smiles at me.

'For the love of God,' barks St Valentine. 'Will you stop grinning or he'll think you're unravelled in the head. Ask him a question. Start a conversation.'

'So you were in the neighbourhood, just passing by?' I ask.

St Valentine rolls his eyes. 'Smooth.'

Sam nods. 'I was.'

St Valentine studies Sam closely. 'He's been in the neighbourhood a lot lately. Let's think about that for a moment, Twinkle.' The saint turns to me. 'Now, didn't you catch sight of a good-looking face peering in through the hedge at Bridlemere the other day? And what about that feeling you had that a handsome, well-put-together fella has been following you to the bus stop?'

I try to ignore him.

'And you're always smelling cigarettes in that garden. You've seen those bushes smoking more than once, haven't you?' He nods at Sam. 'This lad has been keeping an eye on you.'

I glower at St Valentine. I don't believe a word of it.

He leans back in his chair, addressing the saints at the next table. 'Sam doesn't like her being up at the house. He fears for her safety. He's said as much.'

The saints make sounds of agreement. St George growls something about hurling sticks before snapping his visor shut.

The waiter comes over with a look of high begrudgement on his face. Undeterred, Sam orders coffee and an all-day breakfast sandwich. The waiter departs and Sam watches me, his manly fingers playing with the lid of the ketchup bottle.

St Valentine grimaces. 'Get in there, say something sugges-tive, sexy voice, play with your hair, bite your lip, stick out the chest. Every second counts.'

Sam glances out of the window as a black car passes by.

'He's losing interest,' says St Valentine.

I glare at him. Haven't I enough on my hands with looking like Deborah Kerr?

Then Sam, his eyes fixed on an old man struggling past with shopping bags, asks, 'How's Mr Flood?'

'He's grand.'

'Any more mad crazy stuff up at the house?'

Only the poltergeist in the kitchen. 'No. Not really.'

Sam nods. 'You're too sensible to be swayed by it anyway.'

St Valentine winces. 'Ah Jesus, *sensible* is it? Hit back, Twinkle—'

'I'm not in the least bit sensible.'

Sam smiles. 'Pragmatic then?'

'Not at all.'

'Practical?'

I frown.

'Rational?' Sam ventures.

'I'll take that.'

Sam laughs.

St Valentine breathes out.

The waiter brings the drinks.

Sam smiles at me. 'Just a coffee, that's right?'

I smile and nod and poke the froth on the top of the cup with the teaspoon.

'Any sign of Gabriel?' asks Sam in a low voice when the waiter has himself anchored back behind the counter.

'None whatsoever.'

'Let's hope it stays that way.' He takes a taste of his coffee. 'Although, that was a great plan of his: getting the old man out of the house. With a clear day to sift through the rubbish God knows what someone might find.'

'So there we have it, Twinkle,' announces St Valentine. 'This here fella wants to get into the house and not your knickers. That's what he's after.'

I scowl at him.

St Valentine winks back. 'Although, all is not lost, of course, if he's planning to get into the house *via* your knickers.'

At the next table St Rita shakes her head and St George sniggers behind his visor. I hear it; it comes with a metallic echo. St Monica in the corner throws him a sullen look.

St Valentine holds up his hands. 'Wha'? I'm only saying what you're all thinking.'

Sam mops up ketchup with his sandwich. 'I'm not going to suggest again that you let anyone in the house – me or Gabriel. You've made your position clear, Maud,' Sam hesitates, 'and I respect you for that.'

'Sure he does,' says St Valentine. 'Look at him, isn't he full of respect?'

I look at Sam lounging on his chair with his grey eyes shining. The waiter brings the food order. Sam watches him walk away and then he turns to me with a wide, rakish grin.

'Of course, if you do change your mind I'd be more than happy to have a root around.'

St Valentine laughs gleefully.

I ignore the lot of them as I measure three sugars into my coffee and stir it. I don't take sugar but I like the whole routine of it. It's calming. I stir until I find myself equipped to change the subject.

'So I expect you'll be heading back up north soon, Sam?'

Sam puts ketchup in his sandwich. 'Not for a bit. I thought I'd stick around and see how things pan out here.'

I take a sip: it's far too sweet. I add more sugar. 'What things?'

'The investigation for a start; I want to see if any more clues surface.'

I measure in another spoonful. 'I wouldn't hold your breath.'

'Oh, I don't know.' Sam shrugs. 'Renata tells me you are starting to gain the old man's trust.'

I wonder what else Renata tells him. I glance at St Valentine but he has his toothpick out and is deep in thought, going after his few teeth.

'Maybe Mr Flood will enlighten you one of these days,' says Sam. 'And unravel the mysteries of Bridlemere.'

'I doubt it.'

'And then there's the envelope. The one you found at the house. Another message from Mary Flood?'

'Renata told you what was inside it?'

Sam pushes his plate away, glancing up at me, perhaps catching a note of censure in my voice. 'No.' He smiles. 'Renata said you were waiting until I came round to open it – when the gang was all together again.'

Of course she did.

Sam picks up his coffee, swirls it a little, eyes lowered. 'You know you can call me if you ever need to. If things get out of hand.'

St Valentine glances up, then he stops picking his teeth and stares at Sam. A look of wonder dawns on the saint's dim raddled face.

He points at Sam with a trembling finger. 'Look—'

'If you're ever in trouble.'

'Mother of God,' whispers St Valentine. 'Would you look at his ears?' He turns to the other saints. 'The tips of them: reddening. Do you see them?'

St George gets up and lurches over to Sam. Leaning down, his armour grinding, he pushes open his visor and studies Sam intently. Then St George straightens up, his face red with effort, and gives a curt nod.

'I bloody knew it,' mutters St Valentine. 'Son of a gun.'

Sam shifts in his chair. 'Any time you need me—'

'Ears lit up like two little beacons,' sighs St Valentine.

'Any time at all—'

'Like two little flags.'

'I'd be there for you.'

St Valentine gazes at Sam with an expression of rapture. 'It's working down to his cheeks.'

'I mean it, Maud.'

'He's going scarlet!'

'That's kind, Sam,' I say. 'I'll keep that in mind.'

'He can't help himself.' St Valentine turns to me. 'Can you believe that? Jumping Jack Flash is *blushing*.'

'So if anything kicks off, anything at all, in that house . . .'

'Yes, Sam?'

Sam gives me a smile that appears to be located somewhere between apology and confusion. 'Then I'm your man.'

'He is!' roars St Valentine. 'By God, Maud, he's your man!'

St Valentine clears the table with a cry of joy and runs a circuit of the cafe with his red cloak flapping. St George laughs and shakes St Valentine's hand and they pat each other on the back. St Rita throws me a congratulatory smile and St Monica purses the thin line of her mouth.

I give my coffee one last stir and gently put down the spoon.

Chapter 24

There's no dance when I return home and open Renata's gate. No dress ring knuckles at the kitchen window and no bobbing headscarf. I am puzzled; this is not a day that Lillian usually visits. As I round the house I see that the front door is open and the chain has been broken. Renata's shoes lie scattered across the hall and Johnny Cash looks up from the doormat, his frame buckled and his face properly pissed off. Jesus Christ is nowhere to be seen.

I walk into chaos: kitchen cupboards open, smashed crockery, the fondue set in the sink. In the living room the bookcase is toppled and novels are ripped in half; pages confetti the room. The display cabinet is smashed; twinkling gemstones stud the carpet. The moon rock has landed in the fireplace.

The string cockerels in the picture are no longer fighting; someone has put a foot through them. The drinks cabinet is empty; liquid runs down the wall behind the television: Advocaat congealing in yellow drips, splattered veins of blue curaçao.

What have I done?

I think of the shattered shot glass in Cathal's kitchen.

Did I raise this? Did I call up angry spirits?

I run past the wreckage, shouting for Renata.

The bathroom door opens. Under the mess of tears and make-up is a frightened man I've never seen before.

'Are you hurt, Renata?' I force an even tone. 'Did they hurt you?'

She puts her hands up to her poor head, as if to hide it from me. It is hairless, pale, with a few fine grey strands at the sides.

I put my arms around my friend.

There are no saints for this.

There were these three young guys: one had a crowbar, one had a hammer and one had an adjustable wrench.

It sounds like the start of a joke.

They had pushed their way in, filling the hallway and shutting the door behind them.

At first Renata was calm. She walked forwards into the living room like they told her to. Adjusting her headscarf, raising her eyebrows, she asked them what it was they wanted in a light, even voice.

They ignored her and said things to each other that she didn't quite catch. They spat out the big gobs of spit that they worked up in their throats. One lit up a cigarette and one glanced at the television. Then they went to work. One stayed in the living room with her, the others spread out. Renata could hear them crashing about in the other rooms.

He pulled the novels off the bookcase, flicking through each of them with a cigarette in the corner of his mouth, as if he were looking for a good read. He tipped out her drawers and rifled through her papers. Renata had stood motionless.

He glanced up and asked her what she was looking at. *Faggot.*

He walked over to her. What was he, seventeen or eighteen? With the whey-pale look of the badly fed, the underfed, the fed full of crap. A thin, bland face, with spots around the mouth. His trousers were slung low, halfway down his arse with his underpants showing. Renata fought the urge to laugh. She fought the urge to tell him to pull his bloody trousers up.

He walked up to her, close to her, and in his too-high, whining, strung-out voice asked her what she was fucking looking at. *Nonce.* It was a ducking, edging kind of walk; he could be a crab scuttling sideways, his arms out as a counterbalance. As if he was walking through an earthquake—

Crashes in the other room: as loud as colliding tectonic plates, slamming, shattering, rending noises, then pauses and exclamations.

He told her to walk to the mirror. She didn't understand. He pointed. She moved, numb, dulled. She didn't think to refuse.

Take it off.

She didn't understand.

He pointed to her headscarf. *Take it off.*

She had reached up and he had watched her. She fumbled with the knot. He put his cigarette in his mouth.

Here, Faggot, he murmured.

He ripped it off her head.

Time slowed and stopped.

Together they looked in the mirror, him standing over her shoulder. She saw her face through his eyes. Sad old clown. She was surprised by how naked her head was, how obscene, with its skin puckered, scaly even, and the little wisps of grey hair above the ears. He stood smoking, on his face an expression of disgusted fascination.

What is fucking wrong with you, man?

He swore emphatically, stepped back and swung his crowbar. Not at her but at the gemstones in the cabinet, aiming for the moon.

We stay in the bathroom, the only room they did not destroy. I bring two chairs in from the kitchen, shaking splinters of glass from them. Then I close the door against the carnage.

I can call the police, Renata agrees grudgingly, but only when she's decent. I clean her face very gently, with baby lotion and cotton wool from the bathroom cabinet. Sometimes she grabs my hand and holds it against her. Sometimes she just sobs for long furious moments on my shoulder. I find her shower cap and carefully pull it down about her head and she nods and breathes out. In her bedroom I find spilt boxes of make-up. I gather what I need along with a hand-held mirror and take them into the bathroom.

Renata sits quietly in her shower cap and kimono, with her face clean and blank: small, pale and genderless.

I hold the mirror in front of her but her hands shake too much to use tubes and wands, applicators and brushes.

'Do your worst, darling,' she says with a stiff little smile.

She looks for the longest time in the mirror. She is not herself but it is enough for her to face the world. My version of Renata's face is softer, smudged in places, so that she looks a little baffled.

When the police arrive I find Renata a headscarf to

replace her shower cap. When Lillian arrives we find paper cups and make coffee.

Renata sits at the kitchen table with her hands folded on her lap and I sit next to her. The police officer, a tall heavyset girl with a ponytail, sits opposite. She calls Renata madam and asks if she has been a victim of hate crime before.

Renata glances over at the sink. Lillian has her back to us but I can see that she has stopped what she is doing; in her stilled hand she holds the broken crockery she's pulled from the plughole.

'Yes,' says Renata.

'Recently?'

'Ten years ago.'

The police officer writes in her pad. 'So no connection to today's incident?'

'No.' Renata reaches for my hand.

The police officer looks at her. 'Was there a conviction?'

Renata half turns to me and I squeeze her hand.

'No.'

'And that was . . .'

Renata's voice is suave and careless, as if she's extending an invitation to a top-drawer party. 'Indecent assault, darling, behind Waterloo Station.'

'I'm really sorry,' says the police officer, who looks like she really is.

Lillian puts the crockery in the dustbin, dries her hands on a tea towel and walks out of the room.

The police have gone and Lillian is sweeping broken glass into a black bag in the living room, picking out the rock samples as she goes. The string cockerels are not salvageable, but no one liked them anyway. Jesus Christ has been found in the bedroom with his face against the wall, still exuding calm and perfect radiance. Like Johnny Cash, he has been restored to his rightful place in the hallway.

Renata opens the oven door and pulls out a manila envelope.

'The newspaper cuttings?'

'Now you know where I keep the valuables,' she whispers. 'It was what they were looking for.'

I frown. 'Really?'

'It was obvious. They went through every book, all my papers and they stole nothing.'

I speak as gently as I can. 'But if it was a hate crime—'

'It wasn't.' She looks me dead in the eye. 'I know it wasn't.' She taps the envelope. 'It was this they were after.'

'But who knew we had it?'

'The old man, his son?' Renata says. 'Someone must have seen you take it from the house.'

'But how?'

'I don't know. You feel watched in there, don't you?'

I nod. Ghosts, cats, mechanical card-playing stoats, you name it, to say nothing of an ancient shape-shifting giant who can stand a foot away without me knowing.

'What made you hide the envelope, Renata?'

'Instinct.'

'So what next?'

Renata's face is sober. 'We keep going. This shows that we're getting warmer.'

Chapter 25

There's an arrow on the kitchen table sketched in spilt custard powder. It appeared in the time it took me to turn and take up a cloth. Not just any arrow but an arrow fletched with feathers. This ghost is quick on the draw.

The arrow is pointing to the pantry.

I open the door and see scrubbed shelves and orderly packets, regiments of tins and rows of bottles. Cathal eats like a man under siege, preferring the preserved to the fresh. Everything is arranged with a pleasing neatness. I nudge a tin of minted peas into line; there are no clues here.

To the left of me, a jar of pickled beetroot edges forwards diffidently. Its neighbour, a box of savoury crackers, follows suit with more conviction. As does a bag of sugar and a bottle of brown sauce, sliding boldly out of their places as if they are offering themselves up for a dangerous mission.

I wait. Nothing else happens. I clear the shelf, checking each item I move. Then I see it. A key, taped underneath the shelf above.

Bright black iron, long-shanked.

There is the door we mustn't open.

I peel away the tape, put the key straight into the pocket of my tabard and emerge from the pantry to see a nose nudging through the back door. Then a snout, then two eyes and a gaze of molten honey. The fox comes cautiously, ready to retreat. His musk reek is bolder; it stalks into the room, signalling his arrival before he has entirely arrived. His shoulders follow, so that Larkin stands half inside, with his front paws on the doormat. He gives a yawn that comes with a faint whine and closes his muzzle with a snap. Then he looks at me *meaningfully.*

By the time I've crossed the kitchen to the back door, he's at the bottom of the steps standing on the garden path.

I know better than to follow a fox in life.

Larkin leads me past car batteries and suppurating bin bags, beyond bedframes and rusting bicycles. I wonder if we might stop at the caravan but we don't, although he hesitates there, one paw held up.

We weave through bushes and shrubs, stacks of roof tiles and broken window frames. I tread gingerly through piles of scrap metal and rotten planks of wood with proud nails. Even in my excitement I'm mindful of the risks of lockjaw and septicaemia and ear spiders from the webs that break over me like sticky curses.

Larkin shuttles forwards and back, perhaps impatient at my slowness.

Out past the refuse there's an untouched jungle of plants: legions of fat-stalked weeds furious with bristles and wonderful mushrooms in unreal shapes and colours. Some speckled scarlet like brilliant, cautionary tales, others the shape of baby ears, sprouting neatly all in a row.

Stems snap with pungent smells, leaving sap on my legs. Twigs break and twist. Burrs stud my cardigan and thorns pull at my skirt. Soon my hair is spotted with ladybirds and my ankles are ringed with ants. On my shoulder a caterpillar rides: a ferocious orange-quilled monster in his world.

Sometimes I lose sight of Larkin; when I do I trample to a standstill and wait for the bushes ahead of me to quiver.

With every step I seem to shrink and the plants grow taller and the light grows greener.

Then all at once we come to a clearing.

There is a round brick structure set into the ground: a half-buried beehive, an old ice house.

Leggy saplings dot the surrounding bank, dappling the afternoon sun that shines into the clearing.

I follow Larkin down a flight of steps. Nature has reclaimed this place: the brickwork is vivid with mosses and the path is thick with brambles. The iron gate is held open by a clump of nettles and just beyond leaves are piled high against a riveted wooden door. I kick them away and see the door is gnawed at the bottom. Larkin noses along it.

'Would there be rats in there, Larkin?'

As if in answer, Larkin snorts.

I try the key. It turns surprisingly easily.

The doorway is squat and the air inside clotted with the smell of damp and leaf litter. And it's cold, so cold you feel that the sun has never trespassed here.

In the light from the doorway I can see that the floor falls abruptly away to form a great bowl, perhaps ten feet deep. There is a narrow walkway all around it. Ice would have been stored here, packed in straw, kept intact by the subterranean chill of the building. From this dank place frozen slabs were carved and spiked and heaved up to the house to keep food fresh, to make cool drinks and sorbets. There is nothing in the bowl now but leaves and twigs and the remains of fallen birds: matted bundles of feathers and tangled wings. I hesitate to go any further, for the little building has the strange sad air of a plundered tomb, a disturbed burial site.

Larkin turns away from the door and runs back along the path, stopping halfway down, his attention focused on the bank above.

I cross the threshold, my hands on the doorframe, picking my way forward to the start of the walkway. I follow it, keeping close to the wall, although my clothes will be ruined, as the bricks run with moisture and are wet to the touch. The smell is overpowering: as if the belly of the earth has opened. The primordial smell of hidden places, deep dark places, where life ends and begins again, a cycle of rot and germination.

I run my hand along the wall but there is nothing to be found, no loose bricks or cubbyholes, no messages in bottles or hidden envelopes.

It all happens so quickly. A figure fills the doorway, backlit. The ice house darkens. The door is pulled shut and the key turns in the lock, a single resounding click. These sounds are spun, amplified and become echoes.

It's not quite pitch-black, I tell myself. There is a strip of light under the door and a small barred window high above it.

I make a simple plan. I will keep moving through the dark towards the light, sliding my foot against the wall, keeping my shoulder to it. Edging along, slowly, calmly. Not minding the space below me, above me, and all the solid black air that fills it.

It flies into my face. I throw up my arms.

I roll onto my side, swearing, and then onto my knees, to crawl around the bowl of the ice house, my hands scrabbling at dead leaves, feathers, something. My voice is taken up, spun around in the dark, mocked and repeated. Next time I move I'll grit my teeth and stay silent.

When the echoes stop I hear his voice.

There are rungs. Sam guides my hands to them, climbing behind me. At the top he pushes me up and over. He gets me to my feet and half carries me out of the underworld into the light. I'm careful not to look back. Instead I look at my found treasure. In my hand a white ribbon bow on a broken hair slide.

Sam steps into the road to flag a cab. By the time we're halfway home he has stopped telling me that we ought to be going to the hospital. He was coming to meet me, he says; he heard me swearing from the street. I've a set of lungs on me. I laugh and flinch; he takes my hand and squeezes it.

My hand is in Sam's hand.

But all I can think about is Mr Flood's dinner half-made. The jam sponge sat waiting for the custard and the salad waiting for the tinned ham, and the little white bow in my pocket. And beyond this, another thought: the silhouette of a figure the moment before the door of the ice house closed, before the key turned.

Could something in their size, their build, give them away? I barely saw them.

Did I hear them? Of course not.

Would I really have heard the silent scuff of a loafer, or the hushed shuffle of a shape-shifter?

★   ★   ★

Renata is standing at her front door. Sam tells her he will take me up to my flat, for a change of clothes and to get patched up. Then we'll be straight down. Renata nods and I can tell by the look on her face that she wants to follow but she can't.

I take off my clothes in the bathroom while Sam waits in the hall. There are bad grazes on my back, legs and arms. I put on pyjamas and splash my face in the sink.

I call out and say I'm fine. I'll be out in a minute. Then I sit down on the side of the bath and try hard to stop crying.

I hear him in the kitchen, finding mugs, washing them, boiling the kettle, sniffing the milk and pouring black coffee. I step out to a bright greeting and a flat that's different because he's in it. Everything feels festive. The unwatered plants have perked up, the curtains look less drab, and the corners are cleaner than I expected.

He tells me to sit down on the sofa and rolls fabric up over my arms, then my legs. Taking new pieces of cotton wool each time and wiping gently.

'Let me see your back.'

I turn a little on my side.

'Can I?'

He pulls up my top with hands so gentle I start to cry again.

'Done,' he says, and sits with his hand resting lightly on my leg.

I dry my face on my sleeve and we smile at each other.

He puts the cotton wool in a plastic bag and goes into the bathroom to throw away the disinfectant.

I sip hot coffee and feel the pressure of everything in the room waiting for him to return.

'So you were following the fox?' He sits down next to me with a distracted smile.

I shrug. 'It seemed like a plan.'

'And did you find anything in the ice house?'

'No.'

I don't know why I lie. Only that I can't bring myself to show him yet the forlorn little ribbon clinging to the plastic comb, the comb with half its teeth gone. Was it dragged off her head? Was it stamped underfoot as Maggie tried to get away?

'Maybe it's time to let go of this, Maud.' Sam's face is grave.

'You know about what happened to Renata, don't you?'

Sam nods. 'She phoned me.'

'Did she tell you what was in the envelope? The one they ransacked her place for?'

Sam looks at me in despair and perhaps a little pity. I recognise this look; I have given it to my clients often enough.

'You have a sister, don't you, Sam? You told Renata.'

He stares at me. 'What's that got to do with it?'

'If she disappeared, like Maggie Dunne, would you just let it go?'

'I don't see—'

'Mary knew something, or suspected something, that's why she kept the newspaper cuttings. That's why she took such trouble to hide them. Everything started with Maggie's disappearance.'

Sam takes a sip of his coffee.

'You wouldn't let it go, would you, Sam?'

He puts his mug on the table and throws me a look, and for once I know what's coming next.

Chapter 26

Sam sleeps with his hair across his face. I watch him until his eyes open. At first a lazy swimming gaze, a sweet beguiled smile. I wait for his expression to change. For that slow-dawning realisation then that quick flood of horror.

It's a look I know well, the look of an ambushed goat on a rope. I wore it myself once when I woke up next to an archivist I'd met on the bus. He had dry papery hands, enjoyed reading about canals and winced whenever I spoke.

Yes, he would love a coffee, Sam says, the scaffold of his smile just about holding.

When I pull the door behind me the panic will set in and he'll be up out of the bed, searching the room for his things, hopping into his cowboy boots. He'll be swearing softly to himself and cursing the perils of kindness and proximity.

So long, Pardner.

I put the kettle on and get into the shower.

I don't have to check that the flat is empty; I know as soon as I get out, as soon as I wrap the towel round me.

St Valentine is lolling around outside the bathroom door, swinging his dingy rope belt. 'That went well with your man,' he says.

I throw him a caustic glance. 'And you can keep your opinions to yourself.'

He grins. 'He was very shook looking, coming out of your bedroom. But then he recovered himself and by God he put the good leg under him. I've never seen a man move so fast.'

'And you the saint of love saying this? And I'll thank you not to be loitering in my hallway, uninvoked and uninvited.'

'Leaping and hopping out that door.' St Valentine fixes me with one eye; the other wanders at will. 'Like a rabbit he was. No, like a fox, running with the pack an inch away from his arse.'

'Breaking and entering no less.'

'He left a note.' St Valentine nods towards the living room.

Propped up on the coffee table, my telephone pad. I wander over, feigning indifference. In a hasty scrawl:

Sorry M. Have to run.

'He's slipped your hook.'

'I wasn't trying to hook him,' I utter through gritted teeth.

'Well, you'll have more chance of hooking a dose of the clap the way you're carrying on.' St Valentine wags a dim finger at me. 'How long have you known him? Five minutes? He gives you the soft eye and you drop your knickers.'

I glare at him. 'There must be some way I can report you?'

'Fair play to you though for getting a go on that. Jesus, who'd have thought it?' He gives me a jaunty wink and drifts off through the wall.

★　★　★

'You're late. Half the morning has gone.' Cathal glowers through his eyebrows at me.

He's wearing a smoking jacket and a beret. I almost laugh. But I don't. Not with the recent communications from Mary Flood on my mind.

'A bit of dry cake and not a drop of fucking custard,' he growls. 'Tardy little fecker, are you coming?'

He heads off down the hallway and I follow him.

He stops outside the door to his workshop. I notice that he has reinforced his fortifications overnight. On each side of the doorway there is a wooden hat stand topped with stuffed animals, totem-pole-like. Surrounding this Mr Flood has made a corral of plastic storage boxes filled with jumble. I recognise much that has been stolen back from the bins under the cover of darkness.

'Have you anything in your pockets?' he mutters.

'No.'

'Then keep it that way.'

He unlocks the door and flicks on overhead strip lights, illuminating a large cluttered workshop. A workbench runs the length of the room. Above it, a thousand dismembered creatures gather dust on shelves, like a taxidermy accident and emergency unit. Beneath the workbench lie boxes of cogs and levers and half-stripped mechanisms. Tools hang on the wall, between strange carved marionettes. There are princesses and witches, crocodiles and clowns. In the centre of the room there is a glazed booth about the size of a Punch and Judy show. Red velvet curtains are drawn inside the window. Above it is a sign, painted in dull gold letters:

Madame Sabine
Tomorrow's Fortune Today.

Cathal rummages in a jar on the shelf and hands me a coin. He nods at the slot at the front of the machine. 'Put a penny in.'

The coin drops and there's a whirring noise. The curtains open jerkily, getting stuck halfway across the window with a plaintive drone.

Cathal swears under his breath, takes a hammer from the bench and wanders round the back of the booth. The curtains sway open to reveal a terrifying life-sized automaton. A small-waisted, plump-bosomed woman, dressed in a corseted gown of black bombazine. She has long necklaces of jet, huge lustrous eyes and a disproportionately small mouth with tiny white teeth. Over her dusty coiffure she wears a coin-spangled veil. Between her be-ringed fingers sits a crystal ball. The painted backdrop is of a gypsy caravan. There is a little stove with a bright kettle on the hob and a line of patterned plates. To her right is a wire birdcage containing two fat taxidermy chaffinches. A stuffed black cat at her left elbow looks on.

With a clank of the mechanism she lifts her slender wrists and passes her hands across the crystal ball. The two fat chaffinches shake their wings and the cat opens and shuts its eyelids.

'The birds sang once,' Cathal says. 'And the cat purred, would you believe?'

With a terrible grinding Madame Sabine's head drops forward and she regards me with a sudden awful scrutiny, her black irises glistening. Her hands make one last pass and drop lifeless back onto the counter. Her head yanks up with a clinking of her veil.

A card is dropped into a recess below and the curtains fitfully draw themselves closed.

I pick up the card.

Madame Sabine says:
If you meet a squinting woman be sure to give her the time of day lest MISFORTUNE befall you.

I frown at it until Cathal takes the card and ushers me through double doors into a large interconnecting room. A garden swing seat, complete with sun canopy, occupies a central position surrounded by saucers of lapped and sour milk. At least four cats sway on worn cushions and tangled sheets.

'You don't sleep on that, do you?' I say incredulously.

'I do. It's lovely. Go on, try it.'

'I will not. I bet it's crawling. When did you last change your sheets?'

'Now that I can't remember, Drennan.'

I follow him through the room and out into the conservatory. He has the painting covered.

'I was hoping to see it.'

'At the end you will.'

I sit on the chair and he tells me to move my arm, my head. He looks down at me.

'Your hair is wrong.'

'You told me to wear it up.'

'I did not,' he says. 'May I?'

I nod, surprising myself.

He carefully, gently removes the pins. 'That's better. It softens the line of your iron jaw.' He shakes out my hair then tucks a strand behind my ear. 'Grand so.'

'Get on with it then, Rembrandt.'

He pats me on the shoulder and goes over to the easel. He uncovers the canvas. 'You'll be wanting a story, no doubt?'

'To pass the time.'

I watch him shambling backwards and forwards in front of the canvas. He has a wayward veer to him today; I wonder if he's been at the turpentine.

I look at the painting of Mary in her yellow dress and Gabriel walking next to her, with his sketchy scowling face. 'Tell me about Gabriel, as a boy.'

He squints at the canvas. 'For fuck's sake.'

After a while he speaks. 'He was an all-round sneaky shit. Hiding, slinking, spying. Like a chameleon, changing his spots to stripes to blend in.'

I wonder if he inherited this trick from his father.

Cathal pulls a grim face. 'And torturing. He enjoyed maiming things.'

'Aren't all boys like that? What about yourself and the wasps?'

Cathal looks at me. 'They are and they're not. Gabriel was cruel. And hard. You could shake him until his teeth rattled and he'd admit to nothing. You could belt him all shades of blue and he'd stay silent.'

I frown.

'But Mary thought the sun shone out of his arse.'

'They were close?'

He glances at me. 'No. He hated her as much as she loved him. He took every chance to be spiteful to his mother, playing tricks, hiding things or breaking them. Causing accidents about the house.'

'Gabriel caused accidents?'

'I caught him at it a few times and gave him a good clatter. Mary wouldn't hear anything against him; she always took his word over mine.'

Overhead the sun goes in behind the clouds and the

conservatory darkens. It is quiet but for the shuffling sound of Cathal's slippers and the faint hiss of air sucked through his dentures.

A picture begins to grow in my mind, of Mary, rolling down the stairs.

A young Gabriel stands on the landing, watching her fall; it's a long way down from top to bottom. She goes headlong. Her face a mask of panic, her legs, arms, the base of her spine hitting the steps, one sickening thump after another. Little round vowel sounds come out of her, along with funny squeaks, like the sounds of a bagpipe being tuned. On the turn of the stair her head hits the balustrade. She is quiet for the last stretch of steps.

Or maybe Gabriel had nothing to do with it.

Mary and Cathal argue at the top of the stairs, she has a newspaper cutting in her hand. He moves towards her, looming large on the landing . . .

I close my eyes and listen to the slap and rasp of brush on canvas.

At the bottom of the staircase Mary Flood has survived the fall, but only just. She lies on her side. Her fingers twitch, her breathing is ragged. A red peony flowers on her temple. She mouths a name. As Mary loses consciousness perhaps she is reunited with her daughter. It is said that the dead always come to the dying, to help them cross into their world.

Perhaps she meets Maggie too.

The smell of earth comes up through the floor of the conservatory to vie with the smell of turpentine. The clouds move overhead. Silence falls over us, so that when I finally speak my voice sounds unfamiliar and overloud.

'Tell me about Marguerite.'

Cathal stops painting.

'You had a daughter, Cathal.'

He starts to paint again. I wait.

His voice, when he finally speaks, is soft, uncertain. 'I did.'

'I'm sorry. It's hard, losing someone.'

He frowns. 'People are easily lost.'

'What was she like?'

He looks up at me with his pale, pale boreal eyes and he smiles, suddenly and guilelessly. 'A fine forthright girl. She gave Gabriel a run for his money.'

'You were close?'

He nods, puts down his paintbrush and selects another one.

He turns back to the canvas. 'Now hold still, Drennan,' he says. 'This is the tricky bit.'

Chapter 27

There is a change in the air tonight at Renata's maisonette. The jokes are fewer and we drink our home-brewed krupnik the way it's supposed to be drunk: arduously and without pleasure.

Renata's rock collection is boxed up and her bookcase is empty; her walls are scrubbed and stained and there are cigarette burns on her carpet.

But this doesn't explain our mood.

We are weighed down by one feeling: this thing is too big for us. It is larger than one of Renata's crime stories. This is real: the true-life story of a missing schoolgirl and an innocent woman who may have met with a questionable death.

The ribboned comb sits on the table; from time to time our eyes return to it. Renata has checked every newspaper cutting in case Maggie Dunne was pictured wearing it. She wasn't.

'It could have been Marguerite's?' I say.

But this doesn't seem to make us feel better.

The saint pacing the floor over by the window does little

to help; I'm glad Renata is spared the sight of her. St Rita of Cascia is paler than she's ever been, with an anxious look in her kind hazel eyes. She flickers and glows intermittently, like a strip light on the blink. The wound on her forehead burns a fierce red.

What we really need is some kind of celestial truth drug, a bolt of revelatory lightning strong enough to unearth Bridlemere's secrets. I imagine the house hurling all manner of clues at us: train timetables, diaries, a full range of murder weapons. Ghosts would drift out from every corner, grave-eyed and rubbing their cold little hands, ready to give sworn statements. Every last one of the family's skeletons would be accounted for: out they would come, with their bones numbered, chattering their teeth and pointing their bony fingers.

Cathal Flood would be there, with his hand clamped over his mouth and his eyebrows raised in astonishment at the words of disclosure spilling out of him. And Gabriel too, heaving up confessions involuntarily, with his upper lip wet and his shark eyes blank with panic.

And Maggie Dunne, would we finally find her?

Slumbering unquiet under the floorboards, shut down and hopeless in the cellar?

For here are puzzles we don't understand and jeopardy that may return at any moment, wielding crowbars. The windows are locked and the chain is across the door. Renata has the police station on speed dial.

I wonder if our nerves will hold.

I glance at my friend. Renata smells strongly of pipe tobacco and her headscarf is lopsided. From time to time she absently rolls up the sleeves of her kaftan. She doesn't ask where Sam is and when it gets way past the time he's supposed to arrive she sets the plates out on the coffee table and we eat the food she has reheated in the microwave.

We both know there are more important matters than Sam Hebden's whereabouts.

If I could find the words I would tell Renata that she shouldn't expect to see Sam anytime soon. But then maybe I don't have to. Renata has had her share of doomed romances and with the hard-won wisdom of the scarred at heart she won't ask me where Sam is, or if he's coming back. For this I love her.

I could pretend I'd dreamt him, if it wasn't for his cigarette ends in a saucer and the smell of him on my sheets.

The film shows again, a little skewed now, for one night only.

Slow-motion molten glances. Cinematic moments and those less rehearsed. The awkwardness of clothes and the stilted tripping journey from sofa to bed. Then the freedom, the joyful rolling, plotting boundaries and finding landmarks, directions cut off mid-sentence. I see it again, or some version of it: involving limbs and hair, saliva and teeth, the electricity of fingertips and skin scorched into an awful fervent feeling. The urgent consensual stare and the act of near violence that followed; the screwed-down, locked-down grind of tension to a point here and now and no other never.

Then parachuting into sleep. Me, folded silk, strapped to his back. He held my hand fast, as if his life depended on it.

With a pull of the ripcord he's gone into the still, grey light of morning. He tied back his hair, fired up the Ducati and headed back to—

Renata collects our plates.

St Rita stops pacing and stands looking out of the window with her shoulders hunched.

We finish our krupnik in silence and I reach for the bottle and pour us another. Renata raises an eyebrow.

'For the fat on our brains,' I say.

We drink in silence, then Renata rummages in her handbag. 'Lillian left these for you.'

A rape alarm and a family-sized pepper spray.

'What for?'

'I asked her to get them, in case Mr Flood gets frisky and attempts to murder you.' Renata purses her lips. 'You should charge your phone too, in case of an emergency.'

'It doesn't work at Bridlemere: there's no reception. Look, it's kind, but I don't need these.'

Renata purses her lips. 'I'd feel better if you took them.'

I roll my eyes.

'Maud, I am sleeping with a bread knife under my pillow.'

'And Bernie.' I nod at the ornamental urn on the mantelpiece. 'He's well and truly out of the spare room now?'

'My love stays close by me. Thank God those bastards didn't find him.' She wears an expression of deep revulsion. 'Who knows what they would have done with him.'

'Don't go there.'

'Please be careful, Maud.'

'Cathal won't hurt me.'

She looks at me closely and says, not unkindly, 'What makes you think you can trust him? What makes you think you are safe around that old man?'

It's a fair question. One I should be asking myself: *why trust any man alive?*

'He paints you and tells you stories. He charms you with words so that you can't see he's evil. He is the spider and you are his fly.'

I think about the brooch in the red bedroom, the garnet-bellied spider reeling in his prey. 'I'm no fly, Renata.'

'You must be guarded, Maud. Learn to tell your enemies from your friends.'

The phone rings in the hall.

Renata is angry. I can tell this by the way she tugs at her headscarf as she retakes her seat.

My heart flounders. 'What is it?' I immediately think of Sam.

'Cedar House.' She smoothes down the folds of her kaftan. 'The children's home Maggie Dunne was living in when she went missing. Only now it's called Holly Lodge.'

'What about it?'

'They refused to comment.'

'What did you ask them?'

She shakes out her bangles and inspects her fingernails. 'The ins and outs of Maggie's case.'

'You told them who you are?'

We look at each other. Taking a moment to consider who Renata really is.

'I said I was a journalist.'

'There's probably all sorts of rules in place to stop them talking about ex-residents.'

'Even so.' Renata frowns. 'I said I wrote for a reputable newspaper and I was doing a tasteful piece on unsolved missing-persons cases; you'd think they'd oblige.'

'Perhaps you sounded shifty?'

Renata takes it well. 'It's possible.' She pours us both another shot. 'They're not like this on the television, investigations, are they? Two downcast women in a maisonette with a bottle of krupnik.'

'It wouldn't make good television.'

She studies her glass disdainfully. 'Not when there are car chases and procedures and DNA.'

'You got out your flip chart. That was very exciting.'

Over at the window St Rita raises her head and starts walking the floor again, slowly at first and then picking up speed to a decent stride.

Renata nods. 'So we'll keep on?'

'We will.'

'We're beavers after all.'

'I thought you were a goat?'

She downs her drink in one, her eyes hardly watering. 'I've defected.'

Chapter 28

It is raining in Cathal Flood's kitchen. Droplets fall from the ceiling in sudden scattered showers or else drip ponderously. I scurry about with buckets and bowls to catch the worst of it, noticing with surprise that pale-green shoots of ivy have begun to emerge between the cracks in the kitchen tiles and ramble up the walls, stretching up towards the dusty cornices.

A fell wind howls in the capped chimney in the scullery, hitting high notes a banshee would be proud of. An earthy smell rises from the linoleum and up through the sink. The room has darkened, so that I would switch the light on but for the steady dribble through the light fitting.

While outside it is dry and bright and hasn't rained for days.

The smell makes me think of the ice house and I wonder if I should go back with a torch. But even the idea of it makes my heart turn over.

Cathal sails into the kitchen wearing a raincoat over his pyjamas.

I point to the buckets. 'Will I get someone out? For the leaks?'

'Not at all; it does this from time to time.'

'It rains in your kitchen?'

'Somewhere a crow is dropping too many stones in a pitcher,' he says cryptically.

Cathal is in a good mood. This is not unusual. Nowadays he smiles more and roars less and has started to whistle. We eat breakfast together in the kitchen and, newly domesticated, he grooms his fierce white mane with the brush and comb set I found for him.

But then there is that glint in his eye and that curl to his lip and that sarcasm in his voice. The savagery is still there, only it has dropped below the surface, for now.

He settles at the table. 'We'll go ahead with the bath today.'

I stare at him in mock surprise. 'Good man yourself.'

He dips his toast in his runny egg like a good old boy. 'If you promise to desist with your fecking nagging.'

I pour him a juice. 'So you'll let me go upstairs and get the bathroom ready? Through the Great Wall of *National Geographic*s, along the hallway and up the stairs, first floor, third door on the right. Just the one room, as agreed.'

'That's where the bathroom is. I've locked all the other doors on the landing against your beak.' He glances up at me. 'And you can keep your eyes in your head and your hands to yourself. I don't want you touching my curiosities.'

'I've no interest in your curiosities. When did you last have a bath?'

'1998.'

'A while then. Let's just pray the boiler behaves itself.'

He sips carefully from the glass, as if he's getting accustomed to using his paws.

I wash up, glancing at his long thin back bent to his breakfast. Sometimes I wish there were no mystery; sometimes this is enough. There are moments when I don't think about Mary or Maggie Dunne; I just get on with my job here. The process of packing and sorting, scouring and cooking, having the cats come and go after the mice.

'Is there no fecking toast in this house?'

'If you've manners there is.'

He throws me a look of disgust and sucks his dentures. I butter the old man more toast and put it down in front of him.

'It's my birthday soon,' he says to his egg.

'It is.'

'I don't want to spend it alone. I'm a tragic old bastard.'

'That you are.'

He frowns. 'Would you have dinner with me, Drennan?'

Without thinking, I say it, 'I will of course.'

He beams down at his plate.

The bathroom is a vast dusty space, as inviting as a mortuary. I was expecting greater opulence: a roll-top bath with lion's feet and gold dolphin-shaped taps. Something showy, like the red and white bedrooms with their doves and fountains on the walls, their secret passages cats can disappear down

This bathroom feels too real.

A tall window disseminates a cheerless light. Everything is cold to the touch and the whole place asserts itself with a fierce smell of unbridled mustiness.

There are two sinks, both cracked, a lavatory and a bidet, along with a massive trough of a bath: a giant's bath. Everything is spaced out, as if the sanitaryware is avoiding one another. The tiles that cover the walls and floor are white, veined with varicose blue. Dead moths, flies, beetles and the hollowed-out carcasses of wasps litter the room, particularly the windowsill, which is swagged with cobwebs. I turn on the sink tap and it chugs with disuse, vomiting rust. I rinse the sink out and move over to the bath.

And I see her.

Her pale toes are curled over the lip of the bath, the nails unpolished, almond shaped. The ends of her hair are wet, dampened to dark blonde, fair at the crown where it's still dry. Her eyes are glazed, unseeing, gelid marble. She raises her hands in a languid kind of gesture, a kind of sleepy backstroke, and slips down into the water. Feet, legs, narrow chest: all are submerged. I see them float under the surface.

Maggie Dunne raises her arms again then stops mid-stroke and I see: her arms are ribboned with red; it runs down her arms, twisting patterns. She looks up at me, her face a pale pearl. Then it is under too. She drowns in gore.

I'm halfway out the door before I look again. There is nothing in the bath but dust and desiccated spiders.

Cathal shuffles in wearing a dressing gown. 'Just so you know. There's no way I'm going to let you stand there gawping at my flute.'

'I've no interest in your flute.' I look around me, dazed. 'What's the matter with you?'

'Nothing.'

I run the water until it's clear, find a plug and check he has towels, sponge and soap. I set up the portable hoist I'd ordered last week, in case his arse gets stuck in the bath.

He frowns at it. 'What's that contraption for?'

'In case your arse gets stuck in the bath.'

'What kind of a gobshite gets stuck in a bath? Why would I get stuck in my own bath? Aren't I nimble yet?'

'You can certainly sling your leg over your rubbish.'

He looks at me blankly. 'What rubbish?'

'All right so, I'll leave you to it.'

He takes off his dressing gown.

I'm waiting in the hall outside the door. This is what we have agreed. Cathal has set out a chair for me and left me a pile of magazines. I can hear the echoes of his splashing, the squeak and groan of the bath as he moves his long limbs in it.

My eyes feel sore, tired.

In the next room Cathal farts, then starts to sing a dirty song.

I glance across the landing at the painting but Mary won't meet my eyes. She has faded into the dark backdrop: a dim white blur of face and hands.

Mrs Cabello, from the big house next door, is standing on the back doorstep with her nostrils flaring impressively. She looks at least twenty years older close up. Her hair is blow-dried into cascades of black waves and scraped back from her high-domed forehead by designer sunglasses. Her lipstick carries way beyond her lip-line and her eyes are ringed with black kohl. I think of Renata and how she would appreciate Mrs Cabello's gloriously embellished outfit, from her gold sandals to her tight black cigarette pants.

Mrs Cabello has a wide emotional range, from furious and distraught to angry and venomous. Despite her erratic mix of Spanish, English and lyrical profanities, I have ascertained two things.

One: she hopes the old man will be buried alive by an avalanche of rubbish.

Two: the old man has stolen her valuable Sphynx cat.

She has seen Mr Flood's gaunt shape flitting around her property late at night. She has found empty boxes of cat biscuits in her bushes.

'He has been trying to lure my baby outside for weeks,' she says. 'He waits for me to slip up and leave a window open. Manolete is a house cat. One of a kind.'

She curses the eyes in Mr Flood's head and demands an interview with him.

'He's in the bath at present. Is Manolete one of those bald varieties of cats?' I ask politely.

Mrs Cabello stops mid-rant and stares at me. 'What are you talking about?'

'Mr Flood has a lot of cats,' I say patiently. 'What does Manolete look like? Is he bald?'

Mrs Cabello blinks. 'No, he has down. Like fine chamois.'

'And he usually lives inside?'

Mrs Cabello nods and, perhaps reminded of Manolete's singular beauty, begins to cry, making resentful little sobs. She rustles in her handbag, finds a photograph and passes it to me. It is of a singularly ugly cat. A pale grey alien with protuberant yellow eyes crawls over a satin cushion, wrinkling its brow glumly.

'I see.'

'He is very beautiful.' Mrs Cabello puts the photo back in her bag.

'I'll look out for him.' I glance over my shoulder and lower my voice. 'You didn't happen to know Mary Flood at all, by any chance?'

'What has Mary Flood got to do with my cat?'

I pause. 'I just want to find out a bit more about the family.'

Mrs Cabello snarls and points a long-nailed finger up at the house. 'Can't you ask him?'

I keep my voice low. 'He's not very forthcoming.'

'He's a bastard.' Mrs Cabello crows in satisfaction. 'His wife was lovely.'

'You knew her well?'

She nods. 'She gave me a rose bush when I moved in.'

'You must have been upset to hear about her accident?'

Mrs Cabello wrinkles her nose. 'It was no accident.'

I glance behind me. 'You really think that?'

Mrs Cabello shrugs. 'Maybe, but what would I know?'

I lower my voice. 'Did Mary ever mention feeling threatened?'

'We only talked about her garden.'

'Nothing else?'

She points. 'There was an arbour there, with roses over. This was a beautiful house when Mary was here.' She shakes her head. 'It is so sad, how he let all this go. Everything stopped, everything died when she died. The only thing growing here now is rubbish.'

'Did she ever mention her daughter?'

'They have a daughter?'

'Her name was Marguerite; she died very young.'

'That is sad.' Mrs Cabello looks sad. 'Mary never once spoke about her daughter.'

I duck into the kitchen and write down Renata's number and give it to her. 'If you remember anything else about Mary, however small, will you phone this number?'

Mrs Cabello pushes the paper into the pocket of her cropped leather jacket and smiles at me grimly. 'And you'll look for Manolete?'

'I will.'

She puts her sunglasses on and picks her way back down the stairs. At the bottom she waves and retreats up the garden path.

Cathal has spent most of the day in the bath and, with the help of a flannel and a rubber bath mat, he emerged without incident and with his modesty intact. He has put on an old dark suit with a black tie. His washed hair has been carefully combed and he is clean-shaven. He looks like a disreputable guest at a wake.

He now stands ready at the canvas watching me take my position on the chair.

'How much longer will you be dragging this painting out?' I ask.

'It will be finished by Friday. We'll have the big unveiling on my birthday.'

'Is there anyone else you'd like to invite? Friends, neighbours, your son?'

Cathal regards me with disdain. 'You really are a gobshite.'

'I'm only asking.'

'When you know that I'm a hated man? Hated and hating. Sure what would I be doing inviting people round to detest me in person on my birthday?'

'Talking of antagonism,' I say, 'Mrs Cabello called, she's lost her cat.'

'Has she now?'

'She thinks you might have stolen it.'

Cathal looks around him. In the conservatory there are multiple felines. Curled up between paintings, lolling at the feet of my armchair and prowling around the legs of the easel.

'I've cats; she can take her pick.'

'This is a special cat. A bald one.'

'Her cat is not bald; it has a soft down, like a wrinkled grey peach.'

I frown at him. 'You've stolen Manolete.'

Cathal dabs at his palette, his face impassive.

'Don't try to deny it. Mrs Cabello saw you flitting about her garden at night trying to lure him out. You've stolen him, haven't you?'

He squints at his painting. 'I haven't at all. Hush your mouth from flapping.'

'The poor woman's frantic.'

'She's always frantic. The poisonous old mare.'

'She seems nice enough. She was a friend of Mary's, wasn't she?'

Cathal looks at me in disgust. 'Is that what she said? Then she's a bloody liar as well as a filthy brasser.'

'So they weren't friends?'

He scowls. 'That one was always slithering around here, inviting Mary to garden parties and gin palaces and fecking orgies. Mary held no truck with her. Mary was a decent woman.'

'She was a religious woman, Mary?'

'In a way.'

'Fair play to her, the church is the place to be,' I say coyly.

Cathal's reply is steeped in scorn. 'I never had you down as a sheep.'

'St Joseph's is no trek and Father Quigley lays on some nice hymns.' I watch him out of the corner of my eye.

He rinses his brush in the little pot clipped to his palette and wipes it dry on a bit of rag. He selects another brush and carries on painting as if absorbed in his work.

Finally, he says, 'If you want my advice, steer clear of priests, especially that one. He's a great man for meddling in other people's business.'

'You know him?'

He glances at me. 'There's a surprise. I suppose you'd like a tale about that?'

'If you like.'

'I think you've had enough stories now, Drennan.' Cathal concentrates on the canvas, the tip of his tongue touching his top lip. 'I've told you where sticking your coulter in will lead.'

Chapter 29

Renata sways into the room, a look of high intrigue on her face.

'It's Father Quigley.'

'On the line?'

She nods. 'He wants to know if Inspector Drennan can make a house call. He has some information for her.'

'Tell him she's out in the patrol car after a cat burglar but she'll be with him as soon as she can.'

Renata smirks. 'He asks if she can come directly, before the housekeeper returns.'

'She'll see what she can do.'

The priest himself opens the door and practically lifts me inside, checking up the path behind me. There is no one there but St Valentine, who has dogged my step since I left Renata's, scuttling invisibly by my side and spitting on the pavement.

I follow Father Quigley into his study. His Fuengirola tan hasn't quite packed its bags yet but there's an ashen edge to his complexion that comes with long hours shut in confessional boxes or drinking tea in hospices.

He shakes my hand. 'Thank you for coming, Maud. I'll make this brief just while Mrs O'Leary is out, you know. She has a great ear for conversation.'

He waves me to an armchair.

St Valentine settles on the edge of the priest's desk with the expectant air of an audience member taking his seat. He removes a toothpick from the sleeve of his robe and applies it to his few remaining teeth.

'Her heart is in the right place.' Father Quigley glances towards the window. 'But I've never known anyone with such a thirst for a drop of scandal or a dribble of gossip.'

'Is this about Mary Flood, Father?'

'No,' he says. 'It's about Marguerite. And it isn't at all good.'

'Marguerite was sent to a children's home?'

The priest nods. 'The church had connections with the place, so Father Creedo knew a few of the residents, including Marguerite.' He hesitates. 'I hope you didn't mind me being proactive, so to speak.'

'Not at all, Father.'

'Only I noticed Father Creedo's name on the Mass cards.'

'Of course. We had previously made enquiries—'

'And you heard nothing? Well, Creedo is a devil to get hold of.' He beams at me. 'He's in Paraguay now, would you believe? That's where I found him.'

'All credit for tracking him down, Father.'

Father Quinn looks delighted. 'I'm a bit of a one for solving the mysteries on the television there. What great gas being a detective.'

'It has its moments.'

'As that wee Belgian fella said, it's all about the little grey cells.'

'It is, Father.'

'Putting two and two together.'

St Valentine stops picking his teeth. 'Get him to speed up a bit. You've fifteen minutes: O'Leary's waiting at the bus stop with a bag of chops.'

I address him brightly. 'Now, Father, tell me what you want to say, or else Mrs O'Leary will be through the door with her ears wagging.'

Father Quigley nods. 'Marguerite was a long-term resident at the home. Father Creedo saw her arrive as a kiddie and met with her over the years. Although he lost contact with her when he moved to another parish.'

'So Marguerite didn't die?'

The priest is grave. 'No. She attempted to murder her brother.'

'She tried to kill Gabriel?'

'She took the little fella by the hand, led him down the garden and tried to drown him in the pond. Afterwards the girl showed no remorse. In fact, she solemnly promised to try it again, so they sent her away.'

St Valentine tuts. 'Siblings.'

'So Marguerite is alive.' The thought thrills me. 'She's out there somewhere?'

'According to Father Creedo.'

I frown. 'Cathal Flood didn't contradict me when I spoke of his dead daughter.'

'He didn't? Well, in a way Marguerite was dead to her family. That rumour, terrible as it was, might have been easier to bear than the truth.'

'Maybe.'

Father Quigley looks reflective. 'Jim Creedo said he'd never met a more charming kid. The family came up and visited a few times, although they always supervised her around the boy, in case she took the opportunity to have another pop at him.'

And then it dawns on me. 'Did Father Creedo tell you the name of the home?'

'Cedar House.'

'The Cedar House that's now Holly Lodge?'

'I wouldn't know about that, Maud. It was a special home for maladjusted children.'

I try to keep calm. 'When did Father Creedo know Marguerite?'

'Seventies to mid-eighties.'

My heart leaps in me. 'Then Marguerite must have known Maggie Dunne. They would have been living at the home at the same time.'

St Valentine lets out a muted whoop.

The priest looks confused.

'Maggie Dunne was also a resident of Cedar House, Father. She was fifteen years old when she disappeared and was never found.'

'Is that right?'

'I believe Mary was investigating Maggie's disappearance: she kept cuttings.'

'Well, I wouldn't know about that either, Maud, but there's something else that Jim Creedo told me and that came from Mary Flood herself.'

'What was it?'

Father Quigley frowns, his face suddenly older, harrowed. 'Mary suffered badly in her marriage to Cathal. It was a union she didn't want.'

'How so?'

'It all started way back in Wexford, with this rich widower. A man notorious for his dissolute ways and his liking for young girls. Mary's family sent her to work up at his house as a maid. Of course, it wasn't long before Mary, who was a renowned beauty, caught the old man's eye. Mary's father forced a marriage to make an honourable woman of his daughter, intending to benefit from the match. For Mary's father was both corrupt and cunning.'

The priest purses his lips. 'The old widower, who was on his last legs when the match was made, was gone within the year and no sooner was he dead in the ground than his son coerced Mary into a second marriage. So the poor young woman kept the name she was already cursed with: Flood.'

'So Mary was married to Cathal's father?'

Father Quigley nods. 'Just so. Cathal never loved her; he talked her into marrying him in order to claw back his birthright. You see, Mary had inherited the whole of the old man's estate.'

St Valentine is gripped; one of his eyes is riveted to the priest and the other watches the garden path.

The priest continues. 'Mary was young and friendless, you understand. Her own family had forced her into wedlock with Flood Senior for their own financial gain.' A look of triumph crosses the priest's face. 'But Cathal underestimated Mary. She began to fight back. She invested what she could and began to amass wealth in her own name. She hid this wealth from Cathal, who was a terrible spendthrift, libertine and gambler in his youth. So bit by bit Mary gained control of the estate.'

Over the mantelpiece a clock marks time.

'O'Leary has just got off the bus,' reports St Valentine. 'She's called into the newsagents for a packet of mints. Two minutes, tops.'

'Mrs O'Leary will be here soon, Father.'

'Soon enough Cathal realised he owned nothing but the trousers he stood up in and perhaps not even those.' The priest pauses. 'Whether this state of affairs gave Mary immunity from Cathal's temper is debateable. But I believe it fuelled an already flammable situation.'

'What do you mean?'

The priest frowns. 'Cathal was a demon when roused, so is it not possible that he directed some of that rage against the woman who had taken command of his inheritance for a second time?'

'Are you saying that Cathal was abusive to his wife, Father?'

'I can't prove anything of course, but I believe Cathal may have added significantly to Mary's burdens.' Some dark thing crosses the priest's face, some bleak cloud of thought. 'I suppose I saw her terrible unhappiness, loneliness even. But she was such a private woman that I never encouraged her to share it.'

St Valentine shrugs and puts his toothpick back inside his dingy robe. 'Least said and all that.'

The priest looks contrite. 'I could have helped her more, Maud.'

We sit in silence for a few long moments.

And then I break it. 'So you don't think Mary's fall was an accident?'

Father Quigley takes a deep breath. 'I hope to God it was.'

Chapter 30

*She's moving along the hall under the carpet, the woman. See the
ripple she's causing. The pattern undulates with her. She moves
quickly, following the sweep of the staircase down. Feet first like
a breech birth she comes. Arms crossed high over her chest like a
mummy. At the bottom step she bunches up, curls and swells,
pushing against the edge of the carpet. Then with a rush like
waters breaking, she pools out, a liquid shadow, a dark puddle on
the tiles. Behind her the carpet flattens as if nothing at all has
happened.*

Her shadow grows and deepens. I watch it saturate the floor.

I look down into a deep, dark puddle.

*I see a face reflected, but it's not mine. It has a wide smile. I
look up and there she is, sitting cross-legged on the floor next to
me with a white bow in her fair hair. She opens her mouth to talk
and an earwig falls out. She giggles and clasps a hand over her
mouth. She tries again. She opens her mouth and a whole host of
them tumble over her chin.*

She is no longer smiling.

*She spits out tangle after tangle of black-bronze insects with a
panicked look in her eyes. They tumble and writhe, hitting the floor*

and crawling up under her school skirt and into her shoes and down the cuffs of her socks.

Then I notice: Maggie Dunne isn't quite herself.

There's a certain thinness to her arms and legs, her eyes are sunken and her teeth are loose. She spits them out onto the ground after the earwigs, with little exhausted coughing sounds. With effort Maggie stands. She looks down in dismay at the pearly maggots on her blouse. She picks them off, a sheepish smile on her green lips. Then she's away, a clumsy run, an awkward skip, her shoulders hunched.

Then I see: the frayed bandages on her wrists, her hair pulled out in clumps, the bruises—

'If I were you I'd lay off the crime tales.'

I sit up in bed, bathed in sweat and in the rays of golden light coming from the wardrobe.

'The krupnik might not help either.'

I shield my eyes.

'Wait, I'll adjust the brightness,' he says.

And then I see him: the inordinately beautiful St Raphael (lovers, insanity, nightmares). He folds his wings with a demure whirr and sits down on the edge of the bed, looking at me with his eyes large and dark in his heart-shaped face. Even on his dimmer switch St Raphael shines. His eyes, lips, skin and hair: all are burnished and lit by some radiant sun. Only his wings are in shadow: two arched black shapes that move behind him with a faint rustle.

'The nightmares are back, Maud?'

I nod.

'Perhaps it's best you give up the case. Take the quiet life.' He pushes a bronze curl behind his ear and leans forward. 'You know you'll only bring grief,' he whispers.

I try to think of some words I can put together, to explain.

'Give it up, baby.' He smiles.

'I can't,' I answer. 'I have to find out what happened.'

He folds his shimmering arms and looks through his eyelashes at me. 'Raking over old coals can be dangerous; some of them are still burning.'

'Is Maggie Dunne still alive?'

He frowns. 'I can't tell you that.' Velvet shadows flit behind him. I hear a wing beat, a sudden soft whirr. 'But I know who might be able to.'

'Marguerite?'

He ignores me, glancing over to the empty side of the bed.

'I don't think he'll be back.' As I say it, I realise how near I am to crying.

St Raphael looks at me with his dark eyes burning with kindness. 'Who can say?'

To my shame, I start to cry. 'Will he be back?'

'Are you still waiting for a happy ending, Maud?' His smile is so sad that I want to look away.

'No,' I say, 'I just want to know what to expect.'

He nods. 'Warp and weave, Maud, warp and weave.'

And then he's gone, leaving the day all the greyer.

★ ★ ★

Cathal is in evil spirits today. He comes in for his breakfast with a face on him.

'Come on now,' I say. 'It's nearly your birthday.'

'That Spanish tart has dealt me a good one.'

I'm hardly listening. I measure tea into the pot.

'Her next door, the wagon.' He pushes a cat off the chair and sits down at the table. 'Coming round here giving out about her bald pussy.'

I laugh, and Cathal looks at me sourly, for this is no joke.

'She's going to call the agency, and the fecking police. She says they'll get a warrant to search the house. That thing was worth a lot of money; she charged for it to go with lady cats.'

'Mrs Cabello is a cat pimp? Who'd have thought it?' I pour hot water into the teapot.

'This isn't funny, Drennan.' He taps on the table, one finger after another, and glances up at me. Underneath the table his knee will be jiggling, no doubt. 'They'll all be round, battering the door down. Swarming through the place. Another raid.'

'They'll not be given a warrant to find a cat.'

'It's not the police I'm worried about.' He rubs his forehead. 'It's her. She'll get me now. Even after all this.' He waves his hand around the tidy kitchen.

'Who'll get you? Mrs Cabello?'

'No, that fat agency bitch. She told me she would do for me the minute I misbehaved again. Jesus, she's terrifying.'

I laugh. 'Biba Morel?'

Cathal isn't laughing. 'She told me I was a dirty old bastard and if I put a toe wrong she'd have me banged up as quick as Jack Shit in a home for the bewildered.'

'I doubt Biba Morel said that.'

'She fucking did. Those same exact words. So I told her I'd make sure that there wouldn't be a home that would take me.' Cathal scowls. 'I threatened trouble on a biblical scale.'

'Of course you did.'

'She said I had one last chance.' Cathal looks at me in despair. 'I could stay in my house but if she heard even a peep out of me she would personally come and sedate me with an injection right up my arse.'

'You're joking.'

'I am not. She said she'd repeat it five times a day if she needed to. And there I'd be, propped up with all the other old people, dribbling peacefully in some corner.' He lowers his voice. 'A *reformed character*.'

'You couldn't have heard her say that.'

'I could.' His eyes widen. 'I've got fucking ears, haven't I?'

'When then? When did Biba tell you that?'

He purses his lips. 'That day you threw out all my cartons. She came round that morning, toting her syringe.'

My breakthrough day.

Cathal frowns. 'She told me that if my idiot son was happy to pay good money to keep me in this hellhole, who was she to argue? She said if I wanted to live out the rest of my days *compos mentis*, I would put up and shut the fuck up.'

I sit down next to him and watch him bite his fingernails, making unsavoury noises with his dentures.

'And you say Biba had a syringe?'

He nods, his face stricken. 'She showed it to me. She opened her bag and it was all in there. She had this look in her eyes, like she was itching to stick it up my hole. If your woman next door phones the agency I'm done for.'

I am staggered. I wonder how many other clients Biba Morel has threatened and if the real secret behind my magic touch is a case manager with a loaded syringe.

'Do you have Mrs Cabello's cat?'

He grimaces. 'I don't.'

'I'm trying to help you, Cathal. Do you have the cat?'

He begins to pat down his pockets looking for his tobacco. After a while he says, 'It died, unfortunately.'

'Oh, Jesus, what did you do with her cat? You killed it?'

'I didn't at all. Now why would I kill a poor little bald fecker like that?' he roars, indignant.

'Cathal, will you just tell me the truth for once?'

He extracts papers and a twisted nub of tobacco from his breast pocket. I watch him start to roll a cigarette.

'Well now, it was late and I'd been smoking something.' He smiles apologetically. 'To help with the sleeping, you know.'

'You were smoking . . . ?'

His smile widens. 'Well, it wasn't Old Holborn now.'

'Jesus, Cathal—'

'I looked up and in front of me was this apparition.' He sucks at his teeth. 'It was a fright to God. All boggle-eyed and wrinkled, just like the alien fucker in that film. Before I knew it, I'd given it a clatter.'

'You gave it a clatter?'

He nods. 'I did. With a broom handle.'

'You clattered Mrs Cabello's pedigree Sphynx cat with a broom handle?'

'When I saw my mistake I buried it in the garden.'

'Ah no—'

'All Christian-like; I may have said a few words, even.'

I suddenly feel very tired. 'Where did you bury the cat, Cathal?'

'Of that, I've no idea, Drennan. I was motherless on skunk.'

I am standing in Mrs Cabello's hallway with a gift box and an ingratiating smile. It takes her a moment to identify me because she is wearing sunglasses. Whilst she does, I stay very still and quiet because I sense she lives life close to the edge. An antique table the size of my flat runs the length of the hallway. Above it is a life-sized photograph of Mrs Cabello posing in gold thigh-high boots in a wide-legged power stance on a shagpile rug. A young and dynamic Mrs Cabello, caught in that irreducible moment – the one before she turned to demand more maraschino cherries and more bubbles in the Jacuzzi. She is wearing hotpants, a middle parting and a knotted cheesecloth shirt.

Underneath the picture a considerably older Mrs Cabello stands with the same look of passionate nature in arrested motion. Her hair still flows, although her face is less mobile and she is favouring a pair of leopard-print capri pants today.

'Mrs Cabello,' I begin. She must detect a hint of bad news in my tone for she stares at me with horror.

'You have found Manolete?' She rests a bejewelled hand on her highly polished table.

'I'm afraid so.' I wave the gift bag in my hand.

Her eyes are anchored to it.

'Shall we go through and sit down, Mrs Cabello?' I say brightly, cursing Cathal Flood, his broom handle and, above all, Biba Morel.

I listen to myself telling a story. It's a wonderful story, about the young doctor who was driving home from his shift at the children's hospital when Manolete, chasing a butterfly, rushed out in front of his Ferrari. The handsome young paediatrician, who was driving well below the speed limit, was unable to stop or steer his car away (to the left of him a nun was about to cross the road, to the right was an oncoming school bus). I saw it happen. Manolete fell gracefully and the handsome doctor scooped him up and wrapped him in his cashmere sweater. He drove Manolete, as quickly as the speed limit would allow, to a highly skilled veterinarian surgeon. The surgeon struggled for hours to save little Manolete. The handsome paediatrician told the vet to spare no expense and he waited the whole time, pacing the corridor outside. Manolete fought a brave fight but just as the sun came up he breathed his last, a sweet sigh. Everyone with him raised their eyes to God and prayed for the soul of the beautiful cat.

I glance at Mrs Cabello. In one hand she clutches a large glass of Chardonnay, in the other a balled tissue. Her tears fall reverently on the box full of cat litter on her lap.

'So you see, Dr Fortune felt that the last thing he could do for you was to spare you the sight of Manolete's broken body. He organised to have him cremated with all due respects paid.'

Mrs Cabello nods. One of Manolete's peers is stretched across the sheepskin rug that lies in front of the fireplace. It fixes me with the uncanny lamps of its amber eyes. It doesn't believe a word.

Mrs Cabello puts down the box of cat litter and the wine and stands up, fuelled by drunken purpose. 'Wait. I have something for you. But in all this,' she flaps her hands, 'I had forgotten.'

She lurches past the glass-topped coffee table. The bald cat on the hearthrug watches her leave, before returning its gaze to me. It regards me with unblinking disgust. I don't blame it.

I look around the room. It's like being inside a mad wedding cake. The windows are dressed in froths of white and gold voile and the sofas are plump crescents of white leather. In the corner of the room there is a kidney-shaped cocktail bar made of white marble, like the fireplace. Which is a wonder to behold, covered, as it is, by permed cherubs. Above the fireplace is another portrait of Mrs Cabello lolling in soft focus with her mouth open and her eyes glazed. She is wearing see through harem pants and a bra made from coins

I wonder idly whether Mrs Cabello is a porn star

She wanders back in again with her eyes wide and devastated

and a package wrapped in brown paper in her hands.

'Mary Flood gave this to me just before her accident.' She sits back down heavily on the sofa. 'You take it. I never opened it.' She pushes it across the table.

'I don't understand. Why would you want to give it to me?'

Mrs Cabello picks up her wine. 'One morning, early, Mary knocked on my door and asked me to hold on to it.' She takes a sip. 'She said that someone, a friend, might call when she wasn't in and I would need to give this to them.'

I look down at the package. 'Did Mary give you the name of this friend?'

Mrs Cabello shakes her head emphatically. 'No.' She begins to cry, softly. 'And no one ever called for her. Not a single living soul.'

I open the package. It's a notebook: leather-bound, heavy, with thick blank cream pages. I open the front cover. Inside, written in a small neat hand:

M D
Don't be afraid to tell our story.
M F

Chapter 31

I am climbing the stairs at Bridlemere. It's slow going, what with my legs sinking up to the knee with every step. Mice fly past me and cats glide down the bannisters. I upset a box of glass eyes and they cascade, winking, down the stairs.

The painting on the landing is empty now but for a trail of rose petals; the woman in black has disappeared.

In the white room the air is cold. Curled furls of wallpaper hang down; rashes of mould dapple patterns on the wall beneath. Spores draw hieroglyphics, coded sentences — dire warnings. The patterns begin to flicker and shift across on the wall, like images seen through a zoetrope.

Beckett nests on the counterpane, decomposed to no more than a ragged pelt, a twist of rot where a sleeping cat once lay.

I walk over to the dressing table, lift out the jewellery box and then the necklace. It breaks and scatters. The pearls hit the carpet and unwind, turning to maggots before my eyes. I watch them wriggle under the bed.

Closing the door behind me, I walk along the hall. I feel something brush my ankles and look down to see Beckett, dressed in shreds of blighted fur, lumbering on atrophied legs. He grins up at me: all skull and jawbone.

I open the door and he pushes into the room ahead of me, his tail of mottled bone snaking.

In the red room the air is alive with flies. They dance around puddles of dark clotted liquid. It's Countess Báthory's bath time! Gouts of blood arc across the walls and run down from the ceiling in slow drips. Indescribable gobbets fleck the furniture. Beckett jumps up on the bed and circles around, his remaining fur turning red. I walk across the carpet to the dressing table and open the drawer.

Inside, an unready baby, a small coil of head and limbs, eyes fogged and sightless, face veiled with gore, feet as narrow as hooves. Gripped in the bud of its fist, a photograph. Two girls stand on a boarded walkway flanked by sand dunes. The marram grass starts to sway and a gull turns lazily in the sky.

The fist twitches; the tiny wound of the baby's mouth opens.

I hurriedly close the drawer and look up at the mirror. Smeared in red there's a word:

MAUD

Chapter 32

Biba Morel ignores my glare. She has been on the phone ever since I walked into her office approximately twenty minutes ago. I wouldn't be surprised if she's talking to no one at all. She holds the phone in the crook of her neck against her raised shoulder, leaving her hands free to search out stray crisps from under her keyboard. She has an air of pathological coldness, like a social-working Don Corleone in an outsized floral dress.

Now and again she lets loose her terrible salacious laugh, then reverts back to a series of noises: from grunts and shrieks of interest to dismissive clicks of her tongue. But really her attention is on the half-eaten coronation chicken torpedo roll in her in-tray. She laughs again, a sudden, startling, munificent laugh running up and down octaves, communicating open-handedness and gritty honesty.

As she reaches for her sandwich, stretching her easy-care suit jacket to the limits, Biba's genius becomes clear. Her wizened, miserly soul – a soul incapable of human kindness – is masked with the suggestion of generosity and abundance;

from her wide face and well-proportioned bosom to her voluminous hair.

She is ballast. She keeps the agency afloat, commanding the biggest desk nearest the window. Her harrowed and careworn assistants scuttle backwards and forwards doing a real job of work, whilst Biba sits in state, in rotund magnificence. The office, like most offices, has the fake-cheerful feel of death row, with its jokey signs and personal possessions. This is a place that sucks up time and energy on pointless tasks and futile activities and leaves little to show for human endeavour but a growing collection of novelty mugs.

Not for the first time I count myself lucky that I am free-range in my enterprises and not imprisoned in some administrative battery farm, breathing air heavy with regret and thwarted dreams. In my work I make a simple and constructive difference to people: to eat or not to eat, to have a clean arse or not to have a clean arse.

Biba Morel puts down the receiver and turns to the papers on her desk, shuffles them, then begins to type rapidly on her keyboard.

'You wanted to see me, Biba?'

She looks at me with bored disgust, then opens a drawer, takes out a folder and begins to flick through it. 'Your employment with this agency has been suspended pending the investigation of a serious complaint against you.'

'What are you even talking about?'

'It has come to our attention, Maud, that you attempted to extract money from a relative of your client on the pretence that you were taking said client on a day trip to the seaside.'

I narrow my eyes. 'That's a damn dirty lie.'

'The complainant has also informed us that not only were you seeking money for this venture, you were also planning on taking the client on this day trip without notifying the agency or undertaking the necessary risk assessments.'

'Gabriel Flood said that?'

Her face is smug. 'I'm not at liberty to divulge the identity of the party who made the complaint, Maud.'

'But it was Gabriel Flood.' The bastard. A thousand curses go through my mind.

Biba takes a bite from the chicken torpedo then licks her fingers in a manner both grotesque and suggestive.

She pushes a pile of papers across the desk to me. 'This outlines the agency's disciplinary procedures and gives you the details of an ombudsman service should you have any complaints about your treatment.'

'I have a complaint: Gabriel Flood took me to a cafe and asked me to get his father out of the house for the day while he searched it. Then he offered me money.'

Biba shakes her head. 'Maud, you know better than to fraternise with the family of your clients. You have overstepped all kinds of rules and regulations.'

'And you haven't?'

'What do you mean by that?'

I lower my voice and look her dead in the eye. 'I think you know full well, *Nurse Ratched*.'

Biba returns my gaze with an expression of suppurating hatred. 'No matter, the job is finishing anyway. A place in a residential home has been found for Mr Flood.'

I stare at her. 'You told him that he could remain at his home if he toed the line, and he's been toeing it. You promised him, that day you went visiting with your syringe.'

Biba shrugs. 'Yeah, well, plans change. Dr Flood is concerned about the deterioration in Mr Flood's mental acuity and I must say I agree.'

'There's been no deterioration.'

'That's not what I've heard.'

'Gabriel has changed his tune. What happened to the idea that his father should be supported in the home?'

Biba looks at me blankly; she really doesn't give a shit.

'When do you propose moving Cathal?'

'*Mr Flood* will be transferred to his new accommodation in three or four days at the most.' Her eyes light up a little, waiting for my reaction.

I take a deep breath and struggle to control my emotions. I think of Atticus Finch with the rabid dog in his sights. The corner of Biba's lip twitches in a snarl. I need to keep a steady hand.

She forages in a folder and pulls out a form. 'You still have a key to the property?'

Damn right I do. 'Not with me.'

She tuts and puts the form away again. 'You'll need to drop it into the office directly.' Biba fixes me with a look. 'I don't have to remind you that pending an investigation you are not permitted to return to the house in any capacity. Nor are you allowed to contact the client or their relatives.' Her smile is malignant. 'In *any capacity*, Maud; it would mean immediate dismissal, not to mention prosecution.'

I can't bear it. 'Who will help him pack? He'll need someone there to support him during the move, to reassure him.'

'We have people.'

'But what about the house, all his things?'

'That is his son's concern now.' Biba turns to her computer screen, pushing back her bountiful hair and sighing.

'Has anyone told Cathal any of this?'

Biba glances at me. 'Dr Flood thought it would be preferable not to worry his father about the move.'

'So you're not even going to tell him? Warn him?'

I can see it all: Cathal, a noble, aged zebra, with a long frightened face and white mane, bolting through the house with a pack of orderlies running after him – jackals all. The old man will be brought down, netted and tranquillised. They'll drag him out by his heels with his tongue lolling and crate him. He doesn't stand a chance.

'You're scared of him.' I smile with bitter triumph. 'And so you should be; he may be decrepit but he broke Sam Hebden. I hope he leads you a merry dance.'

Biba sneers. 'Mr Flood did not break Sam Hebden. Sam dealt with the situation admirably and as a consequence was moved to a senior Geriatric Conflict Resolution position in Hull.'

'Good for him.' Then I say it before I can stop myself: 'When did Sam go?'

'A day or so after the assault.'

I freeze. 'Are you saying he's been there all this time, in Hull?'

Biba looks at me oddly. 'Yes.'

'And you're sure of that?'

Biba takes up her torpedo. 'Well, that's where he's supposed to be. But that's his own agency's concern, isn't it?'

As I watch Biba massacre the last of her sandwich, a terrible creeping feeling comes over me. 'You've met him, what does Sam look like?'

Biba looks frustrated. 'Average.'

My heart turns over. 'Tall? Blond?'

She narrows her eyes. 'Average.' She picks up her receiver. Her voice is cold. 'We're done here, Maud. Remember to bring the key back. Call us in a week; if the complaint is dropped by then we'll see if we can place you with another client.'

For a moment I watch her type numbers into the phone. She waits a second before treating the talking clock to her ribald laugh.

★ ★ ★

Gabriel is barrelling down the garden path as if his arse is on fire. When I step out from behind the buddleia he nearly dies.

'Maud.'

'You sneaky, underhanded fuck.'

He looks at me in astonishment. 'There's no need—'

'There's every need. Besides setting me up you promised that old man in there that if he complied you'd leave him be. What harm is he doing?'

Gabriel clutches his manbag to his chest as if it would shield him from my biblical disgust. 'He's done his harm and he's moving on now; he'll live out his remaining time peaceably.'

I think of Biba with her syringe and shudder.

'And you've told him this? That you've shafted him? That's why you came here today?'

He purses his sweaty mouth.

'Of course you haven't. You really are a repellent bastard.'

Gabriel's eyes dart towards the gate; I'm blocking the path. My trainers planted, my centre of gravity low. He's trying to figure out how to get round me.

I take a step forward, keeping my chin high. 'What was it that the old man had on you, Gabriel? Come on, you can tell me. Whatever it was that has prevented you pulling the house down around him and turfing him out on his ear.'

A sly look steals across his face. 'I don't know what you are talking about.'

A thought dawns on me. 'You've got it, haven't you? Whatever it is you wanted from that house. Whatever it was he was holding over you.'

'You're talking drivel.'

'It's probably there in your handbag.'

His knuckles whiten on leather. I wonder if I should mug him and how I would set about doing that.

'You've been suspended, Maud. You shouldn't even be here. I'll call the agency. The police.'

'Go on then.'

'I suggest you leave this property right now.'

'This isn't your property; Cathal is here yet.'

He sneers, a little nervously. 'Cathal, is it? It sounds as if you have designs on the old man.'

'God, you're an awful arsehole.'

His face seems to implode. His mouth splutters and his jowls begin to shake. 'I don't have to take this,' he whines. 'Get off this property.'

I square my good strong jaw. 'Or what?'

He fumbles in his manbag and brings out his phone and holds it up in front of me as if it's a talisman. 'I'm calling the police.'

In the work of a moment I have it snatched from his hand and hurled over the toolshed.

'You mad bitch.' His voice is high, hysterical. He almost jumps in his loafers. If he wasn't scared of me I am sure he'd slap me.

Instead, he grips hold of his manbag and rushes past, leaping over an abandoned mattress, making a dash for the gate. I have to hand it to him, he moves nimbly for his size.

I narrow my eyes. 'I'm going to find out exactly what's been going on here. Then I'll be the one going to the police.'

Gabriel laughs at me from a position of safety behind the closed gate. 'To say what? That you're a mad bitch who makes up crime stories?'

I stare at him. 'You've been spying on me. You shut me in the ice house. You sent thugs to threaten my friend.'

Gabriel stabs at his temple with his finger. 'You're fucking mental.'

'I'm going to get to the bottom of what happened to Mary and Maggie. I'm not going to stop.'

His face reddens. 'You've been warned to steer clear—'

'I'm not surprised your sister tried to drown you. I'll be tracking down Marguerite to find out what she has to say.'

The colour drains out of Gabriel's face. It turns from pink to white, as if a tourniquet has stopped his blood. Even in my distracted state I find this remarkable.

'Marguerite cannot be contacted,' he says. 'She went away.'

'I'll find her and bring her back. With any luck she'll want another pop at you.'

'This is not a family to mess with,' says Gabriel with a look of wholesale horror on his face.

'Or else? You'll send round more criminals? We're not scared.'

Gabriel narrows his eyes. 'You really don't want to escalate this; you won't know what hit you.'

'Neither will you, you bollix.' I bend down and pick up a brick with which to knock Gabriel's head off. By the time I straighten up to take aim he's gone.

Cathal sits silently at the kitchen table. It's not a position of defeat, not quite. It's one of introverted thought: eyes lowered, breathing quiet.

I expected roaring, shouting.

I reach forward and take his hand. He glances up at me, his eyes watery under still-dark brows. He covers my hand with his big paw.

'What will you do?' I ask.

He smiles. 'I'll have a birthday to remember; you'll still come?'

I nod. 'I will of course.'

'Then God blast the rest of them to hell.'

'What about all this? Your house, your things.'

He laughs. 'Jesus, don't be so mournful, I haven't left yet.' He squeezes my hand.

He looks tired, fantastically frail, his eyes puzzled, blinking, startled. He gets up from the table and walks across the kitchen with an uncertain tread, as if he's testing to see if the ground is still real.

I should tell him about Mary and Maggie and Marguerite. Tell him what I know and what I don't know, before he is kidnapped into geriatric care and permanent sedation. But when I look at him, I can't. Not right now, when the man has just found out he's losing his home from under him.

At the door he looks up at me. 'You never lost your temper, Drennan, and wasn't that a good thing for the both of us.'

He pats the doorframe and wanders off down the hall.

Chapter 33

Jimmy O'Donnell looked out through his thick girl's eyelashes at me. This usually made me laugh, only not today. It didn't make him laugh either. I believe his heart wasn't in it.

We sat in Granny's kitchen looking out at the weather collecting all around the bungalow. The sky was petrol-dark, banked with great sulking rain clouds. But then there was a sudden rift, and the sun, heavy with the molten gold of a summer evening, came lancing through it.

The sun shone on the clothes that dripped limp on the washing line (wetter now than when they were put out to dry) and the empty birdfeeder on the patio. It spilled through the kitchen window and alighted on the table, on the sticky oilcloth, the sauce bottles with claggy tops, the trails of crumbs left by other, earlier, meals. It lit Jimmy O'Donnell brightly and almost entirely (with the exception of his right hand and the parts of him under the table). So that, in a way, you could imagine that illuminating Jimmy O'Donnell was the sole purpose of this last ray of evening sun. He was burnished to the sheen of a saint: his eyes shining in his heart-shaped face, his hair lustrous bronze in the radiant dying last-ditch light.

Jimmy had a cast-iron alibi: he was at his uncle's house in Ballyshannon plumbing in a bath. Even with the speeds Jimmy drove he couldn't have been back at Pearl Strand in time for Deirdre to go missing. Wasn't that the case?

He told me this with his hand shaking, as his cigarette travelled from the table to his mouth and then back again. And then flick, flick, flick, worrying the end of that cigarette with his thumbnail, ash in the sugar bowl, ash everywhere.

Jimmy looked at me and I looked back at him.

Behind him his shadow changed shape on the kitchen wall, malformed and five times the size of him. Jimmy with brooding shoulders and hooked claws for hands. I watched his shadow creep and slouch, grow and retract, with every movement he made. It was easier than looking at his face. For in that resplendent light Jimmy didn't seem himself. He seemed tired and scared.

He'd had threats, people spitting at him on the street.

When the guards gave him the all clear he'd leave town, no messing, no forwarding address, just like Deirdre had.

Only, unlike Deirdre, Jimmy had no one to hand him an envelope full of cash.

Jimmy grimaced. He ran his fingers through his hair. 'You know why she had to go, don't you?'

I nodded.

He looked relieved. He screwed his cigarette out in the ashtray. 'And you haven't heard from her yet?'

'No.'

'She's taking her bloody time,' he said, his eyes on the drive.

It was a big risk, him being here. Mammy and Granny would be back soon. They were down in the town putting posters up. Jimmy had waited at the end of the lane for them to leave.

I no longer loved him but I promised him anyway, as I had promised Deirdre.

'We never saw Jimmy O'Donnell on the beach,' I repeated to him. 'There was only ever us.'

He squeezed my arm as he got up from the table. 'Good girl yourself.'

Chapter 34

Renata doesn't flinch. She listens carefully, without interrupting. She smiles grimly at the part where I pick up a brick and looks thoughtful when I relay Biba's description of Sam Hebden.

St Dymphna listens too, leaning forward in the easy chair, her legs crossed under her and her veil slipping down. She smiles too, more than Renata and sometimes at the wrong moments.

When I've finished talking Renata gets up and rambles out of the living room, returning with her pipe. She puts the stem of the pipe in her mouth and sits back down.

'Just pretend,' she mumbles.

St Dymphna throws Renata an evil look, then turns to squint at the television, chewing the end of her plait. The sound is turned down on *Inspector Morse*. I wonder if normal life will ever resume.

'Have faith,' says Renata, in a doubtful voice. 'This is a case where nothing is as it seems. We are walking on shifting sand. But really it is perfectly simple if we remain focused.'

'Well and good,' I say. 'But there's another pressing problem.'

'Which is?' Renata strikes an invisible match and sets an imaginary flame to non-existent tobacco.

'If I didn't sleep with Sam Hebden, then who in the world have I slept with?'

St Dymphna smirks in my direction.

Renata mimes a succession of deft puffs on her pipe. 'Biba's description was not so clear.'

'That Sam is average as well as in two different places simultaneously?'

Renata shrugs. 'Biba only knows where he should be, not where he is.'

'Maybe,' I say doubtfully. 'But would you consider Sam to be average?'

Renata smiles. 'Darling, is he a slice of chocolate fudge cake? No? Then to Biba he is average.'

Renata is a picture of effortless elegance today in her knotted headscarf and kimono with her kohled dark eyes, the effect skewed a little by the pipe clamped in her teeth and her air of dogged determination. 'All is not lost, Maud.'

'Isn't it?' I ask. 'The case is in tatters. How are we going to solve it when I'm not even allowed near the house?'

'We talk to Doreen Gouge. We tell her about your incontrovertible communication from the afterlife.' She nods at Mary Flood's notebook, open on the coffee table.

'Who the hell is Doreen Gouge?'

Renata fishes down the side of her armchair and hands me a slim book.

I glance at her. 'Where did you get this?'

Renata smiles slyly. 'I sent Lillian to the spiritualist church.'

I inspect the cover. The book is titled *The Reluctant Clairvoyant: A Spiritual Awakening*. There is a photograph of a fluffed blonde in a peach sweater. She has a lipsticked grin and an expression of committed insanity in her wide blue eyes.

'Lillian must have given you hell for this.'

Renata adjusts her headscarf. 'At least she didn't read chapter four.'

I immediately turn to chapter four.

Many psychics first meet their spirit guides in dreams. They will fly through the air or swim through water to be with you, metaphorically of course! The real substance they move through is celestial space and time.

I think about my nightmares, remembering Mary Flood in her nightie, and I wonder . . .

Your spirit guide is your dedicated escort through the realm of the afterlife. They are uniquely bound to you. You do not choose your guide; your guide chooses you. My spirit guide, Johnny Big Tree, is an Apache warrior who died fighting the Spanish in the 1850s. Johnny first came to me in a dream wearing no more than a pair of moccasins and a crow feather in his hair. He fixed me with his enigmatical dark eyes and held out his hand. With Johnny I always feel safe, he leads me with his silent step and his head held high through the ranks of the departed. They dare not touch us as we pass through the desolate murk of the otherworld. Bringing messages from the dead to the living.

I cast Renata a caustic look. 'And you've read this shite?'

She nods. 'I found it very informative. It explains why I feel Bernie's constant presence.'

I try not to glance at the urn on the coffee table. Renata and Bernie have become inseparable since the visit from Gabriel's henchmen. She even pours him a glass of krupnik from time to time.

I read on.

*In most cases your spirit guide will be of the opposite sex.
They will be well-matched to their psychic in terms of phys-
ical attractiveness and interests. For example, Johnny and I
have a mutual love of good conversation, food cooked outdoors
and ecstatic dancing. My good friend and fellow medium,
Stacey Barrett-Mold, has published widely on the subject of
the psychic–spirit guide relationship. Stacey has a profound
love of numbers and order. Her spirit guide, Mr Sidney Curd,
an accountant who was stabbed to death with a letter opener
in 1954 by a bankrupt client, shares these interests. Mr Curd
doesn't have a bow and arrow like Johnny; he rather deflects
unwanted attention from unsavoury spirits by opening his
briefcase and rustling spectral tax returns.*

I shake my head in despair.

'Before you judge,' says Renata with offended dignity and
a voice of deep-napped velvet, 'you should read the testi-
monials.'

*'Doreen is one in a million – her ears are open to the faintest
voice of the dead. No one understood my late aunt for the
last five years of her life due to chronic laryngitis but Doreen
gave her a voice again!'*
Mrs V. B. Pritchard

*'Doreen, what can I say? You reunited me with my beloved
husband. We are closer than ever now, I am reassured to know
that he watches over me – and the prize-winning marrows I
grow in his memory.'*
Mrs S. Bolick

'Doreen is the real thing: a fully fledged Ghost Whisperer.'
Sam Stroud, Author of They Come in Droves: A
Beginner's Guide to Mass Historical Hauntings

'Has it really come to this?' I close the book and put it
down on the table.

'I think it has,' says Renata. 'Give it a try. What have we
got to lose?'

I look over at St Dymphna, who rolls her eyes, then turns
back to the television. I stay as silent as the afterlife.

Chapter 35

Sam Hebden is standing on Renata's doorstep. He is wearing espadrilles. Jesus Christ looks approving; Johnny Cash sneers. Renata and I stand at the door with our arms crossed.

Sam nods at us with a rueful air. 'Renata. Maud.'

Renata nods back, her black brigand's eyes giving nothing away.

Undaunted, Sam smiles. 'I'm sorry for not calling.'

It's a slow, warm smile. It makes my heart gasp for life, despite itself.

Renata glances at me, thin-lipped.

'I know how it looked,' Sam ventures.

'You have five minutes,' I say.

Renata squeezes my arm and wanders into the kitchen to put the kettle on, tightening her headscarf against the squalls that lie ahead.

Sam is driving me to the spiritualist church in his green Golf with a dented passenger door. This does not mean that I have forgiven him; I make this clear with my testy demeanour. St Valentine and St George, perhaps picking up on the tension, are squabbling in the back seat.

Sam takes a wrong turn.

'You should have gone left,' I point out.

We sit in silence behind a red traffic light.

'Look, I'm sorry, Maud, really I am. I should have called but something came up.'

'Right,' I say.

'I know how it looked.'

'So you said.' I will the light to turn green and it does. 'Renata could have done with your support,' I say, my voice flat. 'After what happened.'

'You're right. I should have been there for her.'

'She sleeps with a bread knife under her pillow and carries Bernie's urn everywhere.'

'I'm sorry.'

There is a sceptical jeer from the back seat. I turn round to see St Valentine making a derogatory gesture at the back of Sam's head. St George has his visor up and is wearing a comprehensive scowl.

I open the window and lean out a bit, avoiding Sam's smell of wolf in sheep's clothing: citrus soap and cigarette smoke.

'Can we start again, Maud?'

I glare at him. 'Start what?'

'I won't let you down.' He smiles and glances back at me with his hot grey eyes.

With my resolve weakening I ask myself this: what kind of a man wears espadrilles? Renata didn't say but surely they are a mark of some horrific variety of deviance.

'I had a great time that night, by the way,' he murmurs.

I wait for wisecracks from the back seat but none are forthcoming.

'Good for you,' I say. Then I switch on the radio and turn it up.

In the bag at my feet is something more tangible than the vicissitudes of men: a gift from Mary Flood, from beyond the grave.

Don't be afraid to tell our story.

I won't, but what is our story, Mary?

Maybe Doreen Gouge, Psychic to the Stars, will tell me tonight.

I'm not hopeful. Doreen Gouge, Psychic to the Stars, stands behind a balustrade, on a wooden box, in front of a lectern. Doreen is as wide as she is tall, the Queen Victoria of the spiritualist world. Her small head, dainty feet and tiny hands are separated by the expanse of her body, so that she looks like a human kite. She is wearing cheerful pastels in chiffon layers and has a long rope of popcorn-like beads around her neck. Her hair and make-up are just as exuberant as her clothes. A frothy blonde halo surrounds her pink face, where her eyes gleam in patches of shimmering blue and her lips shine frosted-peach. I wonder if this is all an attempt to offset the morbidity of her profession.

It's a turnout: at least fifty people, and apart from Sam and I the audience appear to be regulars. They greet each other with nods and smile at us. Some seem normal, with a kind of worn-down averageness. Others look verifiably strange, as if they are unused to company or hairbrushes. I wonder at the desperate lengths people will go to for solace in the face of death and mortality.

We start by singing a Westlife song, to lift the energy in the room and stir the dead into action. Doreen sings with us, sweetly and enthusiastically. I take a moment to be thankful that the saints are still outside in the car park, most probably where I left them. St Valentine glaring at St George with an expression of wall-eyed fury and St George mouthing expletives back at him over the bonnet of a people carrier. Then I wonder what I'm doing here, when Cathal's world is falling apart, Renata is at home with the door locked and a paring knife up the sleeve of her kimono, and Maggie Dunne is still missing. The singing rises in a crescendo, I follow it on my hymn sheet. Where else would I be?

The woman to my right nudges me. I look up into the rumpled face of a professional smoker with a drawstring bag of a mouth. She is wearing a sweater with a picture of a corgi howling at a moon.

She smiles lugubriously, revealing a tumbledown set of tawny teeth. 'Is this your first time?'

'Yes.'

She draws nearer and whispers loudly, 'She's very good, you know. We were lucky to get her. She should be in Woking tonight but she intuited an accident on the M3.'

'That's lucky.'

'My uncle came through last time she was here. Big man, Welsh, unusual death in Llanelli.'

'Is that the case?'

'He died of coronary heart failure after being attacked by a flock of seagulls. Doreen got him pegged, even the habit he had of hitching up his trousers before he sat down.' The woman pulls at the knees of her slacks. 'Doreen said he didn't suffer.'

'Sure, that's the main thing.'

She nods. 'He'd been eating biscuits, you see. A digestive had fallen into the hood of his coat and that's what the seagulls were going for. They hadn't meant to kill him and that was a relief to know.'

'I'm sure it was.'

The music trails off abruptly. At the lectern, Doreen clears her throat. 'I'm very lucky to be here tonight, amongst friends old and new.'

She smiles at Sam, who smiles right back at her. Doreen gives him a cordial wink. She obviously isn't averse to a man in espadrilles.

'Right now,' she purrs, 'the crushed and bleeding wreck of my body should be lying on the intersection between the M3 and the M25. But it's not. Tonight death by motorway carnage is not my fate and for that I thank the spirits who walk with me, who have always walked with me.'

Several members of the audience nod and smile, grateful that Doreen isn't a crushed and bleeding wreck.

Doreen continues, her voice grave. 'Since I was a little girl, the spirit world has revealed itself to me in all its myriad glory. This marked me out as different, unusual.' She looks down at her folded hands. 'But I was never lonely. Not when my earliest playmates were the dear departed.'

I think of Cathal's sister, rendered psychic, or just unhinged, by a rake of wasp stings, a belt with a stick and a dip in a magical horse trough. I wonder if Doreen suffered a similar initiation. Then I think of the pair of martyrs currently brawling in the car park. Then I decide not to think any more.

Doreen glances around the room. 'I am honoured to be here tonight to share my gift of mediumship with you and to offer you proof of the continued existence of the spirit in the afterlife.'

She talks like she's sealing a deal. 'Before we start, I want to remind you that I have one rule and one rule alone. You all know what it is, don't you?'

The audience nod and smile, of course they do.

'I'll say it again for the sake of our newcomers: *don't feed me.*' She grins and gestures towards her generous flanks. 'Heavens, don't I look as if I've had enough to eat?'

Everyone laughs politely and a few idiots shake their heads.

She leans forward on the lectern. 'If I say something you can relate to, or you recognise the presence of a friend or loved one, then raise your hand and I will talk with you. If I talk with you, keep your answers brief, confine yourself to "Yes" and "No" please, folks. And speak up, loudly and clearly.'

The audience nod obediently, their tissues in their hands, ready for a good cry.

Doreen pulls a serious face. 'A conversation with those who have passed is not like a regular chinwag over a cup of tea, such as you or I would have. For the spirit realm both coexists with our own world and lies infinitely beyond it. A good medium can sweep back the curtain separating these domains and gain access to the deepest depths of mystery. As you can imagine this is a difficult, and sometimes unpredictable, undertaking.'

I wonder about this otherworldly curtain. With Doreen it's likely to be chintz or plush velour. I imagine the spirits of ages, coughing and shuffling behind it, like amateur actors waiting for their scene.

Doreen draws herself to her full tiny height. 'Tonight some of you will receive messages and some of you will not. I'm only a conduit, you see; the deceased tell me what they think you need to know. Please be aware that this may not necessarily be what you *want* to know. And, of course, they may not come at all for you this time.' She smiles coyly. 'This is because they are not yet able to communicate or you are not ready for what they want to say to you. Can I have silence now, please.'

A thin, wild-eyed spinster with thick tights and hair that's a haunt for wildlife dims the lights.

Doreen takes several deep breaths and fixes her eyes on a far-off point just over the top of our heads. She begins to nod and beckon. The audience turn in their seats to look with curiosity at a bookcase and a stack of chairs at the back of the hall, perhaps to witness the legions of the dead, awoken by Westlife, shuffling through the wall.

Doreen folds her hands on top of her chest and closes her eyes. She nods from time to time, listening intently. Sometimes she sways. Then she opens her eyes and steps closer to the lectern. She scans the room.

Her tone is brisk, efficient, like that of an auctioneer. 'I have a tall man, brown skin, a Cypriot I think, with a bowel obstruction. Can anyone take this?' Her hand lifts an imaginary gavel.

The audience looks glazed: no one wants to bid for the Cypriot.

Doreen closes her eyes and nods again, a little impatiently. 'He suffered gastrically, very badly.' She opens her eyes and grabs hold of her large stomach, cradling it in her arms. She points towards the back of the room. 'He wants to talk with someone over there. Can anyone take this? I'm hearing the name Tony or Anthony.'

A woman raises her hand hesitantly. 'My postman, he was a Tony,' she suggests. 'But he was from Blackburn.'

'But he liked a holiday? He was a sun-worshipper?'

The woman ponders. 'He might have been. I didn't know him all that well.'

Doreen ignores this and closes her eyes again. 'Tony passed very quickly. But he says he lived life to the full.'

'He did, Doreen.'

'Tony is telling me that there's a Peter, Paul, Pam, Paddy. Now he's showing me a clock. He's pointing to the dial.'

The woman shakes her head. 'I don't know, love. I have a neighbour called Pat. She has a carriage clock.'

Doreen closes her eyes again. 'She recently had a procedure.'

The woman looks amazed. 'She did, last year.'

'Yes . . .' Doreen gives a fruity giggle. 'I can't say that, Tony.' She opens her eyes and looks at the woman. 'Tony is showing me legs. Pat had her legs done.'

'She did, her varicose!'

Doreen smiles. 'Tony knew her well. He says to tell her to wear the surgical stockings and put her feet up more often. And he says that you're not to worry about him; he's gone to a better place.'

The woman in the audience nods, pleased that the postman she hardly knew is in a better place. Later she'll knock up Pat to give her the message from dead Tony.

Doreen, satisfied, goes back into her trance.

I look around the room, at the snaggle-arsed audience bathed in Doreen's charlatan glow. Over the lectern is a picture of a kneeling angel, painted on Perspex and backlit by fluorescent light. It shines down its benediction on Doreen Gouge as she interprets the senile ramblings of the imaginary dead. I watch Sam. He is engrossed, his hair falling around his face, his lovely grey eyes trained on the podium. He glances over at me and gives me a quick grin. My heart flips. I study his espadrilles.

Doreen has earned her money tonight. Standing on her box before the lectern she has mimed a myriad of unfortunate deaths. Tonight, she says, we are at suicide central, with two 'accidental' deaths by sleeping pills and a tortured soul called Janet who made a bid for perpetual freedom from the top of a car park in Shepherd's Bush.

Doreen chillingly mimes Janet's splayed free fall onto tarmac on a dark February morning ten years ago, which narrowly missed a bread van and a Renault Clio.

The devil is in the detail.

None of us can lay claim to Janet. But we are reassured she feels no pain in the afterlife. We let her story die with her. We let her go. There she'll be, forever falling from level fifteen, spiralling through the air like a sycamore seed, caught on eddies, her coat flapping. Hitting the deck like a bag of blood.

We sing another song, this time an ABBA one, to top up the energy. In the second half Doreen concentrates on immedicable infections and malingering sicknesses, interspersed by DIY accidents.

Doreen likens the afterlife to the Underground, so that we can get things in perspective. You have your cancer at Oxford Circus and your heart disease at King's Cross – these stations are always busy. Whereas for something like decapitation with a circular saw you'd need to be heading out of town towards Chesham. Sam smiles and nods; I watch him enjoying this exhibition of dupery. Taking lessons, no doubt.

It takes me a moment or two to realise that Doreen is looking directly at me.

'I've a small man wearing built-up shoes. Shifty expression. Standing behind you. Can you take it?'

I stare at her.

Doreen smiles back, unfazed, and talks very slowly. 'Built-up shoes, dear. He's showing me a stage, footlights. I believe he was in show business. Can you take it?'

Several members of the audience turn round in their chairs to look at me.

'I don't know,' I say.

'A dapper little man in tails and a top hat, pulling something out of his sleeve.' Doreen mimes behind the lectern.

'A string of hankies, bunch of flowers, cagey aspect to him.'

And then it comes to me. 'Bernie Sparks,' I say with a surge of jubilation.

Doreen narrows her eyes. 'Don't feed me, but that's him.' She concentrates hard on a point above my head. 'He's showing me a white rabbit.'

'He was a magician.'

She scowls. 'I can see that.' She closes her eyes. 'He says time is running out for the poor little girl all alone in the dark. It was a long, long way to fall. She's at the bottom of the rabbit hole and she needs to climb back out, tick-tock.'

Other audience members glance at me with interest. This isn't the usual kind of message. They purse their lips and wait for Bernie to talk about kidney disease or where he hid the premium bonds.

'Pussy's in the well,' lisps Doreen, baby-voiced, with a malevolent smile on her face. 'Ding-dong bell, right down the well, Bernie wants you to know—'

She freezes and the smile drops off her face. 'The Red Queen is coming,' she says, with more than a hint of Irish brogue.

My heart turns over.

Doreen is staring straight ahead with a look of riveted horror. I watch as her hands find her popcorn necklace and begin to turn it, winding it tighter and tighter around her throat. Her face twists too, into a grimace.

The audience begin to whisper amongst themselves. This doesn't normally happen. They glare at me accusingly. My dead friend and I have conspired to short-circuit Doreen.

Doreen starts to whimper.

Her wild-eyed assistant clambers onto the stage with a

look of panic and pulls urgently on Doreen's sleeve. Doreen grinds into gear again, blinking and looking around her.

'I've lost the connection,' she says weakly. 'I've lost the connection.'

Sam looks pale as he slips his hand in mine, and I let him, for I feel oddly chilled. Doreen recovers well. Delivering a swift succession of life-affirming messages and finishing on the upbeat advice of a dead council clerk called Jean who stresses the importance of seizing the day and following your dreams. A woman in the back row says she will, she promises she will, she'll book a mini cruise.

By the time Doreen leads us into our final song, an uplifting hit from the Carpenters, and the dead shamble back through the wall to the boundless tundra of all eternity, the audience seem to have forgotten her strange aberration.

Afterwards there are light refreshments and a chance to mingle. The wild-eyed helper starts taking bookings for psychic portrait paintings. Sam is deep in conversation with her as I step out of the hall.

Along a narrow hallway smelling of incense and stagnant mop buckets there's a door with a cardboard star. I knock once and open it, not giving the occupant a chance to turn me away.

In a room the size of a broom cupboard, Doreen Gouge is leaning out of the window, smoking. She has her shoes off and a quarter-bottle of vodka on the windowsill next to her.

'May I have a word?'

She narrows her eyes through the smoke. 'I do private readings by appointment, love, every second Thursday. If you step back outside there's a leaflet.'

I open my bag. 'I'm sorry, I can't wait that long. I need you to take a look at this.'

She frowns at me, her mouth slack and her eyes full of bored venom. She looks a lot younger close up, under the make-up.

I notice a pair of biker's boots in the corner and a crash helmet. I start to wonder who the real Doreen Gouge is.

'Twenty-odd years ago a woman was investigating the case of a missing schoolgirl when she herself met an untimely death. Just before she died she left this with a neighbours, saying that someone would come looking for her – it was almost as if she had some kind of premonition.' I pull out the notebook. 'It has my initials inside and a message.'

Doreen takes another drag on her cigarette and turns back to the window.

'This woman, Mary, kept cuttings on the case she was investigating – I'm sorry, are you even listening?'

Doreen glowers over her shoulder at me.

I try again. 'I'm here because I think you could help me find out what this dead woman discovered, and potentially even find the missing girl. What you said tonight—'

'I can't help you.'

'Doreen, please, if you really saw something . . .'

She turns, balances her cigarette on the edge of the table and holds her hand out for the notebook. She reads the dedication; she touches the writing.

She hands it back to me. 'Nothing. Sorry.'

'But you saw something earlier?'

Doreen picks up her cigarette and takes a deep drag. 'I can't remember. I don't know what I say half the time. One minute.'

Doreen flicks her cigarette out of the window and pulls her dress up over her head. A cushion is tied around her middle with several woollen scarves. I watch as she unwinds them and lays them one after the other on the back of a chair.

She stands in front of me, a thin young woman in an Iggy Pop T-shirt. 'They prefer their mediums with a bit of padding. It lends gravitas. So, how do you know the book is for you?'

'Those are my initials.'

'Plenty of other people with those initials.'

'Are you going to help me or not?'

Doreen Gouge smiles.

Her real name is Eleanor Kemp, she says, and she struggles with her imagination. She tells me that she is brim-full of voices, songs on a loop. She sees faces daily, and sometimes all day, distorted as if pressed against a window, laughing, sobbing or just looking in. Like the voices, the faces come and go, ebb and flow. On her worst days the dead are relentlessly real; they stand in front of her scratching their arses, demanding and bickering. On better days they dampen to a whispered word, the faint smell of lilac, then she can buy shoes and pay her gas bill. Eleanor sometimes wonders who is more alive, her or the dead, for she can lose days at the mercy of the dear departed.

Then there are the sudden vivid pictures, memories that don't belong to her: dappled shade on a veranda, the face of a sleeping baby, the whip and billow of sails against an Aegean blue sea. Or a hand that's not her own: on a bottle, on a bridge, on a swing, on a knife.

Sometimes she's medicated, sometimes not. When she's medicated, she sleeps more; the dead come either way.

Wasn't it always like this? She smiles wryly. The madwoman and the visionary dancing hand in hand, sharing the same tambourine?

As for the practicalities, she knows how to work the room because her father was a market trader, selling knock-down crockery. It's the same thing, only she's selling dead people and she doesn't collect the money now; someone else does that for her.

'Do you ever see saints?' I ask.

She frowns.

'You know, martyrs, with robes, halos?'

She looks at me blankly. 'I know what a saint is.'

'It doesn't matter. What did you see tonight?'

Eleanor pulls on her boots. 'Red-haired woman, pale face.'

I want to sit down but I can't move. 'The Red Queen?'

'And a girl holding her hand,' she says, throwing her gear into a sports bag.

I can hardly speak. 'What did she look like?'

'The girl?' Eleanor zips up her bag. 'Big smile, blonde hair.' She screws the lid on the quarter bottle and slips it into the pocket of her jacket.

'And the well? You said something about a cat in a well?' For a moment I think of Beckett.

Eleanor shrugs. 'Most likely a metaphor; the dead like a metaphor.'

'A metaphor for what?'

'No idea.' She picks up her crash helmet. 'One more thing: that guy you're with.'

'Yes?'

'He's not who he says he is.'

Chapter 36

My heart is submerged; she lies low. A tin can covered with bar-
nacles, a wrecked submarine skulking through murky depths. I follow
her, brushing the silty seabed with my hair. I see the tiles are still
there. We swim in an octagon, my heart and I, past rusty arches.
Above us little creamy moons shine with halos of light.

When I catch my heart I will drag her to the surface and crack
her open. I'll take a flashlight to her dank leaking chambers. All
blighted iron and worn rivets. I'll find the skeletons and ripped-up
ticker tape. Maydays unsent, warnings interrupted – she couldn't
get a message out; they came scrambled or not at all, salt water in
the mechanism, bugs on the line.

There's a flash in the water. A woman swims towards me, sleek-
limbed, white moon of a face. She hesitates in the water, dead-eyed;
hair billows around her face. Then she barrels past, filling my eyes
and nose with bubbles. Beyond there is an explosion of red, a cloud
that spreads through the water, unfurling in swirls and curlicues.

The backs of my knees are wet. I wipe my face on a corner
of the sheet, tasting salt on my lips.

I look at him, in the bed. I take it all in. His hair, a darker blond at the nape of his neck, the muscles on his back and the shape of his spine narrowing downwards to the curve of his buttocks. His left hand is over the bedclothes. I lean forward and study it again, closely, although I don't need to. I know it well enough now. The scar on the bulb of his thumb, the freckles on the back of his hand and the barely perceptible dip on his ring finger where his wedding band usually is.

In his hometown the day is dawning with a chill in the air.

In a while his wife will make breakfast and get the children up for school. Maybe they'll ask where Daddy is. Maybe she'll cry into their lunchboxes or slam the door of the fridge too hard. Or maybe she'll just stand at the sink, staring out of the window, a cup cradled in her hands. How would she not know about the other women, that there would be other women? You only need to look at him: his smile, his body and the wolf behind his eyes.

For he is a wolf, a snaggle-fanged, handsome wolf, easy-limbed and grey-eyed.

He's not who he says he is, not that he's doing much saying.

I slip out of bed and pick up his jeans. Closing the bedroom door behind me, I pull out his wallet and open it.

A wad of cash. Nothing else.

No photos of the twins, or the son he takes to the park for a kickabout every Sunday. No driving licence, cards . . . I should be surprised but I'm not: it's the wallet of an adulterer. I close it and push it back into his pocket.

When I steal back into the bedroom he's rolled over, his breathing slow and regular. Loping feral in some dream forest, his flank twitches in his sleep. Or maybe he's pretending that too.

I see a movement out of the corner of my eye.

A dim hand comes around the bedroom door holding a spectral rose, long-stemmed, glowing red.

I hold a finger over my mouth and St Valentine follows me into the living room.

'Well now, isn't love grand?' he gloats. 'There's Johnny Quicksilver back in your bed, like he never left. A fine-looking man and a handsome man, with those brilliant grey eyes and all the skills he has in the sack. A fierce and energetic lover, and imaginative. God, the things—'

'Do you ever stop?'

St Valentine sits himself down and pats the sofa next to him. On the coffee table I notice the local paper opened at the lonely hearts column. The page is covered with iridescent golden circles.

'Did you do that?'

'It's good to keep your options open, for when your man moves on. How about a widower with a semi-detached in Hounslow? Likes walks.'

I sit down, narrowing my eyes. 'Get to the point, little man.'

'And have you figured out who he is yet, himself in the bed?'

'He's Sam Hebden.'

St Valentine snorts. 'And here you are a great one for the collecting of evidence and the prying into all the corners of a person's life.'

I maintain an aloof silence.

'Wake him up and ask him.' St Valentine has a steely look of challenge in the eye that's fixed on me. The other is drifting towards the living room doorway. 'Give his credentials a thorough inspection.'

'I'll do no such thing.'

St Valentine frowns and picks at his ear. Then his face brightens as a thought dawns on him. 'You're scared, Twinkle.'

'I am not.'

He grins and his halo momentarily glows with a sickly light. 'He already thinks you're a bit touched, doesn't he? Seeing mysteries where there are none, aren't you? Turning your cracked little mind onto him, are we? That could dampen a man's romantic antics, couldn't it?'

'That isn't it at all.'

St Valentine stops grinning and looks thoughtful. 'Then you're scared of what you'll find out.'

And there's that thought again. The wife in the kitchen, staring out of the window, a cup cradled in her hands while the twins bray for their breakfast and the boy kicks a ball down the hall.

'Ignorance is bliss,' proclaims St Valentine.

'If you've had your say—'

'I haven't. All in all, your one had some premium messages last night.'

'What of it?'

'She saw Mary and Maggie, didn't she? Anything else, Twinkle?' St Valentine assumes a patronising air. 'Then I'll give you a clue: it has a bucket and a whole rake of wishes and there's one at Bridlemere.'

'Jesus – she spoke about a well.'

St Valentine grins from ear to ear. 'Ding dong.'

I dress quickly and bring a torch. St Valentine insists on accompanying me; he enjoys a bus ride and delights when we pass over Richmond Bridge. He presses his nose through the window to gaze at the Thames, which is still and perfect and shrouded in mist. We watch a skein of geese fly over, dipping and rising, the ballast of their bodies carried by the long strokes of their wings. They adopt a V formation as they head downriver. St Valentine takes it as a good omen. I say nothing.

★　★　★

St Valentine says he will wait at the gate for me.

'Go on now, Maud, find the well and have a wee look in it.'

He glances over his shoulder. A vague form is clanking along the empty early-morning street. As it draws nearer I make out St George.

I frown. 'What's this, a convention?'

St Valentine looks offended. 'Here we are, showing our support.' He points at St George. 'Myself and this lad.'

St George shrugs; armour grinds. 'I'd get on, if I were you. The old man will be awake soon. Don't lean over too far and don't fall,' he adds. 'Like you did in the ice house.'

'If you can't see anything, then throw a good roar in. That'll rouse whatever's down there.' St Valentine glances at St George. 'She has a sharp class of voice that could wake the dead.'

I narrow my eyes. 'So you're coming in with me, for moral support?'

The saints shuffle and peer off in different directions. I turn on my heel.

The garden is silent and wet with dew. A few cats come running over to me. When they realise I'm not here to feed them they saunter off again, threading through rubbish and jumping up onto the roofs of sheds and outhouses. I pick my way between upended wheelbarrows, car parts and broken furniture, black bags and rusted tools. I won't know what I'm looking for until I find it or fall down it.

It's at the edge of the garden, in a clearing of sorts, surrounded by rubble and covered with a sheet of corrugated iron held down by bricks. I put down my bag, clear the bricks and slide off the cover.

I lean over and the smell hits me: the cold seeping damp of deep wet places, of sunless, starless places. I can see into it several feet, a few curved rows of blown and ancient bricks, then the dark takes over. The torch does nothing; the beam is nowhere near strong enough. I pull a coin from my bag. Not for a wish, but something else, perhaps a tribute, or to pay the toll of some well-guarding sprite. I let the coin go and listen. I don't hear it drop.

A breeze strikes up, snatching sand from a pile of rubble and blowing it over me. Was Cathal planning to fill the well in? I look around; under an old tarpaulin I find bricks and cement bags, mostly empty, a few full and weathered solid.

What was he trying to cover up?

I lean over the edge as far as I dare and I shout.

Is anyone there?

My echo comes back to me, high and mocking.

Is anyone there? There? There? There?

I wait: there is no other voice. There is no one in the well.

Then all at once the wind changes direction. It blows across the top of the well, like lips over a milk bottle, a fell high note. The kind a banshee would be proud of.

Chapter 37

Lillian has been busy today. She has dusted Renata's collection of gemstones and arranged them in the new second-hand cabinet. She has wallpapered over the curaçao stains on the living room wall and cooked a casserole for Cathal's birthday. She leaves as I arrive, taking the living room curtains to the dry-cleaner after a brief but fierce skirmish over the alleged resurgence of Renata's pipe.

Renata, in a floral apron and headscarf like a housewife in a 1970s sitcom, gives me a resigned smile. She always has a shrunken, well-rinsed quality after Lillian has been round, like something delicate put on a boil wash with the dog's towel.

Renata sets about making coffee. 'Is Sam joining us, to go through the itinerary?'

I sit down at the kitchen table. 'I haven't invited him.'

Renata glances at me. 'He's going to Dorset with you?'

'No, he's not.'

Renata raises an eyebrow and sets the coffee pot on the stove.

How can I tell her that I don't trust the man I keep sleeping with? And, what's worse, I don't want to find out why.

'I'd rather go alone,' I say.

'You know best,' she says brightly, and wipes her hands on her apron.

I look at the pad: a plan has most definitely come together.

Trip to Dorset for the Purposes of Investigation

Day One:
AM: Langton Cheney
Check into B&B (Castle View, Renscombe Road, double en suite)
Visit Holly Lodge residential home, for reasons we've yet to invent, to ask about Marguerite Flood and Maggie Dunne.

Question the villagers of Langton Cheney.

PM: Dorchester
Meet with Frank Gaunt, retired police constable who was in charge of investigating Maggie's disappearance and who thinks you are coming to buy a whippet.

Day Two:
AM: Wareham
Attend Mass at Our Lady of Lourdes Roman Catholic Church.
Interrogate congregation over tea and biscuits.

I look up from the pad. 'What's with the whippet?'

'When I phoned the station they told me that Frank Gaunt had retired and is only interested in breeding whippets.' Renata shrugs. 'I told them that was exactly what I wanted to ask him about, so they gave me his number.'

'That's one way to do it.'

'He has a fawn bitch; you can bring it back if it's nice.'

I stare at her. 'You have a dog phobia.'

'It's more a dislike of rabies.' Renata tears the sheet off the pad and hands it to me. 'Hydrophobia makes life very difficult – drinking, showering, that sort of thing. It's best to take precautions.' She narrows her eyes. 'On that note, pack your pepper spray for dinner tonight with Mr Flood. I'm still not convinced it's a good idea.'

I glance at her; perhaps she's getting soft. 'This could be my last chance to speak to him. We could have the case solved tonight.'

'Well, try not to provoke him at least.' She frowns. 'This will also be his last chance to do away with you.'

I have a casserole, an iced birthday cake, a bottle of Józef's finest and a gaudy cravat that belonged to the late Bernie Sparks. I pull them behind me in Lillian's shopping trolley. In the front pocket, where the bus pass ought to go, there's a fully charged mobile phone, a rape alarm and a pepper spray. As I get off the bus I wonder if I should just keep walking. Forging onwards, over roads and motorways, hills and fields, to the edge of the land where I could sail away to sea. Bobbing along on the shopping trolley.

The casserole would last me a few days, until I sighted land again. Somewhere hot, with lizards and outsized fruit. I could get a job in a bar and carouse every night with the locals. I'd be brown and thin from all those days at sea and men would plague me like mosquitoes. I would keep the shopping trolley though, battered and sun-bleached, to remind me that when-ever things get too much I could pack up and sail away again.

Cathal greets me at the door with a raffish grin and a bow, like an unsavoury butler. His white hair is neatly brushed and he is sporting his funeral suit, with a red spotted handkerchief in the pocket. He wears no tie or socks and has his slippers on.

'I've set this new agency one to work today. I had him running up and down, roaring at him. Wait until you see what I've done.' He points at the shopping trolley. 'What's in there?'

'A bit of dinner.'

'I've put the pâté and crackers out, but.'

'We'll have a bit of everything, will we?'

He shrugs, then he's off back down the stairs into the garden, bouncing the trolley behind him. I follow him through the bushes into a kind of twisted wonderland.

In the clearing, in front of the caravan, a table is laid for a party. He must have plundered all the remaining flowers in the garden, for dozens of vases and teapots and jam jars are crammed with them. There are rusty storm lanterns, their candles burning with a slow-dancing flame behind glass, and an old oil lamp, its wick quick-burning and brilliant.

The caravan has been decorated with fairy lights: colourful strings of bulbs that dip and ride along the roof. The door is still padlocked but now two large dead potted plants stand either side with tinsel wound round them.

'It's lovely,' I say.

Cathal nods, his eyes bright.

On a platter at the centre of the table there are lines of crackers decorated with twists of cucumber. A nearby tray of pâté is attracting cats.

Cathal gives a shout and they flee. 'Feckers, all.' He inspects the pâté. 'I'll give it a wee scrape and it'll be grand.'

A record player is set up at the end of the table.

He pulls out a chair. 'Would you care to take a seat, Maud?'

The sky gets darker. It's a mild night for the time of year but there's a blanket on the back of my chair if I want it.

We sit alongside each other. A few cats populate the empty seats ranged around the table.

'Why've you got so many chairs?'

Cathal smiles grimly. 'The agency gobdaw, I told him I was having a birthday dinner and he set all of this.'

'They're for your imaginary friends.'

He laughs. 'The best kind.'

'Who would you invite?'

Cathal grins. 'To start with: Picasso and Mata Hari.'

I join in. 'Jimmy Stewart and Genghis Khan.'

'There'd be Brendan Behan; he'd be hopping.'

I nudge him. 'And Greta Garbo on the piano.'

He's delighted. 'Is it music you want?'

And he's up and fumbling at the record player, cursing the failing light and then with a quick slip and scratch of the needle a few bars of—

'Are you dancing, Maud?'

'Are you asking?'

We take a turn around the table to Frank Sinatra, watched only by the cats skulking in the lamplight or licking crumbs from the tablecloth.

With my hand in his big paw I look up at him. 'Is there anyone else you would want here?'

He stops shifting in his slippers and looks down at me. 'Don't say it, Maud. Please, not tonight.'

We eat casserole from paper plates and then turn to the cake Lillian has made: a sponge with a lemon filling and the top iced in a brown ellipse with little dabs of food colouring.

'It's an artist's palette,' I say after a while.

Cathal nods respectfully, perhaps touched by the effort someone has gone to for a stranger.

'You've told your friends about me.' He smiles. 'That I'm an artist and worse, a bollix, no doubt?'

Much, much worse, Cathal Flood.

I keep my head down, rummaging in the shopping trolley for his birthday gift.

Happy birthday, Bluebeard!

Perhaps, after all, the idea of Cathal is very different from the real thing. The Cathal of our fiction, mine and Renata's, is not the same at all as the raggedy old giant with the still-dark brows and the shock of white hair who looks up at me with eyes lit with humour.

He opens his present, making pleased noises, and carefully folds the wrapping paper and puts it in his pocket.

I tie the cravat for him.

'Well now, Maud, how do I look?'

'A fine figure of a man.'

He smiles up at me, gratified, in the dead man's cravat. On a whim I reach over to one of the vases and break off a blousy yellow tea rose. To his amusement I thread it through his buttonhole.

'Now you're perfect, Cathal.'

He grins and holds out his hand.

We take to the floor with Louis Armstrong.

Even the cats feel it: the sense of something ending, the slow sinking of the ship. Meanwhile, the music plays on and the lights twinkle. A cold inky blackness waits offstage, lapping at the edges of our scene, starting to trickle in. We will be swept away. But not in this moment, not right now.

All of the felines have turned out for the occasion. I see Beckett, a pale blur snaking under the table. The others prowl on the outskirts or lie along the table. There is a pattering of claws on metal and I look up to see the snout of a young fox peer over the roof of the caravan.

'What will you do with them?'

Cathal looks around him. 'They'll find their own ways. The rest is in Gabriel's hands now.'

'But your house?'

'We weren't going to talk about this.'

'I know.'

He smiles. 'It's only a house. All things come to an end, Maud. The trick is to go with the flow.'

I shake my head. 'Is there nothing we can do?'

'Do? No. Unless it's to have a wee bit of that cake.'

I set the candles on the cake without counting, figuring that if there's enough years you lose count anyway. I pour him a drink in a plastic glass and we have a toast.

'To you on your birthday, Cathal Flood.' I smile.

'To you on my birthday, Maud Drennan.' He smiles.

'Now make a wish,' I say.

As seriously as a child he closes his eyes, then he nods. He's ready. I hold the cake near him and he blows out the candles.

'Will you come and see this creation you've inspired now?'

'The painting, is it finished?'

'It is. You're a fine muse, Maud.'

'Am I not a little on the square-jawed side for a muse?'

'I made do.' Cathal stands up. 'It's inside the house. You'll come in?'

I'm halfway down the garden path before I remember the pepper spray but I don't even think about going back.

The house has a different quality at night. The fittings cast a flat tungsten light that is far less mysterious than I thought it would be. There are dark corners, but they are dark in an unswept kind of way. The smell is heightened, as if the rubbish, slumbering, is freely giving off its noxious fumes.

I follow Cathal's impossibly tall form down the hall. His walk is faltering tonight, his body a little hunched in a suit older than days. His jacket swings short of his backside and his trousers end shy of his ankles.

The gap in the Great Wall of *National Geographics* is wider than ever. I can move through it touching the dusty strata on either side with my hands outstretched. Cathal has to duck his head and turn sideways.

He fumbles for a light switch and we are in fairyland again. Strings of tiny lanterns weave amongst the display cases, the instruments and taxidermy. There is a clanking and a whirring of curiosities coming to life, welcoming their master. Stoats throw down losing hands, the raven, back on her podium again, ruffles her wings. The glass eyes spin delightedly and even the shrunken head looks happier: the sewn pout has become a smile.

We carry on past them and past the four-headed angel at the foot of the staircase who wrinkles her snouts in greeting.

We continue down the hallway, further than I've gone before.

'Look at this wee fella,' he says.

Together we peer into a dimly lit fish tank – the face of a startling creature smirks back. The creature leans on one elbow in a sea of painted waves with its tail outstretched. It appears to be smoking a pipe.

'The Feejee Merman.' Cathal smiles. 'Half capuchin monkey, half salmon: a work of genius; you can hardly see the join.'

'It's something else.'

'Over here,' says Cathal. 'Have you a strong stomach?'

'It depends.'

He pulls a string and a set of curtains open.

'The Flayed Man,' he announces.

A life-sized man sits cross-legged in a glass case resting his elbow on his knee and his head on his hand. His skin has been planed away from the right side of his body. Gory ribbons of flesh are still attached to his wrist and ankle. In some places the cuts have gone deeper, revealing muscle, nerves, bones and subcutaneous layer. One side of his face is unremarkable, on the other a naked jawbone grimaces and an eyeball lolls in an open socket.

'Merciful Jesus.'

Cathal looks at me proudly. 'Have you ever seen anything like it?'

'In my fecking nightmares I have.'

He grins. 'The Hunterian Museum has been after this for years. Made by an Italian master of anatomical wax modelling.' He opens a long wooden case. 'But this is what started it all off.'

Inside, nestling in corresponding depressions of faded velvet, is a saw, knives, chisel and tourniquet.

'This amputation kit belonged to my great-grandfather, Thomas 'Butcher' Flood, a surgeon in the Crimean War.'

'That's some heirloom. Did you not think of taking after him?'

'I drop at the sight of the real stuff.' Cathal frowns. 'Will we go and see your portrait?'

He takes a bundle of keys from his pocket, searches through them and opens the last door in the corridor.

It's a beautiful room. Long and narrow, with paintings ranged the length of it on forest-green walls. The gallery, Cathal calls it. The floor is polished wood and the bigger paintings are lit with brass lamps attached to the wall. There are land-scapes and seascapes and even the odd still life.

I turn to Cathal in surprise. 'None of them are by you.'

He gives me a bitter smile. 'These are Mary's paintings; she bought each and every one of them.'

Something else strikes me. 'And there are no portraits.'

'She didn't like the eyes looking at her.' He gestures at the easel. 'Are you ready?'

In the middle of the gallery stands a square ghost: the canvas on an easel with a sheet pinned over it.

Suddenly I feel nervous. I'm an unwitting Dorian about to face my true self captured in oil paint. I wonder what it will be like, my true self. Maybe it will be a wizened strip of a thing, as spare as a fell runner. Or maybe it will be like one of those nocturnal mammals, round-eyed and unpre-pared, shocked-looking and a little otherworldly. I glance up at the old man and nod.

Maud stares out of the canvas. She sits with one leg folded under her and her head resting on one hand. At first sight she is still, self-contained. But when you look closer you see the clenched set of her jaw. And there's a rise to her shoul-ders as if her hackles are up. Her hair is half-pinned, half-falling, giving her an unravelled look. Her mouth plays with a tense smile. For all her wariness she is tired, dog-tired and bone-tired; I can see it in her eyes. Like a soldier who has never been told to stand down, she has kept it all at bay for so long.

I start to cry.

Cathal upset is a broken toy, an old tin soldier, wound-up and wobbly headed. His eyebrows waggle as he tries out different expressions. He fixes on a sad frown. He holds me awkwardly to his chest as I cry, patting my back as if trying to wind a baby with colic.

I cry for the people who are dying from bowel obstructions and car crashes, heart attacks and lingering diseases, unhappiness and fluke DIY accidents. I cry for old rogues holed up in their clutter and brave souls too scared to go out. I cry for dead wives and bad sisters and disappeared schoolgirls. I cry for those who can't remember and those who can't forget and those who are stuck somewhere in the fucking middle.

As all the sadness in the world swells around me Cathal Flood holds on. But he is all smoke and mirrors, roar and bluster. For now I feel how fragile he is, how dry-boned and thin-skinned, made from paper and dust. Just like those big blousy moths flailing in the Belfast sink in the pantry of the Bridlemere of my imagination.

'Come on now, Maud,' he says. 'What in the world have you got to cry about? Is it the painting? Do you not like the look of yourself? Is it your jawline?'

I shake my head.

'I didn't think so,' he says.

But the tears are abating and knowing this, Cathal lets me go and takes the ancient musty handkerchief from his pocket and wipes my nose and eyes with it, roughly, brusquely, as you would a child late for school.

'There.' He smiles down at me. 'You're grand now.'

Cathal Flood walks me to the back door; Bluebeard willingly lets me leave his castle. He no longer wishes to kill me, if he ever did, for we are friends now. He opens the door and we watch the moths race each other, breakneck, to the strip light.

'I'll visit you, at the home,' I say.

He shakes his head. 'Ah no, Maud. I'd like you to remember me how I am now: fine, fierce and fighting.'

Suddenly I realise that this is the last time I will see him.

'I need to find out what happened,' I say quickly.

A raised eyebrow, a hint of a smile; he doesn't quite catch my meaning.

I keep going. 'To Mary and Maggie.'

I watch for his reaction: the beginnings of a frown perhaps, a drawing down of the mouth. Nothing dramatic.

'Mary kept cuttings on the case of a missing schoolgirl called Maggie Dunne. I found them hidden in the red room upstairs.'

The old man stares at me with an expression of disbelief. 'You've been searching the house? Going through her things, my wife's things?'

I try to keep my voice slow, composed. 'I didn't go looking, not as such; they came to me. As if they were being shown to me.'

'You're touched.'

'The missing girl lived at Cedar House at the same time as your daughter. Mary must have known Maggie; either way she wanted to find out what happened to her.'

'You're cracked.'

'Just tell me, please, before they take you, before you go. Is she alive? Is Maggie here?'

He stands in front of me with his head bowed, strangely expressionless. Shut down and blank, like a seaside shopfront in winter. 'You've said your piece and now I'd like you to leave.'

'You knew her, Cathal. Don't deny it.'

'Good night and good luck so.'

I can hear my voice rising and feel a surge of indignation. 'Look, I've respected you, considered your feelings, tried to help you.'

He shifts in his carpet slippers. His old hand goes up to his chest, bumps along where his heart might be. 'Is it a medal you want? For not asking me things that are none of your business?'

'It is my business if a crime was committed, if a young girl has been taken, to be held against her will or even killed.'

'Jesus, would you ever cop yourself on? There's no crime, there's no one taken, there's no one killed.' He stabs at his head. 'It's all up there.'

'You can talk to me, Cathal.' I speak gently, calmly, as if I'm coaxing him back from a ledge. 'You trust me, don't you?'

His face falls, crumples. 'You little bitch. Ingratiating yourself, is that what you've been doing? To get the senile old bastard talking, get him to admit to some shit you've dreamt up?'

'It wasn't like that.' I shake my head. 'Please, Cathal. I need to know.'

'So that's the reason you came here tonight. Last-chance saloon. Before the old fucker is carted off and anaesthetised, propped up in a chair drooling.'

'Please.'

He looks me dead in the eyes. 'You think that I could hurt Maggie Dunne? You think I could kill her or keep her here? You think I'm a monster?'

Maybe my eyes tell him I do, for his expression is one of slow-dawning disgust.

'You sat and drank with me, you shared a meal with me, thinking I was capable of that?'

'If you're scared I can help you. We can go to the police together.'

He holds up his hands, palms out, as if he's stopping a horse, as if he's holding off a siege. He is beyond rigid. But behind the savage blue glare of his eyes he is breaking up. I see it in his mouth; it shapes the start of a sob.

'Please let me help you, Cathal.'

The gates are stormed and the castle falls. Cathal Flood withers. His eyes brim with sudden tears. There is no anger. Here is only pain, his old face says, and betrayal, and love extinguished.

He closes the door. I hear him slide the chain across, then the bolt: sound effects with the right kind of finality. I bang on the door for a while and shout. Then I knock on the door and plead. Then I give up and stand silent in the garden and watch as the lights are put out one by one and Bridlemere sinks into blackness.

I imagine him tottering back through the house – wasted limbs and scarecrow suit. His old head wobbling and his eyes in it bewildered, the backs of his big gnarly hands brushing over the surfaces of his hoard.

Hot waves of remorse run through me. My stomach is a pit of shame. What have I done?

I fight the urge to get down on my knees.

Chapter 38

If you really want to repent, make self-mortification your friend, along with piety and hardship. Familiarise yourself with all three by having a good hard kneel. This is supplemental to the prayers you will already be doing for the absolution you know will never come.

I had been on the gravel for twenty minutes the day Granny caught me. I told her I was doing penance but she made me get up and took me inside and sponged my knees with disinfectant. As she dipped the sponge in the bowl she glanced up at me from time to time with a strange expression on her face, like she was trying to work out a difficult sum.

She dried me off with a clean tea towel while the boiled sweet in her mouth made a series of quick clicks as it ricocheted around her teeth. I never knew Granny not to have a sweet in her mouth and I could usually gauge her mood by her consumption of it, for she sucked sweets faster when riled and was known to crunch them when furious.

Granny straightened up and pulled down the hem of my skirt and patted my leg. She told me it wasn't my fault that

Deirdre had disappeared, that I should know this and remember it. Granny sounded exactly the same as she did the time she lied to Mrs Walsh over the church flower rota.

Deirdre was gone but that wasn't my fault. I had been left behind but that wasn't my fault. None of it was my fault.

The guards would find her. Or Deirdre, being Deirdre, would slouch through that door any minute now, scowling and saying, 'Surprise! It was all a joke.'

I sat up at the table and Granny gave me a tub, a scraper and a pile of carrots. Then she stood by the sink looking out, at the empty bird feeder, the weather and the road leading up to the bungalow. The sweet in her mouth clicked faster and faster as it reached warp speed – soon it would disappear too.

Chapter 39

It's late but Renata is up waiting for me.

'Don't let me think,' I say. 'Just talk.'

'What about, darling?'

'Anything.'

And she does. For almost an hour Renata holds forth on subjects as diverse as mail-order kimonos, the wonder of Steve McQueen and fondue. I look down at my hands on the kitchen table.

I feel Renata's eyes roaming over me for signs of attack: pulled hair, slapped face, unbuttoned clothes, bruises and bite marks and fractures, snot and tears.

St Dymphna wanders up and down the hallway. Now and again she casts me a look; I'm not sure whether it's pitying or mocking.

Renata keeps talking. Halfway through an in-depth analysis of the merits of the tanga over a full brief I start to cry.

Renata takes my hand in hers and waits.

Then, in an easy, downy voice she says, 'Tell me about it, Maud. Tell me everything.'

Everything.

Lightly, quietly, she says, 'This is not just about Flood, is it?'

'No.'

St Dymphna looks up at me from the hallway; an expression of dismay streaks across her face and she's gone.

I don't have to look around to know where she is: she's right behind me. Quick as a ghost. So real I can feel her standing next to my chair; her robe brushes against my arm, her breath moves my hair.

She holds her hand an inch from my mouth. I see it before me.

I smell that medicated soap Granny always bought, and perfume stolen from the chemist, and the sickly strawberry sweetness of bubblegum.

If I try to speak of it, she'll stop me with the pale flat dead palm of her hand.

'There's nothing to tell,' I say. 'Nothing happened.'

Chapter 40

I follow her, the red-haired woman. She leads me across a furrowed field, through a wooded copse, and on, deeper, deeper, into the trees, her white feet sinking into the loam. Above me, light-dappled branches, leaves saturated with colour — a vivid living green — and beyond a sky of cloudless blue. I wade through bracken and stumble over tree roots.

I am not frightened while I hear birds sing. For I remember that birds fly away when something bad is about to happen: they sense what's coming. And the birds are singing all around us, brightly, persistently.

Here's a clearing and there's a stream. On the bank opposite, two children play in the water, sailing acorn cups. When they hear me they look up and smile. A dark blond boy and a bright blonde girl with the same slow, wide grin.

As I smile back I realise that the birds have stopped singing.

Chapter 41

St Valentine sits next to my weekend bag in the back seat of Sam Hebden's green Golf with a dented passenger door. We're making good time down the M3; with St Valentine's intercession we will no doubt be in Langton Cheney by lunchtime. The saint travels with his head out of the window like an excited dog, blessing vehicles travelling below the speed limit and gesticulating at van drivers as they pass by texting.

Sam is quiet, distracted. Perhaps surprised at my last-minute invitation, at my change of heart. Or perhaps it's because with every mile we draw nearer to the place where it all began. I wonder when he will admit he's not who he says he is.

Someone will recognise him. Surely there'll be someone in the village who knew him as a child, who knew his sister?

You just have to watch his face – wait for it – there's the same wide grin as Maggie's.

Only he's not smiling now.

I glance at him, in his T-shirt and trainers with his lovely grey eyes on the road. I don't know what he's thinking but I know what he has done.

He took the job to get close to Cathal. To investigate, in his own way, his sister's disappearance, knowing that the Floods were somehow involved. He had revealed his identity to the old man, or perhaps Cathal recognised him; either way it led to the assault.

But why lie to us? To Renata and me?

He checks his rear mirrors often, as if someone's tailgating him. I glance behind me and so does St Valentine.

'We're being followed,' says the saint.

A new black BMW is keeping a polite distance, pottering along the inside lane in a way new black BMWs never do.

And I'm about to exclaim when St Valentine leans forward, his voice cold. 'Don't say a bloody word, Twinkle.'

We drive on in silence, with Sam checking his mirror.

I steal another glance. St Valentine is halfway out of the rear window trying to get a glimpse at the driver.

'Is everything all right?' asks Sam.

'Just looking for my handbag.'

'It's there, by your feet.'

'So it is.'

Sam frowns at me.

'Tell him to pull in,' urges St Valentine. 'See if we can't get a handle on the situation.'

'Can we stop at the services, Sam? I need the bathroom.'

Sam checks his mirror and pulls into the inside lane, indicating early, slowing down, checking his mirror again.

'Your fella not only knows we're being followed, he's encouraging it,' says St Valentine. 'And you'll never guess who's in that beamer.'

I would.

I sit down on the toilet and look at my phone. There are five missed calls from Renata.

She answers at once. 'Where are you?'

'On a toilet in a motorway service station being followed by Gabriel Flood.'

There's a pause. 'He's following you? Are you sure?'

Someone in the next cubicle flushes. I wait. 'Yes, I'm sure. What did you call me for?'

Another pause, then her voice flat and stern. 'Sam isn't Sam.'

'No, I know. He's Maggie Dunne's brother.'

She sounds surprised. 'What gives you that idea?'

'Look at the photograph of Maggie. It's the same smile. He came undercover as an agency worker to investigate the Floods. But Cathal found out and that's why he threatened him.'

'It would fit.'

The words *vacant cunt* are etched on the toilet door in foot-high letters; I try not to take it personally.

'Only there's a real Sam Hebden,' says Renata. 'I've just spoken to him.'

'How?'

'I got his number from one of the girls in the agency. Biba is off with a mild dose of gout.'

It's as simple as that.

'He confirmed that he worked with Mr Flood until he was run off the property. Then he was transferred to a new gig in Hull.' Renata's tone softens. 'The real Sam Hebden is of medium height, bald, with a goatee beard and a port wine stain on his left buttock.'

I frown. 'So what does that mean?'

'No idea, but there's something else: Mary Flood was a major figure at Cedar House.'

'Tell me.'

'I sent for a brochure and it arrived today, surprisingly glossy. Nowadays Holly Lodge offers tailored care for older people in a faith-led environment. There's a whole page on the history of the place; it says Mary Flood built a wing.'

'I don't see—'

'I'm working on a way to get you in. How are your acting skills?'

'You are kidding.'

There's a smile in Renata's voice. 'Answer your bloody phone, Maud.'

Sam is waiting outside with takeaway coffees. 'Are you ready?'

St Valentine is standing next to him, only now he has friends: St Dymphna and St George, St Rita and St Monica stand alongside. St Dymphna chews her plait and St George holds a sack in his gauntleted hand. St Rita and St Monica stand a little apart, ignoring each other like socially awkward party guests. I'm almost glad to see them.

Sam hands me my coffee.

The saints perk up and start to watch him closely.

'He's nervous,' announces St Dymphna to her plait.

'Agitated, more like,' says St Valentine. 'Look at his eyes, there's a fair twitch to the left one.'

I gesture at a concrete planter. 'We'll sit here a moment, Sam, just while we drink.'

'I'd rather press on.'

I smile. 'What's the rush? Our meeting with Frank Gaunt isn't until three. He's the police—'

Sam looks at me, unsmiling. 'I know who he is.'

He sits down next to me and puts his coffee on the ground. He searches in his pocket for his cigarettes, lights one and gazes out across the car park.

'This is crazy, Maud. Let's just go back to London. It's all gone far enough.'

'What's gone far enough?'

He takes a deep drag and exhales. 'This fictional crime case.'

The saints glance at each other, then at me. St George puts his sack down and grasps the hilt of his sword.

I take a cautious sip of my coffee, moving slowly, counting to ten. 'Mary Flood had a dubious accident; that's not fictional. Maggie Dunne disappeared; that's not fictional either. Mary kept the cuttings; she did that for a reason.'

Sam squints back at me through cigarette smoke. 'People keep newspaper cuttings all the time; it means nothing.'

'In this case, it means something.'

'This is madness.'

'You have a sister.'

He stares at me. 'What?'

'You have a sister. I asked you before. I said, "If she disappeared, like Maggie Dunne, would you just let it go?"'

'Nice one.' St George nods under his visor.

Sam's voice is low and full of contained anger. 'None of this is any of your business.'

'You're lucky: you know where your sister is.'

He screws out his cigarette in the planter. 'I thought you had more sense. I can see why Renata does it, all that time on his hands.'

The saints tut. St Dymphna mutters an expletive under her breath.

I watch Sam walk off across the car park. If I had a brick in my hand I'd be taking aim.

He opens the car door from the inside. I get in, putting my handbag on my lap primly. All the saints slide into the back seat. As we pull out of the service station I see a brand-new black BMW parked by the petrol pumps. The man in the driver's seat ducks. Sam looks straight ahead and dawdles towards the exit.

I have to make a decision. I am in a car with a man who isn't who he says he is and we are being followed. And he not only knows we are being followed, he's encouraging it.

I look down. My phone is hopping in my bag, vibrating through the canvas: Renata.

The saints nudge each other and St Valentine leans forward. 'The next service station is just up ahead. Get him to pull in there.'

'Can we stop again, please, Sam? That coffee's gone right through me.' I sneak a look at his face. He is beyond irritation.

I sit on the toilet for the longest time studying my phone. It's entirely out of charge.

I flush the cistern for something to do, until St Dymphna pushes her head through the cubicle and tells me its high bloody time I came out.

As I line up for the hand dryers with a dead phone, my itinerary and a gaggle of ladies on a beano to Weymouth, a plan starts to take shape in my mind.

St Dymphna is leaning on the sanitary-towel dispenser with her lamp in her hand and her robes arranged nicely. She flashes me an encouraging smile. She looks very sweet when she smiles non-sarcastically; she even has dimples. She could be the face of sainthood.

'Remember how convincing you were when you delivered that box of cat litter to Mrs Cabello?' she says. 'She believed you and she's a savvy old high-class hooker. You can do this, Maud.'

I frown at St Dymphna and she nods at me. For once I know she's right.

I take a deep breath and feel the tears collect in my lying eyes.

The woman in charge is called Wendy; I can tell this from her name badge. I know she is in charge because she is the one holding a clipboard. She's a little out of place in her anorak and walking sandals in a sea of appliquéd nylon and cork wedges. Wendy tells me that she's a retired teacher who misses the headache of escorting ill-behaved miscreants on trips to heritage sites. The Dorking Nifty Fifties Latin Formation Team fills this gap in her life; she doesn't dance but a trip away with them is a workout by itself.

This weekend there is a semi-final in Weymouth, a trip on a steam train and a cream tea at Corfe Castle to contend with. All this and being in charge of two hobby kleptomaniacs, three habitual brawlers and a committed sex addict who's been plaguing the coach driver to distraction. Wendy shakes her head as an argument breaks out in front of the mirrors as thirty women simultaneously attempt to apply lipstick.

I take the opportunity to relay my tragic story and throw myself on Wendy's mercy. She eyes me with alarm over her clipboard as I begin to cry, her long greying hair giving her the appearance of a concerned spaniel.

St Dymphna gives me the thumbs up.

'I'm sure it contravenes all manner of health and safety rules,' says Wendy, 'but we do have extra places on the coach due to an outbreak of shingles.'

I grin like a lunatic.

'You'll have to join the troupe as a temporary member.

I have a form.' She rummages in her rucksack. 'But what about your car, dear, can you just leave it here?'

'I think the main thing is to get to the home in time to say goodbye to my aunt.' I dab at my eyes with the tissue Wendy gives me. 'Of all the times my distributor could fail—'

'I quite understand. I once had a very temperamental Hillman Imp.'

She glances across at the mirrors; the fight seems to be escalating. One of the Nifty Fifties has taken off her shoe and another is putting down her handbag and rolling up the sleeves of her batwing jumper.

A weary frown crosses Wendy's brow. 'If you'll excuse me.'

We emerge like the close-knit group we are; I am already linking arms with a woman with hard-boiled blue eyes, short red hair and gums like a carthorse. She introduces herself as Fun Julie, shows me a half-bottle of vodka in her handbag and threatens to share it with me on the coach. I am careful to steer Fun Julie towards the middle of the group as we stampede, roaring and singing, across the car park. I see Virtual Sam waiting outside the entrance. He is speaking on his phone and kicking a bollard. He glances over his shoulder in the direction of the noise, then looks away, frowning.

A chorus of dim saints are drifting across the car park led by St Dymphna, who, with her dark eyes flashing and crown glinting, waves me on board the waiting coach.

Wendy counts us on. I climb up the steps with the relief of an airlifted soldier. I encourage Fun Julie into the seat by the window and keep my head down until we are underway.

As we pull out of the car park, I see the black BMW

parked by the exit. Gabriel Flood, in dark glasses, leans on his car door shouting into his phone.

I take the bottle Fun Julie is offering me.

Under different circumstances the coach ride would be one of my life's highlights. By the time we are out of the car park the entire coach, including the driver, know about my broken-down car and dying aunt, and now we are on a mission.

The Nifty Fifties will see me all the way to the residential home. They will get me there before my aunt dies and fuck the complimentary scones at Corfe Castle. To settle my nerves I have a few more slugs from Fun Julie's bottle.

Someone hands around paper cups of warm Lambrusco and three rows behind a ne'er-do-well sparks up a Café Crème, incurring the wrath of Wendy, who pads down the aisle on the verge of tears with her long hair flapping.

By the time we hit roadworks in Ringwood we have sung most of the soundtrack to *Dirty Dancing* and the girls have decided to set up a vigil outside the home. After the event they'll bring me on to Weymouth and their seafront hotel with the all-day happy hour. They will teach me to merengue and kit me out with a pair of gold dancing shoes.

By the time we reach the village of Langton Cheney the girls are in a nostalgic mood. It's inevitable they should turn to their losses: lost virginities, lost chances, lost time, lost parents, lost terriers, lost friends and lost lovers.

Doreen Gouge would clean up.

The back row begins to sing a spontaneous Edith Piaf tribute; the rest of the coach goes with Elvis at his most reflective. But as the coach crawls up the drive towards Holly Lodge Residential Care Home the group are united with a rousing performance of the chorus of 'An American Trilogy'.

It somehow seems fitting.

Fun Julie hands me the vodka bottle with a wink of a metallic eyelid. 'Something tells me you're going to need this a lot more than me, kiddo,' she says.

For a moment I feel homesick for Renata.

I shake hands with Wendy and the coach driver before stepping down onto the driveway and watching the coach depart. The saints are drawing in across the ornamental flowerbeds. They collect outside the entrance, nodding to each other, hands clasped, like wedding guests lining up for a photograph.

The Dorking Nifty Fifties Latin Formation team collectively salute me. It's a dignified send-off, only slightly marred by one member of the troupe lifting up her blouse. An elderly gardener looks on in amusement, leaning on his rake.

I watch until the coach is out of sight and then walk towards the long red-brick building that's going to provide me with a whole load of answers.

As I stand in the entrance hall I am mindful of being fluthered. I concentrate on acting normally and ignore the disapproving glances of the receptionist and the amused gaze of the Blessed Virgin Mary, whose statue graces an alcove above me. In the opposite alcove the man himself is hanging out on a cross, fine limbs, jutting ribs, eyes closed, head heavy.

This would be a Catholic care home then. I glance around me to find that my saints have melted into the shadows. No doubt lured away by the raft of expert petitioners in this place.

'Are there nuns around here?' I whisper, feeling a bubble of hysterical laughter rise in me. For I love nuns. I wonder if they would take me in and let me live with them. If I behave properly and stop drinking and swearing and sleeping with hot men who lie about their identities.

The receptionist, a joyless woman with thin eyebrows, frowns. 'We don't have nuns but there's a priest who visits. Did you want to see him too?'

'I don't. I've come to see the manager.'

The receptionist fixes me with a look. 'I've told Mrs Chapman you are waiting and that you would prefer not to divulge what you want to see her about.'

'Grand so, I'll just wait here, with you and Jesus and herself.'

I sit down on one of the visitors' chairs and try to think of one good reason why the manager should talk to me about Maggie Dunne. I blow into my hands and inhale, nearly knocking myself out with the fumes. A quick rummage in my handbag yields a cough sweet; the paper is half-off and it's a little gritty. No doubt of a similar vintage to those I shared with Cathal. I sit looking at it with an immense sadness, until the sight of the sweet in my hand grows blurry.

This is how Mrs Chapman, Duty Manager of Holly Lodge, finds me.

'Maud Drennan, is it? You're here about your aunt?'

I stare at her: all my fictions are coming true.

I follow Mrs Chapman into her office. She waves me to a chair next to a desk. The office is high-ceilinged and painted a bilious green. There is a wall calendar with a picture of the Pope against a backdrop of bishops.

Everything is neat and orderly, including Mrs Chapman herself in her navy suit and low-heeled courts.

She smiles at me. 'I apologise. At first I gave your mother short shrift. You see, we don't give out personal information to just anyone.'

'Certainly not.'

'But when she explained about the family connection I said I was more than happy to help.'

'Thank you.'

'Your mother said you that you are writing a family memoir about Mrs Flood's philanthropic work.'

I don't know what to say, so I just smile.

'Your mother, she sounds—'

'She's from Rotherhithe.'

'Rotherhithe?'

I distract her with a few quick questions. 'They visited often, my aunt and uncle?' I ask. 'In their caravan?'

'I'm sorry, that was before my time. But Máire Doherty would know; she's been here for years.' She hesitates, smiling apologetically. 'Will you also be writing about your cousin?'

'My cousin?'

'Marguerite,' says Mrs Chapman. 'Although she was known as Maggie Dunne when she lived here of course. She went under her mother's maiden name.'

One and the same: Marguerite Flood, Maggie Dunne.

'Of course,' I say. 'And Maggie had blonde hair.'

Mrs Chapman nods. 'I understand that Maggie changed more than her name while she was here.'

'Before she disappeared.'

Mrs Chapman frowns. 'I'm really sorry,' she says, and looks like she really is.

She pats me lightly on the arm. 'I'll go and find Máire for you.'

On the wall opposite, the Pope and his crowd of bishops look down at me with mocking faces. *Retrospect*, I mouth.

Máire Doherty has a strong flavour of nun about her, the non-terrifying kind, who wear socks in their sandals, do

Internet surfing and drink cappuccinos. She's a thin woman with an unflattering haircut pitched somewhere between Julie Andrews in *The Sound of Music* and an Amish elder. There's a small bump on her nose, and her eyes, like those made from currants on a gingerbread man, are set in a deeply lined face.

She'll see right through me with those sharp little eyes.

I'll act sober and try not to lie unconvincingly.

'You're here about your aunt?'

I nod.

'Will we go and sit outside, Maud? It's such a fine day.'

The gardens at Holly Lodge are still in bloom: blown roses, blousy dahlias and bronze chrysanthemums. Late-flowering clematis scrambles around French doors that lead into a dining room. I look inside. Several of the residents are still eating and the tables are being cleared by a short woman in a plastic apron who is making a big point of scraping the leftovers into a dustbin.

I walk with Máire along a path, through neat stepped lawns. We sit down on a bench overlooking a pond. A nymph in a nightie gazes down into the water, her expression placid. Around her feet stony-eyed fish cavort. I recognise her as a more modest relative of Bridlemere's nymph. Instead of a conch shell she holds a jug against her hip, the spout dipped slightly.

'That's a lovely fountain.'

'Your aunt put that in. She built that wing too.'

Máire motions towards an ugly extension to the right of the building. Otherwise the home is three-storeyed with legions of windows: an old, purpose-built sanatorium.

She glances at me. 'So you're writing a memoir, about your aunt's charity work?'

I nod with conviction. 'Did you know the Floods well?'

'I did.'

'You knew Marguerite?'

'I worked with her.'

The old gardener rounds the house with a kneeler and a bucket. He gets down to weed the flowerbed.

'What was she like?'

Máire looks out at the fountain. 'Maggie was very bright; she could be utterly charming.'

'But she was a handful?'

'She was challenging.'

'She wasn't too fond of her brother?'

Máire glances over at the gardener and lowers her voice. 'Now it wasn't as simple as that, Maud.'

'No, I don't suppose it was. So, the last time you saw Maggie was—'

'The morning of 20 August 1985.'

'The day she went missing?'

Máire pauses. 'Yes.'

'Were the Floods visiting at the time?'

'They'd returned home the week before.'

'And Maggie was never found?'

'No.'

'What happened?'

Máire's wrinkles rearrange themselves into a frown, her currant eyes all but disappearing. 'I believe Maggie ran away. She'd been doing it for years, despite all the measures we had in place. Mostly she'd return under her own steam. But this time she didn't and the police failed to find her.'

'Did she leave with anyone?'

'There were sightings, of parked-up cars and strangers in the grounds, that kind of thing. The police investigated every lead.'

'And they found nothing?'

Máire looks at me. 'That's just it, Maud. Not a trace of her.'

We sit in silence, watching the progress of the gardener.

'How did Mary take it?'

The gardener gets up and drags his kneeler and bucket to a spot further along the flowerbed.

'It destroyed her.'

St Dymphna saunters out through the wall of the dining room, just next to the open French windows. She prefers to take walls rather than doors just because she can. She pigeon steps through the flowers with a look of studied piety.

'Sometimes it's worse, not knowing.'

Máire glances at me. 'I think it is, Maud.'

We sit in silence for a while, looking at the nymph. The nymph tips her jug; from its spout runs a stream of clear water.

'But Mary loved her son and she loved to draw.'

'She drew?'

'She did; she was very good at it.' Máire laughs, her face transformed, expansive. 'We planned to put together a book, just for ourselves. I would write it and she would illustrate it.'

'What was it about?'

'Stories about each of us growing up, you know, and how it was back then, in a different time.' She smiles sadly. 'There are some of Mary's drawings in the library. Would you like to see them?'

I would.

Máire leads me along empty corridors; the residents will be in the day room now, she says. There are activities most afternoons. The hallways are painted pink, like bad medicine. Residents' art works jostle with framed portraits of saints. I recognise all of the saints, even the obscure ones. Some of the portraits are more accurate than others.

Máire opens the door to a large, sunny room with old sofas and bookcases and a view out over the lawn.

She points to a picture above a filing cabinet.

'That's by Mary.'

I move closer to a framed drawing of a sleeping girl of around seven, with her hand furled against her face. It's lovely, rendered in vivid detail from the pin-tucked front of her dress to her upturned nose and the curls at her temples.

'This is also one of Mary's; she used pastel here.'

The same child, older, sits reading. A ribbon is coming loose in her hair. Her hair is a soft bright auburn.

'It's Maggie, isn't it?'

Máire nods.

I look at the child in the picture: Mary's little girl.

'What went wrong?'

Máire shakes her head. 'I can't answer that.'

'Are there any pictures of Mary, photographs I mean?'

'There are.'

Máire walks over to the bookcase and searches through a row of albums; she picks one out and hands it to me.

'The residents made this to commemorate the opening of the new wing.'

A priest with a pair of shears cuts a ribbon. Father Creedo himself. People look on smiling. Over the page there's Mary in a shirt dress with shoulder-length red hair standing at the fountain. Behind her, water falls in blurred arcs through the air.

This is not the Mary I see in my dreams, blank-eyed, swooping. Nor is she the Mary of Cathal's paintings, the pale muse with burning hair. This is a real woman in a real moment, having her picture taken, her face caught somewhere between a smile and a grimace.

'Are there any of Cathal?'

Máire shakes her head. 'He wasn't so involved. He tended to use his time here to paint.'

I turn the pages until I reach a photograph taken on the lawn at the back of the home. Trestle tables are set for a party. There are paper cups and bunting and jugs of squash, seated children and adults looking on.

'Maggie is there, look.'

Maggie in a T-shirt and shorts, her bleached blonde hair scooped into a ponytail, secured with a white bow. She has her foot up on the rung of a chair and is smiling.

But I'm not looking at her.

Because sitting at the other end of the table is Sam Hebden. Very young, very thin, but unmistakable.

'Who is this?'

Máire peers at the photograph then looks at me oddly. 'That's Gabriel.'

Next to him sits a fat child with black hair. A youthful version of the Gabriel Flood I know. 'And this?'

Máire looks again. 'Stephen, Mary's sister's boy.' She glances at me. 'Not a relation on your side?'

I shake my head.

'He was often with the Floods. Mary's sister wasn't always in the best of health. The two boys were inseparable, more like brothers, really.'

Máire offers to walk me back to the entrance hall. She doesn't ask me about my fictional memoir, nor volunteer any information on Mary Flood's fundraising. But she does let me borrow two photographs from the commemorative album.

As we part, Máire Doherty looks at me kindly with her shrewd currant eyes and wishes me the best of luck.

And then I realise. I open my bag and take out the notebook. 'I think Mary meant for you to have this.'

M D
Don't be afraid to tell our story.
M F

As I walk down the drive of Holly Lodge and turn out onto the road I hear a car slow to a crawl beside me. I don't need to look up to know it's a green Golf with a dented passenger door.

Dr Gabriel Flood pulls over and winds down the window. 'What happened to you?'

He is livid, white-faced and his eyes are brutal.

The same man only different.

I glance around me. The road is deserted. On one side, a high wall, on the other, a wood. St Dymphna sails out from the trees and across the road, her face graver than I've ever seen it.

'Are you going to get in, Maud?'

I could. Or I could run back up the drive to Holly Lodge, a long lonely drive.

Would he mow me down? My running could spark off predatory urges. I remember that the worst thing to do when faced with a creature possibly intent on harming you is to show fear.

St Dymphna glides to my side with her crown sparking and her robes deepening to a richer green.

'You are more than a match,' she whispers, 'for this sneaky lying bastard.'

I take a deep breath.

'I'm sorry, Sam.'

The name hardly rings true; I glance at St Dymphna.

She nods. 'Go on.'

I go on. 'I got talking to this group of ladies on a coach trip. When I came out I thought you were gone. I couldn't see your car; I looked everywhere.'

'Nice,' says St Dymphna.

'You were pissed at me,' I add. 'You said it was a waste of time us coming here. I thought you'd just driven off.'

Gabriel frowns at me. I can't tell if he's buying it.

'I pulled the place apart looking for you,' he says.

'I'm so sorry, Sam.' I look him dead in the eye and he seems to soften.

I hear St Dymphna breathe out. 'He believes you.' She sounds relieved.

Gabriel gestures towards the entrance of the home. 'You've been in there? You've spoken to them?'

'There was no one available. So I sat in the grounds until they moved me on. They said for me to come back after the weekend, when the manager is around.'

He switches off the ignition and runs his hands over his face. 'So what do you want to do now?'

'I don't know. Maybe check into the B&B?' I walk round to the passenger seat and get in. 'You'll stay?' I smile at him.

'Of course.' He smiles back stiffly.

I pull my seat belt on, amazed at my performance. He starts up the car.

'Nice grounds up there, lovely fountain, like the one at Bridlemere.'

'Oh yeah?' his voice is low, uninterested.

I glance at him. He looks straight ahead, jaw tensed, as if battling some inner demon. I should imagine he has a few of them.

'Get him to pull over,' says St Dymphna from the back seat. 'Somewhere busy. Then make a run for it, Maud. His intentions are not good.'

My heart turns inside me.

As we drive into the village I see a newsagent; there are parked cars, people all around.

St Dymphna whispers in my ear, 'Here, Maud.'

'I'd die for a cold drink. Can we stop?'

He frowns and pulls over. I have my seat belt off but he's already out of the car.

'I'll go,' he says. 'What do you want?'

'Just anything, thanks.'

I watch him until he's inside the shop.

'He's left the keys in the ignition,' St Dymphna observes.

For a few minutes I just keep driving forwards, using any road, through town, out of town, just to get some distance. Then I start to calm down a bit and my heart stops jumping out of my chest and the blood stops rushing in my ears.

'Will he call the police?' I ask St Dymphna.

'Will he ever,' she mutters. She's in the passenger seat with her lamp in her hands, squinting furiously into the flame.

'What is it?'

'He's calling his greasy sidekick.' St Dymphna looks up to the heavens and winces. 'I didn't tell you that, if anyone asks.'

I check the mirror for signs of a black BMW.

'Should I be scared of him?' I glance at St Dymphna.

She avoids my eyes. 'Yes and no.'

'Tell me.'

'I can't; I'd be struck off.'

'I'm sure you've done worse.'

St Dymphna looks at me and bites her lip. 'Stop the car, Maud; check the boot.'

When I open the boot my knees almost give way.

Inside there are folded sheets of plastic, rolls of paper towels, refuse sacks, electrical tape, cable ties and a box of disposable gloves.

I get back into the car with my hands shaking. I can hardly start the ignition.

St Dymphna's face is grim. 'Lock the doors, Maud.'

At the next roundabout I turn the car in the direction of Dorchester.

Frank Gaunt opens the door to a peal of barking. He is a small bearded man flanked by slim hounds. The dogs come forward to nuzzle my hand, tails wagging.

I smile down at them and then I smile at Frank.

Frank pulls the larger of them back by the collar. 'You're here about the puppies?'

'I'm early. Should I come back?'

'Not at all, now is fine.'

I follow Frank through the hallway and out into the kitchen.

Everything feels a little surreal. Like I've slipped out of real life into a different dimension and now I'm just visiting normality.

I look around me; the kitchen is neat and well-proportioned. The dogs that greeted me ramble over to their beds in the corner of the room where there is a pen full of squirming, writhing, wriggling puppies, chewing each other's ears, licking each other's eyeballs, falling into their water bowl, standing on their back legs looking out.

'So what are you after then?' Frank is businesslike but not unfriendly.

I look out into the garden. Mrs Gaunt is pegging out washing on a rotary airer. The lawn has just been mown and Frank has yet to put the mower away.

I've a stolen car parked out the front of his house with a comprehensive homicide kit in the boot. When I leave it's likely there will be a black BMW trailing me. I'm a marked target. The invisible saint that's just taken a seat at his kitchen table has told me as much.

'To be honest, Mr Gaunt,' I say, 'I've come about a lot more than a puppy.'

To his credit, retired Chief Constable Frank Gaunt hears me out. He makes us coffee and we sit down at the kitchen table. The puppies tumble and nip until one by one they fall asleep. Their parents sprawl nearby; the brindle bitch watches me with her dark eyes, her sensitive muzzle on her long paws.

Mrs Gaunt comes in and, understanding some subtle signal, disappears into the hallway with a nod and a smile. Frank doesn't interrupt and his face remains largely expressionless. Although he frowns very slightly when I mention Stephen's bribe and Gabriel's lies and almost certainly hides a smile when I recount being picked up by the Dorking Nifty Fifties.

I leave out the part about the spiritualist church, the dead hand of Mary Flood and sleeping with the enemy. I would leave out the theft of Gabriel Flood's car but what's in the boot is far too compelling.

Frank gets to his feet and picks up our empty mugs. 'Another drink?'

I watch in silence as he fills the kettle, spoons out the instant and finds the milk. I know better than to interrupt him; the man is obviously thinking. In the corner a puppy wriggles in its sleep; in the room next door Mrs Gaunt has put the television on.

He hands me my coffee and sits down. 'I don't know how to help you with this, Maud.'

His hands are tied. He's retired; he mows the lawn and breeds dogs. Gone are the days when he dealt with the criminal underbelly of Dorset.

'I thought you might be able to shed light on Maggie's disappearance, maybe something that was unreported in the media?'

'There's nothing I can add. We had very few leads at the time.' Frank scratches his beard. 'And Maggie was a seasoned runaway.'

'From the home?'

Frank nods. 'Sometimes she went back; sometimes we found her. We figured that this time she didn't want to be found.'

St Dymphna throws me a knowing little half-smile.

I look out into the garden and watch Frank's underpants and his wife's slips dance on the rotary airer.

'What about the Floods? Did you interview them at the time?'

I take two photographs from my bag: Mary in her floral shirt dress and Gabriel and Stephen at the summer party. I put them on the table.

Frank picks them up. He taps the photograph of Mary. 'I remember her well.' He taps the other photograph. 'And this guy.'

'Gabriel.'

'And him.' He points to Stephen's fat head. 'We travelled up to London, spoke to them at the house.'

Frank's voice is changing, growing gruffer. He is forgetting the dogs and the lawn and remembering his old life.

The brindle bitch snores in her sleep, a wheezy high note.

'How did you find them?'

Frank thinks. 'The mother was charming actually; the two boys were a little subdued.'

'And Cathal Flood, the father, did you speak to him?'

Frank shakes his head. 'He was away.'

I proceed slowly, trying to keep my voice in check. 'Gabriel is a liar. He had me believe he was someone else entirely. What if he's responsible for Maggie's disappearance, him and his cousin here, who's still in league with him?'

'Lying is one thing, Maud—'

'It's not like Gabriel didn't have a motive: his sister had tried to drown him. Maybe he finally got his own back.'

Frank frowns. 'Even so.'

'Can't you reopen the case, bring them both in for questioning?'

Frank speaks kindly, choosing his words carefully. 'I would agree that this family appears to be a little complicated, but without good grounds we can't take this any further.'

'What about the murder kit in the boot?'

Frank shakes his head. 'The police can't bring someone in for owning a few tools and a length of plastic sheeting.' He looks at me. 'But if you feel threatened call them, straight away.'

One of the puppies, a pale fawn with one white foot, wakes and yawns. It rolls over and looks at me through the bars of its playpen.

'They're lovely.'

'They're our last litter; it doesn't seem right to keep on when there's so many dogs in the world needing homes.'

I nod.

'And my wife wants to go abroad, a cruise maybe. You can't do that with the dogs.'

'That would be nice.'

The puppy gets up and has a stretch for itself.

I put my coffee down and go over; it mouths my hand, licks it. 'With a dog like this you'd need to spend a bit of time outside?'

'At least twice a day.'

'A dog is great for getting people out and about?'

He laughs. 'I can't think of anything better. That one's a little girl.'

The puppy licks my hand again, wagging her tail hard enough to fall over.

I straighten up. 'Thanks for your time.'

He smiles. 'No problem, Maud. I'm just sorry that you're leaving here empty-handed.'

She's in a crate next to me, strapped in the front seat of Gabriel's stolen car. I push my finger through the wire and she licks it.

'The best time to acquire a puppy,' I say to her, 'is when you're in the middle of a missing-persons investigation and the man you've been sleeping with is planning to dispatch you with a crowbar and wrap you in plastic sheeting.'

St Dymphna, relegated to the back seat, rolls her eyes.

The puppy gives my finger an encouraging nip.

Chapter 42

The dog, still unnamed, has chewed up Renata's feathered mules and had three accidents in the hallway. But Renata loves her already. I can see that from the way she lets the puppy lick the make-up off her face and hang by her tiny fangs from the hem of her kimono.

And now the puppy is asleep, nestled in Renata's lap. Renata looks like a new parent: exhausted and happy, shell-shocked and full of marvellous intentions.

'So what now?' she whispers.

'I don't know.' I glance out of the front window at Gabriel's car. 'I'll have to get rid of that, I suppose.'

'Drive it somewhere and dump it. But for God's sake be careful, Maud.'

The phone rings. The puppy wakes and bites Renata lightly on the chin; she tucks her under her arm as if she's been toting canines forever.

Renata comes back into the room. 'It was one of the girls from the agency. She thought you should know that Cathal is in hospital. It's serious.'

★ ★ ★

I park Gabriel's car outside the hospital and go inside, past the chain-smoking patients strapped to drips and the bickering taxi drivers.

I made Renata promise to check that all the doors and windows were locked and to call the police at the first sign of Gabriel or Stephen. I've left St Dymphna with her, scowling at the puppy, for all a saint can do for someone who can't see them. But as I walk through the corridors I feel an overwhelming sense of unpreparedness, like I've forgotten something important, like I've made a dire mistake.

At the nurses' station I say that I'm his daughter and ask if he's had any other visitors.

No, not yet.

'How is he?'

A doctor guides me to the relatives' room.

'Your father suffered a major stroke event brought on by an accident.'

'An accident?'

'We believe he fell down the stairs at his home. The carer found him.'

For a moment I can't speak. Then: 'Is he in pain?'

She shakes her head. 'We've made him comfortable. He hasn't woken today.'

I look at her face, young, tired, at the end of a three-day shift, and I thank her.

'How long?' I ask.

'That's up to him, really.'

He's in a room of his own. The window is open and a breeze blows the vertical blinds.

There he is on the bed.

My heart falls apart.

I've never seen him without his teeth. He's always insisted on cleaning them in private. But here he is with his cheeks sunken, his mouth a slack pocket. Suddenly a thousand years older. Then there's his colour, the waxy look of him. I've seen this before, this withdrawing, this escape. I move to his side, avoiding tubes, to stroke his hair and hold his hand. His big curved nails are blue, his fingertips cold to the touch.

He's sunk into a grave kind of anonymity. But for his still-dark eyebrows, lifted a little, perhaps in astonishment, I would not know him.

Cathal Flood has moved beyond himself; he's roaming in another dimension. Where facts and histories, likes and dislikes, the stories we tell and are told, mean nothing. Where he doesn't need to hold a brush or a pencil or remember his own name.

A nurse comes in towing a monitor behind her. She speaks loudly to me, to him. He didn't touch his food and why ever not? Wasn't he hungry?

I look at the jelly on the tray and the beaker of orange juice.

I wonder if I should tell her to feck off on his behalf.

'Look at him,' I say. 'The man is unconscious. How do you expect him to feed himself?'

She eyes me with hostility while she takes his pulse.

I'm sure his mouth twitches, a ghost of a smile.

'You're his daughter?' she asks.

'And I'm a care worker. You need to bring me some mouth sponges.'

She writes in his chart, then clatters out of the room, pulling her trolley behind her. I throw her a look and walk back to the bed, slip my hand into his big paw again and kiss him on his forehead.

'Come on, you old bastard,' I whisper. 'Throw a shape on yourself.'

The breeze blows the vertical blinds.

I must have fallen asleep, still holding his hand with my head on his arm. The room is darker. Someone switches a light on. There's a voice next to me. A different nurse; she's telling me he's gone.

I almost laugh. Where has he gone? He's there in the bed. I don't understand.

Then I look up at him. His face is on one side. He must have turned towards me as I slept, maybe to say something. His eyes are open just a fraction, the still-dark eyebrows frowning just a little.

The nurse from before comes in with a tray of mouth sponges and puts them on the table.

And then I'm crying, swearing, shouting. Over the mouth sponges being too late and the jelly uneaten, over the draught from the window and the surly nurse. Over unfounded accusations and the breaking of an old man's heart.

There is some form-filling that needs to be done. The doctor says she's very sorry; I'm not sure whether for the forms or for the death.

My brother will be along, I say. If you've notified him, Gabriel will be on his way.

Would I like to take my father's personal effects?

I would.

I wait in the relatives' room and a nurse returns with a white plastic bag marked 'Patient's Property'.

I'm to sign a sheet which lists.

Shirts x 3
Jumpers x 2
Vest x 4
Trousers x 2
Woollen scarf x 3
Socks x 3
Tobacco
Cigarette papers
Engraved lighter
Set of keys
Hairpins x 2
Half a packet of cough sweets
Notebook.

I open the notebook. It is filled with quick line drawings of the cats, or of Larkin, or of me. In one I'm bent over the hob with my hair falling over my face. In another I am holding a bowl up high and laughing while the felines prowl around my legs. The top of one of the pages is carefully folded down. I open the notebook at the page.

It is a drawing of a girl sitting in a window seat, behind her a tall arched window. I stare at it. Bridlemere has four storeys and at the top there is a belvedere glazed with tall arched windows, from where, if I ever got there, I could see for miles.

Maggie looks out from the page, a half-smile playing on her lips.

Chapter 43

Four things were different on the day Deirdre disappeared: it was hot, Old Noel's kiosk was closed, there were no birds in the sky, and Jimmy O'Donnell lost the plot.

The same man only different.

I knew Jimmy O'Donnell had lost the plot by the look in his eyes. Like Boland's bastard collie looking at a bacon rind: an unblinking, unfaltering, locked-on stare.

'Did you tell, Maud?'

It was a simple enough question but my mouth was having difficulty forming words, so I shook my head. I didn't even think of looking away.

'Don't lie to me now; no one else knew.'

Jimmy took a packet of cigarettes from his pocket without taking his eyes from me. He found his lighter without taking his eyes from me. He lit the cigarette without taking his eyes from me.

'Now why would you do something like that?'

I stood with my book under my arm. To my right: sinking sand; to my left: horseflies, behind me: the sea; before me: Jimmy O'Donnell.

Jimmy stared at me with his collie-dog gaze. I was a stray lamb about to make a bolt for it on wobbly legs. One false move and he would bring me to the ground and have my throat out.

'Do you even know the trouble you've caused, Maud?'

I stood very still.

'I've lost my job.'

I stood very still.

'Your mammy called the guards on me.'

I stood very still.

'Everyone thinks I'm some kind of fucking monster.' He spoke through gritted teeth.

Jimmy O'Donnell took a step forward and my body turned to stone and my mind spun like a top inside it.

If I found the right word he would let me go. The right word would bring the real Jimmy O'Donnell back. His fists would unclench. His face would relax. There would be piggybacks and laughing and sweet money.

'Sorry,' I said.

And then I saw in his eyes that there was no Jimmy O'Donnell left at all.

Deirdre's diary was purple with a little pretend lock. She kept it in her vanity case on top of the wardrobe in the bedroom we shared at Granny's. Deirdre filled the diary daily, nightly, weekly, or never, with her big loopy writing. She liked pale-blue ink and dotted her *i*'s with love hearts. Sometimes she would fold things into the diary, like bubblegum wrappers and bus tickets.

Mammy read the whole story there when I put the diary into her hands.

Afterwards Mammy sat smoking cigarettes, looking out for Deirdre and Granny on the road that led to the bungalow.

Then Granny washed lettuce for the dinner, I did some colouring and Mammy knocked Deirdre into next week.

Deirdre appeared from nowhere. All of a sudden she was beside me.

Deirdre in her halter-neck dress, with her angel's wing-bud shoulder blades, bubblegum doing a slow revolve in her mouth.

Deirdre. Her brown hair plaited to the side with wisps at the temples and her lip still swollen where Mammy's ring had caught.

She didn't look at me.

'Leave Maud out of this,' she said. 'She didn't say a word. I told Mammy.'

Jimmy stared at her. 'You silly little fucking bitch. I said I'd get you the money, didn't I? You've ruined me.'

'Wait in the dunes,' she said to me, without taking her eyes off Jimmy.

I waited in the dunes.

She would be back. She knew the tides and could predict the weather. She knew where to tread and where not to.

She would be back. Clothed in sand, crowned with shells, the scowling angel of Pearl Strand.

She would be back and I would promise never to tell on her again.

I waited in the dunes as the day lost its heat and the sky lost its light and the sea turned on its heel and went off to America.

Chapter 44

It is late by the time I get to Bridlemere. I park Gabriel's car a few roads away, walk back to the house and let myself in the kitchen door. I lock it behind me and pull the chain across. I grope for a torch under the sink and switch it on. It reflects eyeshine from the few cats loitering in the kitchen. They follow me hopefully as I move down the hall. Passing the door to Cathal's workshop I hear a thud. My heart stands still in my chest.

I listen again.

Nothing: just the pattering of cats up and down corridors and some far-off creak.

The door to Cathal's workroom is open. I step into a strong smell of wood shavings and varnish. I flash the torch around the room. The curtains are drawn in Madame Sabine's booth. The tools and the cogs have been tided away and the workbench is clear now.

Apart from the head of a singularly ugly creature mounted on a plaque.

I hold the torch beam steady.

'Cathal, you old bastard,' I whisper. 'You didn't bury the thing at all.'

Manolete stares back at me with glassy marble eyes that were never his own, his mouth set in an eternal grimace.

Before I turn to go I take a small sharp chisel with a sturdy handle from the rack above the workbench and slip it into my bag.

I close the workshop door behind me and pass through the gap in the Great Wall of *National Geographics* into the hallway beyond. It's wider than it has ever been. I'm surprised that Bridlemere has not pulled up the drawbridge and lowered the portcullis in Cathal's absence.

But then the house knows me now.

The curiosities have an off-duty, at-ease feel to them tonight. They make sudden cameos in my moving torch-light. The glass eyes are unfocused, peering off in random directions; the raven sleeps with its beak folded into its feathers. The stoats slump over their cards and the shrunken head dozes. Even the four-faced angel seems to be dreaming in the darkness, her wings limp and her muzzles drooping.

I climb the stairs.

Mary Flood, pale-footed, icy-fingered, hare-eyed stare, still scatters rose petals on the first-floor landing. I pass her and keep going.

As I reach the top of the stairs I see the open door with a light on inside.

I can feel it. The room is filled with a breath-held waiting, as if it is crammed with surprise guests ready to jump out at me. I put my hand in my bag and with my fingers closed around the handle of the chisel I move forward.

In the light thrown down by a row of chandeliers I see her.

Life-sized and beautiful, Maggie Dunne, Marguerite Flood.

Set on an easel in front of the window is the portrait Cathal sketched in his notebook, down to the half-smile. But here also is the fiery richness of her hair as it once was. Just like the sun setting on autumn, just like her mother's. I see for the first time that she has Cathal's eyes.

Looking past the canvas to today's scene, the window seat is empty now. But the curtains are still here and the cushions haven't changed: braided black damask.

I imagine the painting of it.

Maggie, turned to the window but looking back into the room, her eyes a little glazed, daydreaming, or perhaps bored by the long minutes keeping still. And Cathal, dancing to and fro before the canvas, conducting light and line with his deft brushes.

Along the opposite wall chairs are arranged as if spectators are expected. On one of them sits Gabriel, watching me.

He leans forward, elbows on knees. His dark blond hair raked on end by his fingers. He is pretending to be calm, casual. But I can see the veins that have risen in his temples and in his forearms and the sweat on his lip.

And I can smell him. The bitter panic of the hours spent tracking me, of waiting for me.

'Cathal's dead,' I say.

'I know. They phoned.' He sits back in his chair and nods towards Maggie's portrait. 'An uncanny likeness.'

'Where's the original?'

'He did away with her, isn't that what you thought all along?'

'Cathal was no murderer, and besides, he loved her.'

'For fuck's sake, Maud,' he murmurs. 'Why do you always take his side?'

I hear a crash below. Gabriel goes to the door and closes it.

'He's here too? Your sidekick?'

Something made of glass shatters extravagantly.

I think of all the terrible priceless objects. 'He's destroying the place.'

Gabriel lights his cigarette. 'He's looking for Mary's will.'

'Her will?'

'Some years ago, Mammy and I fell out. She instructed that on Cathal's death Bridlemere was to be sold and the proceeds given to Cedar House. All of this was hers, you see. Cathal had nothing.'

A muffled thud from below.

'Just before her death she drafted another will that left the house to me.' Gabriel takes a drag of his cigarette.

'What made her change her mind?'

Gabriel breathes out. 'Who knows?'

'And what about Maggie, was she in the will?'

'No.' Gabriel walks over to the window. He looks out at the dark wilderness of the garden.

'Tell me where she is, Gabriel.'

He gestures with his cigarette. 'In the well.'

'She's dead?'

'Of course she's bloody dead.'

He retakes his seat. 'She'd run away again. Only this time she reached London. She got into the house. It was awful.'

'What happened?'

He rubs his hand across his forehead. 'Cathal was away;

she waited until Mary went out and Stephen and I were alone.' He pauses. 'She had a knife. She cut herself and then tried to cut me. We managed to get out into the garden but she chased us. We were petrified.'

Downstairs there's a scraping noise: the sound of someone moving heavy furniture.

'We tried to hide in the ice house but she found us. She slipped and fell.' He glances at me. 'Just like you did. We ran out and tried to shut her in. But she kept on coming.'

He takes another drag of his cigarette and exhales quickly. 'Then I saw she'd hurt herself. So I ran back and I hit her. I thought I could knock her out, like they do in the films. But it's different in real life.' He hesitates. 'So we dragged her to the well.'

'Christ.'

'We just wanted her to stop.'

Somewhere beyond Bridlemere life continues as normal. People make cups of tea, watch television, go to the pub and don't kill their siblings.

'Did Mary know?'

'I went running to her.' Gabriel drops his cigarette on the floor and steps on it. 'I was young. I wept, terrified. She said she would help me fix it. That it was an accident.'

We sit for a while in silence.

'If Mary thought it was an accident, why didn't she call someone?'

Gabriel shakes his head. 'I don't know.'

'And Cathal,' I ask. 'Did he know about any of this?'

He lights another cigarette. Takes a few puffs. 'If he did I'd have been inside by now.'

'But he had something on you? He spoke about an insurance policy.'

'Mary had given him her revised will for safekeeping.

Sealed in an envelope.' He looks at me. 'But what really worried me was her confession.'

A hammering noise sounds deep in the house. A blunt rhythmic thump, like a heartbeat.

'Her confession?'

'She told me that because she couldn't speak her sins she had written a confession. It was to be her secret, hidden where no one, not even Cathal, could find it.' He takes a drag on his cigarette. 'She refused to tell me where.'

Downstairs there's a rending noise, a crash, then silence.

Gabriel runs his hands through his hair. 'My mother was a liability.'

I think of Stephen hopping down the garden path that day, clutching his manbag. 'But you found it? The confession?'

'Not yet, but then neither did Cathal.'

'But he still had Mary's will?'

'Stephen and I leant on him for years but he wouldn't give it to us. The old bastard knew I was desperate to get my hands on it. He thought it was the money I was after.'

'But it wasn't.'

Gabriel frowns. 'How could I let this house change hands with my bloody sister down the well?'

I look out of the window; darkness hides the Armageddon of cats and rubbish and overgrown foliage. I can only see my own face reflected back at me.

The banging starts again.

'Then you came along, Maud,' he says softly.

'And you lied to me.'

'You mistook me for someone else; I just went along with it. At first I did it to stop you from interfering, to keep you away from the house. I didn't want you getting caught up in this '

I almost believe him.

'But you wouldn't drop it. Then it started to look as if the old man was opening up to you. So I took the risk that things might pan out the way I wanted them to.'

'How would that be?'

'With no one getting hurt.'

I stare at him, incredulous. 'You sent those thugs round to Renata's, didn't you?'

'She phoned me and told me about the envelope. I didn't know what the fuck was in it.' He shrugs. 'I told them not to touch her. Just to find it and shake her up a bit.'

I bite my tongue until the urge passes.

'I panicked, Maud. You were getting too close, uncovering these messages. Then I started thinking that maybe the old bastard had found something out, that he was planting these clues to torment me.'

The banging ceases and is replaced by drilling.

'What is he even doing?'

'Securing the house.'

The drill whines then stops again.

'Do you know what it's like to really hate someone, Maud?'

'Yes.'

'She led me by the hand; she held me under.'

I look at Maggie's portrait; she smiles back at me, undaunted, shameless, unrepentant.

'Will you tell, Maud?'

'No.' My eyes meet his. 'I won't.'

He smiles and nods. 'I told Stephen you wouldn't. I'll come down with you, see you out.'

I lead the way. When my fingers are on the door handle, he says it.

'I'm so sorry, Maud. For everything.'

Chapter 45

Mammy treaded the grass like a sick dog, spiralling down
wards to rock on her haunches, crying into her cigarette.
Granny made tea. I put biscuits on a plate nicely. The lady
guard spoke into her radio and the man guard looked out
at the road that led to the bungalow.

Three things happened the day after Deirdre disappeared.
Old Noel crawled from his cottage where he had lain for
Lord knows how long. Someone had broken his nose, three
ribs and his collarbone for him and cleared out his savings.
The fella kept his face covered and drove in and out of the
yard like the devil himself was chasing him. Old Noel,
destroyed, never opened his kiosk again.

The seabirds returned to Pearl Strand. At least I'm sure I
heard them fly over, screaming and cursing, in that direction.

Down in the caves the guards found treasure, right at the
back of the mermaid's larder. A bag: heart-shaped red leather,
pink silk inside, gold-stoppered, its strap a fine slim ribbon
of a thing.

Chapter 46

I am on my back breathing bubbles; something collects at the back of my throat, something is pooling there.

And all the time the acrid smell of bonfires.

And a rushing sound, somewhere in the foundations of the house, like the sea is rolling in, flooding Bridlemere from the basement up.

And then I realise: Bridlemere is burning.

Get up, Drennan.

says a ringside voice, the no-shit-and-nonsense voice of a trainer. My eyes open. Then I'm up on my knees like a prizefighter, spitting iron. The crowd grimaces. Why won't she give in? Why won't she lie still for the count?

It's a hard thing to see, a woman dragging herself along, smashed up, half her hair gone by the roots, bubbles of blood and snot. He's nearly taken the top of her head off – see, another crack just appeared. No light in there, such as you'd find in the mind of a saint, just a bad walnut splitting open with a dull wet sound and then dark—

God blast you. Get up, Drennan.

See the smears of blood and hair along the skirting board, ladies and gentlemen of the jury. They tell a very violent story. In your own time, Maud, in your own words.

This is how it went:

First he grabbed me with his fingers knotted in my hair and pulled me towards him, as if he was going to kiss me, he was that close. Instead he banged my head against the wall, then again, then again.

And his face – what about his expression? Let's get to the nub of it, Maud. Didn't that hurt most? Seeing the look in his eyes, the indifference and the rage? Maybe even hatred? Surely he'd have to hate you a little bit to want to knock the head off you then throw you down a well? It was the betrayal really, wasn't it? Didn't that hurt the most? After being with him. And this the man you—

No: the assault hurt more.

Jesus, Drennan, will you ever get up?

My bag has been kicked under Maggie's portrait, contents spilled. I take the chisel and the keys and crawl towards the door, breathing shallow against the pain. I sit for a while with my head lifting, pounding. When I can think again I check the door with the palm of my hand: it's cool. I try the handle: it's unlocked. When I am ready I will take off my shirt and tie it around my face as tightly as I can bear.

The lights go out.

I am born into carbon darkness, half-slithering, half-falling down the stairs onto the next landing. Coughing despite the pain, retching despite the pain, eyes streaming. I have Cathal's keys in one fist and the chisel in the other.

The house sighs.

Hot ash rises and falls in lethal drifts. Sparks spitting up the centre of the staircase. Burning scraps rising, landing, pathfinders that will start new fires. Shotgun cracks and the fizzle of squibs and the crash of rubbish collapsing and then the flare of new firestorms of vivid flecks.

They mark a pathway, petals of blazing red and ash white, a trail of blood and snowflakes. I close my eyes and look for her in my mind and find her. She's up ahead, walking along the hallway, with burning hair and soot-blackened heels. She glances back at me, her face pale and her eyes beautiful and terrible – for damage lies at their shining core.

And all at once I know where Mary Flood is leading me and why.

I rest my forehead against a locked door. Behind this door is a room of white with a window. Beyond that window is a balcony. I try the keys one after the other, fingers stiffening, clumsy. I count, *one key, two keys*. If this fails I have the chisel. *Three keys, four keys*. The heat off the staircase is fierce now, turning the smoke orange. *Five keys*. I feel it on my face and my hands. My skin peels. My hair crackles and melts. The key turns in the lock. I'm in. Shut the door, quickly, quickly.

Block the gap, Drennan.

My hands find the silky stuff of the bedspread. I pull it, hanging on to the edge, until it gives way and falls with a slither on top of me. I push it with my feet against the bottom of the door.

I get onto the bed, feeling along the wall. Behind the

door high-pitched noises are racing along the corridor. It is only a Catherine wheel; it's bonfire night at Bridlemere! Somewhere deep in the bowels of the house there is a corresponding scream, then a deep groaning slump that shakes the walls. Some great beast is turning, dying.

The house is giving up.

My fingertips search blindly along the wall until they find the edge of the frame.

Before me is a dressing table, damask curtains, cold glass and the sweet, sweet rush of cold night air. Behind me is a superheated door, flames tonguing the keyhole, heat blistering the paint.

Outside there are lights and shouting; the garden is festive with firefighters. I have the best seat in the house. From here I watch a hundred cats run into the night. From here I see Larkin on the roof of the caravan, counting them to safety, each shadowy pelt. As the last cat leaves he turns, jumps down and runs after.

Chapter 47

The ward slumbers in a predawn lull. The patients are asleep. I see their huddled shapes in the light from the empty nurses' station. I hear their breathing and the creaking of their waterproof mattresses. We are like sickly ships sailing through the night, a cargo of drips and slippers, crosswords and catheters. The nurses are nowhere to be seen and neither are the police officers that were here earlier, all civility and radio crackles.

From my bed I can see into the corridor and into the corridor comes an animal. It rounds the corner on light-stepping paws, claws clicking on the floor. It disappears for a while behind the nurses' station to reappear standing in the doorway.

I know better than to follow a fox in life.

The streets of West London are quiet but for the sound of my slippers flapping on the pavement. The saints are waiting outside the house: all the usual suspects are here. St Dymphna is cleaning her lamp on the hem of her robe. St Valentine has his eyes closed and his fingers in his ears, St Monica looks to be admonishing him. St George and St Rita stand side by side, looking up. They're watching the birds turn overhead in the first pink rays of morning.

Bridlemere is untouched by flame; it's as if the fire hasn't happened. I move through the house flanked by saints. The dawn slants in through the windows illuminating the unwashed dishes in the sink, the tin of custard powder on the table, the jumble in the hallway outside Cathal's lair.

I push the door of his workroom open.

Manolete still grimaces on the bench. St Rita blesses herself as we pass by him. In the middle of the room stands a curtained booth. Above it is a sign, painted in dull gold letters:

Madame Sabine
Yesterday's History Today

I rummage in a jar on the shelf, find a coin and put it in the slot at the front of the machine. The coin drops and the curtains judder open.

Madame Sabine grinds into action. Raising her head with a jerk, addressing the room with her glittering painted stare. The saints begin to mutter and draw back into the corners. St George pulls down his visor and St Dymphna gathers her cape around herself. St Valentine stops picking his teeth and St Rita straightens her veil. St Monica folds her arms with a thin-lipped grimace.

The crystal ball has gone. In front of Madame Sabine is a book. Her hands click over it in a series of blessings, a brisk mechanical rite. The book opens.

A wind picks up. Wood shavings skitter along the floor and cobwebs bounce in the cornices. Loose screws and paint pots start to circle the room. Cloaks and robes, veils and chain mail are whipped up and swirled. Halos flicker and dim. The saints stumble and look around themselves for shelter. And now, with the wind, comes a sudden loud clackety drone, not unlike a faulty extractor fan.

St Rita lets out a sob. She mouths something I can't understand before her shape begins to change. She flattens into an arc, a monochrome flash that bridges the room in one sudden streak to pool on the book's open pages. St George follows, his body elongating to a silver dart that hits the book with an incandescent flash. St Monica crumples like a crisp packet and rolls towards the booth. Then she is gone too, up into the book, with a tepid fizzle.

St Valentine races to the door in a bid to escape but he is dragged back. He starts running, but he's going the wrong way on a moving treadmill. He's losing ground. The book waits, open-mawed. St Valentine shoots me a look of wall-eyed panic before his face folds and he is sucked in, disappearing with a sudden flare of cardinal red.

In a lancing rift of light St Raphael emerges from a cupboard, his heart-shaped face solemn and the arched shadows of his wings battered by crosswinds. He raises his eyes and bursts into a blizzard of sable feathers that are whipped and spun into a handsome tornado. The tornado crosses the room and revolves above the booth, a spinning velvet funnel. It pulses there, growing and retracting. Then it descends into the pages of the open book, dissolving with a dark sparkle.

St Dymphna watches it all from the corner of the room. Her veil blown back and her plait unfurling. She looks over at me and smiles. Then, taking up her lamp, she walks forward, holding a still, strong-burning flame before her. And in a moment she too is gone.

The book closes. The black cat at Madame Sabine's elbow gives a metallic purr and the two fat taxidermy chaffinches shake their wings in a desultory fashion.

Madame Sabine's head drops forward. She regards me with a sudden searching gaze, her black irises bright. Her hands make one last pass and then drop, lifeless, back onto the counter. Her head yanks up with a clattering of her coin-edged veil. A card drops into a recess below and the curtains fitfully draw themselves closed.

I pick it up. It's a postcard.

It's been ripped to pieces and put back together again. The repair is illuminated with seams of glowing gold.

Greetings from Pearl Strand

It is a wild empty place, the place on the postcard. A place where the ocean meets the sky and seabirds scream and reel in wide, wide, borderless blue. Where dunes are three storeys high or no more than an anthill. Where the sand has a sheen to it, a certain lustre in the right light (moonlight, starlight, dawnlight). A long crescent swoon of a beach.

I turn the postcard over. In pale-blue ink, big loopy letters, the i dotted with a love heart:

Wish you were here.

Chapter 48

Chief Constable Frank Gaunt, retired, will drive us there: Renata, in dark glasses and a wax jacket, the dog and me.

Frank waits in the hallway under the sour glower of Johnny Cash and the benign gaze of Jesus Christ. Renata finds her handbag, her keys. He remarks on how much Stella has grown.

'She's spoilt,' Renata says with a smile.

I watch them watching the dog and wonder how I will get through this day.

The house is boarded up. At the top you can see empty windows and charcoaled joists. In wet weather the smell of smoke rises again.

They have cleared the grounds of the rubbish that made the fire brigade's job so difficult. It was a warren, they said, impossible to get their equipment down, which is why the damage was so severe. The caravan has survived, along with the ice house and the gate lodge with its mullioned windows. I can see them now, past the cut-down bushes and wooden walkways. The well is still covered with a tent.

We meet the police officer in charge; I don't catch his name but he has hair gel and a shaving rash and a habit of pushing the tip of his tongue between his lips after every sentence. We shake hands and he walks us round. Renata grills him; she's only interested in the forensics and she wants all the details. The police officer looks at her in desperation as he guides her over uneven surfaces. Frank brings up the rear with Stella dancing on her lead.

Renata takes my arm and squeezes it. She still has moments of panic outdoors. When she does we do breathing exercises and sing show tunes. I look up to see if she's struggling. She kisses me and offers a tissue from her handbag. Then I realise it's me that's crying.

'Did the fox ever come back?' I ask the police officer.

He nods. 'It's been seen hanging around.'

'And the cats?'

'A few; some of the builders have rehomed them.'

I wonder about Beckett, but with eyes like his he would have easily found a home. Stella pulls at her lead, as if she's caught a sniff of something. Or maybe it's just the word.

As for the saints: there are no saints today. No faint bobbing of a veil outside the perimeter fence, no flick and slap of a pacing sandal.

Instead, all around me stand Bridlemere's dead.

I can't see them but I'm sure they are there. Mary Flood, relaxed in a shirt dress, puts a steadying hand on my shoulder. Maggie, standing a little apart, flashes me a quick grin. Cathal raises the still-dark caterpillars of his eyebrows.

And the others?

There are no others. There are some fires even the dead can't survive.

★ ★ ★

I lay flowers at the gate alongside wilted bouquets and teddy bears. Marguerites for Maggie. Roses: red and white for Mary, and for Cathal, a single perfect yellow bloom.

Lillian had cleaned it and wrapped it up until I was ready to look at it: the frame I had taken from the wall of the white room as the fire brigade fought to save Bridlemere, as the staircase fell, as the sparks shot up into the night.

The moths were intact, pale and pristine under glass. I worked the back free and found what I was looking for: the counterpart to the envelope hidden in the red room. Inside, on three sheets of paper, executed in small neat handwriting: Mary Flood's confession.

She had read the story on her son's face before he even opened his mouth. She had lost one child. So she promised not to tell.

But she began to fear that she would. That in a moment of weakness it would burst out of her. She'd be at church, or talking to Mrs Cabello, and out it would come.

She had kept secrets before but this one was different. It festered and suppurated. It pressed against the sides of her skull. It was a dark mass at the back of her tongue. It strangled her heart and soured her stomach. She felt it lodged there, heavy and corrupt, like poison. Mary was consumed with the urge to tell, to vomit the whole story up.

She couldn't tell her husband and she couldn't tell her priest; she couldn't tell her doctor and she couldn't bring herself to tell her god.

So Mary wrote it down.

She would sit and stare at her reflection. Sometimes in the red room, sometimes in the white; it didn't matter. Both belonged to Maggie really, not to Mary. Furnished for a princess, not a queen. Neither room had been used by the girl; Cathal had readied them against visits that never happened. For the father doted on the child, despite everything. She was his fairy-tale girl, she could have everything, twice.

Rose Red, Snow White became Alice and fell down, down, down the rabbit hole.

Mary would sit for hours. Sometimes in the white room, sometimes in the red; it didn't matter. For both mirrors showed the same woman: sealed mouth, hair of dust and eyes of stone.

Soon enough there was another face at the mirror alongside the woman's.

Everywhere Mary went Maggie followed, drifting behind, from room to room, twisting the end of her ponytail and staring accusingly.

Every night Mary took a tumble into the well. Her nails scrabbling against blasted brickwork. Her hands grabbing at the strange subterranean plants that grew from the cracks. Her lungs breathing the cold, earthy smell of the bottom of the world as she turned. Every night she was shattered by the impact.

Every morning, when she woke, Mary wondered if she could last.

Stella is asleep on the sofa, snoring softly. Her legs twitching as she chases the cats that slink and hiss through her dreams.

We see Frank Gaunt out and go into the kitchen and sit for a while drinking krupnik how it's meant to be drunk, with a steady hand and a grateful brain.

Mary's confession, the confession we didn't show Frank Gaunt, is on the table between us.

'What do you want to do with it, Maud?' Renata's voice is low, gentle.

I think about Mary, a proud broken fire-haired woman. Signing her name, sealing the envelope. I think about Maggie, safe now in the police morgue, raised from her unquiet slumber under rubble at the well's end. Soon she'll sleep in the family plot, only this time her rest will be eternal.

I think about Gabriel and Stephen, trapped at the foot of the stairs, their exit blocked by fallen debris. The cause of the fire: faulty wiring on a set of fairy lights.

Mostly, I think of Cathal sitting at the kitchen table at Bridlemere, whistling through his dentures, swearing amiably.

He pats down the wild white mane of his hair and smiles. Then he's off, scudding down the cluttered hallway of my mind's eye.

I get up and search the kitchen drawer for matches.

It catches. I hold the paper as it burns, dropping it into the sink when the flame gets too near my fingers.

I wait for a dim figure to step through the wall, with a glowing corona and a muttered prayer. With a cloak, or a robe, or a wall-eyed wink. But nowadays there are only two undaunted women in a maisonette with a bottle of krupnik.

'You've packed your passport then?'

I smile. 'I have.'

'Of course you have.'

'Will you be all right?' I say. 'I'll be back in a week or so.'

'You'll do no such thing.' Renata looks me in the eye. 'You'll come back when you've found her.'

I nod.

'And you will find her, Maud.'

I raise my glass to Renata and she raises her glass to me.